Heartbreak Trail

Heartbreak Trail

SHIRLEY KENNEDY

CAMEL PRESS

Seattle, WA

CAMEL PRESS

Published by Camel Press
PO Box 70515
Seattle, WA 98127

For more information, contact www.camelpress.com

Cover design by Sabrina Sun
Copyright © 2011 by Shirley Kennedy

ISBN: 978-1-60381-831-5 (Trade Paper)

Acknowledgments

My thanks go to Jackie Rowland, president of the Oatman Historical Society, for her help in the research of my novel. Jackie, an expert on Old West history, lives in the historic mining town of Oatman, Arizona, where she owns and runs a remarkable store called Fast Fanny's.

My thanks also go to artist and gun expert, Andy Kohut, of Laughlin, Nevada, who told me what I needed to know about how to load and fire a rifle in 1851.

Chapter 1

*I*n the dining room of her family's mansion on Beacon Hill, Lucy Parker Schneider bowed her head for grace. She had much to be grateful for. In fact, she couldn't remember a time when she'd been happier than at this very moment. What could be more gratifying than being a new bride, having dinner with her family on a Sunday afternoon, her handsome husband by her side?

"Bless us, oh Lord, and these your gifts which we are about to receive from your bounty. Through Christ our Lord, Amen. Pass the potatoes." From the head of the dinner table, Elihu Parker gazed fondly at his older daughter. "You're looking well. It appears marriage suits you."

Lucy cast a loving glance at Jacob, her tall, golden-haired husband who sat beside her. "Marriage suits me well enough, Father."

A suppressed snicker came from across the table where Sarah, Lucy's younger sister, sat. The knowing glance she sent Lucy spoke volumes. Only Sarah knew of the turmoil in Lucy's heart the day her easy-going, widowed father announced he planned to marry Pernelia Robinson, iron-minded leader of the Lady's Benevolent Society as well as the Women's Christian Temperance Union. Since her mother's death eight years before, Lucy had run the household and done a good job of it, too.

Shocked and dismayed, Lucy couldn't believe her beloved father would marry a woman like Pernelia, who hid a ruthless desire to get her own way behind an angelic smile, coupled with a barbed tongue wrapped in velvet. Lucy had always assumed her father also saw through Pernelia's false facade of sweetness. Obviously, he hadn't.

"Don't you worry." Pernelia batted her eyelashes. "You'll always have a place here. In fact, you and I shall run the household together in perfect harmony, won't we, dear?"

Sick inside, Lucy managed a nod but clearly saw her future. Pernelia and her iron hand would soon be running the household while she, already twenty-six years old, would become that most lowly of creatures—the worthless daughter who never found a husband. Though only eighteen, her sister, Sarah, thought the same.

As predicted, after Pernelia became Mrs. Elihu Parker, she swept through the house like a little Napoleon, crushing every obstacle in her path. Sarah soon became betrothed, mercifully to a man she loved. In a state of quiet desperation, Lucy wondered how she could possibly live her life under the same roof as her overbearing stepmother. Then a miracle happened. At Sarah's wedding, she met recently widowed Jacob Schneider. How handsome he was, and a rich farmer besides! She instantly fell in love with him. He'd been courting his dowdy Cousin Winifred, but when Lucy revived her long-unused flirting skills, he didn't have a chance.

Three months later, she became his bride.

So now, on this lovely September Sunday at her father's mansion, Lucy counted her blessings. She had escaped Pernelia. She could hold her head high, the wife of a prosperous farmer, stepmother to his adorable five-year-old son, and mistress of a home of her own—a beautiful old farmhouse so close to Boston she could visit her family whenever she pleased.

Wrapped in a warm glow of happiness, Lucy fondly looked

around the table at the two younger brothers she'd help raise, Sarah and her new husband Daniel, her dear father, and her stepson Noah, whom she already thought as her own. Even pudgy-faced Pernelia didn't look so bad on a beautiful day like this.

While they ate, the talk centered on the recent news about the California gold rush. Lucy was surprised at the fervor with which the three men at the table had taken over the conversation.

"I'd go in a minute," Daniel declared. "Why, I hear there are gold nuggets lying in the streets just waiting for you to come along and pick them up."

Sarah sat up straight and glared at her young husband. "Daniel Williams! How can you even think such a thing? I would never leave Boston to traipse off to the middle of nowhere."

"Many are going." Lucy's father spoke in his usual quiet, authoritative way. "You'd be surprised at the number of farm sales my bank has handled. They use the money to buy oxen and a wagon. Then off they go to the land of gold."

"They're fools." Jacob Schneider's square jaw tensed visibly. "You'd never catch me selling everything I owned to go on a wild goose chase for gold."

"My view exactly," Father replied. "Just look at your neighbor, John Potts. He's pulling up stakes, selling his farm lock, stock, and barrel, and leaving for California in one of those flimsy covered wagons, family and all. Such folly!"

Jacob nodded in somber agreement. "He doesn't care that the risks are huge, what with Indians, drownings, starvation, and God knows what. From what I hear, some of them suffer so many hardships they turn around and come back. Though I must say, Abner thinks differently."

Lucy felt a ripple of apprehension at Jacob's mention of his older brother. She slanted a worried glance at her husband. "Just what does Abner think?"

Jacob flashed a reassuring smile. "He's talked some about going to California. Just talk, though. You know my brother."

Indeed, she did know Jacob's brother, an intensely religious man who, as far as she knew, had never cracked a smile in his entire life. Unfortunately for her, he and Jacob jointly owned their farm, so Lucy was forced to deal daily with Abner and his shy wife, Martha, who lived on the plot of land next to their own. "Tell me he's not serious."

Jacob smiled in that reassuring way he had. "Of course Abner's not serious. We have no intention of joining the fools headed to California."

No need to worry. Lucy felt relieved. Not that she had even considered the possibility Jacob might want to go, but she was glad to hear that he positively did not.

And yet ...

When she'd married Jacob, she had put him on a pedestal. Soon after, she realized her perfect husband had one little fault: he deferred to his older brother in all matters. What if ...? Oh, no! Such a thought was ridiculous. Jacob had just confirmed that he never wanted to go to California, so she had absolutely nothing to worry about.

Two weeks later, Jacob's neighbors, John and Bessie Potts, were about to leave. They'd sold their farm and most of their possessions and bought mules and a wagon. They planned to travel to Independence, Missouri, one of the popular jumping-off places to the West, where supplies would be bought and the wagon train formed. In mid-April, when the mud on the roads began to harden, they would begin the arduous trek west. Lucy hated to see them go. Neither Jacob nor his brother cared much for John Potts, whom they considered too loud and boisterous, and not nearly pious enough. However, she'd made good friends with Bessie, a likeable, down-to-earth woman, originally from the little town of Possum Creek, Tennessee. Bessie was afraid to embark on such a dangerous journey.

"They say it'll take six to eight months to get to California," she wailed one day while visiting Lucy. "Me with six children and expecting the seventh, and there'll be nothing but a covered wagon to call home." Her small frame shuddered with dread. "'Twill be a miracle if we get there alive."

Lucy asked the one question that deeply puzzled her. "Why does your husband want to give up his farm and go west? Is it just the gold?"

"It's mostly the gold strike. John is crazy to go. He thinks he's going to get rich just picking up gold nuggets off the ground. Also, the farm's been losing money these past few years. Lots of farms are losing money."

"I had no idea."

"Ain't you heard? The country's been in a major depression. Farms all over are going broke."

Of course she knew about the depression, but Jacob hadn't said a word about any of the local farmers being in trouble, nor had Abner. Actually, Jacob didn't tell her much of anything. But surely he would have told her if their farm was losing money. She searched for something optimistic to say. "Perhaps you could think of your trip as an adventure, something to write about and tell your grandchildren."

Tears glistened in Bessie's eyes. "If I ever have any grandchildren. If we ain't all scalped by the Indians, drowned in a river, or bit by snakes."

"Haven't you told John how you feel?"

"My whole life is being ripped apart, but do you think he would listen? I'm only his wife, after all. I must do as he says." Bessie's shoulders slumped in despair. "That's the way of it. Our husbands rule. We wives are like oxen, waiting for a whip to be cracked over our heads." She gave Lucy a meaningful stare. "If you ain't found that out yet, you soon will."

Lucy inwardly cringed. Bessie's unfortunate description of marriage certainly didn't apply to her and Jacob. Even so, a feeling of uneasiness crept over her. True, Jacob didn't beat or whip her; yet lately he'd grown more domineering. So far, she'd been compliant with his wishes, eager to please. What if she defied him? Why did she fear his reaction if she did? Well, there was no use thinking about it now, and besides, Bessie's problems loomed large compared to her own.

Lucy searched for words of comfort but could find nothing appropriate. What she really wanted to tell Bessie was how appalled she was that any man would lead his family into such danger. Saying such a thing to Bessie at this late date wouldn't do one bit of good.

The day before the Potts and three other families were to leave for California, the entire farm community held a farewell potluck dinner in their honor at the local church. Everyone in the neighborhood was invited, from the prosperous merchants and farmers to the servants and rough-and-tumble laborers who worked in the fields.

When Lucy, Jacob, and Noah arrived, she found Abner and Martha already there. *What a gloomy pair they are.* Lucy climbed from the carriage and lifted Noah down. Abner and Jacob were alike in some respects. Both presented imposing figures, with their massive shoulders and impressive height. The resemblance ended there. In contrast to Jacob's blond hair and rather bland features, Abner Schneider had the look of a Biblical prophet with his long, dark beard, blazing brown eyes, and all-black attire. He commanded instant attention, especially when he quoted gloom-and-doom scripture from the Bible, something he did with annoying frequency. His wife, a timid little mouse who agreed with everything her husband said, lived in his shadow. She kept herself as unobtrusive as possible in plain black dresses, her dark, lifeless hair pulled into an untidy bun.

Her skin was sallow, and her big eyes always held a hint of fear. Lucy felt nothing but pity for her, especially when she saw Abner treated her more like a servant than a wife. Even worse, Lucy had twice detected a discoloration around Martha's eye. She never asked what caused it—surely Martha would lie—but she wondered what other marks and bruises might be hidden beneath the high necklines and long sleeves of Martha's dowdy gowns.

"Mother, may I go play?" Noah asked.

"Of course you can. Run along." The first time she met the friendly little boy with the bright gray eyes and blond curls, he instantly stole her heart. Now he called her "Mother," which pleased her to no end.

As Noah ran off, Martha looked after him. "Such a dear little boy, and so very bright, too."

"Indeed he is." Lucy heard the longing in Martha's voice and felt her usual surge of sympathy for the childless woman. Countless times Lucy had heard Abner lament the lack of a son, implying Martha was to blame. Apparently Martha thought so, too. That she remained childless after nearly ten years of marriage must be a constant heartache.

Abner greeted his brother, throwing the barest of nods toward Lucy. He pointed to a group of men standing in the churchyard, engaged in lively conversation with a beardless man in fringed buckskins and a soft, broad-brimmed hat, his face bronzed by wind and sun. "I see Clint Palance is here."

Lucy hadn't heard the name. "Who is Clint Palance?"

"His name is well-known in the West." Abner spoke with admiration. "He's been a trapper, trader, and Indian scout. I hear he fought the Cayuse in Oregon in forty-eight. Now he and a fellow named Charlie Dawes are partners. They own a trading company. Lately they've been guiding wagon trains to California. Safely, I might add."

"So, what's he doing here?"

"Business in Boston, something to do with his trading company. Now, from what I hear, he and Charlie Dawes will lead the Potts' wagon train to California. Come, let's hear what he has to say." He started forward, Martha at his side; then he stopped to address her: "Go in and help with the food."

"Yes, Abner."

Watching her sister-in-law meekly walk away made Lucy's temper flare. How dare Abner treat his wife that way! Lucy had never heard her make more than the most inoffensive of remarks and certainly had never once heard her stand up to her husband.

Abner turned to her. "Why don't you go in with Martha? This is men's talk, not suitable for women."

Lucy smiled back at him. "Perhaps not, but I'll be the judge of that. I'd like to hear what this Indian scout has to say." *Good try, Abner.* Her brother-in-law's constant attempts to domineer were highly annoying, but so far she'd managed to conceal her disgust, not only with him but with her husband, who stood by in spineless silence and let his brother make the decisions.

Lucy drew closer to hear what Clint Palance had to say. Something about him immediately captured her attention. Perhaps it was the knife with the very long blade dangling in a buckskin sheath from his belt. Or perhaps it was the lean, sinewy, slightly dangerous look about him. He wasn't especially tall, yet somehow he gave the impression of power as he stood, stance casual, yet with an air of complete self-confidence. He wore his black hair long and very straight, almost touching his broad shoulders. Drawing even closer, she saw his eyes were a deep shade of brown, wide-set, shrewd, and assessing. She also saw a scar, jagged and ugly, at least five inches in length, that ran from the middle of his left cheek to the bottom of his firm chin.

What an intriguing man. Suddenly his gaze shifted. He seemed to be staring directly at her, and in a cool, impertinent way. Her first panicked thought was he knew exactly what she was thinking! Her good sense quickly returned. She told herself to stop being foolish. Of course, he couldn't read her thoughts. Even so, she felt strangely compelled to show him she wasn't available. Fully gazing at the trapper, she stepped closer to her husband and made a show of tucking her arm through his. Almost immediately Clint Palance looked away, but not before she thought she spied the beginning of a smile tip the corners of his mouth.

Several men, including Abner, crowded around Palance, eagerly asking questions. To her surprise, Jacob left her side to join them. She drew closer, too, and heard one of the men ask, "So tell us, Mister Palance, which is the easiest trail to California?"

"There is no easiest."

The trapper's reply brought a clamor of questions.

"What's the safest way to go?"

"What's the best month to leave?"

"Will there be any gold left when we get to California?"

"Gentlemen!" Clint Palance raised a hand, and the voices stilled. "There is no easiest and there is no safest. April's the best time to go, soon as winter's gone. As for the gold you're seeking ..."

The crowd pressed closer. A large, unkempt man with a straggly red beard asked, "Ain't there plenty of gold for everybody?"

Palance firmly shook his head. "Not with thousands already at the gold fields and thousands more on the way."

The man stepped forward. "That's not the way I heard it! I heard there's gold all over the ground, just a'lyin' there waiting for a man to come pick it up."

"That may have been true at the beginning, but not anymore."

"That's bull!"

"That's the truth." Palance's voice was so soft he might

have been discussing the price of wheat.

The large man sneered. "You're a liar! Everyone knows they're paving the streets with gold in California. What's your angle? You aiming for us to stay home so you can keep it all for yourself?"

The crowd instantly stilled. Bessie, frowning with concern, moved next to Lucy. "There's going to be trouble," she whispered. "Just look at the size of that knife dangling from Mister Palance's belt."

"I see it."

"He would use it, too. I just know he would."

The crowd seemed to hold its collective breath, all eyes, including Lucy's, fastened on Palance, waiting for his response.

The trapper stood with an easy smile, hands by his sides, making no threatening moves toward the knife. He regarded the hostile man much as he would a bug, deciding whether or not to squash it. "I'll wager a horn of Monongahela whiskey you won't find gold on the ground in California." His smile widened. "Now you have a choice. You can accept my bet or you can choose to call me a liar again. Which will it be, sir?"

In the taut silence that followed, Lucy watched as the red-bearded man twice opened his mouth to speak then thought better of it. No wonder. Clint Palance had retained his quiet, conversational voice; his smile seemed genuine, yet the ominous set of his chin and the hard glint deep in his eyes suggested only a fool would tangle with him.

Apparently, Red Beard thought the same. With a face-saving shrug, as if he weren't the least concerned, he backed a step away. "I don't want no trouble." He spun around. Amidst an audible murmur of relief from the crowd, he walked away.

Bessie's gaze followed him. "Mercy me, did you see that? I think Mister Palance is a little ... a little ..."

"Frightening?" Lucy said.

Bessie nodded emphatically. "Yes, that's exactly right, a

little frightening, and certainly not a man I would invite into my parlor." She paused for a thoughtful moment. "On the other hand, there's something about him … you must admit he's devilish handsome." Bessie gazed at Clint Palance with admiring eyes. "Don't you think so?"

"He's all right." Lucy wasn't sure why she concealed her true feelings when actually she found him most intriguing, as well as handsome. "How do you suppose he got that scar on his cheek?"

"They say 't'was a grizzly bear. Imagine!"

No, she couldn't imagine. All she knew was that in her entire sheltered, tranquil life, she'd never witnessed such a scene. She felt greatly relieved it had ended peaceably. As the questions resumed, she wanted nothing more than to get away from this disturbing man in buckskins. She moved in close, to where Jacob stood, and tugged on his sleeve. "Let's go inside."

Abner, who stood next to him, shook his head. "I think we should hear this."

"So do I," Jacob replied.

Lucy concealed her chagrin. Why, again, did her husband show this sudden interest in California? Something cautioned her not to ask; then she silently laughed at her foolishness. Jacob was a prosperous farmer, thoroughly content with his life. Never in a million years would he uproot them to join the foolhardy stampede to the West.

Chapter 2

The potluck was over, thank God. Outside the church, Clint Palance stood alone and impatient in the weak, early spring sunshine. He was staying at the Potts farm and was anxious to return. He had much to do before the wagons bearing the Potts family and their possessions left for Independence, along with the three other families who had joined the trek west. They would pick up others along the way.

As he waited, a slender woman with thick brownish-red hair piled atop her head burst through the church door and started down the steps. Ah, Mrs. Schneider. When he first laid eyes on her, only hours ago in the churchyard, he felt a tug of excitement. Now here it came again. Funny. These days, rare was the woman who stirred his interest. During his years as a trapper, when he spent months in his isolated mountain cabin, he set his mind not to think about women. Had himself convinced he didn't need a woman in his life and never would. Now, back in civilization, he hadn't changed. Sure, from time to time he dallied with the occasional woman, but not the kind you married. Never would he be the kind of man who married, had a passel of kids, and settled into a life of boredom and, as far as he was concerned, entrapment. Still ...

Something about Mrs. Jacob Schneider caught his eye. Among the farm women here today, she stood out like a rose among thorns. Slender figure ... bright blue, wide-set eyes ... full red lips ... small, straight nose with its perky tilt. He could hardly keep his eyes off her.

A while ago he'd been amused when she clutched her husband's arm, sending out that silly "I'm not available" signal. Like he couldn't have figured that out. Too bad she was married. Wait. Why should he care? Leading the Potts' party safely to California was all he cared about. He wouldn't allow any female, married or single, to clutter up his mind.

She reached the bottom of the steps. "Mister Palance." She gave a polite nod. Nose in the air, she was about to sail right by.

Oh, no, she wouldn't. "Mrs. Jacob Schneider!" His voice rang out extra loud.

She stopped and turned her head. "You know my name?"

"I made it my business to know your name."

"Oh."

Good. He could tell she was caught off guard and stuck for an answer. "I've been talking to your husband." She turned to face him—one hell of a beautiful woman.

"You talked to Jacob?" She raised an eyebrow. "I do hope you weren't trying to persuade him to join John Potts and head for California."

"Why is that?"

"Because ..."

He could easily see her struggle to remain polite and keep her mouth shut, but temptation triumphed.

"I think it's insane. All these people leaving the only life they've ever known to take off on a wild goose chase for gold."

"It's not entirely the gold. Many plan to settle the land, make new lives for themselves."

"New lives?" Her large blue eyes snapped with displeasure. "How can they leave family and friends behind? Go all that way, in all that danger, and for what? What will they find in the West they don't already have right here?"

Clint shrugged. "It's not for everyone."

"It most assuredly is not, sir. Mister Schneider and I are quite content where we are. In fact, I doubt I shall ever set foot outside of Suffolk County."

He cut off the sharp words that sprung to his lips. Long ago he'd learned there were times it was best to keep his mouth shut.

She tipped her head. "Are you originally from the East?"

"Kentucky."

"A beautiful state, I hear. If you don't mind my asking, why do you make that fearsome journey west time after time? Why can't you stay in Kentucky where it's civilized?"

He could hardly keep from laughing at this prim young matron with her narrow, wrong-headed view of life. Maybe she came from a wealthy background, but he sure hadn't. He'd had a hellish childhood back in Kentucky, all because of a father who thought he needed a beating every day.

"Why don't I stay in your beautiful civilized East?" He repeated the question to gain time while his mind raced west in a lightning journey, soaring over the open plains with their astonishing sightings of tens of thousands of galloping buffalo; over pristine lakes, streams, and forests never seen or touched by a white man; over the mighty snowcapped peaks of the great mountain ranges, to the edge of the continent where he'd stood and watched in fascination the giant waves of the Pacific crash against the rocky shore.

How could he describe the beauty of a land she'd never seen?

There was no way to describe it, no way she would understand unless she saw for herself.

He shrugged matter-of-factly. "I go west to catch the sunset."

"I don't understand."

"That's the best explanation I can give you. West to catch the sunset. If you're wondering, I have yet to catch it. I probably never will."

❦❦

He was smiling at her. For the next few moments, Lucy found herself speechless, gazing like an idiot into Clint Palance's deep brown eyes. His answer had caught her unprepared. She hadn't thought a man who wore buckskins, carried a huge knife, bore the mark of a grizzly upon his cheek, and doubtless had no idea of sophisticated culture, could possibly say something so imaginative. Still, even if he had, he was not of her world and never would be. "Well, Mister Palance, it seems you know your goal in life."

"Seems I do."

"I know mine, and that's to stay right where I am and not go traipsing across the country after a foolish dream."

"Well said, Mrs. Schneider. I wouldn't dream of attempting to change your mind." With a smile and slight bow he touched the brim of his hat and backed away. "Good day."

Disturbed by their conversation, Lucy watched Clint Palance walk away. She wasn't sure why she was disturbed, except she found him unlike any man she'd ever known. At least he spoke well and knew his manners—which was unexpected— yet she sensed the raw, ruthless power that lurked directly underneath all that politeness. The man with the red beard had sensed it, too, and skulked away, tail between his legs.

Jacob appeared. "You ready?"

Oh, yes, she was ready and very much wanted to get back to her home, garden, and lovely quiet life.

On the buggy ride home, Lucy felt a gush of affection for her husband. She snuggled close, tucking her arm beneath his. "We have much to be thankful for."

Jacob held the reins in his hand. "Indeed." He gave a solemn nod, his eyes focused on the road.

She had not expected more. In the months since they had married, she had gradually come to realize that the attentive man who'd won her hand no longer existed. She hadn't expected

Jacob would remain an ardent suitor, yet she hadn't dreamed he'd grow more taciturn, a man with little humor. Perish the thought, but more like his brother every day. Even so, as the months went by, she made every effort to look at his good qualities and forget the bad.

Although ...

Now and then she remembered what Sarah had said shortly after her marriage. "You'll love married life. I cannot describe what Daniel does to me. It's just so wonderful." A blush crept over Sarah's cheeks. "You might say I get carried away on the wings of love, if you know what I mean."

No, she did not know what Sarah meant. Because of her sister's glowing words, Lucy had assumed her wedding night would open the door to a lifetime of blissful nights where she, too, would be carried away on the wings of love. Ha! Such was not the case. Sarah had rhapsodized about "those joyous hours of passion," but Lucy found that about one not-so-joyous minute practically every night would be more like it. After that, Jacob would quickly roll over and go to sleep, leaving her wondering what on earth Sarah was talking about.

Still, she loved Jacob. After all, she couldn't ask for a better provider. Not only that, his honesty and integrity gave him great stature in the community. At gatherings, she always experienced a swell of pride when she stood by her handsome husband's side, sharing the looks of admiration and respect cast his way. Then, too, there was little Noah. She was grateful to Jacob every day that he trusted her to be the mother to his adorable little boy.

Of course, Jacob could be more generous. He'd been the soul of generosity at first but lately had pinched every penny. All things considered, she was happy with her life and grateful to Jacob for making it so.

"I feel so sorry for Bessie," she remarked as the buggy rolled along.

He slanted a glance. "Why?"

How could he possibly not know? "Bessie doesn't want to go to California."

A frown crossed Jacob's face. "Why not?"

"How would you feel if you had a perfectly fine home and six children to raise, nearly seven, and all of a sudden you're forced to live in a tiny wagon for months and months with all sorts of dangers? And end up, if you ever get there, thousands of miles away from home?"

"It's her husband's wish." Jacob cracked the whip sharply, as if to convey a message that the subject should be at an end.

She wouldn't let it end, not yet. "Would you do that to me?"

"Do what?" He stared straight ahead in that maddeningly detached way of his.

"Sell the farm and move west."

He turned his head and looked down his nose at her. "We have a good life right here. You know what Abner says." With a snap of the reins, he recited in the ponderous voice she was now so familiar with, "Psalm twenty-three, Verse five: 'My cup runneth over.' "

Despite her growing annoyance at Jacob's increasingly excessive recitation of the scriptures, she felt better. She hadn't realized it, but Jacob's obvious interest in Clint Palance had caused her unconsciously to worry. Now she felt at ease. *My cup runneth over.* Yes, she should remember that and remind herself every day what a fine, satisfying life she led as the wife of Jacob Schneider.

Days later, Lucy began to suspect she was harboring a wonderful secret. She waited, not saying a word to Jacob or anyone. Two weeks went by, weeks she spent in a state of ecstatic expectation, each day fearing she would find the tell-tale sign that would prove her wrong. It never appeared, and when one day she noticed how her breasts were swollen, and how she felt nauseous in the morning when she arose, she knew for certain a baby was on the way.

Boy or girl? Which room would be the nursery? Her mind churned with questions and plans. When should she give Jacob the exciting news? She could hardly wait. Joyously, she pictured how happy he'd be, how delighted that he might soon have another son.

That night she put Noah to bed early and waited until she and Jacob sat down for supper. She planned on waiting until the end of the meal, but as soon as she sat down, she could contain herself no longer. "Jacob, I have news." Heart pounding, she fixed her gaze across the table and awaited his answer.

With maddening slowness, Jacob placed a large scoop of mashed potatoes on his plate, then covered it with gravy. "What's your news?"

"I am with child!" She couldn't prevent the way her words bubbled or the happy smile that wreathed her face. As it was, she wanted to run around the table and hug him tight but knew him well enough to know he wouldn't approve.

"Are you sure?" His expression hadn't changed.

"Very sure."

"Hmm." He took a sip of water. He dipped his fork into the mashed potatoes and took another bite.

What was wrong? Why wasn't he beside himself with delight? As she waited, she thought her heart would pound its way right out of her chest. "Jacob, answer me. What's wrong? Don't you think it's wonderful?"

Jacob finally laid down his fork. "I suppose now is as good a time as any to tell you."

"Tell me what?" Concern flickered through her. Whatever was coming, it wouldn't be good.

"Abner and I have sold the farm. We're going with the Potts' wagon train to California."

Chapter 3

As the full meaning of Jacob's words sunk in, Lucy gasped and gripped the edge of the table. "What did you say?"

"You heard me."

"You lied to me!"

His voice was cold and exact. "Don't you dare call me a liar. Negotiations to sell the farm took time. I wasn't going to have you nagging at me. It was best you didn't know."

"You have actually sold the farm?" she asked in a suffocated whisper. Perhaps she hadn't heard right.

"It's gone."

"I cannot believe this."

Jacob shrugged. "Abner and I made a joint decision. We have three weeks to move. Actually—" Jacob settled back comfortably in his chair, looking as if he were discussing the weather, "we plan on leaving sooner. As you know, the Potts' party is undoubtedly well on their way to Independence by now. When they arrive, they must wait for the end of the inclement weather. That gives us time to catch up. Although we have no time to lose if we want to reach them before they leave for California."

The truth dawned. "This is Abner's doing, isn't it? *He* was the one who wanted to go, not you."

"I said it was a joint decision."

"No, it wasn't. You always do what your brother wants. You never stand up for yourself."

Jacob's face grew white with anger. "Shut your mouth. I've

19

heard enough."

Shock yielded to fury. "Why is it I had no say in the matter?"

He looked surprised. "I am your husband. I make the decisions, not you."

"The baby!" She knew she was screeching, but she didn't care. "How can I live in a wagon these next few months? Out in the open, never having a roof over my head? Well, I can't do it. It's impossible; the last thing in the world I ever would have wanted."

Jacob nodded, maddeningly calm. "I admit, the timing is unfortunate. Even if I had known, I wouldn't have changed my plans. I know it won't be easy. In talking to Mister Palance, I gather women must take on a huge burden on these treks west. However, I won't be hiring extra help and will expect you to do your share, baby or no."

She felt herself shaking with anger, so distraught she could hardly speak. "I won't go."

"You are my wife. You will go."

"You'll have to drag me."

He returned an expression of pained tolerance. "Perhaps you'd best reconsider. You can't stay here. The farm is sold. You'd be without support of any kind, that is," his mouth spread into a thin-lipped smile, "unless you return to your father and your beloved Pernelia. I know how happy you'd be, living under her roof again."

How did he know? She had never revealed her desperation to escape the clutches of her stepmother. Jacob wasn't stupid. Somehow he must have guessed.

"How long have you and Abner been planning this?"

"Haven't you noticed the price of apples these days?"

"You mean the farm's been losing money?"

"Three years in a row."

The awful truth dawned on her. "You planned this before

we were even married and never said a word?"

"The Lord spoke to Abner. He told him we must go." Jacob cast a pious glance upward toward heaven. "Jeremiah forty-two, Verse six: 'Whether it be good, or whether it be evil, we will obey the voice of the Lord.' "

"Well, the Lord never said a word to me!"

Jacob rose from the table. "I suggest you go to Boston tomorrow. See what your father has to say about a wife who refuses to obey her husband. Meanwhile, you might want to look up Genesis three, Verse sixteen, 'Thy desire shall be to thy husband, and he shall rule over thee.' "

Lucy sprang up from the table, thrusting her chair back so hard it toppled over. "If you quote one more scripture to me, I shall ... I shall ..."

"You shall what?"

Words failed her. "Never mind. I shall go see Father tomorrow." Even as she spoke, she heartily regretted she couldn't fire back with a more adequate response, something stunningly cutting to bring him down. In the shock of the moment, she could think of nothing else to say. Without another word, she fled the room.

The next day Lucy sat across from her beloved father in the old, familiar parlor on Beacon Street. She would never see him again if she went to California, or her sister or two younger brothers. "He never even warned me." Her voice choked. "Never said a word."

Elihu Parker leaned back in his chair, looking old, tired, and very concerned. "Of course, you can move back with us. The door is always open." He regarded her with gentle understanding. "Daughter, do you really want to end your marriage?"

"He lied to me."

"He had his reasons, did he not? Mind you, I'm not

making excuses for the man. In fact, right from the start I ... but no matter. No man is perfect."

"You don't like him. You never did." She stated it as a fact, not an accusation.

"Jacob is a fine man in many respects. What I don't like is he's too much under his brother's thumb. That in itself wouldn't be so bad if Abner Schneider were a man I admired, but the problem is, I find him to be far too rigid and self-righteous." Father offered a small, sly smile. "I confess, there are times when I hear him spouting one of his endless quotes from the scriptures, I would like to take my own Bible and whack him over the head with it."

Despite her despair, Lucy managed a laugh, but her despondence quickly returned. "What shall I do? I cannot go to California. The very thought—"

"Jacob is your husband." Her father sat up straight. His voice grew hard. "You took a vow to obey him, did you not?"

"Yes, but—"

"You are now with child?"

"Yes."

"You now want to deny that child its father?" Her father's voice softened. "The final decision is yours, but think carefully. Do you really want to destroy your marriage? Do you really want to move back home? You're a strong woman. Time and again I've seen you accept your responsibilities without complaint. Why can't you do so now?"

Her own father! What had she been thinking? His question made her realize she had no defenses, no defenders. Everyone would say the same thing. Even her own sister, who understood her better anyone else in the world, would tell her she'd be a fool to come crawling home, reputation ruined, subjecting herself once again to the oppressing rule of Pernelia. *I would be a pariah, living in disgrace for the rest of my life, the fallen woman who did the unthinkable and left her husband.*

At that moment, Lucy realized further complaints were useless. Whether she liked it or not, her life was not her own. Her future lay in the hands of her husband. No matter what her pain and sorrow, she might as well make the best of it. Honor alone would prevent her from acting the coward, leaving her husband.

Tears filled her eyes, not so much from sorrow but from pure anger and frustration. "I might as well try to fight the wind. I have no choice, do I?"

"No, my dear, you don't."

"All right, I've decided." Her voice was bitter-filled. "I shall go to California with my husband, but I don't have to like it."

Elihu Parker gave her an encouraging smile. "Like it or not, you're smart and have got plenty of spunk. You're going to do fine."

"If you say so." Lucy knew she'd need a lot more than spunk to get her through the months ahead.

When Lucy returned to the farm, she announced her decision to Jacob.

If he was pleased, he showed no sign other than a brief grunt. "We leave in two weeks. You must decide which items you wish to bring, but mind you, we're taking only three wagons, so space is limited."

During the next few days, Lucy learned to her sorrow how right Jacob was. Going through her possessions, time and again she discovered items she could not possibly do without, only to learn she must leave them behind.

Her precious books? "There will be little time for reading," scoffed Jacob.

Her sketch book and paints? "No room."

Her lovely clothes? When Jacob discovered she'd packed her blue satin ball gown, he held it up with scorn. "Do you plan on being the height of fashion for the Indians? I assure you, they won't care how you look."

Indians. The very thought struck fear into her heart, as did nearly everything else concerning this insane journey to California.

The night before they left, Lucy lay in bed, Jacob snoring by her side, and vowed from this day forward her husband wouldn't hear one more word of protest or complaint. She would take good care of him and Noah. She would perform whatever duties were required and remain resolute and strong, no matter what hardships befell her.

As for Jacob, she still loved him and would always feel pride in being the wife of a man who was a natural-born leader, admired by all—at least all who didn't know how he toadied to his brother. With a sad heart, she realized she had lost the unquestioning trust she'd once had in her husband. It vanished forever the day she discovered he'd lied. Vanished along with her dream of raising her child in the security and warmth of this sturdy Massachusetts farmhouse that she'd already grown to love.

She would manage, and most important ... Lucy's hand rested lovingly over the spot where the tiny spark of life lay within her. "I vow," she whispered into the darkness, "no matter where we are, no matter what happens, I'll do everything in my power to keep you safe."

Chapter 4

Independence, Missouri
April, 1851

"We're here!"

In the lead wagon, seated between Noah and her husband, Lucy put her arm around her stepson's shoulders and pointed toward the town square ahead. "It's the jumping-off point, son. Civilization ends right here."

Despite her deep reluctance and painful goodbyes to friends and family, Lucy felt a swell of excitement as the caravan of twenty wagons rolled into town. Independence bustled with energy. Even from a distance, she could see throngs of people buying and selling on street corners, crowding in and out of the town's many stores and saloons. Never had she seen such a variety of mankind swarming the sidewalks. Blanketed, painted Indians—Mexicans in bells and slashed pantaloons—mountain men in buckskins—river men and roustabouts—negro stevedores—soldiers from what she later learned was Fort Leavenworth. Covered wagons, parked at all angles, lined the town's central square.

Thus far, the journey from home had not been easy. The rocking motion of the wagon greatly added to the misery of her early-pregnancy nausea. She yearned to lie down and nap during the day, but her newfound duties prevented any such luxury. She was now the cook, not only for herself, Jacob, and Noah, but also for the two young men Jacob hired to help drive the wagons and herd their sixty head of cattle.

At the beginning, when Jacob informed her she must do the cooking, she said, "I have never cooked! I've never even boiled an egg, yet you expect me to cook all the meals for us and the hired hands? Impossible!"

As usual, Jacob remained stone-faced. "I'm not made of money. You will do the cooking."

She was flabbergasted. "Then how is it you've hired two hands to help you with the wagons and the cattle? Surely—"

"The subject is closed." Jacob clamped his jaw, a sure sign he wouldn't tolerate further argument. She said nothing more but still harbored resentment over his miserly ways, especially when she knew he'd hidden a bag of five dollar gold pieces at the bottom of the flour barrel, far more than enough to pay the paltry wage for a cook.

At least they found plenty of farmhouses along the way to Independence where they were able to buy eggs, milk, and chicken—all the fresh food they needed. That was the easy part. The hard part for Lucy was learning how to cook over an open fire, sometimes with a strong wind blowing, sometimes in the rain. With the help of other women in the party, she managed, and true to her vow, she never once complained. Only when she was alone did she permit herself to remember the heart-wrenching scene when she said her final goodbyes to her father, sister, and two little brothers, knowing the chances were slim she'd ever see them again.

She had pretty much forgiven Jacob his deception. Holding a grudge was not in her nature, especially since it wouldn't do her any good. Even so, she found Jacob's subservience to his brother absolutely galling, now even more noticeable because of their day-and-night proximity on the trail. "Please, must we go to Abner's prayer meeting tonight?" she asked of Jacob one evening after a particularly grueling day.

"My brother expects us."

"I'm so awfully tired, and besides, I cannot see the point in going to a prayer meeting every single night. Am I a sinner if I miss one now and then?"

Jacob's instant scowl told her he'd seen no humor in her question. She might've known he'd side with his brother. So, of course, they attended each of Abner's nightly prayer meetings. He was not an ordained minister, but he sounded like one. Often she nearly fell asleep to the sound of her unctuous brother-in-law's fire and brimstone warnings that she could easily be heading straight to hell.

"Keep a sharp eye out for the Potts' wagon," Jacob told her. They entered Independence's town square. Jacob sat tall and straight, with a strong grip on the reins, showing no sign of emotion. In fact, he seemed to grow more serious by the day. Even their arrival at the jumping-off point couldn't raise a smile or even the slightest sign of excitement. "Watch for Clint Palance and his partner, too. We must make arrangements for joining their wagon train."

Clint Palance. His name had crossed her mind more than once as their small caravan headed west. She dreaded the moment she would encounter the trapper again. She could just picture how his lips would quirk mockingly when he expressed his surprise.

She could even imagine his words: "Are my eyes deceiving me? Is this the same Mrs. Jacob Schneider who declared she'd never set foot outside of Suffolk County?"

She told herself Clint Palance's opinion didn't matter a whit, and from that moment forward, she wouldn't give him one more thought. Her advice to herself never worked. No matter how hard she tried, she couldn't stop thinking about him. Worse, despite the embarrassment she'd surely feel when she saw him again, she was acutely aware of certain wicked, unacceptable thoughts that lurked somewhere deep in her consciousness. She *must* get rid of them. They were thoughts no decent, respectably married woman would ever entertain.

"As I live and breathe, Lucy!" cried a very pregnant Bessie Potts. "Oh, my stars!" Awkwardly, she climbed down from her seat on the Potts' wagon and threw her arms around her friend. "I can't believe it! What are you doing here?"

"Abner and Jacob sold the farm," Lucy replied when they broke apart. "Jacob decided to go west. We plan on joining your wagon train."

"What about Abner?"

"He's here, too."

"Oh dear." Bessie bit her lip. "Sorry, I know he's your brother-in-law, but I hate the way he presumes to speak for God. I declare, half the time he acts like Moses descending from Mount Sinai, stone tablets in hand."

Lucy burst into laughter at Bessie's description. "I'm afraid you're right."

Bessie asked, "Did Martha come?"

"Yes."

"Well, of course, she did." They exchanged a knowing glance but said nothing. Poor Martha, what could they say?

Bessie and Lucy spent the next few minutes in a delightful catching up session. "It really wasn't so bad," Lucy referred to their journey from Suffolk County to Independence. No sense recounting all the misery. "Jacob is so well organized and efficient, he planned everything down to the last detail. Beside the cattle, we have three wagons, six oxen, two horses, and six pack mules—enough for all the household goods we brought. He hired two young men to help drive the wagons and herd the cattle."

"A cook?" Bessie asked.

"We left the cook behind." Lucy put on a cheerful face. "I do the cooking. In fact, I've become quite the expert at tossing slapjacks."

A shadow crossed Bessie's face. "Did you know my John hasn't been well? He came down with typhoid. We nearly lost him. As it is, he's not the same."

"He's getting better?"

"He's still so weak ... Oh, here's Hannah." A tall, gawky woman strode toward them. Plainly dressed, she wore her thin, brown hair pulled straight back into an untidy bun. "Lucy Schneider, meet my sister, Hannah Richards."

Hannah stuck her hand out. Her work-worn face lit into a beautiful smile. "I'm mighty pleased to meet you, Mrs. Schneider."

"Call me Lucy." Right away she knew they'd be friends.

Bessie continued, "By the way, all the women in the wagon train are invited for high tea this afternoon. Me and Hannah will be there. Want to come along?"

Lucy could think of no more unlikely place for a high tea than crude, rough-and-tumble Independence, where most of the population undoubtedly had never heard of such a thing as a high tea. She glanced around the square. "Is there a tea room somewhere?"

Hannah burst into hearty laughter. "Come back at four o'clock and bring your own cup. Her majesty figures her fine china is too good for the likes of us."

"Her majesty?"

Bessie explained. "That would be Mrs. Nathaniel Beauregard Benton, who's stuck-up, puts on airs, and figures she's God's gift to society. You should hear her." She assumed a snooty southern accent. "At all costs, we must remain refined and civilized, my dear, even if we *are* living in a wagon."

Lucy smiled as Bessie and her sister broke into laughter at Bessie's imitation. "I'd love to come." Despite her tactful reply, she reflected with regret that she probably wasn't going to like Mrs. Nathaniel Beauregard Benton.

After Hannah left, Lucy, bursting to tell her news, leaned

forward and said, "I have a secret to tell you."

Bessie smiled. "If you're going to tell me you're expecting, don't bother."

"How can you tell?" At barely three months, Lucy was certain nothing showed.

Bessie flicked a glance toward Lucy's bosom. "You're bigger. Besides, it's written all over you—a certain glow. Lots of women have it when they get in a family way, at least for the first, maybe the second month." Bessie placed a palm on her swollen belly and sighed. "When you get to the seventh, there ain't no more glow."

Lucy was about to say more when she caught sight of Clint Palance striding through the square. Today he wore not buckskins but a long, black rifle coat, khaki pants, a stylish vest, and a black gambler's hat with a soft, wide brim. So handsome! So very ... intriguing. As yet, he hadn't seen her. She couldn't face him. "I must run now, but I'll be back for that tea this afternoon."

"See you then. Ask Martha. She might want to come, too."

Not likely. Lucy hastily turned and started away. She hadn't gone more than ten steps when she heard Clint's booming voice. "Mrs. Schneider? Mrs. Jacob Schneider?"

Damnation. She didn't want to stop but had no choice. She smoothed down the starched white apron she wore over her brown woolen dress, affixed a smile to her face, and turned. "Why, Mister Palance, what a surprise."

"Mrs. Schneider? I had no idea I'd see you here."

She knew it! Just as she expected, his eye lit with a mocking gleam. She lifted her chin to a defiant angle. "Well, obviously I *am* here."

His forehead furrowed in feigned puzzlement. "I can't imagine what urgent event has led you to set foot outside of Suffolk County. As I recall—"

"Obviously, my husband changed his mind." This was

every bit as excruciating as she had anticipated. "If you had any manners, out of delicacy alone, you wouldn't bring up the subject."

He grinned, revealing white teeth that dazzled against his bronzed skin. "I've never been accused of having good manners."

"Obviously." What was the matter with her? Why did she feel so uncomfortable? What was it about this blunt man that set her all atwitter? She already knew he' surely bring up her foolish declaration she would never leave Suffolk County, so why was she not prepared? Why was she now feeling a blush creep over her cheeks that he was sure to notice? Well, she would see this through as best she could. She squared her shoulders. "It appears we shall be joining your wagon train to California." She was pleased at the bright, enthusiastic note she'd put in her voice.

"Are you actually happy you're going?"

"I can hardly wait to get started." Just amazing that she hadn't choked on such a lie. "I'm very much enjoying living in the great out-of-doors and, uh, riding in the wagon ... all that wonderful fresh air. I just love cooking over an open fire and ... well, all of that." She could kick herself. He wasn't fooled.

After a moment's reflection, he grew serious. "I have yet to meet a woman who truly wanted to make this journey."

At least he wasn't mocking her anymore. She'd planned another flippant answer but found she could no longer lie. She was equally serious. "I'm making the best of it."

"I'm certain you are."

The worst was over. She was proud of herself for having met Clint's anticipated sarcasm with dignity ... well, something like it. Good manners decreed she ought to stand and chat a little longer, but the problem was, her pulse remained quick and her mouth had gone dry. Why this should affect her this way, she didn't know, except that she'd never met a man so overwhelmingly masculine as Clint Palance. Even in civilized clothes and without the knife dangling from his belt, he had a certain menacing air. She was so acutely aware of him she couldn't act her normal self. She decided to leave before he noticed. "Well, I must be off. There's so much to do."

For a fleeting moment, his brown eyes delved into hers, making her feel as if he could peer into her very soul and know exactly what she was about and what she was thinking. He smiled politely and touched a finger to the brim of his hat. "Then good day, ma'am."

"Good day, sir." She went on her way. Feeling his eyes on her, she forced herself to walk at a leisurely pace and not, as she was sorely tempted, to run as fast as she could to get to her wagon and out of his sight.

◈◈

Rooted to the spot, Clint observed Lucy Schneider. He liked the way she walked—tall and straight, with a lightness of foot few women possessed. She was pregnant. What a shame. The trek to California was hard enough as it was, but for a woman with child it was a tortuous journey. He could never understand why many of the husbands didn't seem concerned. Despite all the difficulties of pregnancy, they expected their wives to endure the hardships of the trail and work their full share. He'd wager Lucy's husband was one of those.

So, Jacob Schneider had changed his mind, had he? What bullshit. The one time they'd talked, that jackass had outright told him he and his brother would be heading for California, soon as the farm was sold. Apparently, he hadn't bothered to tell his wife.

Clint vented his disgust by kicking the dirt with the point of his boot. They'd had only the one conversation, but that was enough for him to peg Jacob Schneider as a poor excuse for a man. His brother, too. Cold and rigid in their thinking. Real pains in the ass and likely to be hard to deal with on the trail. If they didn't cause trouble before they reached California, he'd be greatly surprised.

≫⩽

Stopping by Abner's wagon, Lucy found Martha bending over a large laundry tub, her reddened hands scrubbing clothes on a board. "We're invited to a high tea this afternoon," Lucy said. "It should be fun. I'm going, and I hope you will, too."

Her sister-in-law looked up from her task and frowned. "Thank you, but I have too much to do."

Just the answer Lucy expected. "Nonsense. This is a fine opportunity to meet the women we'll be traveling with for the next few months. Surely Abner wouldn't mind."

Martha used her forearm to wipe the perspiration from her brow. "I'm not so sure. Abner wants this wash done. You know how he is."

Indeed I do know. Poor Martha always invited pity with her soft, timid voice and frail, stoop-shouldered figure. Her large gray eyes seemed to plead forgiveness for merely being alive. Perhaps if Martha had children she might think more highly of herself. Then again, perhaps not. Even a woman with iron resolve would have a hard time standing up to Abner's constant criticism and stern rule.

"I'm sorry you can't go. If you change your mind, let me know." Lucy turned to leave, but to her surprise, Martha called softly, "Wait a minute. I have something to tell you."

Lucy turned back. "What is it?"

"It's just ... it's ..." Suddenly Martha's cheeks flushed a rosy pink. "I think, I think ..."

The truth dawned on Lucy immediately. "Are you expecting?" There could be no other cause for such a blush on Martha's sallow cheeks.

"I ... think so!"

"Why, that's wonderful news!" Lucy threw her arms around her sister-in-law and gave her an exuberant hug. "Have you told Abner?"

Martha's blush deepened. "Not yet. I wanted to make sure, and now ... well, it's been two months since I ... you know what I mean, so I'm almost sure."

"He'll be delighted." *True enough*. Abner would be delighted all right, but just like Jacob, he'd still expect Martha to do her share of the work, and no excuses. That was too bad. Even under normal conditions, frail little Martha might have problems with a pregnancy. Lucy hated to think what could happen to her, considering the hardships of the trail.

❧

So this was high tea in Independence, Missouri!

Lucy suppressed a giggle as she recalled the many elegant teas she'd presided over in her fancy parlor on Beacon Hill. Now here she sat on an overturned barrel beside a muddy street, holding her own tin cup, beside the covered wagon of that former scion of Atlanta society, Mrs. Nathaniel Beauregard Benton. A handsome woman in her early forties with a narrow face and aristocratic nose, Mrs. Benton showed her slender figure to great advantage in an elegant dress of blue silk taffeta over a hoopskirt. Quite a contrast to her guests who had all left their hoopskirts behind, if they'd ever owned one in the first place. Instead, every other woman there wore a plain, long calico or wool dress, laced-up boots, and starched apron.

Upon meeting Lucy, Mrs. Benton exclaimed in a thick southern accent, "So you're from Boston? Beacon Hill? Do tell!" Her manner instantly grew warmer. "You must call me Cordelia. I declare, we have lots in common."

No, we don't. Lucy instantly recognized the woman as just

another Pernelia, only with a southern accent—all soft and cloying on the outside, hard as granite on the inside. A snob besides. She suspected she'd soon be avoiding Mrs. Nathaniel Beauregard Benton. *How could she?* At home it was easy to avoid those she didn't care for, but on the trail? Impossible. On second thought, she'd better make a special effort to get along with everybody whether she liked them or not.

Lucy sat quiet for the most part, observing the approximately twenty women who sat in a circle on an assortment of boxes, crates, and barrels. Each held her cup of tea, poured by Mrs. Benton from her solid silver teapot. Each held a pastry, freshly baked by a young Negro woman named Sukey, whom Mrs. Benton referred to as her slave. Lucy wondered how it was possible to own a slave while traveling on a wagon train headed west. Wasn't this free territory? But now was hardly the time to ask.

So these were some of the women she'd spend the next few months with. Quite a variety. They included Bessie Potts and Hannah Richards, both from Possum Creek, Tennessee. One would never guess they were sisters, what with small, nervous Bessie constantly expressing her fears and tall, raw-boned Hannah coming across as fearless and unflappable. Both were pleasant and friendly, though, compared to a middle-aged, dour-face woman named Agnes Applegate. She, her husband, William, and their six children came from Pennsylvania. She talked a lot but had yet to utter a positive word about anything. Then there was Inez Helmick, a plumpish blond-haired woman in her forties with a broad, Scandinavian face. She, her husband, Stanley, and their five children came from Ohio. "My husband is a preacher, and I'm a midwife." She had an air of great confidence. "In case any of you might need me on the trail."

"Well, ain't that a comfort to know. I just might be needing you." Bessie glanced at Lucy. "And others, too."

Oh, no. She could think of nothing worse than having her

baby in a wagon in the middle of nowhere. But she needn't worry. They'd be in California long before the baby arrived.

"I'm serving oolong tea today." Cordelia seated herself on a box, carefully spreading her taffeta skirt around her. "My favorite. Imported direct from China. Mister Benton made sure we brought enough to last the entire journey." She nodded toward her elaborate sterling silver tea set and the silver tray of pastries, both precariously balanced on a makeshift table. "I plan to serve tea every day of our journey. After all, one must continue to observe the niceties."

Hannah Richards gave an audible sniff. "Well, I sure don't know about that."

Cordelia's ever-present smile tightened. "Why might that be?"

"Ain't you heard of the poor folks who've gone ahead of us on other wagon trains? Many's the time when they run out of food and water, and the poor oxen are dead or about to die, they have to dump all their precious things along the wayside just to lighten the load."

Cordelia glared at Hannah with reproachful eyes. "Throw away Grandmother Benton's precious tea set? And her French Haviland china it took me a whole day to pack? That's not likely to happen."

"Well, I surely hope not." Hannah took up the tin cup that held her tea and raised it high. "Ladies, here's to a safe journey. May we not be kidnapped or worse by them pesky Indians. May we not get drowned in some river, nor any of our loved ones. May we find food for ourselves and grass for the animals and water for all, so we don't have to toss our precious possessions over the side."

"Amen to that." Lucy raised her cup, as did all of the women, with the exception of Agnes, who sat with her arms crossed and a dour expression on her sallow face.

"You all act like you're happy to be here," said Agnes.

No one spoke until someone murmured, "Well, indeed we are."

Agnes returned a disdainful sniff. "If truth be told, there's not a one of you wanted to come on this foolish journey in the first place. 'T'was all your husband's idea, now wasn't it? I'd wager every last one of you was happy and content where you were until your man got bit by the gold bug. Now he wants to go to California and get rich." Agnes glowered, her hazel eyes darting from one to another. "Well now, am I wrong? If anyone here was just dying to live in a flimsy wagon for months and months, and risk death and God-knows-what, then speak up."

The silence spoke for all. Faced with the truth, even Lucy, who usually rose to the occasion, could think of nothing diplomatic to say. Finally Cordelia, her southern accent extra thick, said, "Mrs. Applegate, I find your remark a bit harsh. Don't our husbands always know best? You seem to have forgotten a wife's role is to obey her husband and follow his lead with good grace."

All except Lucy and Hannah nodded in agreement, appearing relieved that Cordelia had provided an acceptable answer to Agnes' tirade. Lucy wondered why she herself wasn't instantly agreeing. After all, she was just like the rest, subject to her husband's commands. As Cordelia pointed out, a woman's lot in life was to obey her husband. She didn't have to like it, though. A thought struck her, one she'd never had before: she most definitely did *not* like it. Much as she loved Jacob and accepted his leadership, she felt an ever-deepening resentment that she was required to obey him. Despite her wedding vows, she really didn't want to obey anybody.

Hannah spoke up. "Just out of curiosity, what possessed your husband to head west? Looks to me like you had a good life going in Atlanta."

Cordelia awarded Hannah an indulgent smile. "It has to do with manifest destiny, Mrs. Richards. You might not understand."

"I may be poor, but I ain't stupid."

Visibly taken aback, Cordelia recovered quickly. "My husband was a noted historian back in Atlanta—"

"I'll tell them." A slight, beardless man of fifty or so stepped into the circle. Well groomed, dressed like a country gentleman, he had the dreamy-eyed look of a scholar.

Cordelia regarded him with pride. "My husband, ladies. Nathaniel Beauregard Benton."

After a greeting, Nathaniel Benton addressed the circle. "For years I've studied the history of The United States and what its expansion implies. Why am I going west? I believe Thoreau said it best: 'Eastward I go only by force, but we go westward as into the future, with a spirit of enterprise and adventure.' " Nathaniel's face lit up. "Not only that, we must claim what is ours. I know in my heart that the land from Atlantic to Pacific should belong to us, not foreign nations such as Great Britain and Mexico who are already meddling in California and Texas."

"My stars!" said Bessie, "I never thought of The United States spreading all the way from one ocean to the other."

"It's going to happen. It's our manifest destiny." Nathaniel Benton had a faraway look in his eyes. "We Americans are especially prone to setting out for the unknown. Like Mark Twain said, 'It's a human instinct like the need to love, or to taste spring air and believe again that life is not a dead end after all.' " He stopped and smiled. "That's why we're going to California."

"Well put, sir." Lucy put down her cup and started to applaud. They all joined in.

Benton returned a smile. "Well, then, ladies, I won't further interrupt your tea." With a courteous bow he walked away.

Cordelia reached for the silver tray. She held it out to Bessie and said with a sugary smile, "Another pastry?"

Bessie declined. "Well, land's sake, I don't know about manifest destiny. All I want is to get to California in one piece and find us a piece of land."

Cordelia smiled indulgently. "You're fearful of the journey, I know, but don't forget we have Mister Palance and Mister Dawes to guide us, and they're the very best. I'm not the least bit worried. Nothing will go wrong while they're around."

Every woman present except Lucy nodded her enthusiastic assent. Agnes noticed and focused sharp eyes upon her. "You don't agree?" Before Lucy could answer, Agnes continued, "I saw you talking to Mister Palance in the square. Do you know him from someplace? You appear to be good friends."

Lucy immediately caught the implication of wrong-doing in Agnes' voice. How ridiculous. Her entire conversation with Clint could not have lasted more than a minute or two, so how much could the sharp-eyed woman know of her private feelings? Yet ... she and Clint Palance had not exchanged one improper word, but with uncanny intuition, Agnes sensed that a vague current of attraction, or whatever it was, passed between them. Well from now on she'd be extra careful. If she didn't put the trapper completely out of her thoughts, that sharp-eyed woman was going to know.

Lucy smiled pleasantly. "I have barely met the man. My husband knows him far better than I."

The disagreeable woman gave a skeptical sniff but had the decency to change the subject. "We leave in three days. Did you know that? I hope your husband will have his wagons fitted and ready."

"Jacob will do whatever needs to be done, and on time," Lucy replied firmly.

A chubby, fair-skinned boy of about twelve or thirteen with a shock of straight blond hair hanging over one eye suddenly burst into the circle. "What's to eat?"

Cordelia's face took on a glow of motherly pride. "Ladies,

this is my son, Chadwick."

The boy acknowledged no one. Spying the pastries, he headed straight for the silver tray.

"Now, dear, only one," his mother called.

Chadwick acknowledged his mother's advice with a pig-like grunt. He stuffed a pastry into his mouth and scooped up as many more as his chubby little hands could handle.

Cordelia reacted with a merry peal of laughter. "You bad boy! Now, sweetheart, you'd better put those back. You don't want to eat too many or you'll spoil your supper."

After another grunt, Chadwick sped away, hands still full of pastries.

"Boys will be boys." Cordelia seemed not the least bit upset over her son's poor manners.

The entire assemblage of ladies had witnessed the episode in polite silence. Now, discreetly lifted eyebrows signaled messages of disapproval. "Did you see that child's behavior?" Bessie whispered. "If one of mine acted like that, John would have him behind the woodshed in no time."

Lucy silently agreed. If her little brothers had acted in such a manner ... But then, they never had because they'd been raised properly. Poor Cordelia. She was going to have her hands full on a journey like this with a child so thoroughly spoiled.

֍

When the tea party ended, Cordelia took Lucy aside. "I'm so delighted you're coming along. What a comfort to find someone of my own kind." She lowered her voice. "I'm sure you'll agree to the difficulty of having to deal with those of a lesser standing, but we'll manage, won't we?"

Lucy bristled inside. She hoped it didn't show. "Of a lesser standing? I don't know what you mean. Aren't we all of equal standing here?"

"Yes, of course. You know what I mean. Good breeding *is* good breeding."

Lucy sensed how useless it would be to argue with someone as condescending as Cordelia. She'd never change. "I must be going. Thank you for the lovely tea." She turned away. If she hurried, she could catch up with Bessie and Hannah. They might be "of a lesser standing," but she already knew who her true friends would be on the long journey ahead.

When Lucy returned to their wagon, she found Jacob with his coat, shirt, and hat off, bending over a basin washing his face. When he saw her, he straightened and grabbed a towel. Wiping water from his face, he broke into a rare smile. "The men of the council had a meeting. John Potts has not been well and has stepped down. I've been elected the new wagon train captain."

"Why, that's wonderful news."

"I wonder why they didn't pick Abner. Of course, he would've declined. His mind runs on a higher plain. It's best he remain our spiritual leader."

Lucy could've told her husband she knew very well why Abner hadn't been chosen. The men didn't like him and made fun of his holier-than-thou attitude behind his back. Some things were best left unsaid, though. "Well, they couldn't have made a better choice for a captain than you." Her heart swelled with pride as she looked up at her husband, so handsome with those strong arms, that muscular chest, and those golden curls glinting in the sunshine atop his noble head. *I do love him.* She regretted that lately she'd begun to find fault. His constantly serious demeanor had grown more annoying, as well as his increased fondness for quoting of the scriptures—just like his brother. Too much like his brother. Then there was the thing that happened at night after they went to bed. She had hoped the lack of privacy on the road would give her a respite from performing the one wifely duty she'd grown to detest, but she wasn't that fortunate. On the trip to Independence, when they stopped at night, Jacob pitched a tent beside the wagon, which only the two of them occupied. On the few nights they slept in the wagon, Jacob hung a blanket across the middle, between their bed and little Noah's. As if a flimsy blanket could conceal the rocking and muffle the sounds! She could only pray her mightiest that Noah remained sound asleep each time.

The worst of it was, nothing had changed. From her wedding night on, never once had she received the least bit of pleasure from the act her sister had referred to as "so indescribably wonderful."

She mustn't think bad thoughts. She must try harder to be the appreciative wife of a man admired and respected by all. A leader of men!

"I'm so proud of you."

"From now on, they'll address me as Captain."

"You deserve it. You have worked so hard—"

"'All things are delivered to me of my Father.' That's—"

"Luke ten, Verse twenty-two. Yes, I know. Thanks to God, you've been elected leader, but I suspect it's thanks to your fine reputation, too."

"If you say so." For one of the rare times in their marriage, Jacob laughed companionably and gave her a spontaneous kiss on the cheek.

Lucy wished his current mood would last forever, but she doubted it would.

That night she was preparing supper over an open campfire when Clint Palance and his partner, Charlie Dawes, rode up. Jacob went to meet them.

"Congratulations, Captain." Clint swung off the black and white Appaloosa he'd told her was named "Paint." "Since you're now in charge, we've come to discuss a few things."

For a while the three stood talking. Lucy found the

conversation fascinating. She continued to cook dinner but listened closely as the two partners described preparations for the trip and the route they'd take.

"... then, when we start out, we'll make our way across the Kansas River watershed, angling northwest," said Clint. "When we hit the Platte River, we follow it, still heading northwest. Along the way, we'll pass landmarks you may have heard of, like Courthouse Rock, Scotts Bluff, Chimney Rock. Then Fort Laramie ... at the foot of the Rockies, five hundred thirty-five miles from the start of the Platte River Road.

"The next stage, one hundred eight miles to Independence Rock, is difficult for the wagons. It's the broken terrain of the Rockies foothills, where grass gives way to sage and greasewood. Then we come to Fort Hall. That's where we'll part company with those who are heading for Oregon territory."

"We've got to get there first," said Charlie Dawes, a lean man with hunched-over shoulders, long, grizzled beard, and weathered face. He shot a chaw of tobacco upon the ground. "When we start, just to get to the Platte it's three hundred twenty miles, and there ain't no trail. I guarantee we'll run into floods and hailstorms along the way, so better make sure you got the canvas on your wagons weatherproofed and nice 'n tight."

Clint spoke up. "While we're on that subject, Captain, there's been some talk about your wagons."

Jacob's pleasant expression disappeared. "What about my wagons?"

"Your wagons are too heavy. I'd advise you lighten the loads."

"There's nothing wrong with the way my wagons are loaded." Lucy couldn't mistake the cold edge in Jacob's voice. "Are you suggesting I simply toss away my belongings at your request? I'll have you know, sir, that everything I carry is essential."

Charlie Dawes raised a cynical eyebrow. "Maybe you won't

be thinking everything is so essential when you get stuck in the mud and it takes a dozen men to push you out."

"I shall be the judge of that." Jacob's tone clearly invited no further argument. *Of course he isn't going to admit the truth.* Lucy had more than a twinge of embarrassment. In Independence, Jacob had purchased the usual provisions for their own use: two hundred pounds of flour, one hundred fifty pounds of bacon, ten pounds of coffee, twenty pounds of sugar, ten pounds of salt, and so on. He, along with his brother, had also purchased merchandise they planned to sell for a huge profit in California, like heavy tools and several barrels of whiskey. No wonder their wagons were so heavy.

Jacob asked, "Now, gentlemen, is there anything else?"

"That's it for now." Clint's easy smile gave not the slightest hint he might be annoyed by Jacob's hardheaded answer. "If all goes well, we leave in three days."

Lucy watched the visitors mount their horses and ride away. Three days! Despite all her reluctance, a little thrill ran through her. Whether she liked it or not, the biggest adventure of her life was about to begin.

Chapter 5

Three days later at dawn, a line of forty wagons headed out from Independence amidst the din of dogs barking, cattle lowing, men shouting, shrieking children darting here and there. At last the Schneider Party had begun the long journey west, the air heavy with excitement, spirits running high.

For Lucy, the departure was bittersweet. True, a small part of her sensed the thrill of a new adventure, but when she thought how every mile they drove west took her farther away from her Boston home, she felt an overwhelming sense of loss.

Her dear brothers, sweet sister, beloved father—oh, she would never see them again! Tears welled in her eyes, but there would be no turning back. What good were they? Finally, she ordered herself to cry no more. She'd look to the future with courage and determination—never complain—rejoice in the thought that a whole new life lay ahead.

During the morning hours, she enjoyed meeting some of the people she'd be traveling with the next few months. They came from all parts of the country and all walks of life. Like Adam Janicki, an out-of-work coal miner from Pittsburgh. He and his family planned to look for free land in Oregon. So would a bankrupt storekeeper and his family from the Mississippi Valley. Some, like the three rowdy Butler Brothers from the backwoods of Tennessee, were hell-bent on reaching the California gold fields. Jacob had already predicted that the disorderly brothers would all go straight to hell, what with their loud cursing and heavy drinking from what seemed like bottomless jugs of corn liquor they passed around.

As the morning wore on, Lucy's newfound determination to make the best of her lot slowly faded. At first, while Jacob drove their lead wagon, she and Noah walked alongside, easily keeping up with the slow pace of the oxen. When Noah's little legs grew tired, she lifted him up to sit beside his father on the wagon seat. After the mid-morning break, she saddled one of the horses and rode until her back began to ache so badly she had to dismount and walk again.

The trail turned muddy. In parts the mud was so deep that several times one or another of the Schneider wagons got stuck in a quagmire, causing the entire train to stop while a dozen men huffed and heaved with all their might to push them out. No one else's wagons got stuck, only Jacob's and Abner's. She couldn't help but remember Clint's warning: "Your wagons are too heavy. I advise you to lighten the loads." She didn't dare remind her husband, though. One thing she'd learned, Jacob didn't care to listen to advice or admit his mistakes. That went double for Abner, and she'd never dream of voicing her opinion to her overbearing brother-in-law.

They stopped at noon. Although tired already, she had no time to rest; she had to prepare the midday meal for the family, as well as Benjamin and Henry, their two hired hands. Both strong, healthy young men, they were working for their passage so they could reach the gold fields. Henry was the quiet one. Lively Benjamin, a clear-eyed man of twenty-two, played the guitar.

"Mighty good tasting beans and biscuits, ma'am." Benjamin squatted beside the campfire, cleaning his plate.

"Why, thank you." Lucy knew he was just being kind. Despite her best efforts, she had yet to conquer the art of cooking while bending over an open fire with the wind blowing smoke in her face.

After lunch, she decided to try and persuade Jacob to teach her to drive the wagons. So far, he had refused. During the morning, though, she'd witnessed several women, firm hand on the reins, shouting, "Gee up!" as they cracked a whip over the oxen's heads, looking every bit as masterful as any man. If they could do it, why couldn't she?

She walked up to Jacob, who stood next to his wagon chatting with Abner. "Let me take the reins for a while. It shouldn't take long for you to show me what to do."

Jacob opened his mouth to speak. She could have sworn he was about to agree, but before he could utter a word, Abner said, "Never." He regarded her with cold, contemptuous eyes. "Driving a team of oxen is a man's job."

How dare he interfere! She could hardly quell her flash of indignation. She looked pointedly at her husband. "It's a long way to California. Surely sooner or later I'll need to know how."

"It's folly," said Abner. "God never meant for a woman to drive a wagon. They haven't the strength or the aptitude. I'd certainly never allow my wife to drive a wagon. Do you not agree?"

"Quite so. I cannot imagine Martha driving the oxen." Jacob's gaze shifted to Lucy. "Or you. I won't permit it, now or ever. Is that clear?"

"Jacob—"

"Enough, woman." Jacob climbed into the wagon seat, took up the reins, and started off without another word. With a look of triumphant scorn, Abner walked away, leaving her standing in the dirt, clutching her fists in frustration. *Damn* Abner! How dare he interfere? Damn Jacob, too, for allowing his brother to rule his life. Didn't he have a mind of his own? How dare he call her "woman" in such a reproachful, degrading manner? In her whole life, she'd never been addressed that way. Acutely embarrassed, she started to walk behind the wagon, hoping no one had overheard.

She tried to calm down. Jacob simply wasn't himself, she finally decided. No wonder he was cross, what with his new responsibilities and his wagons constantly getting stuck in the mud. She should ignore his coldness. He'd never act that way again.

As she walked along, calmer now, Clint Palance rode by on his Appaloosa. He'd been busy all day, riding up and down the line of wagons at least a dozen times, too busy to stop and chat. He would nod as he rode by, though. Their eyes always met, but in the most impersonal way.

Her drifting thoughts came together. She suddenly realized that no matter where she was, at what time of day, she was always aware of the precise whereabouts of Clint Palance. Whether he was ahead leading the train, or riding alongside one of the wagons, or following behind; no matter where, her eyes followed him. What on earth was she doing? Had she taken leave of her senses? Was she not Mrs. Jacob Schneider, a respectably married woman with a spotless reputation to preserve? The very thought she might become infatuated with another man was totally unacceptable, totally absurd.

Finally tired of walking, Lucy climbed into the back of the wagon to get some rest. It wasn't long before the bumping and constant swaying made her nauseated. "Land sick" she supposed she would call it. She had to climb down and walk again. This was only the beginning.

At the end of the day, when the wagons had circled for the night, Lucy joined Martha, Bessie, and Cordelia's slave, Sukey, in carrying sacks to the nearby woods to collect kindling. On the way back, their sacks full, Bessie wiped her brow. "In all my born days, I ain't never been this tired. We only come ten miles the whole day."

"Give me your sack." Herself exhausted, Lucy could tell that Bessie, almost in her eighth month and heavy with child, was about to collapse.

After a weak protest, Bessie handed Lucy the sack. "I don't know how I'm going to make it. I've still got dinner to cook, and then to clean up and put the young'uns to bed."

"You're not the only one." A scowl appeared on Sukey's face. "I cook and clean for Missus Benton, then I got to put up with her little brat, Chadwick, and her nagging besides. 'Do this, Sukey, do that, Sukey,' " she mocked in a fair imitation of Cordelia's southern accent. " 'Work yourself to death, Sukey.' " She wrinkled her nose and shook her head. "I didn't want to come, but she say I'm still her slave. I wish I could go back."

"Wouldn't that serve Mrs. High-and-Mighty right if you did go back to Atlanta," Bessie exclaimed. "That would bring her down a peg or two if she had to cook her own meals and collect her own wood like the rest of us."

Lucy smiled to herself. Already the subject of Cordelia brought endless grumbling among the hardworking women of the wagon train. Not only did they heartily dislike her snobbish ways, they especially resented her having a slave to do her work while she, according to Bessie, "Just sits there in the wagon like Queen of the May."

Trudging back to camp, carrying two sacks instead of one, Lucy found that not only did her back hurt, her whole body felt engulfed in a tide of weariness. She could hardly put one foot in front of the other. Worse, her stomach threatened at any moment to heave its contents.

Bessie pointed. "Oh, look, here come Mister Dawes and Mister Palance. Don't he always look so handsome!"

Clint and Charlie rode up. "Afternoon, ladies." Clint touched the brim of his hat. "I see you've survived your first day on the trail."

Bessie cocked her head and squinted up at him. "I heard we only come ten miles. At this rate, I'll be an old woman by the time we get to California, if I ain't dead first."

The men burst into hearty laughter. "Don't worry," Clint

said. "We'll be averaging fifteen to twenty miles a day before you know it."

Charlie spoke up. "We would have done that today if it weren't for them wagons getting stuck in the mud."

Lucy felt her face go red. He meant Jacob, and Abner, too. But why should she feel any guilt? She wasn't the one who'd overloaded the wagons. Still, as Jacob's wife, she felt responsible.

As if sensing her embarrassment, Clint created a distraction by leaning from his horse and sweeping up the sacks of kindling from Lucy's grasp. "Here, let me take those." In the process, his hand brushed hers. His touch, so unexpected, gave her a thrill of excitement. Their gazes met. For a long, unguarded moment, she looked deep into his eyes, catching the spark of some indefinable emotion. Hastily, she looked away, wondering, what had he seen in *her* eyes?

They had started back to camp when Lucy realized that while talking to Clint, she had subconsciously tugged up the waistband of her white, starched apron, then spread her hand over the swell of her stomach beneath as if to conceal it. She glanced at Bessie whose stomach was so hugely distorted she didn't walk, she waddled. In a few months, she would be waddling, too, so what was she trying to accomplish by hiding her condition from Clint?

She knew the answer, and she didn't want to think about it.

❧❧

Riding alongside Charlie, Clint shifted the two sacks of kindling across the saddle. They were heavy. Mrs. Schneider shouldn't be lifting them. He didn't like to think of all the misery she'd be enduring before the journey's end. That jackass husband of hers wasn't going to help; he could tell.

"Crazy white women," muttered Charlie Dawes.

"What do you mean?"

"Did you see Mrs. Schneider trying to hide the fact she's got a loaf in the oven?"

"It's their culture. Women in our society are taught to believe their bodily functions are so shameful they should be hidden and not discussed. That includes childbirth."

"Hogwash." Charlie spat a chaw of chewing tobacco. "They want us to think they're all virgins? Like they never went to bed with a man?"

Charlie's remarks filled Clint's head with an image of Lucy in bed with that jackass husband and ... No, don't think about it. He blanked the image out. "Indian women have the right idea. To them, having a baby is as natural as breathing. They don't try to conceal it, like it's something disgraceful."

They reached the circle of wagons, handed the sacks back, and watched the women go their respective ways. For a few moments, Charlie rode on in silence, appearing to be in deep thought. "You know what I suspect?"

"What?"

"I suspect you're taken with that pretty Mrs. Schneider." He slanted a sly glance at Clint. "Ain't you now?"

Only the clip-clop of the horses' hooves broke the silence as Clint rode along, staring straight ahead. "Don't give me any lectures."

"Wasn't going to. The stupidest man in the world would know not to mess around with a married woman, and you ain't stupid."

Clint nodded agreeably. No, he wasn't stupid, and Charlie was right. Any special feelings he had for Mrs. Jacob Schneider—whatever they were—had to stop right there.

❧❧

Later that night, legs aching with fatigue, Lucy crawled into the tent Jacob had pitched next to the wagon. Never in her life had she toiled as hard as she had today. Ah, just to lay her head on the pillow would be heaven! Not to mention how much she'd enjoy the luxury of sleeping soundly until dawn. She lay down next to Jacob and had half drifted to sleep when she felt a tug at her nightgown and a hand creeping beneath. Oh, please, not tonight! She didn't think she could bear another of his near-nightly invasions of those personal, private parts of herself she had always kept sacred. Never had she refused him, but she was just so very tired ... "Jacob, please, I would rather not."

His hand kept creeping. "Now, be a good wife," he whispered as he climbed atop her.

She stifled a sigh and submitted, as she always did. At least she knew he'd be quick. Then she could roll over and get some precious sleep.

A few nights later, while most of the members of the party were gathered around the campfire after supper, a wagon headed in the opposite direction arrived. The owner, a tall, one-armed man named Augustus Turner, asked and received permission for himself, his wife, and three children to join the circle for the night.

"I don't care beans about going west anymore," Augustus said. He and his family had joined the others around the nightly campfire. "I just want to get back to Ohio."

Millicent, his grim-face wife, nodded vigorously. "I knew it would be bad from almost the very start, when we started following the Platte. We started passing lots of dead animals— cattle, oxen, and such—and then there were the graves by the side of the trail. It was just the saddest sight you ever did see. Not a day went by when I didn't see one or more. Sometimes the name was marked on a board, but some weren't marked at all."

"Most of the graves were shallow," Augustus went on. "Like the people didn't have the time or inclination to dig a deep enough hole."

"It was just terrible," Millicent said. "Some of the corpses were dug up by animals. Other times the Indians dug them up and stole their clothes."

A collective gasp went up from the listeners around the campfire. Bad enough to die on the trail, but how awful to have some savage dig you up and strip you bare.

"We crossed river after river," Augustus continued. "At one, the current was so swift that we lost our other wagon, two oxen, and a horse."

"Is that when you turned back?" Jacob asked.

Augustus shook his head. "We kept going, and then—" his voice choked.

"We lost our little girl." Millicent's voice wavered. "Our little Leanna was just five. It happened so fast I couldn't do a thing. One minute she was a'settin' on the wagon seat, and the next, out she fell and got run over by a wheel."

Amidst murmurs of sympathy, Augustus took up the tale. "She died right then. We had to bury her by the side of the trail."

"Is that when you turned back?"

"We kept on." Augustus brushed a tear away with the back of his hand. "It was tough going. By then, you should've seen all the furniture 'n' books 'n' bedding 'n' I don't know what, all thrown overboard from the wagons that had gone before ours. People are dumb, thinking they can haul all their fancy possessions clear to California."

"I find that hard to believe." As usual, Cordelia had not failed to dress for the evening and looked quite elegant in her hoop-skirted blue taffeta dress. She cast a skeptical gaze at Augustus.

"It's true, ma'am. I even seen a piano thrown away. You see, there was times we went days without grass and water for the animals. They got weak, and when that happened, they couldn't pull a full load. Nothing folks could do but throw their things away."

Jacob asked, "So is that when you turned back?"

"We kept going. Then the Indians attacked. Comanche most likely." He touched his empty sleeve. "Got an arrow in my arm."

Millicent cast a pained gaze at her husband. "His arm got them red streaks, then it started turning black." She shuddered. "I can still hear his screams when they took it off."

Augustus cast a rueful look at his empty right sleeve. "That's when we turned back."

Later, before turning in, Bessie said, "Did you hear what the Turners said? Oh, Lucy, I'm so scared. When I think of the months ahead and what could happen ... I'll never make it to California!"

Lucy patted her shoulder. "Don't you worry. The Turners had some really bad luck, that's all. It's not going to happen to us. I'm not the least bit concerned, and you shouldn't be, either."

What a lie. Although Lucy had put on her most confident voice, the Turner's sad tale had shaken her as well. The Schneider Party had only begun their journey. Fear knotted inside her when she thought of all the terrible things that could happen during the long months ahead.

Next morning, Lucy woke to the sound of hysterical screams. A woman's voice ... it was Cordelia! "Something's wrong," she called to Jacob. They quickly pulled on their clothes and hurried outside where they discovered an empty space where the Turner wagon had been parked. In its place stood Cordelia, wild-eyed, clenching her fists.

"What's happened?" Lucy asked.

"Sukey's gone," Cordelia screeched. "They took my cook!"

"Who took your cook?" asked Jacob.

Cordelia pointed a shaking finger southeast in the general direction the Turners must be traveling. "Sukey had the nerve, the audacity, to leave with the Turners. She left a note, hardly readable, I might add. I cannot believe this. She said she was tired of me, tired of cooking, tired of my darling Chadwick, and wanted to go to Ohio with the Turners." Panic filled Cordelia's eyes. "Sukey's gone. I can't cook! Captain, I must have her back."

"That is impossible."

"You must go after them! Tell Sukey I'll even pay her wages, anything she asks." Cordelia hesitated. "Within reason, of course."

Jacob firmly shook his head. "Sorry, but we can't hold up the others because you've lost your cook."

By then, a sympathetic crowd had gathered, including Bessie, Hannah and her husband, Elija, and Agnes and William Applegate. Lucy noticed immediately that Clint Palance and Charlie Dawes had joined the crowd.

William Applegate said, "Turner couldn't have gone far. Why not send someone back, or go back yourself?"

Jacob looked down his nose at William Applegate, a blunt, ill-mannered man he despised. "The sooner we reach the Platte, the better. That's my plan. I won't deviate."

"Please, Captain," begged Cordelia.

John Potts stepped forward. "Hells fire, we don't mind waiting." The crowd murmured its agreement.

"Well, perhaps ..." Jacob's face softened. Relieved, Lucy observed he was about to give in.

"We shall not turn back!" came Abner's thunderous voice.

In dismay, Lucy watched her brother-in-law lift his head and assume his I-am-the-prophet stance, a sure sign he was about to quote a scripture. Now was not the time. He wasn't ... he couldn't ... Lord help us, he was.

"Philippians two, Verse fourteen. 'Do all things without murmurings and disputing.' " Abner cast a stern glance at his brother. "Is that not so?"

Not to Lucy's surprise, but to her great chagrin, Jacob

nodded in agreement. "I cannot argue with the scriptures."

"So you refuse?" Cordelia's lower lip trembled.

Jacob's tightening jaw and cold eyes told Lucy in advance what his reply would be. "I have spoken."

My husband is an idiot. Lucy caught herself. How could she think such a thing? But who, other than an idiot, would allow his brother to make his decisions?

"Don't you worry," called Bessie. "There ain't nothing to cooking. We'll show you how."

Hannah nodded in agreement. "We'll have you flipping slapjacks in no time."

"I ... don't ... cook!" White-faced, Cordelia stalked to her wagon and disappeared inside.

Hannah clucked in sympathy. "Poor thing, what's she going to do?"

Bessie chimed in. "Well, she ain't going to find a new cook in the middle of nowhere."

"Cordelia either cooks or she starves." Agnes gave a nod of satisfaction. "That goes for her mealy-mouthed husband and Chadwick, too. Serves her right for being so uppity."

Lucy had heard enough. Amidst the continued murmurings from the crowd, she returned to their tent, pitched next to the wagon. She was rolling up bedding when she heard voices outside. Peering out, she saw her husband and his brother returning, followed by Clint Palance.

"Hold up, Captain!" Clint called.

Through the small slit opening, Lucy watched Jacob and Abner halt reluctantly. "What do you want?" Jacob asked. "If it's about going after Sukey, I refuse to break my rule for some crazy woman."

Clint smiled pleasantly. "I'm going to ride after the Turners. Maybe I can get Sukey to change her mind, maybe not. It's worth a try. Don't wait. Start without me, and I'll catch up."

Abner's eyes blazed. His mouth took on an unpleasant

twist. "No, you won't. My brother is the leader of this wagon train, duly elected. You are under his command and will do as he says."

Clint pushed back the wide brim of his hat with his thumb. He slung his hands to his buckskin-clad hips and rested his tough, sinewy body back on his heels. Ignoring Abner, he addressed Jacob. "Here's the way it is. Charlie Dawes and I were hired to lead your wagon train to California, and that's what we'll do. What we won't do is take any of your shit." He flicked a glance at Abner. "Or your brother's, either."

Abner's face suffused with red. His eyes bulged out as if he were about to choke. Before he could speak, Clint spoke, still addressing his remarks to Jacob, who stood sputtering. "Anything else? Have I made myself clear?"

Clint turned to leave, but Jacob grabbed his arm. "Don't you dare turn your back on me! I'll take this to the council. I'll—"

"You do that." Clint made no move to loosen his arm from Jacob's grasp. Instead, he regarded Jacob with the cool, fearless eyes of a man who had fought a band of savage Indians and won, and an angry grizzly bear and survived. "Now take your goddamn fucking hand off my arm."

Jacob dropped his hand so fast it could have been touching a red hot iron. Clint started to walk away. Puffing himself up with righteous wrath, Jacob boomed after him, "Exodus sixteen, Verse eight, Clint Palance, 'Your murmurings are not against us, but against the Lord!'"

Clint stopped in his tracks and turned. The merest hint of a smile hovered around his lips. "Ecclesiastes seven, Verse sixteen, Jacob Schneider. 'Be not righteous over much; neither make thyself over wise.'"

He walked away, leaving both Jacob and Abner with their mouths hanging open.

Oh, hilarious! The look on Jacob's face! Self-righteous

Abner for once at a loss for words. Lucy had to clap her hand over her mouth to stifle her laughter. She wondered how an irreverent man like Clint could have delivered just the right scripture. Seconds later, she was making herself busy with the bedding when Jacob stepped into the tent, face still red, his breathing heavy from his rage. "Did you hear that? That profane man has taken the name of the Lord in vain! He must be dismissed. I shall not tolerate—"

"We'll never reach California without him."

"Didn't you hear him? He blasphemed!"

"Then cover your ears next time." Arms full of blankets, Lucy shouldered her way past her husband and out of the tent. Back in the wagon, it occurred to her that she'd never shown him such defiance. Because of it, her spirits soared in a way she couldn't quite understand. What she perceived was, it was about time she spoke up, time she stopped allowing Jacob to bully her. In future, she'd speak her mind more often.

As for Clint, she ought to be incensed that he'd made a fool of her husband, shocked by his salty language, appalled at his disrespect. Instead, she kept picturing his fearless, nonchalant manner. Jacob was taller than Clint, and heavier, yet she sensed if he hadn't instantly removed his hand from Clint's arm, he would've found himself ass-over-tea-kettle on the ground, his dignity in tatters.

hroughout the morning, the wagon train made slow but steady progress. By noon Clint had still not returned. Cordelia stayed hidden in her wagon, leaving Nathaniel, Chadwick, and their two hired men to fend for themselves for their meals. Some of the wives, including Lucy, gladly gave biscuits, beans, and pancakes to the hungry men, but all knew such generosity couldn't continue.

At the noon break, Bessie stopped by Lucy's cooking fire. "That Sukey had better come back soon." She rolled her eyes heavenward. "Jesus wants us to share, but John doesn't like to keep handing out all that extra food."

"Jacob's the same." Lucy didn't care to describe her husband's flare of temper when he saw her doling out food from their precious supply.

"We only have enough for ourselves," he'd thundered. She'd talked him into being generous for one more meal, pointing out that a leader of men should not appear stingy. He'd reluctantly conceded. "But just one more meal. We're not going to feed the whole camp. The Bentons can starve, for all I care, or better yet, turn around and go back home."

She and Jacob were sitting on the wagon seat eating their noon meal when in the distance she saw Clint Palance riding back alone. With growing apprehension, she watched him draw closer. Jacob hadn't said a word concerning this morning's ugly scene. She wondered if he'd be polite to Clint or if he was still in a rage over the man's failure to obey and his so-called blasphemy.

Clint rode straight to Jacob's wagon and touched the brim of his hat in greeting, casually, as if the earlier confrontation never occurred. "Sukey won't come back, Captain. She's hell-bent on going to Ohio with the Turners."

Lucy held her breath while her husband sat silent, his broad face expressionless. No doubt he was trying to decide whether to lash out at Clint again or stifle his anger and resentment. Jacob cleared his throat. "That's too bad. Will you inform Mrs. Benton?"

What a relief! Jacob sounded none too gracious, but at least civil. He wasn't going to dismiss Clint and Charlie, thank the Lord. "I'll inform Mrs. Benton if you like, Mister Palance," Lucy said.

Clint smiled in relief. "If you wouldn't mind. I don't relish being the one to tell her."

Minutes later, Lucy approached the Bentons' wagon, wondering what had possessed her to volunteer for the unpleasant task of breaking the bad news to Cordelia. She went around to the rear of the wagon and knocked on the backboard. "Mrs. Benton? It's me, Lucy Schneider."

She heard a sharp "Go away," from inside.

"I have news of Sukey."

Cordelia poked her head through the opening. "Good or bad?"

"For you, bad."

Tight-lipped, Cordelia jerked back the canvas flap and climbed to the ground. She faced Lucy with crossed arms and a frown. "Sukey refused to return?"

"Mister Palance said he tried, but Sukey wants to go to Ohio. It's a free state. I doubt she'd ever want to return to Atlanta where she'd still be a slave."

"That little ingrate! I treated her well. Never whipped her once, and this is the thanks I get."

"Apparently, she just wants to be free."

Cordelia's shoulders sagged. Her thin, aristocratic face grew haggard, the lines around her mouth more drawn. "What am I going to do? Nathaniel won't even consider going back to Atlanta, and I can't cook. I won't cook!" She extended her dainty white hands palms up. "These are the hands of a lady. They weren't meant for hauling wood and baking biscuits and God knows what. All my life I've had servants to wait on me. I've never had to dress myself or comb my hair. I have never once cooked my own meal, and I can't change now. It's too late."

Lucy looked down at her own hands. Like Cordelia's, they had once been soft, smooth, and alabaster white. Now they'd begun to brown and roughen. An ugly red burn from a cooking pot marred her palm. "I know it's not easy, but—"

"I never wanted to come on this trip!" Cordelia wailed. "This was all Nathaniel's idea, him and his manifest destiny. I'm much too delicate for this, much too ... too ..."

Spoiled and pampered were the words that sprung to Lucy's lips, words she forced herself to suppress while Cordelia sputtered. She couldn't suppress her anger. Just who did Cordelia think she was, some sort of princess? Better than the rest? The remains of the sympathy she'd felt for this mollycoddled woman vanished, replaced by mounting scorn. "Do you realize your husband and son have nothing to eat?" She was none too kindly. "To say nothing of your hired hands."

The distressed woman fluttered her eyelids in bewilderment. "What do you mean?"

"Because you won't fix them a meal, your husband and son, as well as your hired young men, have been begging food from your neighbors. So far, everyone's been generous, but believe me, it won't last."

"Perhaps I can hire one of the women—"

"Not likely. Every woman in this wagon train is already worked to death, and furthermore ..." She paused, surprised at herself. What had come over her? She would never have uttered such a sharp retort in the fancy parlor on Beacon Hill. Instead, she would've mouthed the usual shallow platitudes, never dreaming of saying what she really thought. Now her cultured, cozy little world lay far behind her. On a journey like this, no one cared about genteel manners, idle chatter, or polite little lies. Simply surviving each grueling day was all that mattered.

"You have no choice. You must do what needs to be done. It's as simple as that."

"You're suggesting I *cook*?"

"We'll all help. Bessie and Hannah have already volunteered, as well as—"

"I don't care to be beholden to women like that."

"Women like what?"

"You know, of a lesser standing. Really! I suspect some of them don't even know how to read or write."

"Who cares? You should be grateful they're willing to help."

"I couldn't possibly! I'm much too delicate, and frankly, such manual labor is simply beneath me."

Something snapped. She'd had enough. "My dear Cordelia, let's not get into a discussion concerning what's beneath you and what's not. Maybe you were the leader of Atlanta society, but you aren't anymore. You're no better than the rest of us. You'd best remember you squat behind a bush just like the rest of us."

Cordelia gasped. Her hand flew to her heart. "Why, Mrs. Schneider! I find your remark to be ... to be ..."

"Yes, I know, extremely crude, and you're shocked. Well, that doesn't change the fact you'd better pull yourself together and start doing your part." Lucy could hardly believe she'd just said that. Perhaps she'd gone too far, yet it was high time someone set this snobbish southern belle straight.

Cordelia remained silent for a very long time. Finally, she

heaved a resigned sigh and muttered in a very small voice, "I see I have no choice. Very well then, I shall try."

On her way back to the wagon, in high spirits after her success with Cordelia, Lucy passed by the one small wagon that belonged to Palance and Dawes. She saw Clint in front, building a fire. "Mrs. Benton says she'll cook!"

"That's good news." Clint strolled over to chat. "Mrs. Benton has some funny ideas, but she's got a lot of grit. I suspect once she gets the hang of it, she'll be fine."

"I think so, too." Remembering the events of the morning, Lucy tried to stifle her curiosity but couldn't. She tipped her head to one side. "By the way, wherever did you come up with that quote from the Bible? Was it just luck or do you know the scriptures as well as Abner and my husband?"

"You heard?" The lines around Clint's eyes wrinkled in amusement. "Were the Captain and his brother properly impressed?"

"Oh, yes." She let loose a bubbling peal of laughter. "Properly impressed, indeed."

Clint nodded with satisfaction. "My father taught me the Bible. Yes, I could match your husband scripture for scripture if I had to." There was a pause in which he seemed to debate whether to say more. "Back home in Kentucky, my father was a preacher."

"How nice."

"Not really. He raised me with a Bible in one hand and a birch whip in the other. I got tired of being beat. Left home when I was twelve."

"Oh, I'm sorry." She sensed he'd just revealed a confidence not often shared.

"Don't be sorry. It was the best thing I ever did. I never looked back. Since then, I've led the life I wanted to lead." He folded his arms and regarded her with curious eyes. "What of you? Are you leading the life you want to lead?"

She responded with a cynical laugh. "Now what do you think?"

"What do I think?" He paused, seeming to gather his thoughts. "You view this journey as the worst thing ever happened to you. I predict that some day you'll think otherwise. That's because I see depths in you that you don't even know you have."

"Really?" She was astounded.

"Yes, really. I see strength, determination, a will to survive. I see a woman who was meant for something more than sitting in a fancy Boston parlor serving tea, much as you might believe otherwise."

"So far I'm hating it. So far I'm scared to death of all the things Augustus Turner talked about. Accidents, drownings, Indians—"

"You're a survivor. If ever I saw a woman meant to pull through, no matter what, it's you."

Struck speechless, she wondered if he was only trying to flatter her. She searched his sun- and wind-burned face, marked forever by the jagged scar from the grizzly, and saw only honesty in his eyes. She should have known. Clint Palance was a man who didn't tell lies, not even little white ones. She found herself immensely flattered. Aside from her father, none of the men she'd known had gone beyond mouthing meaningless blandishments about her pretty eyes, pert little nose, soft, silky hair. Come to think of it, Jacob hadn't even said that much. Since they'd left Massachusetts, she'd spent endless hours cooking, scrubbing, and taking care of his child, yet he hadn't expressed one word of thanks or appreciation. She doubted he ever would. "Thank you. That was kind of you to say."

"Truly meant."

She wanted to stay and talk, but standing in the middle of the campground, she could almost feel the sharp eyes of Agnes

Applegate drilling into her back. "I'd best be off."

He touched his hat. "Good day."

"Good day." Her spirits high, she wiggled her fingers at him in a bubbly little wave. When she turned, sure enough, there was Agnes staring directly at her with a wise little smirk on her face. *You old gossip.* She gave a gay wave to Agnes, too. Clint's flattering words still in her head, she walked toward her campsite with buoyant steps.

She was almost there when she saw Jacob standing beside the wagon awaiting her return, fists clenched, face livid. Dear Lord! Had he seen her laughing conversation with Clint? The gay wave? The happy spring in her step?

"What were you doing talking to Palance?" Jacob demanded when she drew close, the volume of his voice lowered only by his awareness of the sharp ears of close neighbors.

"I—"

"I won't have you talking to that man, do you understand?" His chest heaved. His breath came in short, angry pants.

"Jacob, I—"

"Do ... you ... understand?" His quiet words came hissing through barred teeth, reminding her of a wild-eyed, salivating wolf about to spring on its prey. The effect frightened her more than if he were shouting. She fought her impulse to bolt and run—*mustn't make a scene*—and forced herself to stand and listen. "For the good of the company, I must tolerate that blasphemer, but that doesn't mean my wife is to speak to him, ever! Do I make myself clear?"

She tried to answer but found herself unable to speak over the lump of panic in her throat. Thank God for the neighbors. She had the feeling that if Jacob were not aware of their curious ears and eyes, those clenched fists he held tight to his sides would surely have struck her by now. "Jacob, why are you so angry? I was only telling Mister Palance about Cordelia. She's agreed to cook."

She waited, desperately hoping she'd dispelled her husband's fury.

Jacob remained silent, glaring at her until, gradually, his heaving chest and anger-contorted face returned to normal. "You mind what I said. Clint Palance is a wicked, worldly man. You stay away from him. Now get back to work." He spun around and left.

Deeply shaken, she noticed little Noah peering at her through the canvas with round, frightened eyes. He must've heard every word. She wanted to climb inside the wagon and hide from the world, but for her stepson's sake, she forced herself to be calm, act normal.

"It's time for me to wash the dishes, sweetheart. Be a love and help me."

"Yes, ma'am." Noah hopped nimbly from the wagon to the tongue, then to the ground, eager to do her bidding. Once again, this sweet little boy, so kind and loving, so eager to please, touched her heart. He was smart, too, and immensely curious about everything, sometimes spouting questions a mile a minute until the adults tired of answering. "Is Father mad?"

Lucy tousled Noah's blond curls. "He was mad, but just a little bit. Everything's fine now."

She busied herself with cleaning up after the noontime meal, thinking everything was not so fine. She'd already discovered there was no such thing as privacy in a wagon train. Gossip spread fast as lightning. Everyone would pretend otherwise, but Jacob's tirade, muted though it was, had been seen, heard, and carefully noted. Surely tongues would wag. She'd wager that by sunset the whole world would be aware Jacob Schneider had roundly upbraided his wife over her behavior with Clint Palance.

Just what had she done? So unfair! Why couldn't she have a conversation with a man without tongues wagging, without her husband raging at her? After grimly mulling for a while, she forced herself to face the truth. Clint Palance wasn't just any man. He was a man she was drawn to, could not stop thinking about, no matter how hard she tried. Strange, how her unimaginative husband sensed the truth. It was almost as if he could read her mind.

Well, regardless of how harmless this foolishness was, it had to stop. Absolutely, she'd mend her ways. Even though Jacob couldn't read her mind, from now on she wouldn't care if he did. She was a good Christian woman who loved her husband. From this day forward, she wouldn't waste one more thought on Clint Palance.

In the late afternoon, they came to a river so wide and fast-flowing that Clint and Charlie called for all to gather so they could discuss how they were going to get across.

Lucy, standing on the bank with a small knot of women, heard a lot of gloom and doom.

"My stars, how will we ever cross this one?" Bessie watched the water's swift flow with dismay. "It looks so deep."

"We shall all be drowned," said Agnes.

"Do you think so?" Martha's voice sounded small, scared. Lately she'd come out of her shell a bit, Lucy had noted with satisfaction, and now occasionally spoke her mind. Perhaps her pregnancy had given her more confidence.

Only ever-positive Hannah offered hope. "Fiddlesticks! Let's just listen to what Mister Palance and Mister Dawes have to say. I trust they'll get us across."

Lucy agreed with Hannah. She gazed at the two experienced guides sitting casually atop their mounts: clean-shaven Clint lightly holding the reins with strong, practiced hands; grizzly-bearded Charlie regarding the crowd with his old, snappy eyes. Between them, they must have tackled dozens of rivers. They knew what to do. She was not afraid.

After gathering them all together, Clint said, "Folks, so far, the rivers we've crossed so far have been shallow. We waded across, both us and the cattle, and drove the wagons through without getting stuck or losing one wagon or animal."

"This here one's a mite different." Charlie nodded toward the dark, swiftly flowing water. "You got a river what's deep, running fast, and dangerous."

"Can we get across?" someone yelled.

"Of course we'll get across," said Clint, "but you must listen carefully and do what we say. First, you've got to unload the wagons."

"Everything?"

"Everything," Clint answered over groans from the crowd. "Then you've got to take the wagons apart, piece by piece, and that means wheels, canvas, tongues, all of it. Then we water-proof the wagons with wax."

Another groan.

"Then we stretch a strong rope across the river with a tight wagon-bed attached to the middle of it. We'll have men standing on either side to keep the rope tight and pull each wagon across, one by one. When we get all the wagons to the other side, we build rafts to haul the goods from the wagons, same way, attached to ropes. Everything a little at a time. When that's done, we bring the women and children, then we'll swim the cattle and horses."

Shaking his head in disapproval, Jacob stepped forward. "Sounds like a lot of work to me. Surely there must be an easier way. Perhaps we could find a spot where the river isn't that deep and we could simply drive the wagons across."

"Not possible," Clint answered firmly. "Every part of that river is treacherous. Do it the way we said or you'll have drownings on your hands, and I mean people as well as animals."

"I see."

Lucy knew from the cold exactness in Jacob's voice he

wasn't happy with Clint's answer. He argued no further, though, aware that he had no choice but to bow to Clint and Charlie's judgment. He called to everyone, "Very well, let's get to work."

The crossing took two days, during which every man, woman, and child over the age of five pitched in to help, all focused on the momentous task of crossing the river. Lucy toiled along with the rest, helping to unpack the wagons and take them apart. She also caught up on other chores. After baking a supply of biscuits, she heated water in a large kettle and poured it into a big wooden wash tub, set up by the river. In a line of other women, all busy with their laundry, she scrubbed a sizeable batch of wash, spreading clothes and linens to dry on bushes that lined the banks. She was doing Martha's wash as well. The poor woman was suffering greatly from early pregnancy nausea, so Lucy constantly tried to lighten her load.

"Ain't it a pleasure to have hot water to wash in?" Bessie was doing her wash beside her. Up to now, they'd had little time for heating water. Mostly they'd done their wash in cold water.

Lucy agreed what a pleasure it was, then found herself remembering another time, another place that now seemed so remote. Had there ever been a Miss Lucy Parker who lived on Beacon Street in Boston? Whose servants did her wash while she, spoiled creature that she was, never gave it a thought? Lucy looked about her, at the raging river crashing over rocks and huge boulders, at the surrounding forest thick with pine trees. Was there really a Boston? Her former life seemed a million miles away. She extended her hands— red and swollen from backbreaking scrubbing, hard soap, as well as the endless days of sun and wind. "They'll never be the same," she whispered, sadly shaking her head.

Bessie held out her own hands, equally red and roughened. "We'll be out in the weather for months to come. There ain't no way to prevent it, far as I can see. At least you've got your face covered."

Lucy reached up to touch the blue cotton sunbonnet Bessie had made for her. At first she'd resisted wearing one, even though all the other women did. They were so unattractive. The brim poked out over her face in such a ridiculous fashion! What would her stylish friends in Boston think? After a few days in the outdoors, she gave in, forced to admit the ugly sunbonnets were the best protection against the hot rays of the sun.

Bessie looked to a spot along the bank where a woman, separated from the rest, struggled to wash her clothes alone. "Poor Mrs. Benton doesn't want to associate with the likes of us. I've helped her some with the cooking, but she mostly turns up her nose and wants to be left alone."

"I feel sorry for her." Lucy wondered how she could carry on without the friendship and camaraderie of the other women. Even now, in the midst of washing clothes, her companions' jokes and chatter made the backbreaking task infinitely more bearable. Everyone helped one another. Even Agnes, ill-natured though she was, had just helped her spread a bulky wet blanket over some bushes without being asked, not expecting any thanks.

The journey had only just begun, but already Lucy felt a strong bond with these women, even more than she ever felt with her dear Boston friends. Her present companions came from all different backgrounds—some rich, some poor, some educated, some illiterate. Wherever they came from, however imperfect their English, each woman had two things in common: each shared the same heartbreak at leaving her home and family behind. Each worried over the dangers that lay ahead, not so much for herself, but for her husband and children. What a shame Cordelia had chosen to isolate herself. She had no idea how funny Agnes could be with her vinegary outlook on life. Nor would she learn from Inez Helmick, the midwife, who was sharing her vast knowledge of the uses of herbs and other medicines.

Poor Cordelia. Lucy decided she'd try again, just one more time.

When all her wash was done, she made her way up the riverbank to where Cordelia scrubbed her clothes. She had even put Chadwick to work. Face clouded with twelve-year-old resentment, the chubby little boy was busy spreading Cordelia's wash on the bushes to dry. With silent amusement, Lucy noted he wasn't quite as chubby as when she first saw him. No doubt he wasn't eating as much, what with Cordelia's lack of cooking skills. Not only that, Clint had taken the boy under his wing and taught him to ride. Chad, mounted on one of his father's horses, followed Clint around whenever possible.

"Cordelia?" Lucy pressed the back of her hand into the small of her back. It ached after hours of bending over the wash tub. "I just came by to see how you're doing."

Visibly annoyed, Cordelia looked up from her wash. Her expression softened when she saw who it was. "How'm I doing? How does it look like I'm doing?" With a wet, soapy forearm, she shoved a bedraggled curl back off her forehead. With disgust, she looked down at her soiled, wet skirt. "I cannot believe this is happening. Back in Georgia, I wouldn't have allowed my scullery maids to look like this."

"Well, we're not in Georgia now." With an unladylike grunt, Lucy sank wearily to a log and stretched her boots in front of her. "You should join us. There's no sense isolating yourself."

Cordelia's mouth pulled into a bleak, tight-lipped smile. "Thank you, but I have nothing in common with those women."

"You can't ignore them the whole trip."

Cordelia crossed her arms. "Yes, I can, and I will."

"They're lovely women. Granted, some don't have a good education, and some are not, as you say, refined, but never will you find women more generous, more kind and thoughtful, more—"

"I have my standards." Cordelia's voice rang with finality.

Hopeless. Lucy knew when she was defeated. "Well, I hope your standards get you through the next fifteen hundred miles." With another unladylike grunt, she pushed herself off the log. "Meantime, if you need any help, let me know."

"Oh, I will. You know I want *you* for a friend."

Lucy found herself too tired to argue the foolishness of Cordelia's last remark. Instead, she nodded a quick goodbye and started walking through a heavy growth of trees to the wagon. Not walking ... limping would be more accurate. Her back hurt. Her feet hurt. Her whole body ached, and all she wanted was to get back to her wagon and lie down, if only for a little while. Ahead she heard the clop of a horse's hooves. Clint Palance rounded a grove of pine trees. Dear Lord, what if Jacob saw them together? Not only that, her appearance! Never had she looked and felt so bedraggled. Of all the people she did *not* want to see, it was him.

Clint rode close and reined in his horse. "Good afternoon."

In a panic, she threw a glance over her shoulder. "Uh, good afternoon."

He looked down at her, apparently amused. "You're safe. He's across the river."

"So you know."

With one swift, graceful move, he swung off his horse and faced her. "Haven't you found out yet, there are no secrets in a wagon train?"

"Then I guess you know my husband said I shouldn't speak to you."

"Your husband is no fool."

It took a moment for the meaning of his words to sink in. When they did, she felt her face go crimson. How could he be so blatantly honest about what to her was her deepest, darkest, most shameful secret? In the world she came from, certain subjects were never to be discussed. "Mister Palance—"

"Don't worry." An easy smile played at the corners of his mouth. "If your husband doesn't want us to speak, then we won't speak. You should know, though, I find you ..." His smile disappeared. His gaze traveled over her face and searched her eyes, just like the day he helped with the firewood. Her heart jolted as the same intense message flashed from him to her and back again. She had to fight a near-overwhelming urge to lean into his arms and close the space between them.

"Good God." His voice sounded strange. Abruptly, he broke his gaze, stepped back, and let his eyes travel down to the swelling beneath her apron, larger now, too big to conceal. She didn't even try. For a moment, he squeezed his eyes shut, as if surprised at himself. Next moment, his foot was in his horse's stirrup. An easy swing returned him to the saddle. "Time to go."

She knew she shouldn't ask but couldn't quell her burning curiosity. "You haven't finished your sentence. I should know you find me ... what?"

"I'll save my answer for another day."

She knew better than to ask again, much as she wanted to. Best to change the subject. "Will we be safe, crossing that river?"

"Don't worry. I'll be there for you." He rode away.

Chapter 7

Throughout the next day, straining, cursing men, using all their strength, hauled forty wagons safely across the river's swift current. Following that, they brought the rafts across, piled high with goods from the wagons. Women and children came next. At dusk, the final group, Lucy and Noah among them, waded through shallow water at the river's edge and huddled together on what would be the last raft to cross.

Lucy held Noah in front of her, arms locked around him. The child twisted his head around and stared wide-eyed at the fast current. "Will we be all right?"

She wished she knew. She was every bit as nervous as Noah but hoped it didn't show. "Of course, we'll be all right. Didn't you see how the wagons got across safely, then all the other people on the rafts? We've got your father to keep you safe, and Mister Dawes, and Mister Palance, and all the other men. This is going to be fun. Think of it as an adventure."

"Adventure, my foot." Bessie's face was taut with fear. She sat by Lucy, clutching her three little boys.

Roxana, Bessie's oldest daughter, sat on her other side, her fair-skinned face flushed with excitement. She kept a firm grip on her two younger sisters. "Ma, don't worry, Mrs. Schneider's right. The others traveled safely, and we will, too."

Lucy thought that if she had a daughter, she'd want her to be like blond, sixteen-year-old Roxana, who was not only pretty but level-headed and always cheerful besides. She glanced around at some of the others on the raft. Agnes sat cross-legged like the rest, surrounded by her brood of six. For once, her caustic mouth remained firmly shut. The raft hadn't yet left the water's edge, but already she was hanging on for dear life. Inez Helmick, minus her usual self-confident expression, clung to three of her children while Bessie's sister, Hannah, who had no children of her own, held the other two. And, of course, timid Martha, who sat with her eyes squeezed shut, muttered her prayers.

Cordelia sat by herself. Over her objections, Clint had enlisted Chad to work with the men on shore. Chad had gone gladly, happy to get away from his mother's smothering care. Lucy noticed every woman on the raft had one thing in common: fear in her eyes. True, the other rafts had crossed safely, but two of them had almost tipped, one when the rope caught on a rock, and one when a log struck it midstream. The men managed to pull both to the far shore without further incident, but Lucy easily imagined what would've happened had the women and children aboard been flung into the icy water. Most of them couldn't swim.

"Everybody ready?" Charlie Dawes shouted from the bank. "Let's get this raft across."

The men started hauling on the ropes. They started across, everyone hanging on tight. All went well until the middle of the river ... when one of the ropes snapped. Amid frightened cries, the raft spun around and tipped. Lucy gripped Noah tight while a spray of cold water from the river drenched them. They were going to tip over. Were they going to die? Her heart raced. Seconds later, the raft righted itself, and they were again underway. She saw Clint, atop Paint, fighting the swift current but hanging tight to the rope.

"Just look what Mister Palance done," Bessie cried as the raft floated to shore. "Rode his horse right into the river and saved us all."

"Yes, it looks that way." Lucy remembered Clint's words,

Don't worry. I'll be there for you. He'd been there for the others, too, but somehow she knew he'd been watching over her especially, determined to keep his word.

⊱⊰

When Clint got back to shore, his partner gave him a funny look. "That was a dang foolish thing to do. You could have been killed riding into that swift water."

"I wasn't, was I?"

Charlie took his time answering. "Looks to me like if a certain person hadn't been aboard that raft, you never would've taken such a crazy chance."

"Every life is precious."

"Even so ..."

After a swift and definitely annoyed glance from his partner, Charlie closed his mouth. Both still astride their horses, they watched Lucy, Noah in hand, and the others wade to shore, all of them wet, bedraggled, and shivering from a sudden chill wind.

"Thank God, it's over." Bessie called to Charlie Dawes. "I surely hope we don't have to do this again."

Before Charlie spoke, he exchanged a rueful glance with Clint. "There's many a river to cross afore we get to California. This here's just the beginning."

⊱⊰

In the hours that followed, Lucy found herself so busy she barely had time to change from wet clothes to dry or even sit down. Along with Jacob, Benjamin, and Henry, she helped rebuild and repack the wagons. Despite her pleas, the men showed little regard to how, with her tidy nature, she'd originally insisted upon a place for everything and everything in its place. Now they heaped in everything in a complete jumble, causing her to wonder how she'd ever find clothes, dishes, pots and pans—anything at all. Too tired to complain, she collected firewood and built a fire, then fixed a hasty dinner of biscuits and beans. By the time she hauled water from the river, washed the dishes, put them away, and put Noah to bed in the wagon, she crawled into the tent Jacob had erected, totally exhausted.

Jacob lay in bed, sound asleep. *Thank you, Lord.* After such a day, surely he wouldn't wake up now. She would have a whole, wonderful night's sleep without having to endure his near-nightly attentions. Silently, she slipped into her nightgown. Stealthy as a cat, she slipped between the covers and lay next to her snoring husband. *Please don't wake up now.*

Jacob kept snoring. Ah, she counted her blessings. She savored the thought of a few precious hours of peaceful sleep and was just drifting off when she heard the patter of light rain. Drowsily, she hoped it wouldn't get worse, but soon, the patter turned to pounding. Not long after, she felt something damp seep from underneath. She stuck her hand out of the covers to touch the ground. *Wet.* "Jacob!" She shook her husband awake. "It's raining! Water's seeping into the tent!" As if to punctuate her words, a huge clap of thunder broke over their heads, so loud the ground shook. Seconds later, the heavens let loose with such a deluge of rain the tent sagged in, and a stream of water came running through.

"Lord Almighty!" Jacob leaped up and stared at the water.

Lucy cried, "Take the bedding. We must get to the wagon."

They grabbed the mattress and what blankets they could. Through what seemed a wall of water, they ran for the wagon, just as a barrage of hail struck.

Inside they found Noah awake and sitting straight up, shivering with fright. He watched as Lucy and Jacob hastily climbed inside, both soaked to the skin. "Father, will we be all right?"

"Of course, Son. We're under a heavy rainproof canvas, double thickness. Nothing can get through."

Lucy couldn't quite believe what her husband said was true, not with hailstones big as her fist pounding on the cover. Not with the enormous peals of thunder that assaulted her eardrums and the jagged bolts of lightning that flashed nonstop, as if to rip the sky apart. She gazed upward in time to see a split appear in the very top of the canvas, and then another. Water began to pour through the front and back, despite Jacob's tightening the flaps. Soon mattresses, blankets, clothes, everything not packed in the trunks, was soaked through. A chill wind lashed the wagon, so hard she feared it would be blown apart. She was drenched and shivering. "Jacob, what shall we do?"

His face carefully blank, Jacob reached for his Bible, kept dry beneath his coat. "We shall pray."

"Pray?" Sudden rage shot through her. "Here we sit in the middle of nowhere, cold, wet, and the cover ready to rip off any second, and that's all you can do?"

He shook his head as if gently admonishing a child. "Psalms thirty-seven, Verse eight: 'Cease from anger, and forsake wrath.' "

Oh, she could kill him! "You've got to do something. Not just sit there and quote the Bible."

"Are you mad at Father?" Noah's voice was small and frightened. His teeth chattered. He was shaking now, his little face white from the cold.

She *must* calm down. Ranting at Jacob wouldn't do a bit of good. "No, I'm not mad, sweetheart. Here, let's try to get warm." She gathered her stepson and lay down with him on the soaked mattress, pulling him close in her arms. No use pulling the covers up. They were soaked, too. "Jacob, there's a piece of canvas in the trunk that might help. Get it and lie on the other side of Noah. We'll put the canvas over us. Between the two of us we can try to keep him warm."

Her husband seemed unable to move, as if overwhelmed into inaction. "We must pray first—"

"No!" she shot up at him through chattering teeth. "I shall pray when I'm not cold and shivering and wet. Now get that piece of canvas and get down here."

To her surprise, Jacob complied without argument. The three of them lay together in a tight bundle, shivering, thoroughly soaked, sharing what warmth there was. After a time, the hail stopped, but the rain kept pelting the canvas, and the wind did not let up. Tired as she was, she found sleep impossible. She could only hope poor little Noah could sleep despite their misery and that he wouldn't catch pneumonia. As for Jacob ...

Bitterness welled within her. Up to now she'd seen him as a pillar of strength, but tonight, for the first time, she had detected weakness. How indecisive he'd been! How helpless against the frightful storm! She seriously wondered why she married him. Father had warned her about the weakness he sensed beneath Jacob's façade of strength. Sarah, too. No, she wouldn't listen. She knew the reason. She'd been so anxious to escape the clutches of Pernelia, she took the first escape route that came along. Now, as a consequence, she found herself in the midst of the most miserable night of her life. Lying on the soggy mattress, her tears mixed with rain, she pictured her warm, snug bed back in Boston. Oh, how she missed it! Oh, how she wanted more than anything in this world just to be home. She wasn't home because she was trapped in the middle of nowhere with no place to go, trapped with a husband she wasn't sure she loved anymore. Oh surely not! Appalled, she wondered how she could even *think* such a thing. Of course she still loved Jacob. In the morning, when the sun shone again, she'd see all his wonderful qualities that tonight seemed to elude her. Then she'd remember all the good reasons why she married him, and all would be well.

Morning finally arrived but brought no sunshine. Instead, throughout the day, a steady, dreary rain fell upon the soaked, cold, wretched members of the Schneider wagon train. The muddy trail made continuing their trek impossible. They couldn't even build a fire in the heavy downpour. Everyone huddled in their wagons, subsisting mainly on cold biscuits and beans. What Lucy wouldn't give for a hot cup of tea! She spent part of the day sewing patches over the tears in the canvas, not easy when her fingers were numb with cold. The rest of the time she spent hunkered down in the wagon, trying to keep herself warm and Noah warm and entertained. Jacob arose early and left to make the rounds of the other wagons to see how everyone fared after the horrendous hailstorm. She should be proud of her husband, the fearless leader doing his duty, but she wasn't. The memory of his indecision the night before, and his helplessness, hung heavy on her mind.

The next day the rain stopped, but they still couldn't travel. Deep mud bogged the trail. Everyone in camp, all still cold and miserable, had to drag their soggy belongings from the wagons and lay them out to dry. Not an easy task, considering that scattered clouds hid much of the sunshine. As a result, the following morning when they rolled again, the wagons still smelled damp and musty. Lucy spent much of the day comforting Martha, who still fought nausea. Lucy didn't feel so well, either, musing miserably that being pregnant in a smelly, rocking wagon wasn't the easiest of fates.

Mid-morning, Jacob and Abner received a visit from the council, plus Clint and Charlie, after their wagons repeatedly got stuck in the mud. "Either lighten your load or get left behind," demanded Agnes' blunt, strapping husband, William Applegate. The other men of the council, including Elija Richards, Nathaniel Benton, John Potts, and Stanley Helmick, stood behind William Applegate in strong support.

John Potts, recently recovered from typhoid, proved especially loud, as well as crude. "Piss on your wagons, Captain. I'm done."

Mild-mannered, always gentlemanly Nathaniel Benton said, "We simply cannot spend our time hauling your wagons out of the bogs. I, for one, refuse to give you one more push."

After heated debate, Abner gave in, self-righteously asserting that God knew who was right and who was wrong. Finally, Jacob gave in, too. "All right, you've forced me." He scowled. He ordered Benjamin and Henry to remove the barrels of whiskey from the wagons. "Bury them. We'll come back later and dig them up."

Charlie Dawes guffawed. "You think the Indians ain't gonna find them? You've got to pour out every last drop. If you don't, you'll have every Indian twixt here and Fort Laramie so drunk they'll come and scalp us all."

William Applegate glared his contempt at Jacob. "Pour the fuckin' whiskey out."

Given no alternative, Jacob watched while his hired men hauled the barrels from the wagon and dumped his precious whiskey. He couldn't have looked more anguished had it been his own life's blood spilling on the ground.

Two days later the worn and weary members of the Schneider wagon train arrived after dark at the Platte River and set up camp. Next morning, Lucy awoke to bright sunshine. Her spirits rose as the day progressed. She bathed in the river, the "muddy Platte" they called it, and it certainly was. Even though the water wasn't crystal clear, it was more than welcome to one who hadn't been able to bathe for days. She washed her hair, loving its bouncy, clean feel. She donned a fresh calico dress and starched white apron. When she was finished, she felt as good as she had back in Boston after she'd primped and preened for a fancy dress ball.

In the late morning, Jacob and some of the other men went hunting. Before he left, she wished him luck, although so far all his hunting expeditions had been abject failures. So far he hadn't returned with so much as a rabbit. She'd heard Charlie Dawes remark, "Farmers aren't meant to be hunters." Well, she certainly agreed.

Now, sitting upon the wagon seat clutching a rolling pin, she listened intently to Bessie, who stood below, giving her a lesson on how to bake a pie when stranded in the middle of nowhere.

"You take your dough and lay it right out upon the wagon seat. Just make sure there ain't no splinters before you roll it out."

Bessie's words made Lucy burst into laughter, the first time in days she'd found anything to laugh about. "All right, no splinters in my pie. What's next?"

"Then, after you get the apples in, you cook it in your Dutch skillet over the fire. 'Course, if it's raining, you might just want to dig a hole in the ground. You jam in a hollow ramrod what serves as an air shaft, and then you fill the hole with small rocks and bake the pie on those."

"That's a lot of work," Lucy replied. "What if I don't feel like digging a hole in the ground?"

"Then you won't get your pie."

They laughed together companionably, Lucy thinking she felt almost her normal self again, and almost pretty, too. Or as pretty as a woman could look when pregnant.

Suddenly, Bessie quit laughing, pressed her hand to her side, and moaned.

Lucy was alarmed. "What's wrong?"

"I've been having these pains, but the baby ain't due yet." Bessie leaned heavily against the wheel and gave a choked, desperate laugh. "What am I going to do? I don't want to have this baby by the side of the road. What if something goes wrong?

What if—?" She started to cry, covered her face with trembling hands, and whispered, "Oh, God, I mustn't let the children see."

Lucy swiftly climbed down from the wagon and put her arms around her friend. "There, there, it'll be all right. My goodness, you've already had six, and didn't you tell me not a problem in the world? Well, the seventh will be the same."

Bessie laid her head on Lucy's shoulder. "My feet and legs are all swollen. That never happened before. What will the weather be like? What if it's pouring down rain like the other night? Or worse, we aren't going to follow this river all the way, so what if there's no water at all? Can you imagine—?" she pulled away and looked at Lucy with desperate eyes "—no water to wash the newborn in, no water for me! Then afterward, how long do you think the men will let me rest?"

"Well, I suppose a couple of days—"

"Ha! Don't fool yourself. Your husband, my husband, all of them, what do they know? They're so all-fired anxious to get to California, what would they care I just had a baby? They'll want to start again, soon as I pop it out, and there I'll be, lying in the back of that hot, smelly wagon, bouncing 'n rolling, so sick I'll probably die, if I ain't dead by then already."

Bessie's words sent a chill through Lucy's heart. How could she comfort her friend when she harbored the same fears? Bessie had every right to worry. Bad enough to be pregnant, but what could be worse than having your baby by the side of the road? At least they had Inez, but that was small consolation.

Hannah arrived, then Agnes and Inez. They gathered around Bessie. With clucks of sympathy, they soon had her drying her tears. "Sister, you just come with me," said Hannah, "You need to rest, so don't be worrying about that baby."

Agnes chimed in. "It's the seventh, isn't it? Then it's practically going to drop out."

"Besides," Hannah added, "you've got Inez here to look out for you. Ain't that right?"

The midwife firmly nodded her head. "You have absolutely nothing to worry about, my dear."

Lucy liked Inez. With her matronly manner, she acted as a mother figure to them all. When she dispensed her herbal and medicinal advice, she gave the impression of great confidence, almost to the point, Lucy had to admit, of being a bit smug, as if she did indeed know all the answers. Did she really? Did Bessie have absolutely nothing to worry about? Several women in the wagon train were with child. So far, none had delivered, so Inez had yet to demonstrate her midwifery skills. Lucy could only hope she was competent, because the time might come ... no, don't even think it! She would be in California long before her own baby was born. She would never need Inez.

After the women left, Lucy climbed up to the wagon seat again. She was sitting, soaking in the sunshine, when Clint rode up. Thank God she looked her best, and felt her best, too. So did he, judging from his smile and the twinkle in his eye. After a greeting he inquired, "So, what do you think of the Platte?"

She tossed her head. "You call that a river? After all I heard, I thought it would be ... well, majestic. Instead, it's full of mud. Not only that—" she pointed toward a cow standing in the middle of the sluggish current "—I thought the Platte was supposed to be swift and deep. Then I saw that cow. Look, the water's hardly above her ankles."

"What! It's up to her knees, at least."

She smothered a grin. "Her knees then, but that river's shallow no matter how you look at it. I'm *so* disappointed."

He grinned. "The Platte may not look like much, but it doesn't have to be beautiful. We follow it, and it gives us a clear road west."

"For how many miles?"

"Never mind miles. If you start in April, you get to California by October, *if* you're lucky."

"Will we be lucky?"

He shrugged. "No telling."

"Oh." Her spirits dipped. Would her baby be born on the trail? Without thinking, she touched her hand to her stomach. "Such a long way."

His tone was gentle. "You may very well have that baby before we get there. Better be prepared."

She felt herself blush crimson. Certain subjects were never discussed, even within the family, Jacob included. Only once had she tried to express her concerns to him, but he'd stuffily countered with, "Lamentations three, Verse thirty-two, 'Though He cause grief, yet will He have compassion.'"

It was nice to be reminded she had God's support, but she hardly felt comforted. Now here she was, chatting about her delicate condition with a man she hardly knew. To be honest with herself, she shouldn't be shocked. She'd known from the day she met Clint that he said what he pleased, and she shouldn't expect otherwise. Perhaps ... was his honesty the reason she found him so fascinating? Well, she didn't live in Boston anymore where manners mattered, so she wouldn't act like a ninny. If he could be honest enough to speak his mind, she could, too.

She glanced at her bulging stomach, then at him again. "I worry a lot." It felt good, openly discussing the forbidden. "I don't want my baby born somewhere in the wilderness."

He nodded with understanding. "We'll get you there if we can. If not, you'll have lots of help. I'll see to that."

"Thanks, that's reassuring." His words gave her a sense of comfort she'd never received from Jacob.

Just then Benjamin came trotting by on one of Jacob's horses. Bessie's daughter, rosy-cheeked Roxana, sat behind him, arms tight around his waist. "Going for a ride, Mrs. Schneider." Benjamin spurred the horse, and off they went toward the river, both laughing.

Clint looked after them, amused. "Young love. Benjamin and Roxanna. Lately Benjamin's been acting like a lovesick calf. Looks like your husband won't get much work out of him for a while."

"Still, love is a wonderful thing."

"Yes, it is." His gaze traveled over her face and searched her eyes. Here it came again, that look between them loaded with … what? Was she crazy? Was he just being friendly, no more interested in her than any other woman in the company? Or did his eyes reveal forbidden feelings between them that could never be expressed? Here came that jarring, tingling feeling in the pit of her stomach. Oh, he was so disturbing, sitting so easy in the saddle, his every movement so full of grace. Each time she saw him, the pull was stronger.

She forced herself to break their gaze. Frantically, she searched for the first subject that came into her head. "Benjamin's such a nice young man."

One corner of his mouth pulled into a slight smile. "That he is, and Roxana's a fine young lady. They make a good couple. Good day." He picked up the reins he'd rested across the saddle horn and was about to start away when he paused, let the reins drop again, and peered at her intently. "You're a remarkable woman, Mrs. Schneider."

Her pulse leaped. She searched wildly for an answer. "There are a lot of remarkable women in this wagon train."

"None like you." Tipping his hat, he rode away.

She sat on the wagon seat, heart pounding, and faced the truth. This was what it was like to want a man. She had never known before, but now she realized the desire she'd once had for Jacob faded to nothing compared to the searing, nonstop longing she felt for Clint. A desperate shiver of want ran through her. She shut her eyes and instantly imagined his arms around her, his kiss, and then somehow they were entwined together, in bed, and she was beneath him, only it wasn't like with Jacob. It was like Sarah said ...

"Lucy, why are you just sitting there?"

Jacob. She opened her eyes. "Uh ... how was the hunt? Did you shoot anything?"

"What's for supper?"

Fool. "I'm baking a pie, and we're going to have beans and bacon."

"Better get to it. After supper I'll need your help greasing the wheels."

She climbed down from the wagon seat, thinking she ought to feel guilty about her foolish daydream, but she didn't. Maybe she was a terrible person. Maybe she'd rot in hell, but Jacob would never know she wasn't the perfect wife. No one would know, so she'd allow herself her futile dreams. After all, aside from her baby, and a family she'd never see again, she didn't have much else.

True to his word, that night after supper Jacob informed Lucy he needed her help greasing the wheels.

"Can't you ask Benjamin or Henry to help?" She was highly annoyed. She had many chores to complete before bedtime.

"They're busy with the cattle. I want you to hold the grease bucket for me."

"Oh, very well," she said none too kindly.

Jacob had finished one wheel and was lying under the wagon, starting the second, when a shot rang out, followed by two more. "What was that?" He rolled out from beneath the wagon.

"The damn fools!" Charlie Dawes came charging up to the wagon. "This foolishness had got to stop."

"What were those shots?"

Charlie gestured toward the nearby woods. "Some of the young nincompoops in this camp thought they saw a bear and took off after it. Now they're running around the woods like a bunch of idiots, shooting blind, bullets flying all over the place. Nobody's safe."

Jacob drew himself up. "This must stop at once. Come on, Mister Dawes." He glanced back at Lucy. "Keep hold of that bucket. I'll be right back." Lucy watched the two men head toward the woods. Jacob had better not be gone long. She had better things to do than stand around holding a grease bucket.

Before Jacob and Charlie got to the woods, another volley of shots rang out. *Charlie is right, those young men are fools, shooting their guns off so close to the camp ... but something is wrong.* Jacob was clutching his chest and staggering. Why? Her hand flew to her heart. She watched in disbelief. Jacob staggered again, fell to his knees, slowly keeled over, and lay face down on the ground.

"Jacob!" Lucy threw down the bucket, gathered her skirts, and started running across the open field. Halfway there, she tripped and fell hard, but she picked herself up, hardly noticing, and continued to run. By the time she reached her husband, Charlie had knelt by his side, grasped his shoulders, and rolled him over to his back. She flung herself down beside him. "What happened? What—?" It was then she saw the gaping hole in the middle of Jacob's chest, blood oozing out, staining the front of his shirt. "Oh dear God, Jacob!" Her gaze traveled to his face. His open eyes stared, still and sightless, at the sky.

Charlie laid two fingers on the side of Jacob's neck. For a moment, suspended in time, he felt for a pulse. When he finally withdrew his fingers, he shook his head. "He's gone."

"You mean ... Jacob's dead?"

" 'Fraid so, ma'am. Danged if one of those stray bullets didn't go straight through his heart."

Jacob's dead.

Jacob's dead.

The words kept ringing through her head, yet she could

hardly believe that in one stunning, incredible moment she'd lost her husband. She vaguely recalled the cries of shock as people crowded around, little Noah shouting "Father!" running toward his father's body, stopped in time by Clint Palance who scooped him up in his arms and carried him away.

She remembered Abner arriving, kneeling beside his brother's body, tears streaming into his long, black beard. Finally, he thrust a fist into the sky and roared, "God, why did you let this happen?"

Charlie Dawes spoke up. " 'Twas just one of them mindless, stupid accidents. One that only God knows the reason for, and he ain't telling."

She vaguely recalled Hannah and Bessie leading her away from the scene, murmuring words of comfort, their strong arms around her. The next hours passed in a blur. She had a vague recollection of people coming and going, of Cordelia bringing a cup of tea, of Hannah quieting a sobbing Noah and taking him off to her own wagon to care for.

Sometime during the evening, John Potts, hat in hand, visited Lucy's wagon where she sat by her cooking fire surrounded by her friends. "We're all truly sorry, Mrs. Schneider. The captain was a good man and will be sorely missed. If it's all right, we'll bury him first thing in the morning."

"That would be fine." She heard a hollow voice that wasn't her own. As if it mattered. As if Jacob wouldn't be just as dead no matter when they buried him.

John continued, "We don't know who fired that shot, ma'am. We tried, but—"

"It was an accident, wasn't it? Then I'm sure whoever shot him is very, very sorry, and we should just let it go." Why lay blame? What good would it do?

"I'm sure he is, Mrs. Schneider. Sorry, that is, if he even knew he's the one who done it. But that's water under the bridge now." John fumbled with the brim of his hat. An odd expression came over his face, as if he was about to say something he didn't want to say. "You might like to know the committee has elected its new captain."

"Oh?" She couldn't care less.

"Abner Schneider volunteered. We thought it was only fitting, him being the captain's brother and all."

How very odd. She remembered when Jacob was elected, how he'd told her the committee definitely didn't want Abner. Now, no doubt sympathy had played a part in their decision. "Well, I think that's fine."

Agnes spoke up. "It won't matter to Lucy who's elected captain. She can go home now."

John Potts fumbled with his hat again. "I expect that's so, ma'am." He addressed Lucy. "You'll be going back then?"

"I haven't had time to think, but, yes, of course, Noah and I shall return to Boston."

John nodded in agreement. "It's for the best. No need for you to continue on now that Jacob's gone. As you know, hardly a day goes by we don't meet a wagon heading back. We'll see what we can arrange for you as soon as possible."

Grateful though she was for the support of friends, Lucy welcomed the moment when she finally found herself alone, crawling into the tent Jacob had erected by the wagon. How strange he wasn't there. How strange she could crawl under the covers without fear of his hand creeping under her nightgown. The knowledge gave her no comfort. Instead, regrets assailed her. Why hadn't she been more agreeable when he asked for help greasing the wheels? Why, only hours before Jacob died, had she sat on the wagon bench, daydreaming about another man? How wicked could she be? *Oh, Jacob* ...

She had held back her tears, but now she let them flow. Maybe she hadn't loved him as much as she should, but he was a good man, in the prime of life, father of her unborn child, and now ...

It all seemed so incredible. One minute he'd been greasing a wheel and the next, gone forever.

Her tears flowed freely until, after a time, she made herself stop, resolving in the future she'd never put herself and her own feelings first again. She would return to her father's home with Noah, bear her child in the safety and comfort of her own bedroom, cope with Pernelia, and lead a virtuous life filled with good works. Strange, but the thought of going home didn't fill her with the joy she thought it would. How she would miss all these dear friends she'd made! Despite the hardships, she'd miss the day-to-day adventure of this journey, as well as ... *Clint*. How she'd miss him! But he was behind her now, as was this entire insane journey. It was over. Done. She should feel ecstatic that soon she'd be back in Boston where life was dull but safe. Somehow she didn't, and she didn't know why.

She remembered Jacob's bag of gold coins safely stashed at the bottom of the flour barrel. It was hers now. She drifted off to sleep comforted in the knowledge she wouldn't be entirely destitute and dependent. Did Abner know about the coins? She wasn't sure, but if he did, he'd better not try to take them away from her.

∽∾

A sharp cramp in her lower abdomen awoke her in the middle of the night, almost immediately followed by another. For a few moments, she lay paralyzed, knowing what she must do but afraid to do it. Finally, feeling as if her breath had been cut off, she reached under the covers and between her legs. The wetness told her all she needed to know.

What should she do? If Noah were here, she'd send him to fetch Inez Helmick, but Noah was spending the night with

Hannah. She was all alone. Another pain ripped through her, sharper this time. *Must get help.* She threw a blanket around her shoulders and crawled from the tent. On unsteady feet, she walked to the Helmick wagon and rapped on the back. When Inez stuck her head out, her words poured out in a desperate whisper, "I need help."

Had not Inez quickly climbed from the wagon and grabbed her, Lucy would have collapsed on the ground.

Far from Boston, at dawn in the middle of nowhere, a boy was born to Lucy Parker Schneider, so premature he had no chance of surviving. With a grief beyond words, Lucy named him after his father and requested he be laid to rest next to Jacob in the hastily dug grave.

Later that morning, she dragged herself to the graveside services held for her husband and son, so weak she could hardly stand. Grief and despair tore at her heart. Her mind worked endlessly, trying to absorb the shock of losing first her husband, then her precious baby. Beyond tears, she stoically listened to Reverend Helmick deliver a short sermon. Abner followed. Attired in his usual black, ministerial garb, tall-crowned, stiff-brimmed hat atop his head, he launched into a fire and brimstone eulogy for his brother. She remembered how Jacob's blue eyes could occasionally hold a bit of warmth. Abner's dark eyes constantly blazed, as if he must devote every moment to bringing the word of God to those many sinners headed straight to Hell. Would he never stop talking? Abner's eulogy lasted so long Lucy suspected even in his grief he couldn't forgo the opportunity to preach to a captive audience.

After the graveside service, Abner, with Martha beside him, came to talk to Lucy. Still in preaching mode, Abner loudly declared, "Lucy my dear, I want to reassure you you'll have my protection for the rest of the journey."

Lucy squeezed her eyes shut. As if she cared what Abner

did! As if she cared about anything right now except her devastating loss. To her surprise, Martha spoke up. "Abner, I don't believe this is either the time or place to discuss Lucy's plans."

Lucy nodded in agreement. "Martha's right. I'm not in the mood right now to discuss my future."

Abner seemed not to have heard. "From now on, you and Noah will take your meals with us. You can help Martha with the cooking and other chores. I plan to join our herds together, so either Henry or Benjamin will be free to drive your wagon. When we arrive, you'll always have a home with us ..."

Abner rambled on, extolling the fine life Lucy would lead under his care and supervision. Her uneasiness grew as she listened. She could think of no worse fate than living with Abner and Martha for a day, let alone a week or possibly months, possibly *forever*. Worse, even, than living with Pernelia. In her grief, she found it difficult to talk, but she had better speak up. She raised a protesting hand. "Wait. I apologize for interrupting, but you must know I have no intention of carrying on with this journey. We shall be going back to Boston as soon as we meet a returning wagon that's willing to take us along."

Abner's bushy brows raised in surprise. "*We*?"

"Noah and I. Rest assured, he'll have the best care in Boston. We'll stay at my father's home where I know we'll be more than welcome. Noah will have every advantage."

Abner returned an indulgent smile. "I understand how shocked you are at Jacob's sudden death, and the baby, too. Obviously, you haven't thought things through. You must realize Noah is mine now."

Alarm shot through her. She never dreamed Abner might object. "I realize no such thing. I love Noah. You know how close we are. He just lost his father. Are you saying he must lose his mother, too?"

"Martha will make an excellent mother." Abner threw a

look of approval at his wife who wore a worried frown and was twisting her apron, a habit that appeared at the least bit of stress. "She's his aunt, don't forget. I am his uncle, his closest relative now that Jacob has gone to his reward." The remnant of his indulgent smile disappeared. "Did you honestly think I'd let you take Noah away? From now on, he'll be like my own son."

Abner had never paid the slightest attention to Noah, so it'd never occurred to her ... she could hardly believe what she was hearing. "I do think the child will be better off in Boston where it's civilized, and there are good schools—"

"Enough." Abner used a quiet but forceful voice. "I have spoken on the matter, and there's no more to be said. You'd best not forget you're only his stepmother. You have no legal right to the boy. As a matter of fact, Jacob and I bought the wagons— oxen—cattle—all the supplies in both our names, so whatever was his is now mine." His expression softened. He reached and patted the top of her head as if she were a child. "Poor Lucy, you've had a terrible shock—two terrible shocks, actually. But don't fret. If you decide to stay, you have my assurance you'll be under my care and protection. If you wish to return to Boston, then I'll find you safe transportation, but bear in mind, you'll return alone."

In an uncharacteristic move, Martha laid her hand on Lucy's arm. "I do hope you'll stay with us." Her voice was so meek she could scarce be heard. "Noah will miss you terribly if you leave, and so will I."

"Thank you. I ...". A swell of desperation rose in Lucy's throat. She couldn't continue this conversation, let Abner see her lose her composure. She must get away. Must think what to do. "Excuse me, I must go now. We'll talk later." She turned on her heel and walked toward her wagon through the hustle and bustle of a wagon train about to depart for another day on the trail. Vaguely, through her inner turmoil, she heard the lowing of the cattle, the excited barking of the dogs mixed with the oaths of men hitching the oxen and the chatter of women packing the wagons. *How ironic.* Lucy trudged along. At home, several days would have been devoted to solemn mourning for the deceased. Grief didn't last long on a wagon train. Now all thoughts were turned to another day's trek.

She'd almost reached her wagon when she sensed someone come up beside her. A familiar voice said, "Mrs. Schneider?"

She stopped. "Good morning." She hadn't had a chance to talk to Clint but had seen him standing quietly, hat in hand, while Abner ranted over Jacob's grave.

Clint looked down at her, sympathy brimming in his warm brown eyes. "I'm sorry about your husband. He didn't deserve to die like that."

"No, he didn't. Thank you."

"You lost your baby, too. It's beyond me how life can be so unfair to a woman as fine as you."

His voice was so full of sympathy and understanding she almost cried. "Thank you again. It was a little boy, you know."

"I know." There was a silence. "I suppose you'll return to Boston?"

"Yes ... or at least I thought I was, but now ..." Her confusion showed, but with Clint, she didn't care. When he stood looking at her like that, all warmth and sympathy, she wanted to open up, tell him everything. "I planned on returning home, but now ..." She bit her lip. "Now I don't know what to do."

"Why not?" He crossed his arms and regarded her quizzically.

"I planned to take Noah with me, but Abner says he won't let him go."

"Bastard," Clint muttered under his breath. "No surprise there. Abner's the kind of man who'd want a dozen sons simply to boost his ego. So will you go back without Noah?"

"I love that little boy." She paused and continued in a

sinking tone. "It's true Abner's his uncle, but I don't care. Noah's a bright, happy child. I can't bear the thought of what sort of man he'll become if he's raised by that mirthless zealot. If I stay, I can at least make sure Noah doesn't fall under his influence, but ..." She clutched her fists in frustration. "Can you imagine living under Abner's supervision?"

"No, I can't, but let's be practical. Do you really want to go home?"

"Of course. I do so miss my family, especially now."

"A sound argument, but is that all?" He paused, as if to carefully choose his words. "Look me in the eye and tell me you'll have no regrets if you return to Boston. Tell me you won't miss the friends you've made, the excitement of each day's journey."

She nodded reluctantly. "I can't deny I'd miss the dear friends I've made, and yes, even the journey itself. When I wake up each morning, I look forward to the day, despite all the hardships."

"Of course you do." Clint's eyes lit up. "Just think what you've seen already. Mountains, valleys, rivers, green forests—all the beauty that makes up this land. Birds and animals you'll never see if you return to Boston. The best is yet to come." In his enthusiasm, his voice had risen. He gave a rueful smile. "Sorry, you're in no mood for this. I've said too much."

"That's the most I ever heard you say." She smiled for the first time that day.

"I love this land. I wanted you to see it. If you go back to Boston now, I wonder, as the years go by, if you'll grow to regret the choice you made. Something tells me you will."

"You could be right."

"You have a big decision to make, one that will affect the rest of your life."

She gave him a rueful smile. "East or west, which way do I go? Well, you've given me something to think about. It's just that the thought of Abner—"

"You're a strong woman. You can handle the likes of Abner. Think about it. Look into your heart. What do *you* want to do? I've said enough." Clint touched a finger to the brim of his hat and walked away.

Speechless, she watched after him, her mind spinning. Clint so intrigued her. He would be part of the reason she stayed, but how foolish was that? At the end of the journey, he'd disappear, off to guide another wagon train. Still ... how she hated the thought of never seeing him again.

"Mother?"

She felt a tug at her skirt and looked down. Noah, his little face pale and strained, looked up at her with pleading eyes. "Uncle Abner said you're going to leave me. Are you?"

She knelt beside Noah, putting her arms around him, and in that moment made up her mind. "No, Son, Uncle Abner was wrong. You and I are going to California, and everything is going to be fine."

Chapter 8

I'm a widow. I lost the baby. I'm alone in the world. As the day progressed, Lucy lay in the back of her wagon, gathering her strength, slowly coming to grips with her new circumstances. Occasionally, when she had the strength to get out and walk, friends came to keep her company as she kept pace with the slow gait of the oxen. They expressed their sympathy at her loss and their pleasure that she'd chosen to remain. Some were amazed at her choice.

"You're completely out of your mind," said Agnes.

"I just can't understand why you chose to stay," said Bessie. "If I had the chance to go home, I'd surely take it."

Lucy kept her own council. As far as she knew, no one other than Clint even suspected that her concern for Noah was her real reason for not going home. She had to give special thought as to how best to cope with Abner and Martha. So far, except for Jacob being gone, it appeared nothing would change. She and Noah would sleep in their wagon, just as before. She'd watch over Noah, just as before. She disliked the thought of taking her meals with Abner and Martha—those long, long graces before they got to the food—but she'd manage. At least afterwards she could join the others at the nightly campfire, which she always enjoyed.

Maybe living under Abner's thumb would be endurable after all.

All that day, the Schneider wagon train headed due west, following the south side of the Platte River. The barren wastes of the great river valley stretched before them—level plains measureless to the eye, occasional clumps of woods through which coursed winding streams. That day death became even more real when she saw her second grave alongside the dusty trail. She had been walking alongside Abner's wagon. She called for him to stop while she and Martha went to read the inscriptions printed on a pine board at the head of the grave. One read, "Harriet Susan Welsh, born January 4, 1829, died May 8, 1851." The other, "Catherine Amanda Welsh, born May 8, 1851, died May 9, 1851."

Bessie joined them, read the inscriptions, and sadly shook her head. "She must have died in childbirth and the baby next day."

Martha laid a hand over the slight bulge of her stomach. At four months, she was beginning to show. "I do worry so. I send up prayers each day that we'll get to California before my baby arrives."

"I know I won't be that lucky," said Bessie. "Oh, dear." Frowning, she addressed Lucy. "I'm so sorry. We shouldn't be talking about our babies when you've just lost yours."

"Don't worry about it. I'd have to go around blindfolded not to see the number of babies on the way. I can't just ignore them, can I?" Lucy knew she'd grieve for her stillborn child until the day she died, but she wouldn't burden others with her sorrow.

"Martha! Lucy!" Abner shook the reins with impatience. "You'll see plenty more graves before we're done. Get back now."

Lucy returned to the wagon, tears welling in her eyes. Harriet Susan Welsh must have set out for California with her hopes high. Now she and her baby were buried by the side of the road, alone forever in the empty prairie.

She thought of her own lost child, buried in a grave she could never find again. Martha ... Bessie ... pray to God they survive, and their babies, too.

That night, after they parked the wagons in the usual circle, Lucy saw her first Indians. With Martha at her side, she was bent over the campfire by Abner's wagon, baking biscuits, when ten or twelve Indian braves rode into camp. Martha let out a frightened squeal, dropped her cooking spoon, and scampered up to the wagon seat where Abner sat. All around, women were screaming. Men were rushing to their wagons to retrieve their rifles.

"Dad burn it!" Charlie Dawes strode to the center of the campground, waving his arms. "Don't get excited, folks. They're friendly."

Clint followed at his usual easy pace. "They're Sioux, come to trade. Put your guns away. They want bread in exchange for beads and moccasins."

When the camp settled down, the Indians began making the rounds of the wagons. Lucy's heart jumped in her chest when five or six of the tall, copper-skinned savages approached Abner's wagon. What a strange, frightening lot they were with their scowling faces painted in different-colored stripes and elaborate headdresses of feathers and fur. Brass rings hung from their ears and around their wrists and bare arms. She stood frozen, struck by their strange smell, while they milled around her, pushing, getting right in her face, so close that despite Clint and Charlie's reassuring words, she very much feared she'd be attacked and scalped. Even so, she stood firm by the campfire, resisting the impulse to run and hide. She wished Abner was standing beside her, but oddly enough, he chose to remain seated on the wagon seat, rifle across his lap, Noah on one side, Martha on the other. "Give them what they want. Don't let them see you're scared."

Easy for him to say. Abner sat high up, relatively safe.

Shouldn't he be down here? Just why was she the one who must deal up close with these frightening savages? "Good evening." Her voice quaked. "Would you care for some bread?"

She offered her pan of newly baked biscuits. The Sioux accepted with a series of grunts and guttural words she couldn't understand. They all seemed pleased, though, and one held out a pair of beaded moccasins in return.

Clint appeared. She felt a flood of relief just knowing he was there. He took the moccasins and held them out to her. "Take them."

She accepted the moccasins and ran her hand over the soft buckskin. How soft and well-made they were. "Why, they're lovely."

"Save them. You'll have quite a story to tell your grandchildren."

She returned a wry smile. "Then is it your considered opinion I'm not going to get scalped tonight?"

"The odds are you'll survive." His light words reassured her, especially when she caught the glint of understanding deep in his eyes and knew he was well aware of her fears.

Soon the Indians moved on to the next wagon, Clint following. Abner finally climbed down from the wagon seat. "Thieving beggars."

She didn't care for his remark. "It's their land. They didn't invite us here."

Abner snorted with disgust. "A good Indian is a dead Indian."

A rather uncharitable opinion for a man of God. No sense arguing. She had yet to see Abner change his opinion on any subject. One question burned in her mind. Why had he not rushed to her side when the Indians came calling? Until Clint came along, she'd had to deal with them alone while the supposedly brave captain of the wagon train remained relatively safe sitting high on the wagon seat.

The word "coward" came to mind.

The Indians wouldn't leave. All evening they wandered from wagon to wagon. They begged for food, offering beads and moccasins in return. After supper, everyone, including the Indians, gathered around the large fire in the center of the campground. Everyone except Cordelia. Despite Lucy's advice, she hadn't abandoned her "Southern lady of quality" pose and remained aloof as ever. Lately she'd chosen to remain in her wagon, apparently to avoid those-of-a-lesser-standing, although her husband and son always joined in with the rest.

A tenseness hung over the campfire, everyone heartily wishing the Indians would leave. Clint and Charlie advised the jittery group to act normal, as if this were just another evening. As usual, the rowdy Butler Brothers, by now roundly despised by all, annoyed everybody with their crude jokes and drunken laughter. At least one of the brothers, Erasmus, could play a mean fiddle. For a while, he entertained, pleasing the crowd with lively versions of "Rose on the Mountain" and "Billy in the Woods."

After Erasmus, Benjamin sang and played his guitar, an adoring Roxana by his side. Halfway through "I have Something Sweet to Tell You," a piercing scream brought his music to a halt. All eyes turned to the Benton wagon, where Cordelia suddenly appeared through the front opening. With no regard for her customary dignified demeanor, she jumped onto the tongue with lightning speed and leaped to the ground. With a horrified expression on her face, she headed straight for Clint and Charlie.

"Mister Palance, Mister Dawes, do something!" She turned and pointed a shaking finger. "One of those savages climbed right into my wagon."

"Are you hurt?" Clint asked.

"No. I immediately escaped out the front, but I certainly

could have been hurt." Cordelia drew herself up. "What gall to enter my wagon without so much as a knock. Have they no manners?"

Charlie let out a hoop. Clint suppressed a smile. "Indians aren't noted for their manners, ma'am."

"Then they shouldn't be allowed in decent society!"

Before Clint could answer, the subject of Cordelia's wrath stepped from around the back of the Benton wagon and walked toward them. As he grew visible in the firelight, Lucy heard a low murmur of laughter. The murmur turned to a roar when the Indian reached the full light of the campfire.

He was wearing Cordelia's hoopskirt.

Oh, what a funny sight! Never had Lucy seen anything so amusing as that painted-faced Indian strutting around the campground, feathers and fur atop his head, buckskin loincloth and bare legs clearly visible beneath the whalebone rings of Cordelia's hoopskirt.

Watching Cordelia provided even more hilarity. First, her mouth dropped open. Next, her face froze in horror mixed with astonishment. Soon, amidst the laughter, her expression began to soften until finally her lips curved into a smile, and she, too, joined in the laughter.

Clint's eyes were openly amused. "Mrs. Benton, do you want your hoopskirt back? If you do, I'll—"

"Oh, no!" Cordelia waved him off. "Let him keep it. Do you think I'd ever wear it again after this?"

Clint called to the Indian in his own language, then addressed Cordelia. "I told him to take it."

The Indian replied in words Lucy couldn't understand.

Clint grinned. "He says thank you. He also says he likes you very much and will visit you again."

"Oh, surely not!"

Lucy joined in another roar of laugher, this time at Cordelia. She watched the Indian, well aware he was the center of attention, prance about with a big smile on his broad face, making the hoopskirt tilt this way and that. Oh, hysterical! Tears streaked down the cheeks of many in the crowd, Lucy included, as well as Bessie, who surely needed a good laugh, and grouchy Agnes. Even Nathaniel Beauregard Benton was guffawing, his manifest destiny for the moment forgotten. His son, Chadwick, laughed so hard he rolled on the ground, his twelve-year-old funny bone tickled beyond all measure by his mother's part in the humorous scene.

One of the Butler Brothers laughed so hard he fell off his seat and spilled his jug of whiskey. Even Abner's and Martha's ever-sober faces cracked smiles.

The last giggle faded. In the quiet that followed, Lucy perceived the raucous laughter had been more than just a few moments of hilarity over the sight of the hoopskirted Indian. After facing the dangers of the river crossing, the violent hailstorm, Jacob's death, and all the hardships of the trail, they were all grateful for the chance to laugh. What a welcome release, not only from memories of dangers past but from the worry over the uncertainty that lay ahead. Petty conflicts abounded in the Schneider party, as they did in all the wagon trains, but for one brief moment, laughter bonded them together.

When the Indians finally left, Benjamin took up his guitar again and began strumming softly. A full moon rose over the tips of the pine trees; a warm breeze blew gently. Lost in reverie, Lucy faced the truth: once they got to California, and God willing they would, most of these people would take up the same dull, unexciting existence as the farmers they'd left behind. She wondered what she'd be doing. Right now she had little desire to speculate. After losing both her husband and child, all she could do was try to get through each grueling day and not fall apart.

She'd save the moccasins, just as Clint advised. Some day when she was very, very old, she'd dig them out of some musty trunk. They would remind her of the night the Indians traded for bread and one wore Cordelia's hoopskirt, the night she had shared precious moments of warm camaraderie with the other members of the wagon train. She'd also remember how this journey, hard though it was, had given her a taste of something more, a brief escape from her ordinary, mundane life ... given her a sense of adventure, wasn't that what Clint had called it? *West to catch the sunset*. Now she knew what he meant.

If she lived to be a hundred, she'd never forget this night.

Next day, the Schneider wagon train began its trek along the well-marked trappers' trail that followed the Platte River. Edged by a thin fringe of timber lining the river bank, the trail led westward across the plains. They stopped to eat and rest at noon. Lucy was standing by the Potts' wagon, chatting with Bessie, Hannah, and Roxana, when from the distance, they heard a strange roar.

Clint rode up on Paint. "Buffalo. Something's set them off. They're stampeding."

Lucy looked toward the open plain and soon saw her first herd of buffalo. What a frightening sight! The herd was so thick that it resembled a great black cloud, filling the whole prairie and advancing toward them like a moving mountain.

"Should we run?" Bessie's voice was panicked.

"We're all right where we are," Clint answered. "Come look."

He led them to the top of a sand hill, where they stood and watched while thousands upon thousands of the huge beasts roared by, noses almost to the ground, tails flying in midair. Lucy had no idea how many there were, but the stampede seemed endless, the animals' wild snorts and the thunder of their hooves assailing her ears.

After the last buffalo finally disappeared over the horizon, Bessie said, aghast, "My stars, they are horrible looking creatures."

Clint replied, "They may not be beautiful, but I'll wager you'll be eating buffalo steaks from now on, and happy to get them."

"So who's going to hunt the huge creatures?" Bessie wrinkled her nose. "My husband can't bring down so much as a squirrel."

Neither could Jacob. Lucy felt guilty for demeaning the dead. Still, it was true, and that went for Abner, too.

"That's a good question," said Clint. "It's not easy. Takes between fifteen and twenty bullets to kill a bull buffalo, but don't worry, you can count on Charlie and me. We've brought down a few. Meantime, be grateful. Wood will be scarce for a while, but buffalo chips make a good fire."

A frown appeared on Roxana's pretty young face. "You mean we must start collecting buffalo droppings instead of wood? How nasty!"

Clint nodded. "Chips sounds better. The time is coming soon when you'll be grateful to have them." He grew thoughtful. "From now on, be careful. Of all the dangers we face, there's nothing more deadly than a buffalo stampede."

"What sets them off?"

"Lightning ... thunder ... a rabbit dashing across a field ... just about anything."

Remembering the thousands of fearsome animals that had just pounded by, Lucy felt a pang of dread. What a horrible fate to get caught in their path.

Two days later, just as Clint warned, they could find no wood for the campfires. After the train encamped at the end of the day and formed a circle by the river, Lucy, along with most of the women, walked out on the prairie, sacks in hand, to collect buffalo chips. Even Cordelia collected chips. She kept to herself, though, still determined to avoid those-of-a-lesser-standing.

Why must she be such a snob? Lucy had hoped Cordelia would loosen up after the hoopskirt episode, but apparently not. How lonely she must be. It wouldn't hurt to make another offer of friendship. She strolled over to where the snobbish Southern woman was picking up the chips so gingerly they could have been hot coals. "Hello. How are you doing?"

Cordelia smiled a greeting. "I'm as right as I can be, having to pick up these disgusting things."

"We all feel the same way. Why don't you join us? We're in this together, you know. It makes the task a lot easier when—"

"I know what you're trying to say, but don't bother. I told you before, I shall not lower my standards."

Lucy sensed there was no use arguing. "All right, but if ever you feel like joining us, please do."

She left Cordelia and rejoined the others. Tall, raw-boned Hannah tossed a chip into her sack with extra zeal. "So what did Mrs. Stuck-up have to say?"

"She prefers to be by herself, that's all." Lucy would never dream of hurting her friends' feelings by revealing the entire truth. One thing she knew for certain, though; she was done trying to convince Cordelia to come down off her high horse. If the woman made it to California still wrapped in her snooty shell, then fine. Somewhere along the way, Lucy suspected Mrs. Stuck-up would be in a situation where she needed friends. That would indeed be too bad, because she didn't have any. *Maybe I'm wrong.* Maybe Cordelia had already suffered her worse disaster on the trail—losing her hoopskirt to the Indian.

Dressed in their sun bonnets, long skirts, and aprons, the women continued picking up chips, chatting comfortably amongst themselves. Roxana, looking extra pretty in a yellow sunbonnet and printed yellow dress, pointed to a spot much farther out on the prairie. "I see a bunch of them out there. Why don't you quit now and go sit down? I'll bring in enough for the fire."

"I believe I'll do just that." Bessie, awkward and miserable in the advanced stage of her pregnancy, sighed with relief and looked after Roxana with pride in her eyes. "Ain't she the best daughter?" She lowered her voice. "I'm not supposed to tell yet, but last night she told me Benjamin proposed. They want to get hitched real soon."

Lucy joined the others in expressing her delight. "They make a darling couple and are obviously so much in love."

"We'll have a wedding by the campfire," said Agnes, smiling for a change.

"My husband can perform the ceremony." Inez turned to Martha. "Unless ... Your husband's not ordained, is he?"

"No, although he was a deacon in the church. He was too busy farming, but I suspect when we reach California ..." From a distance there came a faint, muffled roar. "What's that?"

They all froze, listening. Through her boots, Lucy felt the ground tremble.

Clint and Charlie appeared at the edge of the plain. "Run!" Clint called. "Drop the sacks and run!"

"Stampede!" Charlie shouted, "Get off the prairie, girls, them's buffalo a'comin,' headed straight toward you!"

Lucy dropped her sack, grabbed up her skirts and started to run. Then she stopped. All the other women raced ahead of her, but where was Bessie? *And Roxana.* She cast a quick look over her shoulder. Dear Lord! With clumsy strides, Bessie was running, but in the opposite direction, out to a distant spot in the prairie to meet Roxana, who was running full-out toward her.

Here came the advancing herd, now so close that Lucy's ears were assailed by the thunderous sound of their hooves. With mounting horror, she judged the distances between the animals and Roxana, between Roxana and the edge of the prairie where safety lay. Her heart sank. No way in the world could

Roxana reach safety in time. "Bessie, you've got to come back. You'll never—"

"Bessie!" Clint called. All at once, Lucy had a sense of Clint sprinting past her, toward the desperate mother. "Bessie, come back. You can't reach her!"

Lucy watched, numb with horror. The huge dark cloud of buffalo was closing in. She saw Clint reach the pregnant woman and take her arm. For a moment, they argued, Bessie frantically pulling away. Clint grabbed her firmly. He began to guide her back to safety, but she still resisted. They were going too slow. They would never make it with Bessie dragging her heels.

Lucy shook herself out of her paralyzing fright and started to run toward Clint and Bessie, her boots fairly flying over the sand and dry sage.

Clint spied her. "Lucy, go back!"

She couldn't spare the breath to reply. All she knew was she couldn't leave her friend to die under a thousand pounding hooves. Strong as he was, Clint needed help. Not only was Bessie fighting him every step of the way, she was so heavy and awkward that she could hardly walk, let alone run.

When Lucy reached them, she grabbed Bessie's other arm. "Run! You must run!"

"Let me go!" Bessie stretched her arm toward the spot far out on the plain where the small figure of Roxana stood, still as a statue, facing the buffalo. She must have known. She wasn't trying to run anymore.

"Let me help my child!" Bessie's anguished cry carried over the prairie.

"It's too late." Clint's jaw was clenched with determination. "Quick, let's move." Between the two of them, they half-dragged, half-carried Bessie, kicking, screaming, sobbing, back across the plain. They reached safety just as the first red-eyed, frothing beast charged past. Bessie collapsed, and Lucy knelt to gather the woman in her arms, holding her while the herd of animals pounded by.

An eerie silence fell across the prairie after the last buffalo passed. Spectators stood helpless, not knowing what to say, what to do. Helped by Clint, both Lucy and Bessie staggered to their feet. Barely comprehending, they gazed in silence at the empty prairie where, only faintly seen, a splotch of yellow lay on the ground. Bessie sagged into Clint's arms. "She's gone, ain't she? My little girl is gone."

John Potts appeared, his face white with shock. "Let me have her." He took his weeping wife's arm and gently led her away.

Clint turned to Lucy. "Are you all right?"

"I'm fine, but ..." she looked toward the prairie. Far out, she saw that small patch of yellow, all that was left of a beautiful young girl on the brink of life. She looked toward the sky. "It happened so fast. I can't believe she's gone. I ..." She choked back a sob.

Clint brought his hand to her cheek. She closed her eyes, feeling the rough comfort of his calloused palm against her skin. "You were very brave."

When she opened her eyes, she caught his brown ones looking directly into hers. They were full of pain, and there again, deep inside, she caught the spark of that indefinable emotion she'd found before.

"Clint?" Charlie called, "we'd best get out there and find what's left of that poor girl before the critters get her."

"You'll be all right." Clint's voice was strong and reassuring. Through her tears, she watched him follow Charlie onto the prairie.

Abner appeared at her shoulder, stony-faced as ever. "Come with me, Lucy."

"Oh, Abner, have you heard? Poor Roxana—"

"I heard." He gripped her arm. "Come along."

She went with him gladly. The shock had left her weak and

trembling. She felt sick to her stomach, too, and wanted very much to lie down.

Abner walked her to her wagon. She made a move to climb in, but he tightened his grip. "No, you come with me." He ushered her past the wagon. They kept walking toward a small grove of trees.

Where were they going? Lucy began to feel alarmed and pulled back, but his grip tightened even more, his strong fingers digging into her flesh. "Abner, you're hurting me." Silence. Again, she pulled back.

"You'll come with me, woman," her brother-in-law commanded quietly, through clenched teeth. He yanked her forward so hard she tripped and nearly fell. It was then she realized he was angry, very angry. She couldn't imagine why.

"All right, I'm coming. You needn't be so rough." Hadn't she gone through enough today? Thoroughly perplexed, she offered no further resistance. They stopped when they reached the center of the grove of trees, a spot far enough from the wagons he could yell, if he wanted, and not be heard. He turned to face her.

She stood waiting, wondering why he was standing there, eyes ablaze, upper lip twitching, obviously so angry he could hardly speak. Finally he loosed his painful grip on her arm and let his hand drop. "Abner—?"

"Silence!"

"What have I done?"

"What have you done?" His voice was heavy with sarcasm and rage. "I'll not allow you to disgrace the family." Before she knew what was happening, his hand shot out and delivered a swift slap across her face.

Stunned, she brought her hand to her cheek, unable to speak. "You dare to hit me?" she finally asked in a horrified whisper.

"You deserve to be punished." Again he drew his hand

back, far back this time. She had easily endured the lightness of his first slap, but now she saw he intended to hit her with even more force. Oh, no he wouldn't! She threw up both hands. "Abner Schneider, don't you dare strike me again!"

He still held his hand at the ready, prepared to swing again.

'You, you ..." She was so mad she choked on her words. She drew in a deep breath that filled her lungs. "You lay a hand on me, and I swear, I'll scream at the top of my voice. Everyone will know. Is that what you want? For the whole world to know Abner Schneider hit a woman?"

Although Abner's eyes still blazed, he lowered his hand and went into the scripture-quoting stance Jacob had imitated—the one she'd come to despise. "Nahum three, Verse five: 'I will show the nations thy wickedness and the kingdoms thy shame.'"

"What is that supposed to mean?"

"I will not tolerate your wickedness."

"What wickedness are you talking about? I was only helping rescue my friend, so what could possibly—?"

"I saw you with my own eyes. You made a spectacle of yourself, flaunting yourself before God when you ran out into that field in front of everyone."

"That's ridiculous."

Appearing not to hear, Abner raged on. "Then you consorted with that wicked blasphemer, Clint Palance. He touched your cheek. I saw him!"

"What if he did? I'm not your wife. Why should you care?" The moment the words left her mouth, she regretted them. Abner would be the last person who could give her a logical answer. She'd never suspected him of harboring lustful feelings toward her, and she didn't now. Rather, his inflexible attitude stemmed from his rigid notions of right and wrong, leaving no room for tolerance. According to Abner, the world would be a better place if he were in charge of everyone's morals. Dear God, what did the future hold? As if she didn't have enough problems, she now must deal with a lunatic who wanted to dictate her behavior. "Abner." She struggled to keep her composure. "I'm very tired. As you know, I recently lost my baby and haven't completely recovered. I absolutely must go lie down. Have you anything more to say to me?"

He blasted, "Stay away from Clint Palance. If you don't, Martha will take over Noah's care, and I shall not allow you anywhere near the boy."

Noah in the hands of Abner? A chill swept through her. She thought of those bruises that appeared from time to time on Martha's face. Lord only knew what was hidden beneath her dress. She thought, too, of Abner's cold treatment of the boy, of how he ordered Noah about, with never a laugh or smile. Oh, never. Noah must remain in her care. "All right, I'll do as you say. Just don't ever even think of hitting me again."

"You're my responsibility, under my command. I'll do what I want with you, and you'd better obey."

How outrageous! She felt her temper rising in response and wanted to set him straight. Increasingly she felt weak and dizzy. If she didn't soon get to her bed and lie down, she'd collapse. She turned on her heel and left Abner standing in the middle of the grove. By the time she got back to the wagon, she felt sickeningly numb, as if her mind couldn't cope any longer with the death of Roxana, Bessie's grief, her own grief, and Abner's unreasonable rage.

She'd hoped she could slip quietly into her wagon, but Henry, their shy, sandy-haired hired hand stood feeding the oxen close by. "Benjamin's down by the river. It's just awful, the way he's been crying over Roxana. They were going to get hitched, you know." His own eyes were red.

"Oh, dear. I shall go to him shortly."

The young man took a closer look at her. "Mrs. Schneider,

are you all right? You look ... your face is so white, like you're going to faint or something."

"I'm just upset over Roxana's death. Such a terrible thing. There's nothing to worry about. I'm fine."

The horrible truth struck her. Clint's words came back to her: "Haven't you found out yet there are no secrets in a wagon train?"

Had she and Abner really been alone in the woods? She doubted they had. A sick feeling swept over her. Soon everybody would know the captain of the wagon train called her wicked and slapped her. Worse, she'd have no way to defend herself because all the gossip would take place behind her back. No one would dare say a word to her face, but everyone would know, just the same.

Chapter 9

Next morning, Lucy gathered with the rest of the somber members of the Schneider party around the hastily dug grave of Roxana Potts. Earlier, when she awoke and looked in her mirror, she cringed at the sight of her drawn, pale face. She really did look bad and could only hope everyone would attribute her wan appearance to her grief over Roxana. At least Abner's slap hadn't left a mark. He'd offered no apologies, nor had she expected him to. This morning he acted as if yesterday's terrible scene never happened.

Now, standing by Roxana's grave, she forgot her own troubles and listened while Reverend Helmick gave a eulogy, followed by Abner reading from the Bible. When he came to "Dust thou art, and unto dust shalt thou return," she couldn't hold back her tears. Hard to believe only yesterday Roxana had been a vivacious young girl, her whole life ahead of her. Now she was gone forever, doomed to lie in a forsaken grave by the side of the trail.

There had been no wood available for a coffin, so they'd wrapped Roxana's remains in a blanket before placing her in the ground. When Abner shut his Bible and stepped back, Bessie said in a choked whisper, "Not even a coffin for my little one."

John Potts, subdued and quiet, wiped his tears away. "My God, I hate to leave her here."

"We must move on," Abner said.

" I can't just leave her," Bessie cried. "She'll be all alone, and I'll be so far away." She sank to the ground and laid her head close to the board placed at the head of grave. Its inscription read, "Roxana Potts, born April 14, 1835, Died June 22, 1851." "I can't bear to think of her here, all alone. What if the wolves get her? Or the Indians? Or—?"

Charlie stepped forward, his hat in hand. "We buried her as deep as we could."

Bessie bowed her head in resignation. "I know." She gazed up at her grieving friends. "I'm sorry for being such a pest. It's just so hard, leaving your dear child alone in the wilderness, knowing you won't even be able to bring flowers to her grave."

John Potts turned to Abner. "We need to stay another day. Bessie will be better by then. Only a day."

"We cannot wait."

Lucy's heart sank. She could tell from Abner's stern, unbending expression he'd never soften.

"Every moment counts," Abner continued. "You've heard of those unfortunate wagon trains caught in deep snow in the mountains? Horror stories abound."

Bessie rose to her feet. "Please, Captain."

"Sorry." Abner addressed the assemblage. "We leave in an hour. Come, Martha, Lucy."

"I'll be there in a moment." Lucy turned to her weeping friend. "I know it's hard, and I'm so sorry."

Bessie stood with her head bowed and, for a time, remained in an attitude of frozen stillness. When she looked up, her eyes were dry. "Don't you worry. I'll be ready. I don't know how I can bear it, but I will." She lifted her head. "We must endure like good soldiers. My mother taught me that."

Lucy's heart wrenched with grief, not only for Roxana but for brave Bessie, laden with sorrow but willing to carry on.

Before they left, Lucy went to Bessie's wagon. Hannah, her plain face pale and strained, stood outside as if on guard. "She's asleep. Best leave her be. Oh, what are we going to do without

Roxana? How could God let her die in that terrible way? I wish we'd never came on this horrible journey."

Lucy could only nod over the lump in her throat. Of the two sisters, Hannah was the strong one, yet even she showed signs of breaking over the death of her pretty young niece.

Hannah went on, "I'm not blessed with children of my own, so I guess I can't exactly feel Bessie's grief, but ..." Her eyes moistened. "I loved that girl."

"We all did. Poor Benjamin couldn't even come to her burial ..." Lucy proceeded to tell Hannah about the young man's grief, how she'd heard him sobbing during the night.

Hannah listened intently. At one point she seemed to see Lucy's face for the first time and gave an almost imperceptible start. When Lucy finished, she said, "You look bad. Your face is all strained and white."

"Well, Roxana's death—"

"Abner done that."

Lucy put her hand to her face. "There's a mark?"

"No, there's no mark, but we all know what happened just the same." Hannah's face twisted into an angry scowl. "That no-good bastard! There's some as don't like the captain. There were some who didn't like Jacob, either, but at least he wasn't quite so self-righteous and smiled once in a while. Abner not letting Bessie stay an extra day didn't set well with a lot of us." Compassion filled her eyes. "I guess you know we all heard how he yelled at you and slapped you, and, bless your heart, you didn't let him give you anymore sass and stood right up to him."

She could almost laugh. "Is nothing sacred?"

"Not around here it ain't."

"Please, don't say anything more."

"You think I don't know you have your pride? Don't worry. I've had my say."

Lucy raised her chin. "It won't happen again. I informed Abner in no uncertain terms that I—"

Hannah's scornful laughter cut her off. "You think he'll listen to you? These men! Well, you're not the only one."

"Has your husband ever—?"

"Elija? He'd better not, the little runt."

Lucy couldn't suppress a quick smile. Hannah was a big woman, taller and heavier than her husband. Come to think of it, Hannah could probably knock the poor little man flat if she had a mind to. She wished she could do the same with Abner.

Hannah patted her shoulder. "You'll be all right. You're strong, and you're smart enough to know how not to rile him again."

Lucy nodded silently.

"I know he's got a hold on you. It's Noah, ain't it?"

She could only nod again. How very perceptive of Hannah. "It's Noah and a lot of things. I feel so trapped. Out here in the middle of nowhere there's no place to run. I couldn't leave now, even if I wanted to."

"You're right, you can't leave." Hannah's voice was practical. "My best advice to you is, stay with Abner for now. You'd best be very, very careful. You know what I mean." Hannah cast a knowing look, as if she knew every shameful secret Lucy harbored in her head concerning Clint Palance. "Meanwhile—" the animation left her face "—say a prayer for Bessie, will you? I worry about her."

"Of course. I know how she loved Roxana."

"It ain't only that. My sister's having problems this time. We used to joke about how the seventh would just pop out, but lately I'm not thinking so."

"I've noticed her feet and legs are swollen. Is there anything else?"

"She's having sharp pains. Not labor pains, just the kind of pain she shouldn't be having."

Not Bessie. Lucy's heart sank at the thought her dear friend might be in trouble. "We can only hope for the best, out here in this God-forsaken wilderness."

Hannah sadly shook her head. "Sometimes I think God truly has forsaken us."

"Bessie said it best. 'We must endure like good soldiers.'"

"Yes, our mother used to say that. 'Like good soldiers.' "

Mere words ceased to be adequate. Lucy and Hannah embraced and stood silently for a time, each drawing strength from the other. When they finally drew apart, Lucy had a wistful smile. "I am *such* a long way from Boston."

"I'm sure as heck a long way from Possum Creek, Tennessee."

Together they shared a moment of laughter, a small consolation on such a dark day.

For days, mile after mile, the bare plain stretched before them. Here and there the Platte River, their constant companion, divided into thread-like sluices wending through the open prairie and through the occasional clumps of woods that relieved the monotony.

Not nearly enough clumps of woods. These were days when not one single tree, bush, or hill broke the horizon. Only endless miles of flatland that stretched on forever. As a result, the lack of shelter made life a daily agony of embarrassment for the women. Their long, full skirts supplied the only privacy for "nature's call." The best arrangement was for at least two or three women to stand together and hold their skirts out, but even one woman extending her skirt was far better than nothing.

"I allow, I'm getting mighty tired of hunkering down in the middle of the prairie," Bessie complained to Lucy and Hannah one day while they stood patiently, their skirts fanned out.

Hannah retorted, "It wouldn't be so bad if you didn't have to go every fifteen minutes."

"Just wait 'til you get pregnant, my fine sister!"

Lucy could surely commiserate with Bessie, as well as her

shy sister-in-law. As the weeks went by, Martha's pregnancy had caused more frequent treks to the bushes. At first she'd suffered agonies of embarrassment. Now, with no bushes at all, she'd grown accustomed to relying heavily on her women friends. Not one woman complained, though. The spirit of camaraderie and helpfulness never ran stronger than it did when each provided the other her privacy.

The lack of any kind of plant life forced even Cordelia to make use of the curtain of skirts. She hadn't changed, though, and acted as if every minute she spent with those-of-a-lesser-standing was a great sacrifice she must endure. By now her popularity had dipped even further. Bessie said it best. "If I didn't have such a kind heart, I'd drop my skirt at just the right moment and let the men get an eyeful of Mrs. Stuck-up squatting just like the rest of us."

Not a day went by that Lucy didn't see at least one grave dug by the side of the trail. Not surprisingly, Agnes kept a record of each and every grave site in her journal. "The road that runs beside the Platte River is like a graveyard," she wrote in her usual glum style. She wasn't far from wrong. They had yet to reach halfway to their destination, but already she had listed over eighty graves. She also took note of the cause of death, included on many of the inscriptions carved into rough boards that marked the graves. "Died of cholera," was common, or "Died of typhoid ... died of measles." Every day, Lucy gave thanks that so far no one in the party had been stricken with one of these deadly diseases. Still, there were always the accidents to worry about. She was keenly aware of the ever-growing list of tragedies in Agnes' journal: "Died of a rattlesnake bite ... died from drinking poisonous water ... died when he accidentally shot himself ... drowned in the river ... killed by a grizzly."

One cause of death was never noted. "Died in childbirth" was much too delicate a subject to identify, but when an inscription listed the names and birth dates of a woman and baby who died the same day, the cause became obvious. Lucy did her best to divert Martha's attention from such grave markers. Each time she saw one, Martha became visibly shaken. "What if me and my baby were the ones buried under the little mound of dirt, with only a rough board for a marker? How awful to lie in a cold, dark hole for all eternity with never a loved one to come and leave a flower, shed a tear, or say a prayer."

Lucy could only attempt to assure her sister-in-law she'd never suffer such a fate. She knew she didn't sound too convincing. After all, she'd lost her own baby, and she wasn't nearly as tiny and frail as Martha. She tried her best to appear confident. Worry was a useless emotion, and besides, she was far too busy to indulge herself. Simply surviving each day on the trail took all her energy.

As the days went by, and the Schneider wagon train rolled on, the shock of Roxana's death faded, along with the memory of the horrible scene with Abner. Lucy felt better. Her color returned. She continued caring for Noah as before. As for Abner, he never mentioned the slapping incident and acted as if nothing had changed between them.

Now she was beginning to look ahead and wonder what would happen when they reached California. Would she have no other choice but to remain with Abner and Martha? Her mind rebelled at such a thought, but the dilemma remained. She would *not* spend the rest of her life with a man she'd come to detest, but on the other hand, how could she face losing Noah? Somehow, some way, she'd solve her dilemma, but at the moment, she could find no easy answer.

To her constant frustration, because of Abner, she strove to steer clear of Clint. The irony hadn't escaped her. She wasn't a married woman anymore, yet because of her brother-in-law's self righteous wrath, she didn't dare go anywhere near Clint. That didn't prevent her from constantly thinking about him. In those moments when she looked into what seemed a dismal future, all she had to do was think of Clint Palance, and her spirits lifted. She pictured him riding Paint, so easy in the saddle, so confident, so honorable and trustworthy, so handsome, too, despite the scar. She thought of the times they talked, when he looked down at her with that glint of humor in his eye. His eyes told her a lot more, too. They said he wanted her. It was so very plain. How unfair life was, never to know the feel of Clint's arms. Now, because of Abner, she must avoid him. She blamed herself for being stupid enough to marry Jacob in the first place, especially when both her father and sister had warned her not to.

If she hadn't married Jacob, she never would've been on this wagon train, and if she hadn't come on this wagon train she never would've gotten to know Clint Palance.

Sometimes in the dark of night, when she was unable to sleep, she'd imagine it was Clint, her tender lover, who lay beside her, that she was thrilling to his touch, just like Sarah said, carried away on the wings of love. She wasn't sure what that meant. She hadn't learned from Jacob, but she had the feeling Clint could teach her.

She knew her secret thoughts were utterly foolish, yet she felt not one twinge of guilt. After a grueling day on the trail, her fantasies of Clint Palance gave her most of the happy moments she could find amidst the toil and heartbreak of her harsh new world.

On a day when heavy showers prevented the wagons from moving, Lucy stayed inside her tent, doing her best to keep Noah and his little friend Jamie entertained. In the late afternoon, she took the boys to the Helmick wagon, then went for a walk to get much-needed fresh air. The rain had stopped for the moment, replaced by a muggy stillness that hung like an oppressive mantle over the camp. There wasn't one person in sight. Everyone must be hunkered down in their tents and wagons, which was most unusual, but how very nice. Privacy was a rare luxury these days, so she welcomed the idea she could actually go for a walk and be all by herself. She strolled out of the camp, through a grove of trees to the river, swollen from all the rain. Finding a log that extended into the water, she sat down, stripped off her boots and stockings, and dabbled her feet, enjoying the feel of cool water running across her toes. For a while, she took in the glorious view across the river, where a herd of deer had ambled down to the edge for their evening drink.

Finally, in the gathering darkness, she stepped to the shore. When she bent to retrieve her stockings, she felt a burst of sharp pain in the sole of her right foot. "Oh, oh, oh!" she cried and began hopping about. Something had bit her, or stung her, she wasn't sure which. She looked down in time to see a horrible looking creature scurrying under the log. It had crab-like front claws and a long body with a high arched tail that curved around. She had never seen anything like it.

Tears welling in her eyes as she stood on one foot waiting for the excruciating pain to subside, clenching her teeth to keep from crying out again. At last, when the pain had lessened slightly, she knew she needed help. What should she do? Stay and wait? Surely, sooner or later, someone would come along. What if she didn't have that much time? What if the creature was poisonous? She could be dead in an hour if she didn't get help right away.

She had to get back to the campsite. Had to get to Inez Helmick. With all those herbs and potions, surely she'd know what to do. Wincing with pain, she picked up her boots and stockings and began hobbling back, stepping on her left foot, gingerly balancing herself with the heel of her right.

When she reached the campsite, she found only one person in sight—Clint, standing by his wagon. He saw her at once, painfully limping along, and immediately went to her side. "What happened?"

"Oh, Clint!" She was so relieved to see him. "I stepped on this ... this awful thing, and it bit me. It hurts! What if it's poisonous? Do I need to see Inez?"

"What did it look like?" When she described it, he looked relieved. "You got stung by a scorpion. There are a lot of them around these parts. Let's have a look." He swept her in his arms, carried her to his wagon, and set her down on the yoke. "Hold out your foot."

Grimacing, she extended her foot. "It feels like I got stuck with a red hot needle. Is it poisonous?"

Clint bent over, clasped her foot gently, and raised it enough so he could see the bottom. "A little, but you'll survive." He gave her a reassuring smile. "It should feel better in a few minutes. It's slightly swollen but shouldn't get any worse. A cold compress helps. I'll get one."

Clint disappeared inside his wagon. Just as he returned, the heavens opened and a deluge of rain began to fall. "Quick," let's get you inside."

Despite the rain, and the dreadful burning pain in her foot, she took a cautious look around the campsite. Still not a soul in sight. She couldn't even feel the prying eyes of Agnes upon her.

Clint regarded her with a mocking gleam in his eye. "Still worried about what people might say?"

Why had she been thinking such nonsense? "Absolutely not. Help me inside."

He helped her into his wagon and had her sit on a bed that wasn't much more than a mattress on the wagon floor. "A sting from a scorpion is pretty much like a bee sting. Hurts like hell, but you're not going to die."

"I didn't think so." She was inwardly relieved. She watched Clint dip a cloth in cold water, then carefully wrap it around her foot. Instantly the burning eased. "That feels better. I'd wager this isn't your first scorpion sting."

"Scorpions ... spiders ... snakes ... you learn a lot when you live in the wilderness." He finished applying the compress, sat back on his haunches, and regarded her with concern. "Is that better?"

"Oh, much." It was. No need for Inez Helmick. She might have known Clint could help her.

"So, how are you?"

"Fine."

"You've just lost your husband and your baby. Don't tell me fine."

Clint's blunt response reached the constant torment in her heart. Since the day her husband and son were buried, she'd mostly grieved to herself. How could she expect sympathy when everyone she knew was simply struggling to survive? "There is nothing worse in this world than losing a child." Her voice quavered.

"I can only imagine what you've been through. You've been very brave."

His deep understanding nearly brought her to tears. She swallowed hard. "Thank you for that. It hasn't been easy."

"Actually, for a city girl, I think you're doing pretty well."

She smiled. "Thank you for that, too." His remark not only jerked her out of her gloomy mood, it caused a warm flood of feeling to course through her. So nice to hear praise for a change. She certainly got none from Abner. "I'm not like Mister Benton and his manifest destiny. I mean, I'm not out to expand The United States or any such thing. I just want to get where I'm going and find a place for Noah and me." She laughed. "And then die in bed of old age, not from having my scalp removed by an Indian."

He nodded agreeably. "I admire all you women. To endure what you do every day takes great courage."

"This may surprise you, but in some ways this journey isn't

as hard as I thought."

"It's not? In what way?"

She paused to put her thoughts together. "Sometimes when we're riding along and I see the beauty of the mountains we pass, and the rivers and forests, I realize these are all things I would never have seen had I stayed in Massachusetts. I wouldn't have even known they were there."

For a long time he didn't speak. "West to catch the sunset," he said in an odd yet gentle tone. "You see that now."

"Oh, yes." She looked around his wagon, crowded but neat. "I've never been in here before."

"Well, I wonder why." There was a trace of laughter.

"Umm, you're right. Now it's different. I'm not a married woman anymore."

He raised an eyebrow. "You might as well be."

She didn't want to think about Abner right now. She sighed and searched for a change of subject. "Where's Charlie?"

"Gone to try and find a trapper friend of his. I don't expect him back until tomorrow."

We're alone. "Oh really?" She tried to sound casual.

He shot her a gaze that swept over her, soft as a caress. "Really."

The look he gave her made her forget the pain from the scorpion's sting. She grew acutely aware of her surroundings. Only a thin layer of canvas separated her from the world outside, yet she felt snug and warm, sitting on the bed in Clint's wagon, listening to the soothing patter of the rain. "We've never been alone like this."

He sank down beside her. "No, we haven't." He lifted a hand and touched her hair. No sunbonnet today. She wore it loose, streaming down her back. "I've wanted to be alone with you since Independence." He thought a moment. "No, since Boston, when you were such a little snob."

She began to laugh. "And said I would never set foot

outside Suffolk County."

He joined her laughter. When it stopped, he regarded her a moment, then his breath caught and his arms went around her. Almost of their volition, her hands slid around to the back of his buckskin coat. He pulled her close. She pressed her fingers into the broad shoulders she'd admired from afar for so long. Their lips crushed together in a kiss so long overdue that she felt him tremble and knew she was trembling, too. She returned his kiss with reckless abandon, her mind spinning in several directions at once. How wonderful to be in his arms. How incredible. She could hardly believe her impossible dream had finally come true.

When they finally broke apart, he looked into her eyes, his face only inches from hers. "I don't want this to end."

She understood his meaning. He was giving her a chance to say no. For a clearheaded moment she faced the fact that although the campsite was temporarily deserted, chances of discovery were still high. Like him, she didn't want to stop. How could she when a crazy jumble of feelings were pouring through her? None had to do with caution. They were all about excitement, yearning, and her burning desire. "Neither do I."

He gripped her wrists, lowered her all the way to the bed, and lay beside her. He began kissing her again, and she eagerly responded. Somewhere, during a frenzy of kisses, they undressed each other: first her dress went, then his coat, pants, and boots, finally her bloomers which, in a heavy-breathing moment for both of them, he slid slowly down her hips, over her silky mound, continued down over her legs, then clear off. She knew not where he tossed them, or cared.

"You're beautiful." He looked down on her, his eyes brimming with admiration.

She lay naked beneath him, basking in the warmth of his gaze, experiencing a wanton delight that every inch of her was exposed to his gaze. With his swelling manhood pressed hard against her hip, he began to swirl gentle fingers around her pink nipples, watched as they hardened, then with the lightest of touches, teased them harder still. The gentle massage sent currents of desire running through her, and when he whispered, "You have beautiful breasts. I've been wanting to kiss them," her whole body throbbed. When he lowered his head and sucked her nipples, running his rough tongue over each in turn, her body arched, and the pleasure of it made her bite her lip to keep from crying out.

"Oh, that was good," she gasped, "very, very good."

"He took her hand and guided it to his manhood. "Hold on to this while I do some things to you."

Heart pounding with excitement, she clasped the most intimate part of Clint Palance, marveling at how thick it was, how long, and how very, very hard. Next, just like he said, he began doing things to her, incredibly exciting things like running his thumb deliciously over her palm, nibbling at her ear, moving his hands magically here and there over her body. Often he returned to her breasts, where his hands roamed intimately, and he nibbled, sucked, and kissed until she thought the exquisite feeling would drive her mad.

She now experienced such ecstasy that she moaned, frantically eager for his next touch. When at last he slipped his hand between her legs, the sweet sensation of his fingers touching the most intimate part of herself was so intense ... "Oh, I can't bear it. I need you inside me. Now! I shall die if you don't."

"Happy to oblige." His voice was thick with passion. He reached to spread her legs apart, and she eagerly slid them open. Slowly he guided his shaft inside her, causing her to emit little groans of pleasure each time he moved. By now she'd abandoned all logical thought, her mind nothing more than a mass of delicious sensations, all centered on that pleasure spot where they were joined. At last, when he was all the way in, he paused and looked into her eyes. "Feel good?"

"Oh, yes, I'm in heaven. Don't stop!"

"I won't, not until you're pleasured."

"Oh, I'm pleasured all right," she managed to gasp through her rapturous haze. "Do keep on."

He began a series of rhythmic strokes, each one driving her to a higher arousal. In return, her hips rose and fell in a natural rhythm that matched his own. His own passion turned wild and hard until finally he stopped. "Are you almost there?"

"Yes!"

He drove in hard, pushing her over the brink into a sensation so fantastic, so incredibly wonderful she was forced to press her lips together, muffling her screams of ecstasy against his shoulder.

At the same time, he, too, experienced an explosive pleasure and soon lay spent and panting beside her.

While the rain pattered on the canvas above, they lay for she didn't know how long, wrapped in each other's arms, their beating hearts slowly returning to normal. Finally, voices in the distance brought her back to the real world. She sat up. "I'd better go."

"Yes, you had." He immediately arose and pulled on his clothes. "I'll be outside. Let me know when you're ready."

Alone in the wagon, she washed herself as best she could and pulled on her clothes, all but her right shoe. Her foot still throbbed from the scorpion sting. Funny, but when she was making love with Clint, she'd entirely forgotten. When she was ready, she called softly, "Is it clear?"

"It's clear."

She slipped from the wagon and took a quick look around the rain-soaked camp. No one was in sight except Clint. "It's clear for the moment," he said. "You'd better go."

Her heart swelled. There were so many things she wanted to say to him, but already her mind had turned to matters more practical. Time to start dinner ... Noah would soon be back ...

where was Abner? Hard to believe only minutes ago she was in such a state she wouldn't have cared if the whole world had seen her making love with Clint. Now apprehension coursed through her. What if Agnes had seen her? What if Abner found out? What if ...? No more euphoria; she was back on earth again.

"Goodbye." She gave a wicked little smile. "Whenever I see a scorpion, I shall think of you."

Not waiting for his reply, she hobbled away, wondering how she could've been so flippant with the man who'd just turned her whole world upside down. *Carried away on the wings of love.* Yes, she had been, and yes, she knew there'd be sleepless nights ahead when she remembered the sheer bliss she'd experienced on this bleak, rainy afternoon.

"Lucy, what happened to you?"

Damnation! Agnes' voice. Lucy turned to see her gossipy friend's head sticking out of her tent.

What happened to me? Well, if you must know, I just finished making mad, passionate love with Clint Palance right under your very nose. By the way, do you have any idea how large he is? It was so long and hard it drove me wild. In fact, he's such a good lover, I had to bite my tongue to keep from screaming and waking the whole camp up. It was just so wonderful. So what do you think of *that*, Agnes!

"I got stung by a scorpion."

"Oh, you poor dear. It must have been terrible, getting stung like that."

"Yes, it was pretty bad, all right. If it isn't one thing, it's another, isn't it?"

"It's just awful, the hardships we must endure."

"You're so right." Lucy nodded her head in solemn agreement and hobbled on her way.

A few days later when the wagon train was underway again, Noah called, "Look, Ma, what's that?" Seated on the wagon seat between Benjamin and Lucy, he pointed to the distant horizon where a lone pillar of rock reached toward the sky.

"I don't know what that is."

Just then Charlie Dawes appeared, pacing his horse to the slow plodding of the oxen. "Son, that there is Chimney Rock. They call it a great natural wonder."

"Why do they call it a chimney?" Noah asked.

"Because when you get up close, it looks like one. It looks close now, don't it? You ain't going to reach it for two more days. It's the first of our landmarks. It tells us we're five hundred and some odd miles from where we started. Folks like to climb it, at least the lower part. After we pass it, Fort Laramie's just three days away."

Abner rode up. In his usual brusque fashion he inquired, "What's going on?"

Charlie's eyes shifted to Abner. "We're talking about Fort Laramie. By the way, we'll need two or three days' rest when we get there."

Abner stiffened, as Lucy knew he would. His hard-driving ways drew many protests, but he kept insisting they move at as fast a pace as possible. "We must not waste time."

"The folks need a break. There's plenty of wood at Fort Laramie, and grass and water. The people can trade at the fort and bathe and wash their clothes." Charlie Dawes, until now always congenial, regarded Abner with a hard glint in his eye. "I highly recommend you stop for a couple of days. Otherwise ..."

"Otherwise what?"

"These people are tired and worn. They've still got a long way to go, and they need a couple of days to get clean, buy some food, give their animals a good feed, and get their spirits back up. Plain and simple, there's going to be trouble if you don't let them rest."

Abner's jaw clenched. His lips pinched tight. "I shall keep

your advice in mind, but may I remind you the final decision is mine?"

After Charlie shrugged, gave a curt goodbye, and rode off, Lucy couldn't keep silent. "You'd better listen to what he says. We're so in need of a rest, and—"

"God and I shall be the judge of that, not you."

Lucy knew better than to waste another word, even though she was hearing constant rumblings of unrest and dissatisfaction with Abner's leadership. Surely he sensed how unpopular he'd become. She'd even heard rumors many in the party wanted him deposed and another leader elected.

Better than anyone, she could understand why.

"Ain't this grand?" exclaimed Hannah. "Two whole days in Fort Laramie." She, Lucy, and other women from the party, pails in hand, strolled toward the thick woods near the fort to pick berries.

"We surely need the rest." No need to mention the heated argument Lucy had overheard between Abner and the members of the council. A shouting William Applegate threatened to depose Abner as leader if he didn't allow a two-day rest in Fort Laramie. All the other men agreed. Lucy silently applauded when Abner finally gave in to the pressure.

Fort Laramie, situated on a tongue of land formed by the junction of the Laramie and North Platte Rivers, offered a heavenly abundance of water. How wonderful to wash all over and feel really clean! Lucy had spent an enjoyable day with her women companions, bathing, cleaning out their wagons, and washing all their clothes, while Abner joined the men in mending wagons and equipment, and turning the cattle out to graze on the plentiful grass. Now, in the late afternoon, she strolled toward the woods feeling better than she'd felt for days ... weeks! She wore a newly laundered blue calico dress and left the hated sunbonnet behind. How nice, the carefree feel of her freshly washed hair falling loose around her shoulders.

She wished Clint could see her now. Since they had made love in his wagon, he'd constantly been on her mind. She longed to be with him, away from prying eyes, but the chances of that happening again were slim to none.

She pulled her thoughts back to earth. "I'm going to make a berry pie for dinner, and one for Bessie," she called out to Hannah, Agnes, Martha, and Inez when they spread out to collect berries. Poor Bessie, who was near her time, remained behind.

Engrossed in her berry picking, Lucy soon found herself alone, although she hardly noticed, so intent was she on filling her pail with the plump gooseberries and chokeberries she found in great quantities. Finally, when she had filled her pail to the brim, she stopped, raised her head, and looked around. Surprised, she found high walls on either side of her and realized she must have worked her way into a canyon filled with tall trees and thick undergrowth. Where was she? How still it was. Where were the others?

"Agnes?" she called. "Hannah? Martha? Inez?"

No answer. Only her own words echoed back at her. She called again, louder, and listened intently, but the only sounds she heard were the caws of a passing raven, the gurgle of a brook, and the rustle of soft wind through tall pine trees.

"You can't be lost," she muttered to herself, annoyed but not alarmed. Her friends couldn't be far. All she had to do was retrace her steps, and she'd be sure to find them.

Which way? Clutching her pail of berries, she turned in a slow circle and tried to decide which way she'd come. Trouble was, each bush looked like another, and each tree looked like the next. She had no idea which way to go.

"Agnes?" she yelled at the top of her voice, more impatient now. "Hannah? Inez?" No comforting reply, but she still felt no alarm. She'd find that creek she heard and follow it, and in no time she'd be back with her friends.

She followed the sound of flowing water and soon found a gurgling brook flowing over moss-covered stones, edged by tiny violets and moss roses. How pretty. She'd like her friends to see it, but meanwhile, should she go upstream or downstream? She had no idea. Downstream, she supposed. That was as good a guess as any.

She started walking, finding the way easy going at first because she could follow along the bank. Farther along, the underbrush was so thick in places that she had to wade through the creek in order to get around it. She kept a firm grip on her pail, though. Bessie *would* have her pie. And Noah, too, and Henry and Benjamin. Even Abner.

Over and over, she called her friends' names, but no one answered. She had no idea of the time, but it seemed an hour at least that she'd struggled down the stream with no end in sight. She wondered how she could have wandered so far. Surely, she should've found someone by now. She glanced up at the sun and saw it was about to set behind one wall of the canyon. That meant she was facing west. But from which direction had she come? She didn't know, and soon darkness would set in.

Now she recalled the warning she'd been given at the fort. *Don't stray too far. Indians ... grizzly bears ... snakes!*

A sudden fright overcame her. Soon she'd be all alone in the dark, lost in the wilderness. She sank to the ground, her back to a tree, her heart pumping with fright. She had no place to run, no place to hide, no weapon of any kind. So vulnerable anything could get her! Her mind racing, she remained absolutely still against the tree, terrified something monstrous would leap from the bushes at any moment and pounce on her.

Just then, she heard a slight rustling in the bushes. Must be her imagination. Again a rustling. She turned her head toward the sound and saw, not six feet away, the glittering black eyes of a snake staring straight at her. Panic like she'd never known welled in her throat. *Run!* cried a little voice within her. *Get up and run!* But her body refused to cooperate. The snake, its body a blotched mixture of yellow, gray, and brown, left the bushes and slithered straight toward her. She let out a small scream, pressed her back to the tree. In the wink of an eye, the snake wound into a menacing coil, its head swaying back and forth, forked tongue flicking rapidly. She heard a funny sound. Rattles! A rattlesnake! She could hardly breathe.

Again she told herself she must get away, must run. Barely had she started to put thought into action when she heard a voice.

"Lucy, don't move."

She froze.

"Don't move."

She shifted her eyes toward the sound of the voice. Dressed in his buckskins, knife in hand, Clint Palance stepped through the bushes, his eyes on the snake. With a motion so swift it was just a blur, he sent the knife flying square into the snake's head, killing it instantly. She slapped a hand over her mouth and gazed wide-eyed, unable to speak, first at the dead snake, then up at Clint.

"Good afternoon." He retrieved his knife, slipped it into its sheath, and smiled. "Out for a stroll?"

Hand shaking, she pointed at the remains of the snake. "Get that thing out of here!"

"My pleasure." He picked up the dead reptile and tossed it back into the bushes. "Better?"

"Much better." Her fear gone, she was so relieved to see him she wanted to leap up and throw herself into his arms. Pride prevented her, though. Since that day they'd made love, they'd hardly said a word to each other. As a result, she felt a certain constraint had grown between them, and the intimacy they'd shared was gone. "Well, it appears you've saved me again." She picked up her pail of berries and held it up to him. "Care for a gooseberry?"

He sank down beside her. "Did you know everyone's looking for you?" He took a berry and popped it into his mouth. "Hmm, good. Why didn't you stay with the others?"

"Why didn't they stay with me?" She managed an elaborate shrug. "Actually I wasn't really lost."

He raised an eyebrow. "Really? Not scared, I suppose."

"Not at all. I was just resting. How did you know where to find me?"

He grinned. "You left a trail a mile wide. Footprints—snapped twigs—broken branches. An elephant would be harder to find."

"Really?" She tilted her nose up. "I'll have you know I knew what I was doing. I was following the stream, just like I'm supposed to. Sooner or later—"

"You'd have ended up in Texas. You were going the wrong way."

"Oh." She put her hand over her mouth and started to laugh. "I made a mess of it, didn't I?"

"Pretty much." He weighed her with a critical squint. "You shouldn't have wandered off. There's plenty of Sioux around here. They're not always friendly."

Her laughter stopped abruptly. "I worry a lot about the Indians."

"They're pests more than anything else. You'll see a lot more of them coming into camp, begging for food or anything else they think you might give you. If you don't watch, they'll steal anything that isn't nailed down. You can't blame them. This is their land, and we're stealing it." He paused, as if weighing whether or not to go on. "I won't lie to you. Ahead we'll be running into parties of Shoshones. They're a dangerous lot. Arapahos, too."

"Do you think we'll be attacked?"

"Just keep an eye out and be careful. Tell Ben and Henry to

keep their guns handy, and loaded." A chill ran down her spine, but before she could pursue the subject, he continued, "Do you realize this is only the second time we've been alone?"

"I guess it is."

He smiled ruefully. "I know it is."

A tingle of excitement shot through her. She wasn't going to pretend she didn't understand his meaning. He stood abruptly and cast his gaze to the last rays of sun fast disappearing behind the canyon wall. "Time to go. You wandered a long way. We should get back before dark." Solemn-faced, he reached down. "Take my hands." His powerful arms brought her to her feet with one easy pull. Instead of breaking apart, he remained close, still clasping her hands. She drew a deep breath, catching the dizzying, masculine smell of him: buckskin mixed with gunpowder, and maybe a touch of the towering pine trees thrown in. *I'm almost in his arms again, and all I want is to get closer still.* His eyes captured hers. She could see they'd softened, filled with longing ... passion ... all the things that had been there before, that rainy day he'd taken her in his wagon. With a ragged breath, he moved his hands to her shoulders. She could feel their trembling. She leaned toward him, her heart beating madly. He pressed his lips to hers, caressing her mouth more than kissing it. When she flung her arms around his neck, he claimed her lips with crushing intensity. She returned his kiss with a hunger that spoke of her memory of their passionate encounter in his wagon. When they finally pulled apart, he showered kisses around her lips and jaw. "I haven't forgotten. It's just so damn hard to get you alone."

"Almost impossible." His hands slid a slow, eager path downward. She could feel the warmth of them pressing against the sides of her breasts. Then one slid over and cupped her breast. In a dreamy intimacy, she felt its warmth through the fabric of her gown. A hot ache grew in her throat. *Don't stop now ...*

❧

Clint had to catch his breath. No woman had ever aroused him like this one. Just standing close to her caused such an animal urge within him he wanted to throw her on the ground, pull off those bloomers, and ram it in. He laughed to himself, thinking how thin the veneer of civilization men possessed was. A good thing women couldn't read their minds.

When he heard she'd gotten lost, he was sick with worry. So many dangers out here in the wilderness. As he'd frantically searched, he'd pictured the worst: wild animals, Indians, and of course the snake, which only proved he'd been right to worry. He hated to admit it, even to himself, but he cared deeply for this woman. Since the day they had met, thoughts of her had hung heavy on his mind, especially since they'd made love in his wagon. It wasn't just the sex, although that had been wonderful beyond belief. Her beauty, bravery, saucy attitude—everything about her kept him awake at night. Most of all, he kept imagining how he would make love to her again. No, not throw her on the ground. He longed to bring her to the heights of passion again—hear her moan with pleasure when he kissed her breasts, scream as loud as she liked when she climaxed, and not have to bury her head against his shoulder.

Good God, when could they be alone again?

"Lucy? Lucy where are you?" a voice intruded far in the distance.

With an oath, Clint firmly thrust her away and dropped his hands. "Should have known." She started to speak, but he shook his head. "Out of my mind. Come on, let's go." He scooped up her pail of berries. "Don't forget these."

She took the berries, the turbulence of their pent-up passion still swirling within her. "We're not done yet."

He stared at her a moment, then burst out laughing. "No, we're not. It's still a long way to California."

She bit her lip. "Abner won't be too thrilled when he hears I've been in the woods with you."

He raised an eyebrow. "Do you think I'd let him hurt you?"

"Whether I like it or not, I'm obliged to do his bidding."

"For now."

"Well, you're right. We'd better go. They must be wondering where I am."

On the way back, Lucy followed closely behind Clint, clutching her pail of berries. At first all she could think about was Clint and how they'd kissed. Then she began to think about Abner and what he'd say when he discovered she'd spent time alone in the woods with the man he detested above all others. He was going to be angry. Would he try to hit her again? She would be compelled to take action if he did, but for the life of her, other than screaming at the top of her lungs—which she was loath to do—she wasn't sure how she could defend herself.

When they reached the edge of the clearing between the woods and the fort, she saw people milling about. Agnes and William Applegate were there, as well as Hannah, Inez, and their husbands, and ... *Abner.*

She stopped before anyone saw her and grabbed Clint's arm. "Wait. I must go ahead alone." She heard the panic in her voice but couldn't help it.

He gave her an easy grin. "You don't want to be seen with me? Wonder why."

"You know very well why. Do I have to spell it out?"

"Why don't you?"

She turned to face him. "I have a short-tempered brother-in-law who, for some reason, doesn't want me to associate with you. He most especially doesn't like you."

"I know. He hit you because of me."

"Apparently, the whole world knows."

"There are no secrets—"

"I'm aware of all that." She placed her hand on his forearm.

"Can't you see? How would it look if we came strolling out of the woods together? Lord only knows what he'd do."

"I wouldn't worry if I were you."

"You wouldn't?"

"You're not going to leave me hidden in the woods. Let's go."

"No! Abner will kill me."

"Abner will never hit you again."

"How can you be so sure?"

"Trust me."

"He's going to be very, very angry."

"Trust me."

"You're sure?"

"Positive."

Maybe she was a fool, but if Clint Palance said to trust him, then she would. When it came down to it, she'd trust her life to this man. "All right, if you're sure; let's go."

They stepped into the clearing and had barely started across when Hannah Richards pointed and joyfully called, "There she is!" Seconds later, her friends surrounded her, expressing their relief.

Smiling, Lucy held up her pail of berries. "Bessie's still going to get her pie."

"Lucy!"

Her smile faded.

Abner strode up. "Where have you been?"

"I got lost in the woods. I—"

"Come with me." He took her arm, none too gently.

She could tell from his strangled voice and the tightness of his grip he was furious. All eyes were watching them. Her legs began to tremble, but she returned a pleasant smile. "Of course, Abner."

They had just started off when Clint called, "Captain, I want a word with you."

Abner stopped in his tracks and turned. "Can't you see I'm busy now?"

"It can't wait."

"Are you sure?"

"It can't wait."

"Very well. You go ahead, Lucy. I shall be right with you." Under his breath he muttered, "We have much to discuss."

He turned to Clint. Not disguising his annoyance, he inquired, "So, Mr. Palance, what was it you wanted?"

Chapter 10

*C*harlie Dawes was sitting by his campfire, supper plate in hand, when his partner rode up. "So there you are. I hear you found the little lady."

"Yep." Clint dismounted, went to their wagon, and found the piece of sandstone he used for sharpening his knives. He returned and sat across from Charlie. "She got lost in the woods."

"I seen the captain come by just a minute ago. Had a funny look on his face. Sort of pale, like something just scared the shit out of him."

Clint smiled.

"What happened?"

Clint drew his ten-inch Bowie knife from the sheath that hung on his belt. With great deliberation, he rubbed the sandstone along its curved, sharp edge. "He'll never even think of hitting her again."

Charlie regarded the gleaming, ten-inch blade. "Holy Jehosaphat! You threatened him with that? No wonder he looked bug-eyed."

"I never mentioned it. Never drew it out. Let's just say we came to an understanding."

"What about?"

"Do you remember down in Texas when the Comanche were on the warpath?"

Charlie nodded. "Them Comanches is surely an unpleasant bunch. You wouldn't want to be their captive,

142

especially if you was white."

"Just what I mentioned to the captain. Do you recall that Army sergeant who fell into their hands a few years back?"

"You mean the one where they cut his eyelids off and buried him up to his chin in the blazing sun?"

"That's the one."

Charlie thoughtfully scooped up a forkful of beans. "What about the trader they staked out spread-eagled on a red ant hill? Ain't he the one where they cut off his private parts? Then they stuffed them in his mouth and sewed his lips together."

"The very same. I told the captain about him, too. Made it clear these things could happen to a man, especially one who raises a hand to a woman."

Charlie let out a deep chuckle and slammed his hand to his knee. "So that's why that tight-ass son-of-a-bitch looked like death warmed over when he came by."

"Could be."

"You don't think he'll want to get his revenge?"

Clint slowly shook his head. "Abner's a weak man, as well as a coward. My guess is, he'll have nightmares tonight about someone cutting his balls off and stuffing them in ..." a half smile crossed his face "... I can think of a couple of likely places." Clint ran a thumb along the sharp edge of his Bowie knife. "He won't hit her again, nor that poor wife of his, either. I guarantee it."

ﻬ

Lucy couldn't imagine what Clint had said to Abner. Whatever it was, the unbending captain of the wagon train acted like a different man when he returned to his wagon. She had braced for his wrath. Instead, he withdrew within himself and had never been so quiet. He even cut his nightly prayer service short and didn't quote a scripture all evening long, a record for him. As a result, she felt vastly relieved knowing she didn't have to concern herself about any further violence from her brother-in-law. A good thing, too. She could never have obeyed Abner's wishes and put Clint out of her head. Thoughts were one thing, acting upon them quite another. There were no secrets on a wagon train, and no privacy, either. To be alone with Clint again, she'd have to get stung by a scorpion, lost in the woods, or something equally dramatic. Yet the difficulties made her want him all the more. Who knew what the future had in store? So much had happened since she left Massachusetts. What lay ahead, she didn't know, except that they still had a long way to go.

Two days out of Fort Laramie, the party had stopped for lunch by a small stream when Hannah came running to the Schneider wagon. "Captain, we can't go on. Bessie, it's her time."

"Are you sure?"

"Positive."

Abner squinted his eyes shut in annoyance. "We must adhere to our schedule. We'll keep going, but we'll slow down."

"What!" Hannah jammed her hands on her hips. "How can you slow down from two miles an hour? We will do no such thing. Bessie's come to her time, and I ain't going to have her bounced around in the back of a wagon. Bad enough what the poor girl's got to go through."

Lucy, who'd been helping Martha with the midday meal, spoke up. "We must stop, I—"

"That will do." Abner swung his gaze to his wife, who stood staring at him, wide-eyed. "You, too."

If the situation hadn't been so serious, Lucy might have laughed. Poor, browbeaten Martha hadn't been about to open her mouth.

John Potts came on the half run, frowning with concern. "My wife can't go any farther."

Clint and Charlie rode up and immediately apprised the situation just as Inez Helmick arrived, closely followed by Agnes and some of the other women.

Clint addressed Abner. "It's best we don't move on." He nodded toward the small stream nearby. "We know we've got water here. We don't know if we'll find any ahead."

Charlie added, "Ladies in these situations have got to have water."

"How could you even think of moving on?" demanded Inez. "Mrs. Potts has certain complications, which might be aggrieved if we moved an inch farther."

Grim-faced Agnes folded her arms across her chest. "We're not moving. I don't give a hoot what you say."

For a time, Lucy remained silent, growing increasingly disgusted with Abner's stubborn attitude. Had he no heart? How could he turn a deaf ear on such desperate pleas? She gripped Abner's arm. "We must stay. Can't you see—?"

"Hush!" Abner jerked his arm away. "I make the decisions here."

"Then you'd better make the right one."

Abner chose to ignore her, but the increasing hostility of the crowd must have finally wore down his resistance. "I see I'm outnumbered. Very well, then, against all common sense, I have decided we shall stay." He accompanied his grudging words with an expression so sour he could have been sucking a lemon.

Soon after, Lucy went to see how Bessie was doing. She found her friend lying atop several mattresses piled up in the middle of the narrow box of the wagon with barely enough room for one person to sit on either side. Propped up on one arm, Bessie gave Lucy a welcoming smile. "At least we're in a place where there's water."

Lucy sank down beside the bed. "That's just like you, always looking on the bright side."

"Well, I don't have much choice now, do I?" Gripped by an

onslaught of pain, she winced, cried aloud, and lay back hard on the mattress.

Inez climbed into the wagon carrying a large tapestry satchel. She settled herself at the foot of the bed and gave Bessie a reassuring smile. "I've got everything right here, my dear. Chamomile, valerian, lobelia, skullcap—all the necessary herbs to make you comfortable—packed safe in my bag. Don't you worry. I'll get you through this in no time."

"I ain't so sure." Bessie winced again, her face contorted.

"Trust me." Inez brimmed with confidence. "Your new baby will be here by the time the sun goes down."

Throughout the afternoon, Bessie's labor progressed "nicely," according to Inez. At first, those outside could hear only muted groans coming from the wagon closest to the creek. The groans soon gave way to a series of piercing screams, causing several of the men, including John Potts, to declare they had a sudden need to go hunting, while others discovered some distant task well out of earshot. Many of the women stood in small, anxious groups around the campground while Lucy, Hannah, and Agnes took turns sitting by Bessie's bedside in the cramped, stuffy wagon. There wasn't much they could do other than offer words of comfort, hold Bessie's hand, and lay cool cloths on her forehead.

"Oh, Lord, I'm so tired already," Bessie gasped as the afternoon waned. Hair matted, face glistening with sweat, she gazed at Inez with desperation in her eyes. "I've never hurt as bad as this. Am I going to be all right?"

Inez had just finished an examination. She raised her head. "You're dilating just fine." She dug into her satchel and pulled out a small bottle. "I'm going to give you a few drops of tincture of valerian. It'll relax you, as well as ease the pain."

"Oh, it's vile!" Bessie cried out after swallowing a spoonful of the valerian.

"All in a good cause, dear."

The terrible pains continued. Lucy couldn't see that the valerian helped at all. The sun went down. Despite Inez's prediction, no baby appeared. During the next few hours, Bessie went through pain so agonizing she writhed on her bed screaming. Sometimes after a contraction, weak and panting, she'd apologize. "I'm just such a pest. Really, Lucy, you must be tired. You don't have to stay."

Each time, Lucy would firmly state she wasn't leaving. Her ears might be ringing from Bessie's screams, she might be feeling faint from the stifling heat in the wagon, but as long as her friend needed her, she'd continue to take her turn along with Hannah and Agnes. Despite Inez's optimistic attitude, she grew more concerned about Bessie, suffering so much, yet getting nowhere. Once, when Bessie dozed off, Lucy asked, "Is everything really all right?"

The midwife returned a bright smile. "Right as rain."

"The sun's gone down, and the baby's not here."

"It soon will be. After all, it's not a breech birth. I just wish ..." the slightest of frowns crossed her face "... she should have dilated more by now, but instead she appears to be slowing down."

Lucy exchanged worried glances with Hannah, who sat across, just as Bessie woke up to a contraction and started to scream again. As they'd done already countless times, Lucy grabbed one hand, Hannah the other. "Push, Bessie," commanded Inez. "Hang on to their hands. Push as hard as you can."

Bessie pushed, but once again the baby didn't move. The hours went by with Inez preparing various concoctions: lobelia and flaxseed, motherwort and green tea, both of which, Bessie declared, were equally nauseating and foul. She kept pushing, enduring the pain, but without results.

"Why ain't the baby coming down?" Hannah asked Inez

after a useless contraction left Bessie pale, weak, and weeping. "Looks to me like my sister ain't doing so well. Can't you do something?"

With great self-assurance, Inez reached into her tapestry valise yet again. "It's time for blue cohosh. It'll ease her pains as well as speed up her labor."

The herb called blue cohosh had no effect. Around midnight, the contractions stopped. "My pain's gone, thank the Lord." Bessie was so exhausted she couldn't lift her head from the pillow.

"Rest for a while." Inez nodded to Lucy and Hannah. "We'll slip out while she sleeps."

In the late hour, no campfires remained to cut the darkness. Nearly everyone had gone to bed. Only John Potts and Clint Palance stood in the little circle of lantern light in front of the wagon. Earlier, John had gone hunting in high spirits, expecting to greet his new baby upon his return. Now he frowned with concern. "She's not screaming anymore. Is that a good sign?"

"Nothing to worry about. For some reason, her labor has slowed."

Not slowed, stopped. That couldn't be good. "What do we do next?"

"We're going to make her walk."

Lucy stifled a gasp. "How can she walk when she's so tired she can hardly move?"

"She must walk."

Hannah asked, "Isn't there something else you can do?"

"It's the only way. A little walking should start things up again."

Clint stepped forward. "John and I will help her down."

Soon Lucy had to press her hand over her mouth. It was just so painful watching the two men, carefully as they could, ease poor Bessie from the wagon. She was so weak she couldn't help at all and pretty much resembled a rag doll, her legs buckling when she reached the ground. She would have fallen had not the men held her up. Tears rolled down her strained, pale face. "I just don't know if I can do this."

"You will do it," Inez commanded. "Lucy, you take one side, Hannah the other, and you, Bessie, are going to walk."

They started out, Bessie's arms around Lucy's and Hannah's shoulders, Inez leading the way, holding up a lantern. At first, Bessie dragged her steps. "I can't do it." They walked down to the creek, then around the campground until finally Bessie could almost walk on her own. At last she gave a little cry. "The pain's come back. I think I'm in labor again. How will I ever climb back up in the wagon?"

She didn't have to. While they walked, John and Clint had hastily erected a tent by the wagon and stacked the mattresses inside. Bessie's eyes lit up when she saw the new arrangement. "Thank you! Now just let me lie down and get this over with."

Lucy waited outside, all alone while Inez helped Bessie settle in. In the lantern light, she saw Clint approach. "Are you doing all right?"

"You should get some sleep," she replied. "No sense all of us staying up all night."

He gave her his funny, crooked grin. "The same might be said of you."

"I'm fine. It's Bessie I'm worried about." What was it about Clint Palance that made her want to reveal her innermost secrets?

"Each woman is different. Try not to worry. It's not good for you." Quickly he walked away.

She stared after him into the darkness, grateful for his words. Somehow he knew how concerned she must be, seeing Bessie's suffering, knowing the same could happen to Martha. Where was Abner? As Captain, he should have been here helping when they lifted Bessie from the wagon. He certainly should have helped Clint and John erect the tent. Instead, he lay safe in his own tent sound asleep, not caring one whit what happened to Bessie, Martha, or anyone else for that matter.

Bessie's labor was short-lived. When the contractions stopped again, Inez announced stronger measures were necessary. "We'll do a milk and honey enema. Agnes, I trust you have some milk from your cow? Get it and I'll heat it up and add a slug of honey."

Bessie, back to exhaustion again after her latest contractions, could offer only a feeble protest. "I just hate enemas."

"Well, you must have one. It's sure to work."

The enema didn't help at all, only made Bessie more miserable than ever. By now, they'd reached the wee small hours of the morning. Bessie had suffered for hours, and still the baby wasn't close to being born.

"What next?" asked Lucy. Exhausted, Agnes had gone to bed. Lucy and Hannah, both bleary eyed, remained on either side of Bessie.

Inez reached into her satchel again. "I hate to do this, but it's the only way." She pulled out a quill and a bottle with something red inside.

"What is that?" asked Hannah.

"Cayenne pepper. I'll do what is called 'quilling.' "

Hannah wrinkled her nose. "That sounds awful."

"It is awful," Inez admitted. "What happens is, I dip one end of the quill into the cayenne pepper. Then I stick the other end up Bessie's nostril and blow. The pepper will cause her to sneeze so violently the baby will descend." She nodded with confidence. "It's most effective."

Lucy asked, "But won't that be just terrible for her, shoving pepper up her nose?"

"Yes, but Bessie's labor has lasted much too long, and I don't know what else to try." Inez's mask of unconcern slipped a little. "We *must* get the baby out."

Dear Lord, please don't ever do this to Martha, or me, either! What could be more excruciating than having red hot pepper shoved up your nose? Bessie screamed from the pain. Tears streaming down her cheeks, she sneezed and sneezed, just what Inez wanted, but horrible, nonetheless.

The cayenne had its effect. Soon Bessie was pushing again, this time with success. With the help of Inez, the baby finally slid out. A girl! Before Lucy could express her delight, she noticed how the umbilical cord was tangled around the baby's neck, how the baby was still, her tiny face blue.

Inez grabbed for the scissors and swiftly cut the cord. For the next few minutes an air of desperation pervaded her every move. She hung the baby by its heels, slapped its bottom, breathed into its mouth. Nothing helped. Despite her frantic efforts, the baby never breathed, never lost its blue color.

"The baby was stillborn," Inez finally declared in a voice leaden with defeat. "I'm so sorry."

Lucy wasn't sure if Bessie even heard. She lay so drawn and still, almost as if she were in a coma.

Inez laid the baby aside and examined Bessie. "She hasn't yet expelled the afterbirth." She massaged Bessie's stomach until a gush of blood stained the sheet. At first it seemed normal, but it wouldn't stop. "She's hemorrhaging." Inez grabbed towels from her valise and stuffed them between Bessie's legs. "Quick, get me towels, rags, anything."

With frantic haste, Lucy ripped a sheet into pieces. Hannah rushed from the tent and came back with towels. Inez used everything she had, but the flow of blood wouldn't stop or even slow down. After agonizing minutes, Hannah begged, "Can't you do something?"

"We're losing her." Inez's voice broke miserably. "We'd best get her husband in here. Lucy, Hannah, say your goodbyes."

Chapter 11

Bessie's dead.

Lucy stumbled from the tent. Looking around in a daze, she thought she'd entered another world. The morning sun streamed down through puffy white clouds. The nearby brook gurgled softly. Birds chirped their early morning songs, as if nothing were wrong. She blinked her eyes in numb disbelief. How could this be the start of a beautiful day when her dear friend had just died?

Clint stood outside. Had he been there all night? "She's gone?"

"She's gone, and the baby, too." She took a step forward and stumbled.

Clint caught her arm. "Are you all right?"

"No." She tried to keep her raging emotions to herself. "It's so unfair! Why did Bessie have to suffer like that? She never wanted to go on this journey in the first place. She was such a good person. Oh, Clint, you can't believe what she went through. All that pain, Inez's horrible concoctions, the enema, red pepper up her nose, while all the time ..." a sob welled up inside her "... nothing helped. She went through all that misery for nothing and died anyway. I want to scream, tear my hair out. I want—"

"Hush!" Clint pulled her to his chest and wrapped his arms around her. "Don't think of it now. You've been up all night. You need to sleep awhile."

They were standing behind the Potts' wagon so no one

could see. Right now she didn't care if they did. She rested her weary head on his broad shoulder. She didn't know how long they stood that way. All she knew was that his sheltering arms, the warmth and comfort of his voice, soon made her pulse slow, brought her back from the edge of hysteria. She could stay forever in his embrace, if only the world wouldn't intrude. It would. This precious, private moment couldn't last. She forced herself to break from his arms and step back. "It was very kind of you, staying with us all night."

"She was a good woman." She heard the genuine grief in his voice. "One of the rare ones. Kind, unselfish, not a mean bone in her body. I'm going to miss her."

"It hasn't sunk in yet that she's gone." She gazed at him in despair. "When it does, how can I face not seeing her again? How can I ever not be haunted by the horrible way she died? How can—?"

"You can't." Clint caught her hand in his. "You'll carry on because you must. I do." He was staring off into nothingness. "I knew a man once, name of Jeremiah Todd. He was a trapper like me, crude as they come, barely civil, couldn't even read, but we were good friends. One day we were out hunting when a grizzly came at me from out of nowhere. Had me on the ground, about to rip me apart, when Jeremiah started whooping and hollering. Then he shot off his gun. The grizzly got off me and went for Jeremiah instead. I watched helpless while that bear ripped my friend apart. There was nothing I could do." He ran his finger along the jagged scar that scored his cheek. "Every time I look in the mirror, I'm reminded of how Jeremiah gave his life to save mine. Then I wonder, why him, not me? It's something I live with, a memory that'll never go away. I've managed to go on because I have to." He smiled gently. "You'll never forget Bessie, but you're strong. You won't let her death drag you down."

His voice bolstered her confidence. Everything about him gave her strength. She'd be all right now. She drew a deep breath. "Thank you for that. If I were to guess, you don't share that memory very often."

He smiled. "Never."

"Well, you're right. I'll survive." She smoothed back her hair and lifted her chin. "It's time for me to go. Good night, or should I say good morning?"

"I'll walk you."

"It won't be necessary. I'd best get back. They'll be wondering where I am."

She needn't have worried. When she reached her wagon, Abner's loud snores from the wagon next door told her he hadn't waited up. Climbing into her own wagon, she tried to be as quiet as she could, but her foot slipped, causing a considerable noise. Before she could try again, Abner poked his head out. "Why are you so late?" His voice was hoarse from sleep.

She closed her eyes. "Bessie's dead."

"The baby?"

"Stillborn. It was a girl."

"Too bad." His voice held no vestige of sympathy.

Martha stuck her head out. "Oh, Lucy, that's terrible about Bessie."

"You may as well stay up," Abner told his wife. "Time to fix breakfast. Lucy, you can help."

Was the man totally devoid of sympathy and compassion? "Abner, I've been up all night. Right now I'm very tired. I've got to sleep awhile."

A long pause. "All right, sleep an hour if you must. We'll be getting off to a late start anyway, what with another funeral and having to dig more graves. Or maybe just one if we're lucky. I hope John wants them buried together."

For days, Lucy was haunted by the memory of that agonizing moment when the wagon train moved on, leaving

Bessie and her baby's lonely grave by the wayside, lost forever in the wilderness, never to be visited again.

Only two days after Bessie's death, they left another grave beside the trail. One of the Applegates' young hired hands accidentally shot himself and died an agonizing death, leaving Charlie Dawes livid with rage. "Didn't the boy see all them grave markers with 'Shot himself accidentally' written on them? Didn't he know enough to take the cap out before he stowed his gun in the wagon? Dang it, these people never learn."

"Don't forget that they're amateurs," said Clint. "They don't know how to handle guns. They've never been in the wilderness before. All the stress of the journey makes them tired, and that makes them careless. That's why we have so many accidents."

Lucy could only nod in agreement when she heard Charlie say, "I still call it sheer, pigheaded stupidity!"

They would soon reach the Rockies but first had to deal with the broken terrain of the foothills, far different from the smooth, flat trek along the Platte. The lush grass gave way to sage and greasewood. The streams grew bitter and brackish. Only a few creeks provided enough good water. They had left the land of the buffalo, and that meant no more buffalo chips. Wood and grass for the animals became more difficult to find. Sometimes the trail became so indistinct that often, in the early morning, Lucy saw Clint and Charlie riding out to stake the way.

"It's good we're kept so busy," Hannah remarked to Lucy one day. "God's being generous giving us all these adversities. It don't leave much time for grieving over Bessie."

Lucy nodded grimly. "That's one way of looking at it." In one respect, Hannah was right. Simply surviving each day took all her strength and attention. To her surprise, even Cordelia seemed affected by Bessie's death. "I know what good friends you were," she told Lucy one evening when they were out searching for wood. "She had such a lovely smile."

Lucy thanked her nicely. She hadn't forgotten how Cordelia had looked down her nose at Bessie and Hannah, but now she hadn't the time or energy to waste on resentment. Besides, of late, the snooty Southern lady had become a bit more human. Earlier that day she'd actually joined Lucy and others as they toiled to push the wagons up a particularly steep and rocky trail. On the other side, she'd helped hang onto the ropes, straining along with the rest, using all her might to ease the wagons down again.

If Cordelia had become slightly more human, the tough journey west had prompted even more drastic changes in both her husband and son. Thanks to Clint, who'd taught Chad how to ride, the spoiled, chubby boy who had started the journey was now "lean as a whip," according to Charlie. "Chadwick doesn't mouth off anymore, either. He tries to imitate Clint, and you know Clint, he don't say a word more than he has to."

Nathaniel Benton no longer talked about manifest destiny. No longer the pasty-faced, dreamy-eyed scholar, he now wore the rough twill pants and plain cotton shirts the rest of the men wore. Well-liked, he performed his share of the work and had become a valued member of the council.

Lucy's heart went out to Inez Helmick, who had truly been shattered by Bessie's death. She just wasn't the same person anymore and had dropped the veneer of irritating self-confidence to reveal tormented self-doubt. "I won't be delivering any more babies on the trail. I'm done. I don't trust myself to ..." she bit her lip and looked away.

"What about Martha?"

"She'll be settled in California first."

"I hope so, but just in case she delivers early, we'll certainly count on your help." Lucy smiled, trying to cheer Inez. "You must promise me one thing."

"What's that?"

"I don't care how bad off Martha might be, promise me you'll never, *never* blow red pepper up her nose!"

A week after Bessie's death, Clint and Charlie came up to the slowly moving Schneider wagon and rode their horses alongside. Clint touched the brim of his hat. "Good afternoon, Captain."

"Afternoon," Abner replied. Lucy, who sat next to Martha, marveled at how extremely polite these two were to one another since that day she got lost in the woods. She still didn't understand why.

Charlie spoke up. "There's a river we got to cross up ahead, and it ain't for the faint of heart."

"Is that so?"

Clint edged his Appaloosa closer. "The Sweetwater River. It's treacherous this time of year. Swift currents and quicksand. We may have to detour upstream until we find a place to cross."

Lucy remembered the first river they'd crossed, where they had to take the wagons apart and float them across on rafts. Since then, they'd crossed so many rivers she'd lost track. They were able to simply ford most of them, although they always had to watch for quicksand. Only with a few had they been compelled to take the wagons apart and float them across. Abner hated those crossings and tried to avoid them at all costs. Always in a hurry, he became extremely annoyed when a crossing took days. She hoped this next one would not be too bad. Abner's temper grew increasingly short the more they fell behind his precious schedule.

"Let's hope we find an easy crossing." Abner's speech was clipped, as it always was with Clint these days. He looked at Charlie. "What about the Indians?"

She might have known he'd ask. So far, they'd only had limited contact with Indians and no major problems, but it was obvious Abner couldn't get the threat of murderous savages off his mind.

"We're in Sioux country," Charlie replied. "There are some Snake Indians around, and some Shoshone."

"Are they dangerous?"

Somehow she knew Abner would ask that.

Charlie chuckled. "They're all dangerous. You just got to stay alert. Keep telling your men to keep their guns handy and be vigilant at night." He started to ride off but turned back. "Tomorrow we reach Independence Rock. I know you're in a rush, but you'd best set some time aside. There are people who'll want to carve their name on the rock and climb to the top. That's going to take a little time."

Next day, the trail climbed steeply to the rushing waters of the Sweetwater River, then along its banks to Independence Rock. "It looks like an unshaped pile," Charlie said, "about half a mile long, half that breadth, and one hundred feet high."

Hannah, shepherding Bessie's five small children, stopped by Lucy's wagon. For the first time since Bessie's death, she had a gleam of excitement in her eye. "Come on. Bring Noah. We've got to carve our names and climb to the top."

Lucy called to Abner and Martha, whose wagon was parked next to hers. "Shall we go to the top? Everyone is."

Abner straightened and immediately locked his gaze on Martha's ever-increasing girth, which no apron could conceal. He assumed his I-am-the-prophet voice. "It would not be seemly for Martha to go." He addressed Lucy. "Don't you have chores to do?"

The nerve! If Abner were her husband, she might have meekly bowed to his wishes, but he wasn't, and she deeply resented his ordering her about. "If this were Boston, Martha would be a proper lady hiding in her house by now. This isn't Boston, and she can't hide, even if she wanted to." She tilted her head defiantly. "Independence Rock is the most famous landmark of all, and we shouldn't miss it. You ought to come, too. Don't you want to see it?"

Abner sternly replied, "Deuteronomy six, Verse eighteen, 'Do that which is right and good in the sight of the Lord.' "

Dear God in heaven. Well, she'd at least tried to reason with her fool of a brother-in-law. "That's a noble sentiment, but I hardly think God is against our climbing Independence Rock. Mister Dawes said we've come eight hundred and thirty-eight miles from Independence. Isn't that something to celebrate? What better way than to carve our names and climb to the top." She placed her hand on Noah's shoulder. "We pass this way but once. You don't want your wife and nephew to miss a famous landmark, do you?"

Abner's mouth took on an unpleasant twist. "Suit yourself then. I want no part of such loose behavior." He stalked off without another word.

Lucy looked after him, savoring this minor triumph. Ever since his mysterious chat with Clint, his words seemed to carry little threat. "He's letting you go, Martha."

"Are you sure?"

"Of course I'm sure. You know how he is. That's as close as Abner will ever come to saying yes." She waited for her sister-in-law's reply, thinking how disgusted she'd be if Martha went lily-livered and said she wouldn't go.

Martha's face wreathed in a smile. "Let's go then! I want to carve my name on that rock."

They started out, Lucy delighted with Martha's newfound courage. All thanks to Clint, of course. Whatever he'd said to Abner made all the difference in the world. It wasn't that Martha had suddenly changed into an outgoing, confident woman, yet lately she'd definitely emerged from her shell of timidity. She occasionally spoke up for herself, and her perennial look of fright had pretty much disappeared. She even smiled occasionally, a treat to see. Best of all, Lucy felt as if she and Martha had become good friends. They worked well together, with never a cross word. They shared an intense dislike of Abner, although as yet Lucy hadn't heard Martha make a derogatory remark about her husband. She didn't have to. Lucy knew exactly what the other woman was thinking. These days she felt protective of Martha, much as she would her own sister.

"God almighty," Hannah whispered lightly under her breath as they strolled along. "Defying Old Sobersides? Pretty risky!" Lucy smiled but kept silent. Despite everything, Abner still had a hold on her because of Noah, and there was nothing Clint or anybody else could do. She knew Hannah's reference to Abner as "Old Sobersides" hadn't originated with her. Abner had become increasingly unpopular. Many in the party had started to mock his constant Bible quoting and stringent ways. She was concerned, but today it didn't matter. Today was a day to celebrate. She resolved she wasn't going to let herself wallow in unpleasant thoughts or worry about anything. She, Martha, and Noah were going to have fun.

They reached the rock, already marked with thousands of names of passersby. The adults scratched their own names in the soft sandstone and helped Noah and Bessie's five children do the same. "Children, remember this historic spot," Lucy said. "A hundred years from now, we'll be gone, but these names will still be here."

After an easy climb to the top, they found most of the members of the Schneider party already there. An air of celebration prevailed as they all strolled around, taking in a view so spectacular it took Lucy's breath away. She knelt by Noah. "There are the Rockies." She pointed west where, for the first time, they saw the jagged silhouette of the magnificent mountain range, topped by perpetual snow.

"When do we get there?" asked the bright-eyed boy, still full of questions. Lucy often felt a burst of pride when she looked at him. Many children in the party were unkempt, allowed to run around on their own. Who could blame parents, burdened from dawn to dusk with the problems of simply staying alive? Still, busy as she was, she kept good care of Noah, who was always clean, tidy, and neatly dressed.

Clint strolled up, along with the Benton family. Lucy already knew he was there. Every single moment she knew exactly where he was.

"When do we get there?" Clint repeated the boy's question. "The Rockies are still a long way off, farther than they look. We should get there in two weeks, if we're lucky."

Nathaniel Benton gestured with a wide sweep of his hand. "Take a look, children. Decades ago, fur traders and missionaries were the first to sign this rock. Now it's our turn. We're a part of history."

"Our manifest destiny?" Lucy asked.

"Hardly." Nathaniel regarded her with his gentle gray eyes. "I've come a long way since Atlanta, and I'm not referring only to miles traveled. To tell the truth, I don't think about manifest destiny anymore. I've lowered my sights. Now all I want is for my family and me to survive this arduous journey, just like the rest of you." He placed an affectionate arm around Chad's shoulders. "I can hardly wait to get to California, find a piece of land, and start our new life."

Chad asked, "How much longer will we be on the trail, Mister Palance?" Lucy still marveled at the changes in Chad. Not only had he grown taller and much slimmer, but now, mostly thanks to Clint, he had some manners.

"It's about a hundred miles to the continental divide at South Pass. Do you know what 'the divide' means?"

"Yes, sir! That means the water flows west to the Pacific instead of east to the Atlantic and Gulf of Mexico. How long before we reach California?"

"That's hard to say. At best, two more months, but better not count on it. We've been through a lot, but the worst of the journey is yet to come."

Martha's hand went to her throat. "Two months? I was certain we'd reach California before ... you know." She blushed deeply, embarrassed to discuss such an intimate topic with a man.

Lucy tried to hide her own dismay. For the first time, she faced the real possibility that poor Martha would deliver her child by the side of the trail. *Just like Bessie.*

No! Lucy shook off her gloomy thoughts. Today she wasn't going to think about Bessie or dwell on her fears for Martha. Today was a happy day, and she was going to celebrate this great occasion, their arrival at that famous landmark, Independence Rock.

On the narrow path down from the top, Clint trailed directly behind Lucy. At one place she stumbled over a rough patch, and his quick hands gripped her arms to steady her. Her flesh prickled at his touch, and she longed to be in his arms. Would they ever be alone again? She felt the hot ache in her throat and threw a quick glance over her shoulder. "Thank you."

"Don't worry. I'm here."

"I know."

She was continuing down the path, comforted to know Clint hovered directly behind her, when she started thinking about her friends and family back in Boston. What would they say if they could see the recently widowed Mrs. Jacob Schneider now? How shocked they'd be. How ironic it was that if she'd returned to Boston after Jacob died, she'd be dressed all in black, secluded in her grief behind closed doors. Here in the wilderness? She wished Pernelia could see her now. Patched blue cotton dress ... scuffed boots ... ridiculous sun bonnet tied in a limp bow under her chin. Not exactly the height of fashion. What would her high-minded stepmother say if she could read her thoughts? Doubtless she'd faint from shock because they didn't exactly center around grief-filled remembrances of her dear, departed husband. They were thoughts full of lust, desperate yearning for the man following directly behind her. She should be ashamed of herself for thinking such things, but strangely she wasn't. She did grieve for Jacob—thought about him every day—but life went on whether she wanted it to or not. Simply put, on a wagon train, the future mattered and the past did not.

Meantime, she ached for Clint's touch. *When* could they be alone again?

Chapter 12

Amidst tall pine trees, on a high, moss-covered bank overlooking the Sweetwater River, Lucy stood with the other women, Noah by her side.

"Do we have to cross that?" Noah asked.

"I'm afraid so."

Hannah Richards stared at the swiftly running waters. "Just looking at that water scares me spitless. I hope we ain't going to cross here."

"Don't worry. Mister Palance said they'll find a place upstream where we can cross safely."

Noah pointed below. "Is that a big raft down there?"

Lucy peered down at the water's muddy edge, where Abner, Clint, Charlie, and members of the council had gathered. Judging from the wild gesticulations, Abner appeared to be engaged in a heated exchange with several others. He kept pointing at the raft Noah had just observed. Lucy said, "I believe it's called a skow. A wagon train that came before us must have built it to ferry their wagons across. See the poles?" She pointed toward several long poles that lay close to the skow. "They used those poles to push with. The skow is so big they had to leave it behind."

"I'd wager the water was much lower then and not nearly so swift," Agnes dourly observed. "We would all drown if we try to use that skow now." She crossed her arms in her familiar gesture of disapproval. "Just look at the bunch of them down there, all those men deciding our lives, and we don't have a say."

Cordelia appeared, Chad by her side. "I agree with you. If we women were making the decisions—"

"We would all be heading straight back east," Agnes interrupted. "Back to the homes we should never have left in the first place."

Over the roar of the water, they couldn't hear a word of the conversation below. They could tell, though, from the exaggerated gestures and angry faces that Abner and the guides were in a major disagreement. Finally, Charlie Dawes whipped off his hat and slammed it to the ground. Soon he came charging up the bank. "That dang fool!" Upon seeing Lucy, he stopped abruptly, looking sheepish.

He must be referring to Abner. Lucy asked sweetly, "Is there a problem?"

"Dad blame it! With all due respect, ma'am, your brother-in-law wants to cross the river right here, and I'm against it."

"That can't be right. He can't possibly—"

"You bet your ass he can! Excuse me, ma'am. He's got the council thinking they'll save a lot of time, what with using that skow that was left behind. He says if that other party did it, we can do it, too."

"But we were just saying the water must have been a lot lower then, and not as swift."

"You're dang right it was lower!"

As they watched, Clint, his forehead creased in a frown, came up the bank and placed his hand on his partner's shoulder. "They just voted. Now stay calm. We're going to cross here."

Charlie's mouth dropped open. "Well, I'll be hornswoggled!"

"Only the wagons. We'll swim the cattle across upstream." Clint's voice was so calm he could have been discussing the time of day.

Charlie spat on the ground. "That is surely one piss poor decision."

"I know."

"Didn't those lunatics see all the grave markers that read, 'He drowned in the river'?"

"They've made their decision. Let's not alarm the ladies. Come on, we'd better start gathering rope. We're going to need a lot of it if we're going to cross here. Then we'd better find a place upstream for the cattle to cross."

Just then, a group of six or seven Sioux arrived on horseback. Lucy no longer panicked when she saw Indians. The ones they'd seen thus far were what Hannah called "pesky" more than anything else. Sometimes they wanted to trade, sometimes they begged for food. At night, the council was compelled to post guards because the Indians had made countless attempts to steal cattle and horses.

Clint pointed toward the river. In what she guessed was Sioux language, he spoke a few words to the lead horseman, a toothless old man in an elaborate feather headdress. The old man looked puzzled for a moment then started to laugh, soon joined by his comrades.

"What are they laughing about?" Lucy asked.

"They're laughing at the crazy white men who think they can cross the river here."

After Clint and Charlie left, the Indians not only stayed behind, they lined their horses along the river bank, obviously to get a clear view of the white men below making fools of themselves.

Lucy watched with alarm and a growing certainty that Abner's foolhardy decision meant disaster. She would at least have a talk with him. The chances she could change his mind were practically nil, but she'd try. She started down the wide path to the river but soon discovered it was muddy, slippery, and so steep she'd have to cling to vines to get to the bottom. They'd be bringing the wagons down this path. She didn't know how they could make it. She almost couldn't make it herself. Somehow she managed to reach the bottom safely and found Abner busy inspecting the skow. She gripped his arm. "Abner, please, you can't cross here. It's too dangerous."

"The decision's made." He jerked his arm away.

"You can unmake it, can't you?"

Abner shot her a withering glance. "I won't have you—"

"Look!" Lucy pointed upward toward the river bank where the line of Indians solemnly gazed down upon them, waiting for the show to begin. "They think you're crazy to cross here. They're just waiting for that skow to tip over and someone to drown."

"What do those stinking savages know?" With a look of contempt, Abner walked away.

Well, she'd done her best. All she could do now was pray they'd all get safely across. Maybe they would, but the more she gazed at the turbulent waters of the Sweetwater River, the more her heart filled with dread.

During the hours that followed, Lucy, joined by most of the women, watched the preparations from the river's edge. First, the men had to get a rope to the opposite bank. Since the river was too wide to simply throw it across, Abner asked for a volunteer.

Benjamin stepped forward. "I'm a strong swimmer. I can do it."

Lucy wasn't surprised that their hired hand had volunteered. Inconsolable since Roxana's death, Benjamin kept himself busy every hour of the day, as if hard work could prevent him from picturing his beloved's horrible death. Often Lucy tried to persuade him to play his guitar and sing, but he always refused. He never laughed anymore and kept strictly to himself, shunning friends who tried to help.

Abner seemed satisfied with Benjamin's offer, but Clint

spoke up. "That's a treacherous river, Son. Are you sure?"

"I'm sure." Benjamin's sad smile told Lucy he thought he could make it, but if he didn't, he didn't much care.

Benjamin stripped off shirt and shoes and plunged into the water, rope between his teeth. He began to swim toward the opposite bank, but the swift current carried him downstream. Soon he was fighting his way across. For an awful moment, Lucy thought he'd be swept away. She cheered with the rest when she saw him grab hold of a rock on the opposite shore, pull himself from the water, and hold the rope high.

Soon three more men, clinging to the first rope, brought more rope across. Next, a party of men dragged the skow to the water, attached the ropes, and shoved it in. They rolled the first wagon aboard, centered it, and set big blocks of wood to hold the wheels. "I'll ride her across," declared its owner, William Applegate.

"Are you sure you can manage?" Abner had a slight edge of contempt in his voice. Blunt, outspoken William Applegate was one of the men who had insisted Abner dump his barrels of whiskey. Abner had heartily disliked him ever since.

William Applegate didn't bother to reply. "Come on," he called to three of his hired hands. "Grab those poles, and we'll guide her across."

His wife, Agnes, drew in a horrified breath, then made a beeline for the skow and started waving her arms. "What are you doing! You let the young men do that! Get off that boat right now!"

"Shove off, boys," William Applegate said with great haste.

Men on both sides of the river pulled on the ropes to keep the skow steady. They worked it into the deep water inch by inch, the four men aboard straining on the long poles. Once, in the middle of the stream, the skow began to tilt, drawing shrieks of fright from the women observing along the shore. Soon it righted itself and reached the far bank without mishap.

Agnes had watched with bated breath, hands clenched stiffly by her sides. "Thank God he's all right!" William Applegate landed, jumped to shore, and gave her a hearty wave. Lucy laughed to herself. Her sour-faced friend often referred to her husband as "that old coot." Obviously, she cared more for him than she let on.

Three more wagons crossed safely. Each time, Abner's expression grew more annoyingly smug. Lucy glanced back up the bank, where a line of wagons still waited their turn. "We're not done yet."

"Don't you question me. Ecclesiastic three, Verse twenty-two: 'There is nothing better than that man should rejoice in his own works.'"

She chose not to reply. If she did, she was sure to show her disgust, as well as her fear. How long could their luck hold out?

Chad appeared, followed by Cordelia, lines of worry etched across her forehead. "We're next. Look who's already on the skow—Nathaniel! He doesn't have to, but the fool claims he's going to ride it across. That's insane."

"He shouldn't," Lucy agreed. Nathaniel Benton might have lost his dreamy-eyed view of the world, but still, he was a small man, over fifty, and frail. "He should let the younger men handle it."

"I'm going to help Father!" Chad darted toward the skow and jumped aboard.

With a horrified gasp, Cordelia chased after him. At the water's edge, she stood, hands on her hips, as angry as Lucy had ever seen her. "Nathaniel Benton, you get off that raft right now! And bring Chad with you!"

Nathaniel bent and spoke in Chad's ear. Lucy could see the boy argue, but his father appeared adamant. Soon Chad jumped angrily to shore.

Cordelia glared at her husband. "Well?"

He had a gentle smile. "Sorry. See you on the other side."

He turned his back, the conversation closed.

Two other men boarded the skow: Carl, one of the Applegates' young hired hands, and Benjamin, who had just ridden back across. They secured the wagon with ropes and placed blocks of wood under the wheels. They grabbed their poles and shoved away from shore. Lucy came to stand by Cordelia, who stood watching, her face tense with anxiety. "The damn fool's going to kill himself." Lucy hadn't heard her so upset since the night Sukey had run away.

"I'm sure he'll make it." She spoke in a soothing voice. "All the other wagons have."

Together they watched as men on either side of the river began to tug on the ropes, starting the loaded raft on its treacherous journey.

All went well until they were halfway across. Lucy saw it coming—a large tree branch floating swiftly in the middle of the river. Before anyone could yell a warning, it smashed into the skow, causing it to spin around. A rope snapped, then another. The skow began to tip. "Oh, no!" Lucy cried. This just couldn't happen. The skow continued to tip. Suddenly it flipped over, hurling men, wagon, everything aboard into the frigid water.

An instant later, Lucy saw two heads bobbing in the current. One belonged to young Carl. Flailing his arms, he fought to reach the shore. The other head belonged to Nathaniel. Was he in shock? He didn't appear to be moving. Where was Benjamin? No sign of him. She clutched Abner's arm. "Do something!" She knew there was nothing he could do, nothing anyone could do.

Amidst the helpless yells and screams of the bystanders, Lucy watched the raging waters carry the two men farther downstream, then around a bend and out of sight. For one more agonizing second, she looked after them, then leaped to catch the arm of Cordelia, whose sagging knees would no longer support her. Young Chad, tears streaking down his cheeks, caught her other arm. They lowered his mother to the ground where she lay in a crumpled, sobbing heap.

Lucy looked to where the line of solemn-faced Indians still watched quietly from above. Suddenly, without a sound, they turned their horses around and disappeared.

Clint, Charlie, and a party of men immediately set out to search for the three missing men, but it was the Indians who found them. As dusk fell, they came riding into camp with three bodies slung on the backs of their horses. According to Clint, who interpreted, they'd found the bodies on a sandbar down river. Benjamin had a big gash across the forehead. "Looks like he was struck and knocked unconscious when the wagon turned over," Clint said. "That's why he never tried to swim ashore."

Lucy recalled that sunny day when Benjamin, Roxana behind him, rode jauntily by, so full of life, so much in love. Now both were gone, and Bessie, too. Oh, how could she bear it? She grieved for Nathaniel and Carl, but most of all, she grieved for dear Benjamin, who was so kindhearted and good. How could God have meant for him to die like that?

How many more? When would it end? "We must endure like good soldiers," Bessie once said. Lucy wasn't sure she could endure much more. But then, what choice did she have?

"Dust thou art, and unto dust shalt thou return."

A dreary rain fell as Abner read his Bible over the three freshly dug graves by the river. If he noticed the hostile looks cast his way, he didn't let on.

"It was all his fault," some said.

"He should never have insisted on crossing there."

"He killed those men, same as though he shot them. All to save a little time."

Lucy stood by the graves with her head bowed, keenly aware of the hostile muttering. Next to her, Martha whispered, "They're angry at Abner."

"Yes, they are."

"I don't blame them. He shouldn't have had us cross there."

Martha was speaking out against her husband? This was indeed a new Martha. Lucy, too, found herself dismayed over Abner's poor decisions. The irony was that she, more than anyone, blamed Abner for the tragedy, but family members were supposed to stay loyal to one another. That was the rule. She must play the part of the loyal sister-in-law, despite her personal opinion.

After the service ended, Lucy spoke to Cordelia, who stood with Chad beside her husband's grave. "I so admired Nathaniel. We're all going to miss him."

In a sorrowful voice, Cordelia read slowly from her husband's wooden grave marker, "'Nathaniel Beauregard Benton, 1798 to 1851. Drowned in the River.'" Her eyes filled with tears. "He'll never see California now."

Lucy held back her own tears. "He was a good man."

"He was, and so were Benjamin and Carl. They didn't deserve such a fate." Cordelia gripped Lucy's hand. "You need to know this. I'll be blunt. Resentment runs high against Abner right now."

"I'm aware, and I'm so terribly sorry."

"It's not your fault. I want you to know that. You're a good woman. Everyone loves you and respects you for all the help you've given. Not one single person blames you for what the captain does."

"Thank you for that." She could say nothing more without revealing her own feelings about Abner. "Are you going to stay with the wagon train? I do hope you will. Everyone will help."

"Oh, no!" Cordelia's jaw tightened. "I'm going to turn this wagon around today and go *home*, back to Atlanta where we belong."

"No, Ma!" Chad stepped forward. "I don't want to go back.

Pa would want us to go on. He'd want us to settle in California just like he dreamed we would."

Clint stepped up. He'd overheard. "I wish you would reconsider, Mrs. Benton. We'd all be willing to help if you decided to go on."

"Thank you, but I prefer to go home." Cordelia put a protective arm around Chad's shoulders. "My son is too young to know what he wants."

"I am *not* too young," Chad protested. "I want to go to California!"

Clint addressed the troubled boy. "You must do what your mother says, but meanwhile—" his gaze shifted to Cordelia "—give it a few days. Then if you still want to go back, don't go alone. We're sure to meet someone headed east who wouldn't mind if you joined them."

Lucy silently applauded Clint's advice. The Turners weren't the only returning family they'd met. Every few days the train met others who'd decided to turn back. They had given up for various reasons, like a death or illness in the family, or fear of an Indian attack, or just plain discouragement over the unspeakably hard conditions they found on the trail.

Despite Clint's attempt at persuasion, Cordelia declared she would never change her mind. She would, however, continue on until she could join a party heading east. After she and Chad left, Lucy found herself alone by the graves with Clint.

"How are you?" His eyes were gentle, contemplative. "You've been through a lot, haven't you?"

His concern made her want to cry. Since yesterday's drownings, she'd acted like a member of the captain's family ought to act: dignified, in control, ignoring the scowling glances cast at her brother-in-law. Inside, though, grief intermingled with rage in what felt like a seething caldron about to explode. Abner was responsible for those deaths. How could she be civil to him now?

She couldn't pretend with this shrewd, unpretentious man who stood before her. He knew her too well. Besides, she didn't want to pretend. "Abner was at fault. Everybody knows it. I see how they look at him."

Clint returned a grudging nod. "In his eagerness to get to California, he's made some bad choices."

"Bad choices?" She couldn't control a burst of ironic laughter. "You are most kindhearted."

"It doesn't matter how I feel. Like it or not, he's your family."

"I know. For Noah's sake, I must live with him and make the best of it." She couldn't keep the edge of bitterness from her voice.

He didn't reply. What could he say? Overwhelmed by the futility of it all, she asked, "How long will we be here?"

"We'll have to find another place to cross, and that takes time. Then the actual crossing ... I'd say two or three days at least."

"Time is getting short for Martha. I'm beginning to think she might have her baby on the trail."

"She won't be alone. She'll have Inez and you, and I'll be there, too. I promise I'll help in every way I can."

"Thank you for that. I do worry."

"After Bessie, of course you would."

His kindness was almost more than she could bear. A lump rose in her throat. She wanted to throw herself into his warm, sheltering arms and cry, but instead she backed away. "I must go. Good day." Grief and despair tore at her heart, but never could she let it show. She walked away from Clint with shoulders squared and head held high.

In a sad, melancholy mood, the members of the Schneider wagon train took the better part of three days to cross the river in a safer spot downstream, then pressed ahead toward the

Rocky Mountains. Like everyone else, Lucy set her grief aside. Life went on. What with the never-ending perils of the trail, no one could spare time to mourn.

One day around noon, she was riding with Henry in their wagon, directly behind Abner in the lead wagon. The oxen were plodding along when she saw a cloud of dust. Clint and Charlie had gone ahead to scout the trail. Now she saw them racing back.

"Stop right here," Clint called. He and Charlie pulled their horses to a quick, dust-billowing stop beside Abner's wagon.

"What is it?" Abner sounded annoyed. Everyone knew he hated to make an extra stop unless he absolutely had to.

Charlie swung his grizzled head from side to side, as if he'd just seen something he couldn't quite believe. "Captain, there's a wagon up ahead that's been attacked by Indians."

Lucy called, "Is it bad?"

"Bad as it can get, ma'am."

"People dead?" Henry asked.

" 'Fraid so. Most likely a raiding party of Shoshones done it. They took everything they could get their thieving hands on. There ain't much left except the bodies."

Lucy asked, "Do you think they're still around?"

"Hard to say," Clint replied in clipped tones. "It's a bad scene. We're going to gather a few men together to ride ahead and dig the graves. No sense the ladies seeing more than they have to."

By the time the wagon train reached the burnt-out wagon, four bodies lay discreetly covered with blankets beside newly dug graves. Thanks to Agnes, Lucy and the other women soon learned the gruesome details of the tragedy. Agnes' husband, William, one of the first to reach the grisly scene, returned to his wagon pale and shaken. Not surprisingly Agnes made him tell all.

"William says it was a family of four that was killed." The

group of women were gathered around the Applegate wagon. For once Agnes didn't seem to relish relating the morbid details. "Mister Palance said they'd been headed east, going back home. When the Indians struck, they plundered the wagon and set it afire. All four of those poor folks were stripped of their clothes. The father was hacked to death. The mother had her head beaten 'to a perfect jelly,' according to Mister Dawes, and she bore marks of brutal treatment and had been scalped besides."

Amid shaking heads and clucking tongues, Agnes continued, "William says the daughter was a pretty girl of seventeen or so. She also bore signs of the most brutal violence." Agnes lowered her voice. "He says they thrust a hot iron into her person, down *there* I mean, doubtless while she was still alive."

For one suspended second, the little group of women sucked in their collective breaths, then broke into horrified babbling. *What if that were me?* Lucy knew every woman there was thinking the same thing.

After Agnes finished, Hannah asked, "Are you sure about all that?"

The grim-faced woman jerked her head toward her wagon. "William's still in there, sick as a dog at what he saw. I've never seen him so upset."

"It could happen to us," a woman cried in a near-hysterical voice. "Oh, this is terrible. We'll all be killed."

Lucy felt an urge to give the woman a sharp, surreptitious kick. "It's not going to happen to us. In the first place, that family was all alone. The Indians would never have attacked had they been in a wagon train the size of ours. Remember, there's safety in numbers."

On her way back to her wagon, Lucy tried to convince herself that her own words were true. The image of the young girl killed in such a brutal fashion kept getting in the way. *How can we go on when a band of Shoshones lurks out there in the wilderness, waiting to kill us all and do unspeakable, horrible things?*

When she got back, she found all of the council members, along with Clint and Charlie, gathered by Abner's wagon for a meeting. She stood and listened, along with others. Charlie was saying, "It's hard to say how many Indians there were in that war party. Judging from the hoof prints, at least fifty, maybe a hundred, maybe more."

Abner asked, "Do you think those Shoshones are still out there?"

"Most likely."

"Would they attack a party this size?"

Clint spoke up. "There's no telling. Why take a chance? Do you remember the advance scout who rode by yesterday? He came from a party two days behind us. A big one, over a hundred wagons. Instead of going it alone, let's wait 'til they catch up; then we can join with them."

"Two days?" Abner lifted his eyebrows in exasperation. "Can't be done. That would put us way off schedule. Matter of fact, I hear there's a shortcut."

"What shortcut might that be?" Charlie asked.

"The Thompson Cutoff. Someone left a note on a tree. It said we'd save a lot of miles if we cut off before we reached Fort Hall and went south to—"

"You'll find lots of notes on lots of trees about shortcuts." Charlie's voice was full of skepticism. "All of them written by dang fools who don't know what they're talking about. You take one of those shortcuts, and like as not, you won't find enough food and water for yourselves, let alone your animals."

Clint nodded in agreement. "Charlie's right. It's a foolhardy move to take a shortcut. Now let's get back to the matter at hand." He set his foot on a small log and leaned forward in that easy way he had. "Look at how much stronger we'd be if we wait for the next train. We're only thirty-five wagons now, what with people turning back. That means ... how many men?" He looked at Charlie.

"With the hired hands, we've got maybe sixty able-bodied men to defend us." Charlie shrugged dismissively. " 'Course that includes the fools who don't know their gun from a hole in the ground. They're more likely to shoot themselves than an Indian."

Clint looked back at the captain. "I strongly advise we wait."

Standing quietly in the background, Lucy sent up a silent plea. *Decide to wait. Make a wise decision for a change.*

"I see no need to wait."

A prolonged period of wrangling began. Recovered from his shock, William Applegate joined the group, arguing loudly and forcefully they should wait for the larger wagon train. Elija Richards and Stanley Helmick stood behind William Applegate in strong support. Others argued the opposite, that they'd lose their autonomy if they joined with others. They pointed out that constant wrangling and disharmony were common in every wagon train. The more wagons, the larger the number of conflicts. So why not forge ahead? The Shoshones were probably long gone. Even if they weren't, they'd shown their cowardice by pouncing on a single wagon. They would never attack a wagon train full of well-armed men.

Both Clint and Charlie again advised they wait. There could be no guarantee the war party wouldn't swoop down on them at any moment.

Abner finally ended the discussion. Standing tall upon the wagon, he announced, "Tomorrow we move forward. Those who are afraid can stay behind." He assumed his prophet stance, eyes blazing, noble head held high. "Acts twenty-one, Verse fourteen, 'The will of the Lord be done.' "

Charlie sniffed in disgust. "True, Captain, but you'd just better hope the Lord ain't on the side of them pestiferous Indians."

To Lucy's dismay, no one else stood up to Abner. No one said he'd stay behind, perhaps because if he did, he'd be labeled a coward. Perhaps, too, because Abner was at his enigmatic best when standing noble and tall, quoting the Bible.

Lucy flashed a glance at Clint, just in time to catch a look of concern, quickly replaced by his usual impassive expression. He caught her eye and gave her the barest of nods and the hint of a smile, as if to tell her not to worry, he'd watch over her.

Chapter 13

ext morning, the Schneider party made good time, no
rivers to cross, no wagons breaking down. "I made the
right decision," Abner proudly announced. "With God's help,
we shall soon be out of this territory, away from the Shoshones."

"I suppose." All morning, Lucy stayed close to Martha,
offering what comfort she could. Martha couldn't get her mind
off the poor family massacred by the Shoshones and how the
Schneider wagon train could easily be next. Her feeling of dread
fueled her imagination. "Any second an arrow could pierce me
in the back," she cried fearfully. "Any second a wild, painted
savage holding a hatchet could leap from the bushes and attack
me. I'll be scalped and even worse. That hot iron! That poor girl!
Oh, Lucy, we're all going to be tortured and killed."

Lucy knew poor Martha wasn't the only one concerned.
According to Agnes, "Every woman in this party is sick with
worry. The men, too, although the fools would never admit it."

The extra caution Clint and Charlie displayed brought
home the danger. All morning Lucy sensed their unusual
tenseness as they rode up and down the line of wagons,
ceaselessly scanning the trees and bushes that lined the trail.

Like all members of the wagon train, at the beginning of
the journey she and Jacob had devised a plan in case the Indians
attacked. Now, with Jacob and Benjamin gone and Martha
utterly useless in a crisis, the plan was somewhat altered. If the
Shoshones should strike while the wagons were circled, Lucy
would take her stand behind the wheels of Abner's wagon. He

owned two Hawcan rifles. While he aimed and shot one, Lucy would load the other. Before heading west, she'd never even touched a gun, so she'd had to practice loading, ramming the rod down the barrel swiftly as she could.

Jacob had also owned two Hawcan rifles, but Henry, their remaining hired man, declined to use them. He carried a Colt revolver and would take his stand behind the wheels of Lucy's wagon. An expert shot, he boasted, "The cylinder is loaded with six bullets, and that means six dead Indians, so don't you worry."

"That's certainly comforting to know."

When they stopped at noon, the guides insisted the wagons form a circle, usually done only at night.

"Keep your weapons close," Clint warned.

"Be prepared to shore up them wagons," said Charlie.

Had it not been for her fear of an Indian attack, Lucy would have enjoyed the warm, windless summer day as she and Martha prepared their midday meal. A few puffy white clouds hung over the low, tree-covered hills close by. Birds chirped. Colorful wildflowers dotted the clearing where they stopped. Beside the wagon to her left, Hannah Richards prepared lunch over a campfire while her husband, Elija, cleaned his rifle. Beyond Abner's wagon to her right, Chad Benton helped his mother unhitch the oxen. Lucy never ceased to marvel at how the spoiled little boy they all thought so horrid had changed into a reliable young man, eager to step up and take his father's place.

Nearby, in the shelter of the circle, Noah played quietly with Jamie Helmick. The two five-year-olds squatted in the grass, engrossed in tracking some sort of bug.

Bent over the campfire, stirring a pot of beans, Lucy mused what a perfect day it was, the kind of day when nothing bad could ever happen, the kind of day ...

"Indians! Indians!"

The cry of alarm jerked her from her reverie. She

straightened, saw nine-year-old Timmy Potts standing on a wagon tongue peering outward toward a distant batch of pine trees. "I see them! Indians on horses! Indians a'crawlin' through the bushes!"

Martha dropped a pan of biscuits and burst into hysterical screaming.

"Get in the wagon, Martha!" Lucy called. "Hunker down and don't raise your head."

Lucy watched her sister-in-law scamper into her wagon fast as she could go. Across the campground, she saw both Clint and Charlie grab their rifles. "Men, get your weapons," Clint called. "Shore up those wagons."

Abner and Henry had been greasing one of the wheels. Henry stood up and yanked his Colt from its holster. Abner stood up and looked around in surprise.

Blood-curdling war whoops cut through the air. Between the wagons, Lucy saw mounted Indians with painted faces gallop by, all whooping and hollering. *The children.* Lucy dropped her spoon and ran to her stepson and Jamie Helmick. Tucking a child under either arm, she saw Abner still standing there, as if in a daze. "Get the rifles, Abner!" Carrying the boys, she raced for her wagon and hoisted them inside, then practically dived in after them. "Lie down!" She grabbed a mattress, some pillows, and covered the boys, now both pale and wide-eyed. "You'll be all right." She tried to keep her voice from shaking. "You must stay where you are, and don't you dare raise your heads." She grabbed a pouch containing powder and shot, hopped from the wagon to the tongue—faster than she would ever have thought possible—and dived to the ground.

An arrow flew past, so close she heard its whooshing sound.

A wave of sheer terror swept through her. She wanted to turn back, hide in the wagon with Noah and Jamie, but she couldn't. She must help Abner. Frantic screams caused her to glance around the circle of wagons. Amidst a horrendous, deafening noise, people ran in all directions, women grabbing their children, dashing for cover. Puffs of smoke arose from men crouched behind wagon wheels, already firing rifles randomly, some helped by wives doing the reloading. Outside the circle, she saw Indians on horseback, Indians afoot, all yelling terrifying war hoops.

A barrage of arrows came flying toward her. She ducked behind a wheel. Most of the arrows landed harmlessly, but some, aimed in a high arc, found their mark. Screams went up. She saw Stanley Helmick fall to the ground and writhe in pain, an arrow in his shoulder. She saw Inez rush to his side. She wanted to go to them, but now wasn't the time.

Henry knelt by one of the wheels, his pistol resting on one of the spokes. His gun barked. Lucy heard him holler, "Got him!"

Abner had finally retrieved his two rifles and knelt at the other inside wheel. He aimed, fired off a shot, and yelled, "Quick, Lucy, the other rifle!"

Lucy rushed to kneel beside him. "I brought the powder and bullets," she shouted over the din of screams, gunfire, and whooping Indians. She picked up the other rifle, a ramrod, and small horn. Just as she'd practiced, she used the horn to measure just the right amount of black powder. From the brass patch box in the rifle butt she took a tallowed greased patch cloth, carefully centered the ball on the patch, drove it down the barrel with a smooth thrust of the rod, and tamped it down.

She pulled the rod out and thrust the rifle at Abner. He gave her the first rifle, and she did the same. Abner kept firing. She couldn't tell if he hit anything, but she kept loading, nearly choking on the acrid smell of gun smoke that lay heavy in the air. Back and forth, almost in a rhythm, they exchanged the rifles. Then, through the wagon spokes she saw a pack of Indians afoot. Waving bows, arrows, and tomahawks, they rushed toward the circle yelling bone-chilling war hoops. "Oh, my God!" she heard Abner call.

She continued loading, quickly as she could, her gaze focused on her task. "Here, quick!" She looked up and thrust the loaded rifle at Abner, only to discover the other rifle on the ground and no one there. "Abner?" She glanced around, saw him running toward the center of the compound. "Abner?" An arrow arched down. She gasped in horror, watching it strike him square in the middle of his back. She heard his grunt of surprise, saw him fall to his knees then flat onto the ground.

"Hit bad." He reached a hand behind him, trying to clutch the feathered shaft. He couldn't reach it and winced. "Come help me!"

He could be dying. The pain must be terrible. She wanted to run to his side, but here came the Indians, now practically atop her, and she knew she must stand her ground. To her left, both Hannah and her husband, Elija, blazed away. To her right, Henry kept firing and beyond ... could that be Cordelia firing off a shot? No time to lose. She hefted the rifle to her shoulder. Never in her life had she fired a gun, but she didn't hesitate. She aimed at one of the advancing savages. Could she kill a man? *Him or me.* She fired. No one fell. *Damnation.* She picked up the powder and shot and began a frantic reload.

She had just drawn the rod out of the barrel when a painted, feathered savage, bare except for a breech cloth, leaped to the tongue of the wagon. For a horrified moment she stared at the fur, feathers, and beads dangling from the leather-wrapped tomahawk he brandished over his head. She swung her rifle around, jammed the rifle stock against her shoulder and aimed. *Can I kill a man?*

The Indian raised his tomahawk, a savage, murderous gleam in his eyes.

She pulled the trigger.

A hole appeared in the middle of the attacker's forehead.

His face grew slack. The tomahawk fell from his hand. He crumpled to the ground in front of her. She had killed a man, but no time to think about it. She must reload.

"Mrs. Schneider, give me one of your rifles!" It was Chad, running toward her. "Ma's rifle jammed."

Lucy tossed Chad her rifle. "You've got to reload!" She was reaching for the rifle Abner dropped when a horse carrying a Shoshone in feathers and full war paint sailed through the space between the wagons, causing a cloud of dust to rise where its hooves met the ground. For a few moments, the horse danced around, as if its rider were searching for a target. Chad was closest. Lucy's heart nearly stopped when she saw the rider reach down and grab the boy by his long, blond hair. In his other hand he held a tomahawk raised high. The boy struggled, yelling at the top of his voice but couldn't break away.

"No, no!" Cordelia appeared from out of nowhere and hurled herself toward the Indian. "You let go of my son!" Wild-eyed, clawing and scratching, she grabbed the Indian's bare leg and tried to pull him from his mount. The rider gave her a look of annoyance, as if she were a mere bug he needed to brush away. He drew back his leg, then struck her in the face with one swift, mighty kick. The blow sent her reeling. She fell to the ground and lay there, stunned.

The Indian still held Chad's hair firmly in his grasp. Helpless, Lucy watched as he raised his tomahawk higher. *Oh, no, he's going to scalp the boy!* Suddenly a hole appeared in the Indian's chest. An arc of blood spurted out. His eyes rolled upward as he let Chad go and fell from his horse, stone dead. Lucy took a swift look around. There stood Hannah, twenty feet away, lowering her rifle. "Got him!" She grabbed up another rifle and started shooting again.

Another Indian on foot leaped through the opening, followed by another on horseback. She heard Charlie yell, "They're a'comin in through there, boys!"

Men came running from around the compound. In an instant, Lucy found herself in the middle of a pitched battle, dust flying, men shouting, guns firing. She threw the useless rifle down and tried to run, but the swinging flank of a horse knocked her to her knees. Dazed and hurting, she tried to stand while all around, yelling, grunting men brandishing knives and tomahawks fought hand-to-hand. Foolish to stand. She'd be better off escaping on her hands and knees. She started to crawl, only to have her way blocked by the fallen body of an Indian, blood spurting from a gash in his neck. Hopeless. No escape. She squeezed her eyes shut and waited for the end.

From out of nowhere, a strong arm encircled her waist. She opened her eyes. *Clint.* In one hand he held a rifle. With the other arm he swooped her off the ground. Without a word, he half carried her unceremoniously out of the melee, hauled her to the middle of the campground, and set her down by Hannah, who was wiping blood from Cordelia's bruised face. "Stay here," Clint commanded. "Watch this for me." He laid down his rifle, pulled the knife with the long blade from its sheath and ran swift and sure-footed back to the battle.

"Lucy, are you all right?" Hannah called.

"Fine." Her heart pounding, Lucy bent forward and braced her hands on her knees. She gulped deep breaths, fighting to control the spasmodic trembling. Her eyes followed Clint as he plunged into the hand-to-hand fighting again. Surely he'd be killed. She watched, fearing everyone would be killed, but soon the Indians that were left began a hasty retreat, slipping through the space between the two wagons where they'd entered. In another minute, the last Shoshones had gone.

Through a gunpowder haze, Lucy gazed around the campground, fearful of what she might see. Sure enough, the bodies of three dead Indians lay on the ground. Of their own party, one of the Helmick's hired hands lay dead, an arrow through his neck. One of Adam Janicki's children, a little girl of six, was badly wounded, her stomach pierced by an arrow. Her mother wept by her side, wringing her hands. Inez Helmick tended to her husband, Stanley, now propped up against a wheel.

The boys. Lucy looked toward the wagon. Henry had already climbed inside to take a look. "They're fine, ma'am Just scared."

Abner. Lucy looked to the spot where her brother-in-law had crumbled to the ground. He hadn't moved. He lay face down, the shaft of the arrow protruding from his back. Lucy rushed to his side and knelt down. "Are you all right?" She shook his arm. "Answer me!"

Abner winced and groaned. "My God, the pain! Get the arrow out."

"Somebody help us," Lucy called.

Several men, including John Potts, came running. Charlie Dawes arrived and knelt beside Lucy. The old trapper seemed unperturbed, even though she'd personally seen him slit at least one savage's throat. "We'll get that arrow out, Captain." Knife still in hand, Charlie tugged at Abner's shirt. "T'wouldn't be the first arrow I've dug out. Now this might hurt a bit, but ... well, I'll be hornswoggled!"

Of its own accord, without Charlie touching it, the shaft tipped and the arrow fell from Abner's wound and lay on the ground. Charlie pulled Abner's shirt aside, revealing a shallow cut made by the arrowhead, no more than half an inch long, from which oozed the thinnest trickle of blood. "I do believe he'll live." Charlie's voice held more than a touch of sarcasm. He picked up the arrow and handed it to Lucy. "Here's a souvenir for his wife. Her husband's a lucky man. This here arrow was just about spent before it hit him." He sat back on his haunches and regarded Abner with shrewd old eyes. "How come it's in your back? Was you going somewhere?"

Abner struggled to his feet. For a brief moment he

appeared uncertain, then raised his chin with confidence. "God is my guide in all matters."

Charlie waved his hand in a gesture of dismissal. "Don't worry about it. I've seen more than one man turn tail and run when a pack of Indians was aiming down his throat."

Subdued but audible laughter trickled from the crowd gathered around. John Potts spoke up. "Did God tell you to turn tail and run?"

More laughter. Turn tail and run? Lucy felt her face burn with embarrassment for Abner. Could she now add cowardice to his many faults? Worse, not only laughter rippled through the crowd. She also heard a low, hostile grumble. She had better get Abner out of there. She took his arm. "Come, I'll tend to your wound." She turned to Charlie. "Will the wagon train stay here or must we move on?"

"I reckon those Shoshones are long gone by now, ma'am. We've got wounded that shouldn't be moved, so we may as well stay right here."

Back at their wagon, Martha, pale and wide-eyed, pushed the canvas aside and stuck her head out. "Are they gone?" Her voice trembled.

Poor Martha. "Yes, they're gone."

"I wasn't very brave, I'm afraid."

"Who cares? You're not supposed to be brave. They're gone now, and that's all that matters."

Henry held a crying Noah in his arms, trying to console the child. "Glad you're here. The boy won't stop crying."

"Oh, dear, he must be terrified." Lucy sat by the now cold campfire, took Noah in her lap, and wrapped her arms around him. "Dry your tears, sweetheart. The Indians are gone, and they're not coming back."

Abner stood over the boy, bridling with anger. "Stop that blubbering. If you don't, I'll take a birch rod to your behind."

Noah's cries turned to screams. Lucy gave Abner a hostile

glare. "Can't you understand that's no way to talk to the child? Can't you see he's terrified?"

"I'm in charge of his discipline, not you."

"He's a sweet little boy. He doesn't *ever* need to be whipped."

"I won't have a coward in my family!"

You're the coward, she wanted to shout but bit her tongue. "So you're going to beat him into silence? Your own flesh and blood?"

"Put the boy down," Abner thundered, for once unmindful others might hear. "Get the bandages. Come here and tend to my wound."

"In a minute. You're not dying, are you?" Granted, Abner was upset and no doubt humiliated over his cowardly actions, but that didn't excuse his boorish behavior. Ignoring his bullying command, she held her stepson in her arms, determined to comfort him until he stopped crying. "Get your wife to help you."

"Martha, get out here!"

Soon Martha, still trembling, was cleaning and bandaging Abner's shallow cut while he sat seething in front of the remains of the campfire. Lucy watched in silence, fighting her impulse to ask an explosive question. Noah finally stopped crying. Suddenly filled with indignation, she set him from her lap. "Go play, sweetheart. Everything is fine now." When Noah was out of earshot, she stood up and looked at Abner. "If you weren't running away, what *were* you doing?"

Abner arose, pulled himself to his full height, and glared down at her. "If you question my decisions, you'll live to regret it. Is that clear?"

"Oh, dear," Martha said in her small voice. "Lucy, you'd better not say any more."

Lucy ignored her and glared back at Abner. "I came face to face with death today. Funny, how it's changed my thinking.

The small things don't seem to matter. That includes your threats, so don't waste your breath."

Abner's nostrils flared with fury. "You *will* obey me. You will not address me in such a manner! You—"

"Stop your bullshit!" What a pleasure to see him flinch when she said the bad word, almost as if he'd been shot.

"You dare to blaspheme?" He couldn't have looked more outraged if she'd set the wagons afire and shot all the oxen.

"I'm sick and tired of your ordering me about, and I'm not going to stand for it. Especially when ..." she was about to make Abner even more furious, and why not? "You would be well advised to reflect upon your own faults, and that includes your actions today. Don't keep spouting those quotations from the Bible. You can't keep using God as an excuse. It's not working." How sweet to voice thoughts long stifled. How sweet to see befuddled anger cloud his face.

"How dare you speak to me that way!"

"How dare I? I just gave you my reasons. And another thing—" Again she hesitated. How she would love to tell Abner to his face that he was a coward, that she'd lost all her respect for him. Her own good sense made her stop. For one thing, she would further upset Martha. For another, slamming Abner with the complete, honest truth wouldn't be very smart, even though he deserved to hear it. She still had to deal with him every day. He still held Noah's custody, and she couldn't change that, even though she heartily wished she could.

Reluctantly, she concluded she'd said enough. Time to get away, take her mind off herself. "I don't care to talk right now. I'm going to see how everyone is." She shot Abner a look of warning. "When Noah comes back, don't you dare touch him."

"You're not going anywhere."

She tilted her chin and returned a beatific smile. "Try and stop me." Feeling his eyes drilling into her back, she walked away, refusing to worry. He wouldn't dare try anything in front of the whole camp. Besides, the way she felt now, she wouldn't care if he did. Despite the events of this horrifying day, she felt at peace with herself. Today marked a turning point in her life. Not only had she fought with courage and survived the Indians, she had cleared her mind of all her troublesome doubts about Abner. She would no longer obey him. That was a fact she'd never question again. She had said the things that needed to be said, yes, *demanded* to be said unless she wanted to remain a spineless victim the rest of her life.

At a brisk pace, she began a walk around the campground, first stopping at Cordelia's wagon. "Ma's asleep," said Chad. "She got a black eye where the Indian kicked her."

Lucy recalled those terrifying moments when the Indian held Chad by his hair, tomahawk held high, an image that would stay forever etched in her memory. "Are you all right? That was so frightening, what happened to you."

"I wasn't scared, not much anyway." Chad's chest swelled with pride. "Did you see how my mother fought that Indian?"

"I did indeed. She was very brave."

The boy's face fell. "I sure wish Ma would change her mind about going back home."

"So do I." Lucy meant what she said. She'd grown to like and admire Cordelia immensely. She hated to see her turn back now, but the former Southern belle still clung to her determination to return to Atlanta.

Continuing on, Lucy stopped next at the Helmick wagon to ask after Stanley. "He'll recover," said Inez. "Luckily the arrow caught him in the shoulder." Her face softened. "I saw you shooting at those Indians. Never saw anything so brave. Too bad Abner ..." Embarrassed, Inez looked away. "Sorry. The words just slipped out. You'd best be aware, though; many in the train are really, really unhappy with the captain."

"I know." Right now the last thing Lucy wanted was a discussion of her brother-in-law's shortcomings. She said goodbye and walked on. At the guides' wagon, she spied Clint sitting on the wagon seat, cleaning his rifle. Up to now, her concern over gossip would've prevented her from stopping to chat. Not today, though. She walked to his wagon, heart stirring at the sight of his lean, buckskin-clad form, so tough and sinewy, so very powerful. She felt a tug deep inside when she remembered how he'd scooped her up like a feather in his strong arms and saved her from the Indians.

"Hello," she said.

Surprised, he looked up, then smiled. "Lucy. To what do I owe the honor?" He made a show of glancing around the campground, where more than one pair of eyes were trained their way. "Do you want to ruin your reputation? Don't you know it's not proper for a woman to visit a man not her husband?"

"Blast the gossip." She perched herself on the tongue of the wagon. "I don't give a fig what people say."

"Why, Mrs. Schneider!" He cast a mocking look of surprise. "Have we thrown caution to the winds?" He jerked his head toward Abner's wagon. "What about him?"

"I don't care. But if *you're* afraid, I shall leave immediately."

"Afraid of Abner Schneider?" He laid his rifle down, threw back his head, and let out a great peal of laughter. When he finished, he gazed at her thoughtfully. "So you're all right?"

"Yes, and I came to thank you."

"For what?"

"For saving my life today. That's the second time."

"Second?" He raised a puzzled eyebrow. "What was the first?"

"When I got lost in the woods and you saved me from the snake."

"You weren't lost. You'd have found your own way out."

"You said I would have ended up in Texas."

He didn't smile as she'd expected but instead regarded her with eyes that brimmed with admiration. "Either way, you were worth saving."

All her false bravado slipped away. "Oh, Clint." There came that lump in her throat. She had to swallow before she could speak again. "I needed to hear that. It's ... not been a good day, what with the Indians, and then Abner, the way he ..." She had to swallow again. "What a disgrace."

"No surprise there."

"Nobody else ran. Henry didn't, or Hannah and Elija, and did you see Cordelia and Chad?"

"I saw *you*."

"Ha! When you saw me, I was in the midst of the battle on my hands and knees in the dirt and scared spitless."

"I saw you before that, standing your ground. You fired that rifle like you thought you were Davy Crockett. You did pretty damn good." He grinned. "For a spoiled young lady from Boston, that is."

His simple praise caused her heart to ache. She recognized her desperate need for a few kind words instead of Abner's constant criticism.

"As for Abner ..." Clint picked up his rifle and sighted it, taking his time. "You've got to get away from him."

"Easier said than done. You know the hold he has on me."

"You're afraid for the boy, and I can't say I blame you. I would guess you're concerned for Martha, too."

"So what do you suggest I do?"

He sat silent for so long she became aware of the sounds from around the campground: the low murmuring of tense voices, everyone still disturbed by the attack, the continual, weak crying of the little Janicki girl struck by the arrow, the rhythmic strike of shovels jamming into earth, digging graves. When Clint finally spoke, he lay down his rifle, leaned toward her, and clasped his hands between his open knees. "As Charlie would say, Abner's not worth the powder and shot to blow him to hell. Mark my words, wait long enough, and he'll self-destruct."

"That might not be soon enough." Lucy's laugh was bitter. "I guess you know, when we get to California, he'll want to keep Noah."

"And you as well." A thoughtful smile curved Clint's mouth. "I care about you."

Clint had spoken so matter-of-factly, it took a moment for his words to sink in. When they did, her heart swelled with a feeling she'd never imagined. "Clint, I—"

"Yes, I care. I didn't know how much until today, when I saw that Indian take his tomahawk and—" He drew a deep breath and shook his head. "—I couldn't get to you then. I came soon as I could, but if you hadn't stood your ground and shot him, God only knows. Where the hell was Abner? How could he let you ...?" From the whiteness around his mouth, the tensing of his jaw, she could see he was fighting to control his anger. "Do you know you rob me of my sleep at night?"

She shook her head, so overcome she couldn't find words.

"Well, you do." The beginning of his little crooked smile tipped the corners of his mouth. "You want to hear it all? I won't be saying it again, so you might as well."

"Yes, then." How could she not want to hear?

"At night when I lay under the stars, I can't sleep for thinking about you. I remember the first time I met you, the cheeky girl from Boston with the pretty hair, so sure she knew all the answers. I admired your spunk and your quirky humor. Now I know you better, there's even more I admire. I see you as you are now, so brave, so ..." A self-mocking little smile flitted across his lips "... so very unavailable."

She couldn't begin to express her stunned reaction and searched for something light to say. "Well, I'm not much of a prize at the moment." She glanced down at her shabby clothes. Lord only knew what her hair looked like after she'd quickly plaited it this morning, not even looking in her tiny mirror.

He spoke again in a tender voice, almost a murmur. "I'm a plain man without fancy words. All I can say is to my eyes you're beautiful just as you are." With fleet, swift moves, he sprang down from the wagon and stood close, looking down at her. "Do you remember that rainy day in the wagon?"

"Yes, of course, I do." How could she forget?

"That was only a start. God willing, I'll make love to you again, only better, like you've never been made love to before. I'll make you feel things you never thought possible with that ignorant husband of yours."

She almost blurted, *how did you know?* Then she remembered nothing was sacred in a wagon train, and that included the most intimate, private details of her life laid bare. She cocked her head. "Why are you telling me this now?"

"Because ..." He looked deep into her eyes, his own eyes filled with tenderness and passion. "I've faced death before. Never thought twice about it. Had I died today and not told you how I felt ..." He shrugged. "Let's just say, I wanted you to know."

She sensed the profound depth of his feelings, so carefully concealed behind his casual words. " I've been wanting to tell you—"

"Don't say it." He quickly raised a hand. "What good would it do? Who knows what fate has in store? Perhaps you'll never hear me speak these words again. Perhaps ... who knows? See over there?" He pointed across the campground to where Agnes, bending over her cook fire, quickly jerked her gaze away. "What would you wager that dear lady is trying her best to read our lips? She won't get another chance. When this journey ends, we could very well part and go our different ways." He gave her a look so full of raw desire her pulses went spinning. "Every now and then, give a thought to a man who would have laid down his life for you, would have loved you dearly for as long as he lived.

Would have ... That's enough. I've got things to do."

She felt a desperate need to pour out her feelings for him. "There's so much I haven't told you."

"This conversation is over. But still ..." His eyes filled with longing. "If the right time ever comes, it'll be my pleasure to listen to whatever you have to say."

Before she could answer, Clint strode away, leaving her weak-kneed, feeling as if she were swimming through a haze of doubts and desires. How could she let him go? How could she ever live without him?

She wanted to run after him, throw herself in his arms, tell him she was his forever and nothing else mattered, that he was the only man she'd ever love.

Then she thought of Noah and how he needed her. How Martha desperately needed her, too. Never could she leave them, no matter how much she loved Clint.

So, as she knew she would, she turned her back on Clint and started away, her heart in a turmoil, but knowing she had done the right thing.

Chapter 14

*O*n her way back to the wagon, Lucy spied Cordelia.

"Just look at my black eye!" The former Southern belle touched her hand to her bruised face. "I must have looked pretty foolish when that savage knocked me ass-backwards to the ground."

"Cordelia!" Lucy laughed in surprise. "Since when did you start using that kind of language?"

Cordelia gave her a rueful smile. "Since I came to realize I'm not Atlanta's queen of society anymore."

"Well, you didn't look foolish. You looked very brave, like a mother tigress protecting her young."

"Do tell." Cordelia flushed from the compliment.

"I mean it." Lucy heaved a regretful sigh. "I'm truly going to miss you when you go back to Atlanta."

"I'm not going back."

"*What?* You mean you're going on to California?"

"I surely am."

"That's wonderful news. Why? You were so sure you didn't want to go on."

"Just look at me." Cordelia spread her arms. "Do I look like the same woman who served that fancy high tea back in Independence?"

"Uh, not exactly." Lucy tried to be tactful. "Your hair was beautifully coifed, you wore that elegant, hoop-skirted taffeta gown, and you had Sukey to serve the refreshments."

"Well, look at me now. Did you ever see anyone more

bedraggled?" Cordelia pushed back a strand of untidy brown hair and held out the skirt of her faded blue calico gown. "Today my eyes were opened. I nearly lost my life, and so did Chad. It made me realize if we go back now we'd be throwing away all the hard work, sacrifices, and risks we've taken. All that we've struggled through would've been in vain if we ran back to Atlanta now, 'tails between our legs,' as Charlie Dawes would say."

"Chad certainly wants to keep on."

"He's right, and besides, I don't want to go back to Atlanta anymore. How could I return to that stuffy society where they think they're so highborn they can look down their noses at anyone who isn't like them? I look back and wonder how I could've been such a snob."

Lucy asked, "Am I right in thinking Hannah had something to do with this?"

Cordelia nodded emphatically. "That fine woman saved my son today. I cringe when I remember how I used to consider her 'of a lesser standing,' and I've already told her so. My dear Nathaniel ..." Cordelia's eyes glistened with tears. "I know he would've wanted us to keep on, despite the hardships. He dreamed of a new life for all of us, especially Chad. Well, if God gives me the strength, I'll see Nathaniel gets his wish."

Just then, Hannah, Martha, and Inez arrived, soon followed by Agnes. When they heard Cordelia's news, they expressed their delight. If they held any grudges, they kept them well concealed, but Lucy didn't think they did. Life on the trail left little time for pettiness.

Cordelia served coffee to all. They settled around her campfire, each taking comfort in discussing the horrific events of the day. Hannah asked, "Has anyone heard how the little Janicki girl is doing?"

"Holding her own." Agnes of course would know. "Inez says she'll probably pull through if she stays quiet for a few days."

"We'll be staying here a while?" Martha's voice was timid. *No wonder she's asking.* Every day counted now.

"We can stay if the captain approves." Agnes gave Lucy a pointed look. "You know how he likes to keep moving."

Inez spoke up. "Martha, you're worried about your baby, aren't you?"

Martha managed a casual laugh. "It's beginning to look as if I might have my baby before we get there. Time is getting short, but how could I possibly insist we move on when that little girl might die if we do?"

"You have nothing to worry about." Inez nodded vigorously. "I'll be here."

"I keep thinking of Bessie."

"So do I. After she died, I lost my confidence. Maybe it took that Indian attack for me to realize I can't run away. I must stand my ground, just like everyone else, and do the best I can." Inez bent toward her, her face full of strength and resolve. "What happened with Bessie won't happen again. She had a lot of problems, but you? You're small. You may look frail, but you're healthy as a horse. I promise that baby will arrive safely and you'll be fine."

Hannah said, "Honey, if that baby pops by the side of the trail, we'll *all* be here to help you."

The others chimed in, eagerly agreeing.

Martha looked toward Lucy. "I feel better. Isn't it a blessing to have such good friends?"

Lucy was so choked with emotion that she couldn't speak for a moment. "Thank you, everyone. We may have to count on you." Somehow she felt better, too. Her hopes that Martha would have her baby in California were fading fast. With each day it seemed more likely that she'd be forced to deliver her baby on the trail. At first, the very idea had been unthinkable, but now Lucy felt comforted, knowing that dear friends were standing by to help any way they could.

She could not imagine what she and Martha would do without them.

Early next morning, Lucy carried a pail to the nearby creek for water. She hadn't yet heard how the Janicki girl was doing and wasn't sure if the wagon train would stay another day or move on. Close-mouthed Abner hadn't said. She was about to scoop up some water when a solemn-faced Cordelia appeared, almost as if she'd followed her.

"Good morning. What's the latest news about the Janicki girl?"

"Uh ... I really don't know." Distracted, Cordelia plunged ahead. "Lucy, there's something I must tell you."

Had she picked up more than a trace of distress in Cordelia's voice? Lucy dipped her pail in the creek and waited until it filled with water. She straightened. "Why do I have the feeling this is something bad?"

"It's bad, all right. I wanted to intercept you before you started back."

"Just tell me."

"The council members met in secret late last night. They're on their way right now to talk to Abner."

"Is it about what happened yesterday?"

Cordelia nodded. "They've deposed him."

A soft gasp escaped her. "You mean he won't be captain anymore?"

"I'm afraid not. It's not only because of what happened yesterday. It's a lot of things. William Applegate, John Potts, Stanley Helmick, Elija Richards—all of them. They haven't been happy with Abner's leadership for a long time, as I'm sure you're aware."

Lucy felt the beginnings of a knot in her stomach. "Will they just talk to him, do you suppose? Give him a warning?"

"It's over. They'll demand he resign."

"I see." Funny, despite all her negative feelings about Abner, she could find no joy in his downfall. Instead, she felt sick inside.

"I'm so sorry." Cordelia's eyes brimmed with sympathy. "He's such a proud man. This will be just devastating."

"Oh, yes." Lucy didn't even want to think about the blow to Abner's pride. Poor Martha would also be devastated—just what she didn't need right now. "Who will replace him?"

"William Applegate."

"I see." Lucy tried to hide the rush of apprehension that engulfed her. For her brother-in-law to be deposed was bad enough, but to be replaced by a man he despised and considered his enemy was even worse. She couldn't imagine how Abner would react, but she suspected that those closest to him would suffer the consequences.

When Lucy returned, she found Abner sitting on the wagon seat. His full, black beard concealed much of his expression, but she could tell from the way his dark eyes blazed he was in a rage. "I have been deposed." His voice shook with indignation. "How could they? Who could have been a better leader than I? Now they want William Applegate?" He spit the name out as if he'd tasted something rotten. His eyes widened with fury. "I tell you; it's not to be endured."

She'd been prepared to offer comfort, but his unyielding attitude dampened her sympathy. Could he ever admit he was wrong? Worse, could he keep his anger under control? Lately he'd been constantly losing his temper. "Obviously, they think they have legitimate complaints, or they wouldn't have—"

"The fools!" Too angry to sit still, Abner sprang down from the wagon and stood before her fuming. "They'll rue the day they got rid of me and put that idiot William Applegate in charge."

There was no sense in arguing. Abner would never see anyone's side but his own. "You must calm down," she said softly. "I know you're angry, but what can you do?"

"God never meant for this to happen."

She refrained from mentioning that God didn't appear to be on his side this time. "Don't you think God would expect you to accept the inevitable and try to make the best of it?"

He roared, "God will smite my enemies!"

What was the use? There was no reasoning with this man. "No matter how you feel, you must realize you have no choice."

Stubbornly shaking his head, Abner looked beyond her to where the woods began at the edge of the clearing. He jerked his head in a decisive nod toward a tree-covered hill, then started away.

"Where are you going?" she asked.

He turned and addressed her. "Matthew twenty-six, Verse thirty-nine: 'Not as I will, but as Thou wilt.'"

"What does that mean?"

"It means I'm going to talk to God."

Several hours dragged by. Lucy waited and wondered. It seemed the whole camp was avoiding her and Martha's wagons. Finally Cordelia and Hannah came by. "How did he take it?" asked Cordelia.

"It could have been worse." She inclined her head toward the tree-covered hill. "He's up there. Said he was going to talk to God."

"Just like Moses on the mountaintop," said Hannah. "Well, I sure hope God tells him to get himself back down here. Inez says the Janicki girl is better. We can leave in the morning."

Practical Hannah's remark made Lucy smile for the first time that day. Once again she gave thanks for her understanding friends.

Concerned and uneasy, Lucy and Martha waited all day for

Abner to reappear. They were cooking the evening meal when he finally returned, his face no longer white with anger. Instead, the firm set of his mouth told them he had reached a decision.

Lucy greeted him. "Well, I see you've calmed down. I'm glad you're back. We start again tomorrow."

"Not us."

Martha's mouth dropped open. "What on earth do you mean?"

"I'm through with this wagon train."

Lucy spoke up. "That's nonsense. What does it matter if you feel you were wronged? We'll get to California all the same, go on with our lives. No harm done."

"No harm done." Martha clasped her hands in a supplicating gesture. "Please, we must stay with the wagon train."

"Didn't you hear what I said?" Abner drew himself to his full height and looked down at the two women with contempt in his eyes. "Don't you ever listen?"

Lucy replied, "Well, of course, we listen, but—"

"We're not leaving with the wagon train tomorrow."

"Then what—?"

"I spoke to God. He told me to take the Thompson Shortcut."

After a stunned moment, Lucy asked, "But isn't that the shortcut Charlie Dawes said was no good?"

"I don't take my orders from the likes of Charlie Dawes. We're striking out on our own. At the crack of dawn tomorrow, we shall leave this cursed wagon train behind."

Chapter 15

At first, Lucy stood frozen, mind and body numb, unable to comprehend Abner's words. When they finally sank in, she thought she'd misunderstood.

"What do you mean?" she asked when she finally found her voice. "For a moment I thought you said you want to leave the wagon train, but that can't be true."

"We're leaving." Abner's mouth twisted unpleasantly. "I've tolerated these fools long enough. I should've left sooner. The Thompson shortcut will take days, perhaps weeks, off our time."

"But Charlie said—"

"My decision is final."

"Don't you realize ...?" In desperation, Lucy, assisted by Martha, tried every trick of persuasion she could think of. They wouldn't have a guide, so what if they lost their way? Noah wasn't feeling well. What if he got really sick and Inez wasn't there to help? What if Martha's baby decided to come early? How could she do without Inez and her other women friends? The thought was not only frightening, it was unthinkable.

Abner listened to their pleas with undisguised impatience. "We'll take the shortcut. I've no doubt we'll get to California long before the baby arrives." Lucy opened her mouth to speak again, but he cut her off. "I haven't time for more of your babble. We shall take two wagons. I'll drive one and Henry the other." He seemed to be talking more to himself than her. "Stanley Helmick says he'll buy my remaining wagon and the cattle. They were more trouble than they were worth, anyway. I plan to ask if any of the others care to come with me. I'd wager I'm not the only one who wants nothing to do with William Applegate and his ilk."

Until that moment, Lucy had assumed that somehow, someway, she could dissuade her brother-in-law from his insane decision. Now, as she watched Abner walk away, the realization hit her full force: he meant what he said. What could she do? The very thought of striking out on their own was shattering. How could she bear it? How could Martha?

Clint. If anyone could help, he could. Abner was afraid of him, although she still wasn't sure why.

Forcing herself to walk, not run, she headed toward Clint and Charlie's campsite. She found only Charlie. When asked about Clint, Charlie replied, "He's gone off to scout the trail."

"When will he be back?"

"Not for a couple of days."

"Dear Lord." Clint had been her last hope.

"Set yourself down. You ain't lookin' too perky."

"I'm not." She sat across from the old guide and told him about Abner's decision to take the shortcut.

"Son of a bitch! Excuse me, ma'am, but that's the dad blamed dumbest idea I ever heard of."

"I know, but he's going to do it."

Charlie rose to his feet. "I'll go talk to him."

"Sit down. It won't do any good. Abner's a stubborn man. Once he makes up his mind, he'll never change it."

Charlie's bushy white eyebrows drew together in a frown. "That's the trouble with these long, hard treks across the country. They can bring out the best in a man or they can bring out the worst in a man. You know which applies to Abner."

"You're right. He was always a zealot, but back in Massachusetts he could at least be reasonable."

"Why don't you and your sister-in-law stay with the wagon train?"

"What?" She couldn't comprehend Charlie's question.

"Tell that cussed fool brother-in-law of yours you ain't going to go traipsing off on that shortcut."

" I can't." Such a thought had never entered her head.

"Yes, you can. Did it ever occur to you that you should do what's best for you? There ain't no person on this earth should have to be beholden to someone else, and that includes you, even if you are a woman. I surely couldn't live that way. Been on my own since I was knee-high to a mosquito and never took orders from nobody. Why should you be any different?" The old guide's eyes filled with sympathy. "You and Martha need your lady friends right now. She needs that midwife, just in case. It wouldn't hurt the captain to leave one of his wagons behind for his wife. As for you, why don't you go talk to Mrs. Benton? She's got room in the wagon now that Mister Benton's gone. You tell Abner to go ahead and take his shortcut, you'll meet up with him in California."

"He'd kill me."

"Abner?" The old trapper guffawed. "Not with Clint around. Besides, maybe he'd just as soon leave the both of you behind, what with Martha's condition and all. Noah, too."

As Charlie's words sunk in, she began to think, why couldn't the three of them stay? What a fine idea. If Abner was so hell-bent on taking that treacherous shortcut, he could go by himself, and they could meet up with him later. Surely, he could see his wife would be much better off remaining with the wagon train. So would Noah. And if, later on, it took a while to find each other, no harm done. She thought of the money safely stored at the bottom of the flour barrel. With it, she, Martha, and Noah could surely get by. *Indefinitely.*

She smiled at the thought.

Relief flowed through her. She stood and straightened her shoulders. "Thanks, Mister Dawes. What a wonderful idea."

Cordelia broke into a grin when she heard Lucy's request. "Of course! I would love to have you."

Lucy's spirits lifted. "I'll earn my keep. I'll do the cooking. I'll—"

"I don't care if you just sit and don't do a blessed thing! You just don't know how lonely I've been with Nathaniel gone, but with you staying with me?" Cordelia's eyes sparkled. "Oh, Lucy, this awful journey could almost be fun."

"I can only hope Abner will agree."

"How could he make Martha go on some horrible shortcut at a time like this? How utterly thoughtless and downright cruel. I don't care what he says. You stand your ground. He can't force you to go, now can he?"

"No, he can't." She'd been feeling weak and helpless, but now, thanks to Charlie and Cordelia, her sense of strength grew by the moment. "I'll go talk to Abner right now."

"Absolutely not." The stony contempt in Abner's eyes made Lucy cringe. "How dare you even suggest such a thing? Martha and Noah stay with me. I prefer that you come along. I need you to watch after them, but you're free to do as you please."

"Please reconsider," Lucy replied with quiet, desperate firmness. "You know your wife's condition. She should stay with the wagon train where she can get help if she needs it, not go off on some idiotic shortcut. Noah will be much better off with me. You know I'll take good care of him. We'll meet up in California or even sooner, any place you say."

Abner's stern expression held no vestige of sympathy. "Go or stay as you see fit, but Noah is my son now, and he remains with me."

She kept trying to reason with him, but his loud, dictatorial voice overrode all her arguments. Despite her resolve, her determination began to crumble. She dreaded to think what might happen to her stepson if she wasn't around to keep him safe. In her present condition, Martha could hardly take care of herself, let alone Noah. Abner never paid any attention to the child. Noah could easily get lost, or fall under a wagon wheel, or heaven knew what. He certainly wouldn't eat right. That wasn't all. She had yet to see Abner physically abuse the boy in any way; yet she couldn't forget those bruises that had appeared from time to time on Martha's face. Clint had kept them safe, but with a sinking heart, she realized that on this God-awful shortcut he wouldn't be around.

"We leave at dawn," Abner announced. "Either come or don't come, but you'd better remember Noah's my son, and he's coming with me." With a final look of scorn, he turned and stalked away.

Sick at heart, Lucy considered her choices. If she stayed with the wagon train, she 'd worry herself sick over both Noah and Martha. If she went on the shortcut, she'd face God-knows-what dangers, plus she'd be entirely under Abner's domination. Two choices, both impossible.

Yet, she must chose, and before dawn tomorrow.

By late afternoon, she still hadn't made up her mind. Then Noah came to her, complaining that his stomach hurt and his head ached. She placed her hand on his forehead and found it burning hot. After she put Noah to bed in the wagon, she sent for Inez.

After examining Noah, the midwife shook her head. "Looks like mountain fever. Some call it typhoid. There's lots of it going around. Nothing I can do, I'm afraid. I wish there were a doctor around, but of course there's not."

"Will he be all right?" Lucy held her breath, waiting for her answer.

Inez looked her square in the eye. "Mountain fever is a deadly disease. From what I've heard, it's swept through many of the wagon trains and taken lives. They say about one in eight who are stricken die."

"Is there anything I can do?"

"Nothing besides keep him warm and give him lots of water. He shouldn't be moved. I'll go ask William Applegate to hold up the wagon train, at least another day."

Lucy told Inez about Abner and the shortcut.

"Then I'll go speak to Abner. When he hears about Noah, surely he'll change his plans."

Only minutes later, Inez returned, tense lines creasing her forehead. "I tried to dissuade him, but he says he's leaving tomorrow regardless and taking Noah, mountain fever or no." Her face clouded with concern. "Abner said you weren't going. Is that true? I only ask because Noah will need a lot of care. You know Martha can't help much in her condition."

That settled it. Lucy put aside the despair in her heart and made the only decision she could. "No, it's not true. Tomorrow I'll be leaving on that shortcut with Abner."

Inez's face flooded with relief. "Bless you. I'll remember you in my prayers each day."

"Don't forget." Lucy had a wry smile. "I'm going to need them."

Later that day, she was packing the wagon when Henry appeared. The shy young man removed his hat and started twisting it in his hands. "Uh, Mrs. Schneider, may I have a word with you?" She nodded. "I won't be going on the shortcut, ma'am. Mister Applegate has hired me on. He's needed a replacement since Carl got drowned, and ... uh, frankly, he'd be easier to work for than Mister Schneider. I sure hate to leave you, ma'am."

Another disappointment. She had counted on steady, reliable Henry to help her through the grueling days ahead. She didn't blame him for leaving, though. Abner's overbearing, self-righteous attitude made him a hard man to work for. She patted his arm reassuringly. "Why, that's fine. I don't blame you at all, and I wish you well."

Henry looked greatly relieved. "At least you'll have someone to drive the second wagon. Mister Schneider told me he's talked the Butler Brothers into coming along."

She stared at him in astonishment. "The Butler Brothers? Are you sure?"

"Yes, ma'am. Mister Schneider told me so."

"Uh, yes, of course." Her mind was totally distracted. Along with everything else, now she'd have to put up with those three rowdy, hard-drinking lowlifes.

In a miserable state of mind, she continued making preparations for their departure. Where had Clint gone? Why wasn't he here when she needed him so desperately? She had so much to tell him, whether he wanted to hear or not. Now she'd never have the chance.

She felt such an acute sense of loss she couldn't imagine she'd ever be happy again, but she kept reminding herself she mustn't break down in despair. Noah needed her. Martha needed her. She must carry on.

Chapter 16

E arly the next morning, four wagons set forth on the Thompson Cutoff: the Butler Brothers' two wagons, followed by Abner and Martha's wagon, and Lucy's wagon, driven by Erasmus Butler, at the rear. Lucy wasn't happy about the proximity of the smelly and disgusting Erasmus, but at least he left her free to tend to Noah, who lay pale and feverish in the back.

From the very first, the cutoff proved to be a nightmare, even worse than Charlie predicted. With each passing hour, every jolting turn of the wheels, Lucy's concern increased. Heavy rain the night before had turned parts of the trail into such a bog that one of the Butlers' wagons immediately sunk into the muddy mess and got stuck. Lucy felt like covering her ears so she couldn't hear the uncouth brothers' grunts and curses as they strained to push it out.

The faint trail—what there was of it—grew rougher and steeper as they went along. To make matters worse, Noah's fever shot higher. "Ma, my stomach hurts," he kept crying in a weak little voice, "My head hurts, too."

She kept applying cool cloths to his forehead, caring for him as best she could in the back of the cramped, bouncing wagon, but his plaintive cries grew ever more heart-wrenching. To make matters worse, whenever she checked with Martha, the pregnant woman complained her stomach felt queasy, a result of the wagon's constant lurching and pitching. Lucy didn't bother to complain to Abner. He wouldn't do a thing except quote some useless scripture.

When the wagons finally got beyond the mud, they encountered a hill so steep the oxen hadn't the strength to pull them to the top. Lucy was in the wagon tending to Noah when Abner poked his head in. "You and Noah must get out and walk. Everything's got to be unloaded or we'll never reach the top."

Was he insane? Lucy pointed at Noah, lying pale and limp on the mattress. "Take a look at him. He's terribly sick. Feel his forehead; it's burning hot. You expect him to get out and *walk*?"

Abner's gaze lingered over his nephew until he finally seemed to realize how sick the boy was. "Very well, let him stay in the wagon. You must come out and help us push. Martha, too."

Seething with resentment, Lucy climbed from the wagon and helped poor Martha down. *If only Father could see his elegant, pampered daughter now!* Lucy was becoming ever more resentful. If she were home, at this very minute she might be having a lovely visit with her sister or perhaps the seamstress might be fitting her for a new gown. No! Here she was, wearing an old, patched dress, expected to push wagons up hills while enduing the obscene curses of the Butler Brothers who had to be three of the crudest men on the face of the earth. Worst of all, forced to obey the commands of a man who treated her as if she were no better than an animal.

All my own fault. If she hadn't been so anxious to escape Pernelia, she would never have rushed into marriage with Jacob. He would've married someone else, and then *she*—whoever she was—would be the miserable woman in the middle of nowhere, all sweaty and gasping for breath, pushing a wagon uphill with all her might, ears burning from the vile curses of the Butler Brothers. Oh, life was not fair!

Where was Clint when she needed him? Clint, who as much as said he loved her?

When she stopped to brush away a tear, she heard Martha

puffing and panting beside her. "The baby just kicked me hard." The poor woman put her hand over her stomach. "Oh, Lucy, I'm so scared. What if it comes early, out here in the middle of nowhere?"

Seeing Martha's distress jarred Lucy to her senses. *I think I have it bad. I must stop feeling sorry for myself.* "You're going to be fine." She addressed Martha's bulging stomach, "You're going to be fine, too, little one. Don't you dare decide to come out and see the world just yet! You've got to wait till we get to California."

They finally reached the top. Despite her new resolve, Lucy took one look ahead and her heart sank. Now they would have to go down again on a trail so steep the wagon would overrun the poor oxen unless they pulled on ropes to hold it back.

Ahead, another hill, even steeper, and then another.

For the rest of the grueling day, Lucy alternated between caring for Noah and lending what strength she possessed to pushing the wagons up impossibly steep hills, then pulling on ropes to ease them down. At least Abner had relented after his wife collapsed in a heap, announcing she couldn't go another step. He allowed her to rest in Lucy's wagon where she could keep an eye on Noah.

By late afternoon, exhausted, they came upon a flat, grassy area beside a creek and made an early stop for the day. Lucy checked on Noah. He wasn't better, but at least he seemed no worse. She started to build a campfire. "How far have we come today on this wonderful cutoff of yours?" she asked Abner as he unhitched the oxen. After such a difficult day, she couldn't hide her sarcasm.

"Far enough."

His curt answer so incensed her she knew she'd better keep her mouth shut. Otherwise, she'd surely let loose her scathing opinion concerning his heartless inconsideration for Noah and Martha, as well as his utterly stupid decision to leave the wagon train. She wagered he already knew. The worried knit in his brows told her he was beginning to realize taking the shortcut was a big mistake.

To make a horrible situation even worse, The Butler Brothers, who had built their own campfire nearby, were already passing a jug around. What lowlifes, all three. Huge, burly Sam with his tangled beard. Snaggle-toothed Emery. Sly-eyed Erasmus. She suspected they hadn't bathed since the start of the journey, if then. It seemed highly unlikely that their rag-tag, smelly clothes had ever seen soap and water.

A burst of drunken laughter caused Abner to scowl in the direction of the slovenly three. "Ephesians five, Verse eight. Be not drunk with wine, where is excess; but be filled with the Spirit.' "

"Corn liquor's the only spirit they're interested in," she snapped. He started to reply, but she cut him off. "You have no right to complain. You *knew* what they were like before you started."

He made no reply, which indeed was for the best because she was so disgusted and distraught she would've pounced on anything he said.

Later that night, when Lucy laid her hand on Noah's forehead, she found it alarmingly hot. Each breath seemed more labored than the last. Helplessly, he looked up at her with fever-dulled eyes. "Ma ... I don't ... feel good."

"I'm going to get you well, sweetheart. Don't you worry." This was Abner's fault. How could he have allowed his own nephew to be bounced around all day in the wagon, knowing the boy was so ill? Why had Abner insisted on this insane shortcut in the first place? Now was not the time for recriminations. She waited until she calmed down, then went to Abner's wagon. "You both had better come. Noah has taken a turn for the worse."

During the following hours, Lucy fought to bring down

Noah's fever by bathing his heated body with cold water from the creek. Martha and Abner, Bibles and prayer books in hand, sat beside the boy and prayed.

Their efforts failed. Around midnight, Noah fell into a coma. By dawn, the beautiful little boy Lucy had grown to love so dearly had slipped away.

Next morning the Butler Brothers dug Noah's grave, muffling their curses, at least for a little while. "Dig it deep," Abner ordered. "I don't want the wolves to dig him up."

Even through her overwhelming grief, Lucy felt disgust for Abner's handling of his nephew's death. At first, he'd put on a display of deep mourning, holding the dead child in his arms and weeping aloud. Now, only hours later, he'd assumed a cloak of stoic composure. Not even when he said a few, final words over the little boy's grave did she see a trace of a tear.

"Dust thou art, and unto dust shalt thou return."

Death, nothing but death. Her clamped lips imprisoning a sob, Lucy stood by the grave listening to Abner's dismal words. What use were tears? How could she go on when all she wanted was to lie across her little stepson's grave and wait for the wolves to take her?

"We'll leave right away." Abner closed his Bible.

"All right." She felt icy calm now, beyond tears, beyond everything but a numb sorrow that left her close to complete despair. She wasn't the only one. Martha, wan and pale, sank down beside Noah's grave. "Where's the end of it?" she cried in a tortured voice. "First Jacob, then Roxana, then Bessie ... Nathaniel ... Benjamin—"

"Try not to think of it," Lucy broke in. "You must have faith God will watch over you." By now, she wasn't at all sure about God, but she said what she knew Martha needed to hear. She pulled Martha to her feet. "You must be strong for your baby's sake."

She was pleased to see that her words had their effect, for Martha squared her shoulders and lifted her chin. "For my baby's sake." Her voice was stronger than Lucy had ever heard it. "I shall carry on."

They traveled all day, making little headway over an ever more difficult trail. That night Lucy lay in her wagon, trying to get some precious sleep. Outside, a wolf began to howl and was soon joined by several others. Exhausted though she was, she lay awake listening. The wolves' mournful cries made her feel even more alone, more isolated than ever in this endless, unforgiving wilderness. She thought of her father, the house on Beacon Street, her cozy room with the sunbonnet babies quilt Mother had made that covered her snug, warm bed. She thought of dear Sarah, so far away ...

Oh, Sister, if only you knew about Noah. How I yearn for your comfort right now. How I would like to be home. I miss you more than words can express. I yearn to see you again, and if ever I'm able, I will go back. Oh, how I want to go home!

Early the next morning, Lucy was bent over the campfire cooking breakfast when Abner approached. "At least you'll be able to give us more help today."

Was she hearing him right? Hardly able to contain herself, Lucy slowly straightened and looked Abner in the eye. "You mean now that Noah is dead, I can devote more time to pushing the wagons? Is *that* what you mean?"

Abner met her gaze with eyes like cold stones. "You know what I mean. I know you're grieving, but you'll still be expected to do your part, especially now that Martha's not well."

"You know I always do my part." In a sudden rage, she turned her back on him and bent over the fire. The truth dawned on her as she dished up the biscuits. Her rage disappeared, replaced by wonderment.

Noah was gone, so Abner's hold on her was also gone.

She didn't have to do Abner's bidding anymore! The thought made her giddy with relief. She rose up, pan of biscuits in hand, and gazed at the tall, majestic trees that surrounded her. "I'm free," she whispered to herself. Free! Her grief for Noah prevented her from feeling even the slightest joy, and yet ...

When all this was over, how wonderful her life was going to be. She need no longer cater to Abner's commands. She could be independent. Go where she pleased. Talk to Clint—*make love with Clint*—without having to fear Abner's wrath. She would be financially independent, too. With a deep satisfaction, she thought of that bag of gold buried in the flour barrel.

Not quite yet. Her life was going to be good—very good, just as soon as they came to the end of this wretched, cursed Thompson Cutoff.

Later the same morning, they were on the trail again when Martha whispered to Lucy, "I keep getting these little twinges of pain—" she touched her lower abdomen "—and I don't want to tell Abner because he'd just start to yell."

"I'm sure it's just a touch of indigestion." Lucy ignored Martha's complaint because for her to go into labor now would be unthinkable.

Lucy spent the morning walking beside her wagon, grieving in silence over Noah. As the day wore on, she grew increasingly concerned about their progress. They seemed to be aimlessly wandering first in one direction then another. Around noon she looked up at Abner on the driver's seat. "Do you think we're lost?"

Abner regarded her with scorn. "Of course we're not lost."

"Don't you think you should check?"

Abner's jaw tightened. "I know where I'm going."

By now, the last vestiges of a visible trail had disappeared. At least the steepest hills lay behind them, but as they pushed on, they encountered a forest that grew increasingly thicker. At last they came to a cliff with a drop of several hundred feet. "It looks as if we've come to a dead end." Lucy tried to sound utterly calm. Martha, walking beside her, had experienced two more twinges of pain. Surely it was only indigestion. Surely there was nothing to worry about.

Abner looked ahead at the Butler Brothers' two wagons leading the way. "Those idiots have lost the trail. I'll go talk to Sam." For once, he didn't sound quite so sure of himself.

When Abner returned, his face was etched with concern. "We're lost, aren't we?"

He replied with a reluctant, "It's possible we've lost sight of the trail."

"We must go back." She tried not to show her distress over their having wasted the entire morning and gotten nowhere.

Abner squinted up at the sun. "I need to get my bearings first. Sam and I will saddle up, go back, and find the trail."

She jammed her hands on her hips. "Leave us here alone with Emery and Erasmus? Those two paragons of virtue?"

"What would you have me do? I admit they're a crude pair, but they're not going to hurt you."

Martha clutched his arm. "Please, I've been having these pains—"

"Don't bother me now." Abner jerked his arm away. "This is not the time to be having any pains. I shall be back shortly. Stay in your wagons. Don't go near the Butler Brothers, and you'll be fine."

What could she say? At this point, Abner had no choice but to go look for the trail. *He could let Sam go alone.* No use arguing, though. She cocked her head and had a wicked little smile. "You'd better get going then. I do believe we'll have a party with Emery and Erasmus while you're gone. I've just been dying for a big slug of that corn whiskey." Abner's face began to cloud. The man had absolutely no sense of humor. "Only joking. You go ahead. We'll be fine, won't we, Martha?"

Clint Palance rode back into camp with the satisfaction of a job well done. He had scouted the best routes ahead for the next two days. After a lengthy search, he'd found the easiest place for the wagon train to cross the swift river they'd reach tomorrow and left a marker.

As always, his gaze swept the circle of wagons, not for his own but hers. Not there? He looked around again. Sure enough, the Schneider wagons were missing. So were those belonging to the Butler Brothers.

What the hell?

At his own wagon, he swung from his horse and headed straight to Charlie who sat by the campfire, intent on writing in his journal. "Where'd they go?"

Charlie slowly raised his head. "Schneider got his pride hurt when he got demoted. Figured he'd be better off on his own, so he decided to take the Thompson Cutoff. Good thing is, he took the Butler boys with him. Bad thing is, he took Lucy and Noah, too. That poor little wife of his, of course."

"Son of a bitch!"

"Well, that's the truth of it. Lucy's gone, and there ain't nothing you can do about it."

"When did they leave?"

"Two days ago." Charlie laid down his journal. "I know you're fit to be tied. Right now you're thinking you'll go after her, but you've got to remember she ain't married to you and she's got her obligations."

Clint clamped down his rising anger. "I'd wager she didn't want to go."

"Not hardly. She was going to stay, but the little boy got sick, mountain fever, I think, and that jackass Schneider said he'd take the boy whether she went along or not." Charlie shook his head in disapproval. "That little wife of his wasn't looking any too perky before she left, either."

"What was Schneider thinking? The Thompson Cutoff's a death trap."

"Be that as it may. Just remember Lucy's obligated to Abner Schneider, such as he is, and it ain't much. You'd better not even think about going to rescue her. It ain't none of your business, and you'd best not forget it."

Chapter 17

*T*his can't be happening.

But it is happening.

But it can't be!

Martha was having her baby.

Lucy huddled in the back of Abner's wagon giving what comfort she could to her sister-in-law, who lay on her narrow bed twisting this way and that, gritting her teeth as each pain struck. Once she looked up at Lucy with wide, frightened eyes. "I'm scared I'm going to die, just like Bessie."

"Nonsense! You'll be fine." Lucy's attempt at reassurance sounded weak, even to her own ears. *Where is Abner*? He'd been gone for hours. He should be back by now. He must help her. There was no one else.

She peered out the back flap of the wagon. Nothing in sight except dense forest and the loathsome Butler Brothers sitting around their campfire. They'd been passing the jug around for hours. Their campsite was fifty feet away, yet she could still hear their drunken laughter loud and clear.

She got a towel, dipped it in water, and wiped the sweat from Martha's forehead. "You're doing fine." Truth be told, she had no idea if Martha was doing fine or not. Oh, dear God! Everything struck her at once. All alone ... Martha's baby coming ... Abner not back yet ... the Butler Brothers ...

Abner, please, *please*, come back. You must come back. I can't do this alone!

Martha's agonizing scream cut through Lucy's desperate

thoughts. "I'm going to die!" Her eyes were wide with panic.

"You'll do no such thing." Lucy grabbed the dampened towel and wiped Martha's face. Such a useless gesture, but what else could she do? "You're going to have that baby, and I'm going to be right here to help you." Hearing her own words gave her the courage to carry on. "You can count on me. When Bessie was in labor, I watched Inez, so I know just what to do."

"I can count on you?" Martha's voice was pleading.

"Of course you can." At least that last remark was the truth. The rest? Lucy had seen little of what Inez was doing when Bessie was in labor. What she did see, she could hardly remember. For Martha's sake, from now on she'd act if she were an expert in midwifery.

She heard a knock on the back of wagon. "Hey, Mrs. Schneider?" It was one of the Butler Brothers.

"Yes?"

"You all right?"

She crawled to the back of the wagon and pulled back the flap. Emery stood outside, grinning his snaggletooth grin. "What is it?"

"Just wonderin' if you and the other Mrs. Schneider was all right. We thought we heard a scream."

How could she explain? Lucy's mind raced, looking for a reasonable explanation. In the end she told the truth. "Mrs. Schneider's time has come. If you hear screams, pay no attention."

"Want some help?"

God in heaven. She used her most confident voice. "I have everything well under control. You can help the most by keeping your distance and giving Mrs. Schneider her privacy."

Emery nodded. "Whatever you want. By the way, we was wonderin' where Mister Schneider is. He's been gone a spell."

"I really don't know, but I'm sure he and your brother will be back shortly."

"Sam's already come back."

"What!" Her heart skipped a beat.

"Yep. Sam rode in some time ago. Said he lost track of Mister Schneider."

"Well, as I said, I'm sure he'll be back soon."

Emery's near-toothless grin widened. He gave her a broad wink. "Iffen you get lonely, you can come and set with us a spell."

"That's very kind of you. If I find the time, I shall certainly keep your invitation in mind."

She closed the flap and heaved a sigh of relief. At least the Butler Brothers wouldn't be bothering them. With a little luck, they'd soon drink themselves into their usual stupor and sleep the night away.

"Has something happened to Abner?" Martha called faintly from her bed.

Lucy returned to her side. "He's just a little late, but he'll be here." What if Abner had lost his way? Funny, but as much as she despised the man, she certainly needed him now.

Darkness fell, but Abner didn't return. As the pangs of childbirth increased, Martha twisted and turned upon the mattress. The pains began to cut through her body with such intensity that merely gritting her teeth was not enough. She tried not to cry out. "Oh, please, I don't want the Butler Brothers to hear me!"

Lucy rolled up a towel for Martha to bite on hard whenever a birth pang struck. She sat at the foot of her bed, and whenever a pain struck, clasped her hands. "Push, push!" she said, recalling Inez's orders to Bessie. Just as Inez had done, Lucy assumed a confident air and conducted an examination. "I can see the baby's head. It shouldn't be much longer."

Raindrops began to patter against the canvas. Only a light rain ... so far. She remembered that awful night when Jacob was still alive and their wagon flooded. Surely such a disaster wouldn't happen again.

The hours dragged by. So intent had Lucy become on helping Martha, she hardly noticed when the light patter of raindrops turned into a pounding. Only when driving sheets of water struck against the canvas with deafening force did she become aware of water leaking into the wagon. The leaks came from several small holes in the canvas. As the rain pounded—or was it hail?—the holes grew larger, until a deluge of cold water swept into the wagon, soaking her, Martha, the bedding, everything.

Lying on the soaked mattress, Martha began to shiver and cry. "Another flood. What shall we do?"

"Well, we can't stay here. Don't you worry, we'll find another place." Lucy wished she were as confident as she sounded. Other than fleeing to the Butler Brothers—an unthinkable option—her only choice was to move them to her own wagon, although it might very well be flooded, too. Only one way to find out. "I'll be right back."

When she slipped from the wagon, she was hit by a driving rain that stung her eyes like dozens of tiny, sharp knives. Blinded, she slipped and stumbled her way through the darkness and mud to her own wagon, only thirty feet away, but it seemed much farther. It was dry. Thank God the canvas had held.

Soaked to the skin, shivering in the chill air, she made her way back to Abner's wagon and climbed inside. Martha had to move. What an awful thing. Far gone in childbirth, Martha should absolutely not be moved, but she couldn't stay where she was either, all wet and shivering from the cold. "Come, Martha, we're going to go to my wagon where it's dry."

"I can't, I can't!" her sister-in-law called in a pitiful voice.

Lucy replied firmly, "You cannot stay here with the rain falling in your face. You must move. I insist."

Martha begged, "Can we at least wait until the next pain passes?"

"Of course. We'll do it between your pains."

"They're coming so close now!"

"They're at least a minute apart. That's plenty of time. Try to think of the good part. Soon you'll be dry and so much more comfortable." It was hard, trying to sound confident and cheerful when she wasn't sure she could get Martha to the other wagon, let alone help her climb inside.

A sheet of rain fell through the rent in the canvas, further drenching them both. "All right, I'll do it."

They waited until the next pain struck and subsided. The second it did, Lucy called urgently, "Come on, let's go." She helped Martha to the back of the wagon. In near total darkness, she jumped to the ground, braced herself, and raised her arms. "Just lean into my arms. I'll catch you. Hurry!"

With a groan Martha lowered herself from the wagon. Lucy caught her, glad she'd braced herself. Petite as Martha was, Lucy needed all her strength to cushion her fall. She placed her sister-in-law's right arm around her shoulders. "Lean on me. We'll be there in no time."

Martha leaned heavily against Lucy as they half walked, half stumbled the short distance through drenching rain to Lucy's wagon. Just as they reached the rear of the wagon, Martha cried, "Oh, Lucy, another pain's coming!" She doubled over and let out a long, heart-wrenching scream. Lucy stood helplessly by, hoping she'd have the strength to boost Martha up and into the wagon. *Lord give me the strength.*

When Martha's scream ended, she sagged to the muddy ground and started to sob. Lucy bent over her. "Please, Martha, you've got to stand up."

"I can't! I can't!" With the rain pounding on her, Martha remained on the ground and screamed again.

Lucy bent closer. "Do you want to lie here in the mud? You must help me. I can't lift you by myself."

Sheer desperation gripped her. What if she didn't have the

strength to lift Martha? She was putting her hands under Martha's arms, trying to pull her up, when from behind she heard a man's voice say, "Looks like you could use some help."

Oh, no! One of the Butler Brothers? She looked over her shoulder. She could barely make out the outline of a face ... It was Clint! A cry of relief broke from her lips. "I'm so glad you're here! Where did you come from?"

Swiftly Clint bent and swept Martha into his arms. "We'll talk later. Right now let's get this lady out of the rain."

In the wee hours of the morning, Clint, assisted by Lucy, delivered Martha's baby girl. She wasn't very big—Lucy guessed she was at least a month early—but she possessed the correct number of fingers and toes and let out a lusty wail when Clint held her up by her heels and gave her a gentle slap.

She and Clint had been so busy during Martha's final birth pangs that—other than Lucy relating the tragic news about Noah—they had hardly talked. Now, with the baby swaddled in one of Abner's old shirts and lying snug in Martha's arms, Lucy finally could express her gratitude.

"You were like God descending from the heavens. What would I have done without you?"

"I came to find you." Clint smiled. "Figured you might be in trouble. Even if I hadn't shown up, you would have managed."

"I highly doubt it." She tipped her head. "Where'd you learn how to deliver a baby?" She'd watched in awe as Clint brought the baby into the world with the skill of a midwife.

"I've done a lot of things in my lifetime." His brow furrowed. "That's terrible news about Noah. Are you all right?"

The thought of Noah left her empty and drained. "I'm all right because I have to be all right."

"You've been through a lot. Too much." Clint slipped his arms around her and pulled her close. She rested her head on his shoulder, savoring the strength she drew from his sympathy and understanding.

Clint finally asked, "Where's Abner?"

"Gone ... I don't know where. Maybe he got lost in the woods. Surely he'll be back by morning."

Lucy awoke by dawn's first light. She'd spent a cramped few hours next to Martha's bed and was pleased to see that both Martha and her baby appeared to be doing fine. Clint was gone. She poked her head out and saw that the rain had stopped. Clint was piling wood for a fire. After a greeting she asked, "Is Abner back?"

"No, he's not."

"Then something's definitely wrong. He could be lost, dead, badly injured, captured by Indians—anything!"

Clint struck flint and steel together and lit the kindling. "Don't worry. After breakfast I'll go after him." He nodded toward Lucy's wagon. "Are they all right?" When she nodded, he climbed into the wagon, knelt beside Martha, and picked up the baby. Tenderly his finger traced over the tiny velvet cheek, button nose, and up over the soft, golden wisps of hair. "She's beautiful. Have you named her yet?"

Martha lay limp and quiet on the mattress, so exhausted she could hardly move, but she managed a smile. "Amelia Catherine. That was my mother's name. I shall call her Amy for short."

He held the little bundle up in front of him. "Well, Miss Amelia Catherine Schneider, you may have been born in the midst of a rain storm, but I see you're none the worse for it."

Martha's eyes brimmed with gratitude. "What would we have done without you? I'm so glad you came after us. I never thought ... I wouldn't have dreamed ..." Her face reddened. Lucy guessed she was thinking of last night, how she'd lain there, in such an undignified position, while he did all those intimate, personal things.

Clint must have guessed, too. He smiled gently. "You've brought a new life into the world. What could be more beautiful? It's a shame white women set such a store on modesty. The Indians consider giving birth just a normal, everyday thing."

"Indian ladies aren't modest?"

He smiled. "No, the Indian ladies aren't modest." Martha sighed with relief. "Then I won't worry about modesty."

At that moment, Lucy felt like throwing her arms around Clint and giving him the hug of his life. Never had she felt this close to a man. "You were so good to help us. It seems you're always there when I need you."

"My pleasure. It's because I—" He drew a sharp breath, as if to check himself, then sighed. "Tell me about Abner."

"Yesterday we got hopelessly lost, so Abner and Sam Butler went to look for the trail. Sam came back, but Abner didn't."

Clint muttered a curse under his breath. "I'll go after him. Sam can show me where to look."

"What if you can't find him?"

A quirk of his lips told her he found her question amusing. "Trust me. I'll find him."

She suppressed a sudden urge to reply, "I hope not." She couldn't say such a thing in front of Martha. What would Abner say when he came back—*if* he came back—and discovered Clint had delivered his child? She'd wager he'd be furious, not that she cared. Resentment welled within her. If not for Abner, poor Martha wouldn't have suffered so much. If not for Abner, Noah might not have died. If not for Abner ... oh, so many things. She wouldn't have to tolerate Abner much longer. Her spirits rose at the thought that he no longer had a hold on her.

"Can I please have some water?" Martha whispered. "I feel hot."

Lucy felt her sister-in-law's forehead. Yes, it was hot, very hot. "You have a bit of a fever, but that's no surprise. Nothing to worry about."

Lucy slipped from the wagon to make breakfast, Clint close behind. Away from Martha's hearing, Lucy said, "Do you think Martha's fever is anything to worry about?"

"We'll keep an eye on her. I'm going after Abner now."

She reached out and clutched at his hand. "Oh, Clint, there's so much I want to tell you. I—"

"No, not yet." He pulled his hand back. "We're not out of the woods yet, in more ways than one."

Before she could answer, he spun on his heel and left her standing, her heart full of sentiments left unsaid.

The sun was just setting behind the trees when Clint, Sam Butler, and Abner Schneider rode into camp. At the noise, Lucy left Martha's side and went to greet them. The sight of Abner made her gasp. Ashen faced, eyes nearly shut, he swayed in his saddle. Then he started to fall.

"Grab him!" Clint and Sam sprang into action. "Careful of his leg. Lay him down while we pitch the tent."

Lucy asked, "What happened?"

"Durned if the captain didn't bust his leg," Sam replied. "Busted it bad, it looks like."

Abner opened his eyes and moaned. "My horse stumbled, fell atop me. I lay in the rain all night ... I ... awwww!"

Lucy knelt by Abner's side, her ears ringing from his awful screams. She took his hand, but he jerked it away. His face twisted. At the top of his voice he yelled, "Give me something for the pain!"

Clint gently clasped Lucy's arms and raised her to her feet. "Don't try to talk to him. Get back to Martha and stop worrying. The Butlers can give him some of their moonshine to ease the pain. We'll get him settled in the tent."

"Will he be all right?"

"No telling. Sam's right. It's a bad break." He paused for a moment. "One thing's clear. You can't go any farther on this insane shortcut."

"What will we do? Where will we go?"

"I'm taking you back to the wagon train."

"What if Abner—?"

"Abner's in no condition to decide anything."

"Can we catch up?"

"You let me worry about that."

Joy filled her heart. She would no longer be alone. She would soon see her friends again. What a comfort to know she could share her grief over Noah with friends who would truly care and understand. She could share the happy moments, too, knowing how Cordelia, Agnes, Inez, Hannah ... all of them, would appreciate the story of how Amelia Catherine came into the world.

Only one worry hung over her like a dark cloud. Martha didn't seem to be getting any better. She could not eat and lay on her bed like a limp rag doll, her eyes glazed with fever. She had no milk for the baby, whose weak wailing increased as the hours went by. "Give the babe some sugar water," Erasmus Butler suggested, perhaps the only sound advice that had ever come out of his mouth.

The sugar water helped. The baby quieted and went to sleep. To Lucy's growing concern, Martha's fever refused to come down.

꧁꧂

"Your leg's badly broken in several places, Mister Schneider."

In the hastily erected tent, Clint looked down upon the injured man and made an effort to hide his contempt. He would not kick a man when he was down. "We're going back to the wagon train. I calculate they're about to reach Fort Hall. There's a doctor there."

Abner's whiskey-glazed eyes glared up at him. "How ... dare you ... tell me what to do."

Clint crouched beside the stricken man. "You think I want to haul your sorry ass back?" Abner started to sputter. "I'm not doing this for you. I'm doing this for your wife and baby."

"Baby?" For a moment the dullness lifted from Abner's eyes.

"She had the baby while you were out in the woods with your broken leg."

"A boy?"

"Girl."

Abner's response, a slight sniff of scorn, fueled Clint's contempt, but he kept his voice level. "You're lucky the Butler Brothers agreed to come back with us. They'll drive your wagon, as well as their own."

"This is your doing, not mine, Palance!" Abner tried to sit up, winced with pain, and fell back. "I've no choice but to return. Mark my words, though, you'll rue the day you ever—"

"Schneider, I know you're hurting, but don't be a bigger prick than you already are."

Clint left the tent in a hurry. If he stayed, God only knew what he'd do to that lily-livered bastard. However, nothing could be as bad as the fate God had in store. Abner's twisted leg jutted at an odd angle. A jagged bone fragment poked through the skin. Ugly black streaks tinged with red had already crept beyond his knee and up his thigh. Clint had seen bad breaks like this one before. Abner would be lucky if all he lost was his leg.

Clint was struck by the sorry irony of it all. He was about to make an all-out effort to save the life of a man he not only detested, but a man who had, up till now, controlled the fate of the woman he loved and made her life a living hell. *Ought to leave him here to die.*

He wouldn't, though. Gentlemen called it honor. He called it downright stupidity, but, like always, he'd do the right thing.

❧

That night, as the hours crept by, Martha's condition worsened. Wracked by the raging fever, she lay dull-eyed and weak on her makeshift bed. Clint and Lucy did everything they could, but without medicine they were helpless. In a futile attempt to bring the fever down, Lucy spent hours sponging Martha's burning skin with cool water. It didn't work. The fever raged on. In the end, there was nothing left but prayer.

In the middle of the night, Martha grew delirious. Soon after, she lapsed into a coma. At dawn, the self-effacing "little mouse" who had never harmed anyone in her life quietly passed away.

Just as the sun rose over the trees, Lucy made the sad trek to Abner's tent to tell him Martha was gone. Even though numb with grief herself, she actually felt sorry for Abner. First, his terrible leg fracture, and now the death of his wife of ten years. Surely he'd be devastated.

She needn't have worried. Hearing Lucy's news, Abner turned his face away. Were there tears in his eyes? She couldn't tell. When he finally spoke, he asked in a steady voice, "Will the Butler Brothers dig her grave?"

"Yes, I suppose, along with Clint."

"Well, tell them to dig it deep, like Noah's. I don't want the wolves to dig her up."

"Are the wolves all you care about?"

Abner winced, groaned, and glared at her. "My leg! Can't you see I'm in pain? Leave me alone!"

Lucy could not contain herself any longer. "Just look at what your insane decision to take this stupid shortcut has done. Noah's dead. Your wife's dead. Your leg's broken, and it's all your fault."

Abner turned his head away and didn't answer. No surprise there. Of course, he'd never admit to being wrong. She left the tent without another word. Of course he was suffering, but even so, never had she known a man so calloused, so uncaring.

Shortly after, everyone but Abner stood beside Martha's hastily dug grave. Erasmus, hat in hand, spoke for the Butler Brothers. "She was a good woman. She didn't deserve to come to such a bad end."

Lucy spoke of her kindness and gentleness. "We shall never forget her."

Clint, Bible in hand, finished the service in an infinitely compassionate voice. "Rest well, Martha Schneider. Dust thou art, and unto dust shalt thou return."

Death, nothing but death. Beyond tears, Lucy stood by the grave watching the men shovel dirt over the remains of Martha Schneider.

A wail from the newborn reached her ears, causing her to set her morbid thoughts aside. The baby needed her. Sorrow and despair were luxuries she couldn't afford right now. "All right then," she whispered to herself with a decisive nod of her head. They'd be leaving soon, but first she must find something to feed the baby.

"Clint, I don't know what to feed her." Lucy held little Amy in her arms. "We have no milk. She can't take solid foods when she's just barely been born. We can't—"

"Here, let me have her." Clint took the baby and held her with practiced ease. "She won't be too hungry for a day or two."

"You seem to know a lot about babies." She had always

thought babies were strictly a woman's province. She had hardly ever seen a man hold a baby, much less met one who knew how to care for them. She wondered if perhaps he'd had one of his own, perhaps with an Indian woman.

He grinned. "Let's just say I've learned a lot in my time." He gazed at the sleeping infant in his arms. "For now, Erasmus has the best advice. Get a clean rag, soak it in sugar water, and let her suck on it. That should be enough for two or three days."

"And then?"

"You let me worry about that."

He seemed so positive she asked nothing further. Where, she wondered, would they find food for a newborn in this total wilderness?

Chapter 18

During the trek back, Lucy felt torn between joy over seeing her friends again, grief at the loss of Noah and Martha, and concern for Amy—although for the first two days the infant seemed to thrive on the sugar water. Then there was Abner. Much as she detested him, she'd need a heart of stone not to be moved by his constant moans and occasional screams whenever a bounce of the wagon jarred his mangled leg.

His suffering increased whenever one of the Butler Brothers drove his wagon. They didn't like Abner, never had, and made no effort to avoid bumps on the trail. That he was badly injured and had just lost his wife made no difference. With ill-suppressed glee, they aimed for the largest bumps they could find. Clint drove the wagon whenever he could, and Lucy was grateful. Abner's moans and screams subsided when Clint held the reins.

The baby seemed fine until the fourth day, when she began to fret and turn her head away from the rag soaked with sugar water. Lucy asked Clint, "How much longer before we get back?"

"At least two more days, possibly three."

"The baby could starve by then." She tried to keep the panic from her voice. Already, Amy had claimed her heart. "We can't let her die. We can't—"

"Stop your worrying. Guess it's time. We'll stop for the day." Clint went to tell the Butler Brothers they were stopping. Shortly after, rifle in hand, he disappeared into the thick woods.

Hours later when he returned, he carried something loosely wrapped and held it up for Lucy to see.

"It's an elk's liver. We're going to boil it and make a broth. Then we'll strain it, add cod liver oil, if we have any, and feed it to Amy with a spoon. That should keep her from starving until we get back."

After a few tiny spoonfuls of the liver broth, fortified with a bit of cod liver oil donated by the Butler Brothers, Amy stopped fretting.

Holding the contented baby in her arms, Lucy mused how once again Clint had come to the rescue. What a magnificent man he was, in so many different ways. Just then, Abner let loose one of his many screams. She put the baby down and went to tend him. As she bent over the stricken man, her resolve strengthened.

Just wait until this is over, Abner. You won't have a hold over me anymore. It's Clint I want and Clint I shall have, and I won't let you or anyone on this earth get in my way.

When they finally caught up with the wagon train at Fort Hall, Lucy sat on the wagon seat, the baby in her arms. Despite her grief, her heart lifted at the sight of Hannah, Inez, Cordelia, Agnes—all the dear friends who crowded around the wagon to greet her. She held up the baby for all to see. "Meet Amelia Catherine Schneider, everyone."

"Oh, what a beautiful name!"

"See how pretty she is!"

"What a sweet baby!"

Agnes' sharp gaze swept over the wagon. "Where's Martha? Where's Noah?"

Lucy related the sad events of their ill-fated journey. By the time she finished, tears were shed amidst grim shaking of heads. She tried to conclude on a bright note. "The baby is fine, but we need a wet nurse for her right away. We need a doctor for

Abner."

Not only was there a doctor at Fort Hall, but two women in the wagon train had recently given birth and were happy to share.

Agnes commented, "You've been through a lot, haven't you?"

Lucy nodded, gazing fondly at Amy in her arms. "She was born in the middle of a rainstorm."

"Abner helped?"

"No."

"Not the Butler Brothers!"

She knew Agnes would ask. She'd already decided to tell the truth because they'd find out anyway. "Clint delivered her."

Everyone gasped. Mouths dropped open. The questions came thick and fast as she filled in the details. Just then the doctor arrived, a distraction for which she was most grateful. After the earnest young doctor had finished his examination, he came over to talk to Lucy, frowning and shaking his head. "Gangrene's set in. The leg has got to come off. Otherwise, Mister Schneider will surely die. I can't guarantee he won't die anyway."

Six men held Abner down. Even though he'd been well fortified with whiskey and laudanum, his anguished screams echoed throughout the campsite, causing Lucy to cover her ears in a futile attempt to block the heartrending sounds. Afterward, the doctor explained, "Had to take his leg off above the knee. He's not in good shape. Frankly I don't hold out much hope."

Because of Abner, the wagon train stayed on at Fort Hall. Despite the exorbitant prices, nearly everyone shopped for supplies. Lucy remained at Abner's side. It was hard seeing a man once strong and vigorous lying weak and in pain. He was feverish and groaned constantly. When he spoke, it was only to bemoan the loss of his leg. Apparently he'd already wiped poor

Martha from his memory.

She always tried to sound cheerful. "John Potts has volunteered to make you crutches. Soon you'll be able to get around just fine."

Late on the third day, she was taking a brief break outside Abner's tent when Agnes walked over to talk. "I wanted to tell you how sorry I am about Noah and Martha, and Abner, too." Lucy was about to say thanks when the skinny, sharp-nosed woman went on, "Now tell me, how do you really feel?"

Lucy was slightly taken aback. "About what?"

"About Abner, of course. If he dies, I mean."

"That's a really rude question."

"Of course it's rude. Don't you know why I'm asking?"

"Why don't you tell me?" Lucy knew what was coming. *Damn* Agnes and her eagle eye.

"I just think it's sad you have to sit there acting like the grieving family member, *so* anxious for your dear brother-in-law, when the reality is that you wouldn't be unhappy if he died."

"Why do you say that?"

"Easy. He's an obnoxious, domineering man you never liked in the first place. Didn't he have a hold on you because of Noah?"

What a nosey woman! How very perceptive. Words of defense rushed to Lucy's lips. She didn't say them, though, because she recognized the truth in Agnes' remarks. She would never wish anyone dead, even Abner, yet since he broke his leg she couldn't prevent the occasional stray thought that her life would be a thousand times happier if he were gone. She wasn't about to admit her secret thoughts to Agnes, though. She certainly wasn't going to admit to being relieved that Abner no longer had a hold on her because of Noah. Instead, she raised her chin, assuming all the dignity she could muster. "What's the point of all this? Assuming you have one, of course."

Thick-skinned Agnes wouldn't be deterred. "The point is this. You and Clint are so hot for each other, it's a wonder smoke doesn't arise when you're together."

"So?" She wasn't about to deny anything.

"We still have a long way to go. Six hundred miles to the Humboldt River, then that trek across the desert everyone fears and talks about. Right now you're still in a state of shock from that awful shortcut, and you have a baby to care for. But soon you'll be getting back to normal, and when you do, there you'll be, stuck with a one-legged, scripture-spouting fool when with all your heart and soul you long for Clint. Will you be able to resist? I wonder." Agnes stepped back and folded her arms across her chest. "You may not think so, but I'm your friend. I'd risk our friendship in order to tell you what you need to hear. Now tell me if I'm wrong."

No, she wasn't wrong. Lucy could only stare at the blunt woman, utterly speechless. "Don't concern yourself. I know right from wrong, and I know how to handle myself."

"I hope you do, dear. I'm mainly concerned because I suspect Abner isn't going to die. He harbors a lot of hate in his heart, and I fear he's going to take it out on you. He still has a hold on you, now more than ever."

"What do you mean?" Her heart sank because she knew what Agnes was going to say.

"Amy. Abner's very own child, so he's got you in his clutches again because it's plain to see you love that child as you would your own. Am I not right?"

Yes, Agnes was right. All along, in the back of her mind, she'd known Amy belonged to Abner. She had no right whatsoever to the child. Now Agnes had forced her to face the truth. She lifted her chin. "I have nothing more to say on the subject."

Concern filled Agnes' eyes. "Are we still friends?"

"Of course. I always welcome your opinion."

❧

"Only the good die young," said Charlie Dawes. He and Clint sat with their coffee before the dying embers of their campfire. "That's why I'd put my money on Abner to pull through."

Clint responded with a noncommittal, "Hmm."

"There ain't no use pretending you don't care."

Clint shifted his gaze from the fire and regarded his friend. "All right, you've got my attention."

"You give me one good reason why you'd want that dumb son-of-a-bitch to live."

In deep thought, Clint lingered over his next sip of coffee. "I've never wished anyone dead. Even the Indians I've killed, I did because I had to."

"I've never relished killing Indians, either, not like some. What if Abner pulls through, which to my way of thinking, he probably will."

"So what if he does?" Clint pretty much knew what was coming, but there was no stopping Charlie when he wanted to have his say.

"You're in love with Lucy." At Clint's quick, sharp glance, Charlie continued, "No use denying it. Just the way you two look at each other, it's plain as the nose on your face."

"She's got a lot of responsibilities right now. I'd never—"

"Oh, I ain't doubting for a minute you were the soul of propriety on that trip back, what with a newborn to care for—and I hear you saved the little tyke's life, besides having that sorry-ass religious lunatic in the back of the wagon with his leg broke. What happens now?"

"Nothing happens now."

"What if Abner dies?"

"Then ..." Clint's eyes narrowed under a furrowed brow. "I never thought I would marry. That was before ... A muscle quivered in his jaw. "Yes, it's crossed my mind the son-of-a-bitch might die."

"You wouldn't be human if it hadn't." Charlie's voice was suddenly gentle. "What if he lives? You know damn well he still has a hold on her."

"Whatever happens, I won't do anything until we get to California. If Abner's still around, I'll deal with him then."

Charlie burst into scoffing laughter. "It ain't going to work, old friend. Don't give me a bunch of bull. What with six hundred miles to the Humboldt, and then across the desert, and then the Sierras, human nature being what it is, I'd wager a quart of Old Orchard you won't be able to keep your hands off each other for that long a time."

꿍

On the morning of the fourth day after Abner's surgery, the young doctor emerged from the tent and spoke to Lucy, a big grin on his face. "Good news! Looks like Mister Schneider is going to pull through."

"Why, that's wonderful news. I'm so very grateful." Lucy watched the doctor walk away, pleased with himself for a job well done. Little did he know. Of course, it was wonderful news. Just wonderful. Maybe if she kept repeating those words enough times, she'd believe them. She'd be a terrible person if she thought otherwise.

The wagon train split at Fort Hall. After a well-needed rest, those bound for Oregon continued on a northwest course that would take them to Fort Boise, the Columbia River, and on to the Oregon Territory. Those headed for California turned southwest. They'd cross a blistering hot desert, then the Sierra Nevada Mountains before reaching the golden shores.

The split brought heartbreaking farewells. Hannah

Richards, about to continue on to Oregon, bid Lucy goodbye with sad reluctance. "You're one of the best friends I ever had or ever will have." She hugged Lucy tight, unabashed tears rolling down her cheeks. "We can't even exchange addresses."

"I know. Chances are, we'll never see or even hear from each other again." Lucy couldn't control her own tears. "I'll never forget you." She stepped back and clasped Hannah's hands in her own. "We've been through a lot, haven't we, dear friend?"

Hannah nodded. "It's going through all the hardships together that makes dear friends." She hesitated a moment. "Can I give you a piece of advice?"

"Of course."

"Follow your heart. That's all I have to say, just follow your heart."

Lucy wouldn't even try to pretend she didn't know what Hannah meant. "Perhaps I will." There was a long pause. "I absolutely will."

Chapter 19

$\mathcal{L}$ucy's opinion of Abner sank to new depths as they traveled the six hundred mile stretch from Fort Hall to the Great Basin of the Humboldt River. She wanted to cringe every time she heard his voice, always irritated since his accident. Granted, losing a limb was a terrible thing, but his constant moaning and complaining were a trial to everyone, Lucy most of all. It didn't help that—aside from taking the reins and driving the oxen every now and then—he'd become totally useless, never lifting a finger to help. She was responsible for all the work now, and each long day included yoking and driving the oxen, caring for the baby, setting up the camp, repairing the wagon, collecting firewood, and doing the cooking. Only the helping hands of others in the train made her miserable situation bearable.

If she thought her plight couldn't possibly get any worse, she was in for an unpleasant surprise. The most brutal part of the journey began when the California-bound party headed out over the treeless, alkaline region of the Great Basin of the Humboldt. By the time they reached the halfway mark, food and water were scarce. Wagons broke down, and the oxen, deprived of food and water, were in such sad shape they hadn't strength left to pull. For days the struggling party followed a pathetic trail of cherished belongings left behind by the unfortunate souls who traveled before them. Chairs, tables, bedsteads, mattresses—every article of housekeeping. Clothes, family pictures, all tossed overboard as people tried to lighten their load. Lucy saw many deserted wagons, too, and dead animals.

Now it was their turn. When two of their thirsty, half-starved oxen died, Abner decreed they must lighten the loads in both wagons, causing Lucy to grieve for the loss of her precious family pictures, which must now be left to rot in the sand. She found little consolation in knowing she wasn't the only one. Families all around them were tossing their precious possessions over the side.

"I never dreamed I'd be doing this."

Cordelia Benton carried her tea service to the side of the trail and lovingly placed it atop the alkaline dust. " I do believe Grandmother Benton would roll over in her grave if she could see her magnificent sterling silver tea service just tossed away like trash in the middle of the desert."

Lucy nodded in sympathy. "It's terrible, but we have no choice."

Charlie Dawes rode up. "It don't get any easier, does it?" Face covered with dust and sweat, he halted his hoof-sore horse by the side of the trail, removed his hat, and swiped his arm across his forehead. "Nary a drop of water nor a spear of grass since we started across." He surveyed the never-ending landscape of rock, sand, mesquite, and cactus, stretching out desolate and bleak beneath the blazing sun. Ahead, the wagon train barely moved. Since dawn, two of the Benton's oxen had died, leaving Cordelia no alternative but to lighten the load.

As Charlie rode away, Chad stuck his head out the back of the Benton's wagon. "Hey, Ma, what about this barrel of dishes?"

For an agonizing moment, Cordelia squeezed her eyes shut. "Yes, they've got to go." She watched her son lift the barrel to the back edge of the wagon, then gasped in alarm. "Chadwick, you be careful with Grandmother Benton's French Haviland china!"

"What for?" Chad hoisted the barrel over the edge and let

go. It crashed to the ground, accompanied by the loud, sickening sound of breaking dishes.

"Oh, dear Lord!" Cordelia looked toward the sky. I'm *so* sorry, Grandmother Benton."

"She understands." Lucy placed a comforting hand on Cordelia's shoulder. "I know how it hurts, but the best we can do is put our former lives behind us and carry on." She barely believed her own brave words.

Cordelia wiped away a tear and stood tall. "We're going to make it, never you fear. We'll make Nathaniel proud."

Chad appeared at his mother's elbow. "Not if we try to farm. I want to go to the gold fields."

"Perhaps we will."

"You mean you're not going to farm?" The last Lucy heard, her friend from the South planned to carry out her husband's wish to acquire farmland in California.

"I've decided I'd make a very poor farmer. Besides, from what I've heard, there's money to be made in the mining towns, and not just from panning for gold."

Bright-eyed Chad spoke. "We'll be passing by lots of mining towns before we get to Sacramento. Like Hangtown. That's where I really want to go. You should tell Mister Schneider."

Lucy shook her head. "I don't know if I can even bring it up. Mister Schneider is ... a bit difficult to deal with since his accident."

"A *bit* difficult?" Cordelia looked ahead to where Abner's wagon slowly rolled along the trail. "He's impossible, and you know it. Is he actually driving the oxen today?"

"Yes. He does ... occasionally."

"Hmmph!" Cordelia raised a skeptical eyebrow. "That's the least he can do. I know he can't walk, but in my opinion, he could contribute something more than just lying around reading his Bible and complaining. Furthermore ... oh, dear, I should keep my mouth shut."

"I don't know why. Tell me what you're thinking."

Cordelia appeared encouraged. "Why don't you leave Abner and come with us? You know very well he won't be able to farm, much as he might claim otherwise. Certainly not in his present condition, and it doesn't look as if he's going to get any better. Besides ..." Cordelia hesitated, as if choosing her words carefully. "Far be it from me to pry, but you're not married to the man. Why must you stay with him, anyway? I don't understand."

Other than Clint and Hannah, Lucy hadn't revealed Abner's hold on her. But why not? In his pitiful condition, what could he do to her now? "After Jacob died, Abner made it clear that Noah was legally his and he'd never give him up. What could I do? I couldn't bear the thought of leaving that beautiful child in his hands. Now, with Martha's baby, it's even worse. I love that child like my own. Just as with Noah, I couldn't bear the thought of leaving her with that awful man."

Cordelia nodded. "So that's it. Well, I always had the feeling he had a hold on you. It's different now, isn't it? He's weak and helpless, and it's his own stupid fault, as far as I can see. You should no longer feel obligated to him in any way, even if he is your brother-in-law."

"I don't. In fact, I've decided that as soon as we reach California, I shall leave Abner and strike out on my own." Lucy felt a swell of strength, just hearing her own words.

"What about Amy?"

"She comes with me. If Abner objects, I have only to point out he can hardly take care of himself now, so how could he possibly take care of a baby? Why would he *want* to?"

Cordelia applauded. "Good for you! I don't wish to snoop, but can you afford it?"

Lucy thought of the bag of coins at the bottom of the flour barrel. What a comfort, knowing they were there. "Jacob didn't leave me penniless, I'm happy to say."

"Then that's wonderful news, and I'm so glad to hear it." Cordelia turned to her son. "Come on, Chad. Let's see what other priceless heirlooms we can toss over the side."

After they left, Lucy walked on, reflecting that never in her life had she felt so weary. There were times when she could hardly put one foot ahead of the other. No sense complaining—everyone felt exactly the same way. She must look a sight. If only her fancy friends in Boston could see her now in her faded, tattered clothes, limping because her feet were blistered from walking over the burning sand and flint rocks. Well, one good thing ...

She ran a quick hand over her trim waist and the hard, flat muscles of her abdomen. Her figure had never been so trim. Despite her ragged appearance, she knew Clint had noticed. She'd seen the admiration in his eyes.

"Good afternoon. Out for your daily stroll?"

It was Clint, coming up beside her on foot, leading his Appaloosa. As usual, her heart lifted just knowing he was near. "Good afternoon. Not riding today?"

He fell in step beside her. "Paint's not up to it. I won't ride again until we're through the desert."

They walked in companionable silence for a while, their steps matching the train's slow pace. "Everything all right with you today?"

The deep caring she heard in his voice made her want to cry out, "No, everything's not all right because I can't have you."

Agnes was right. Lucy longed for Clint, so much so that there were nights, exhausted though she was, that she lay awake and yearned with all her heart and soul to be in his arms. She almost wished they'd never made love in the first place. Then she wouldn't know what she was missing. Now that she knew what "lovesick" meant. Her desire for Clint seemed to deepen each day, to the point she could hardly act like a good, well-brought-up Christian woman was supposed to act. In fact, if he touched her right now, she suspected she'd fall at his feet in complete surrender, in front of God, Abner, Agnes, and everyone else.

"I'm doing just fine today, and the baby, too. She's asleep in the wagon." She reached to wipe the dampness from her brow. "I'm such a mess."

He threw her a glance. It was quick, but not so quick she didn't catch the passion in his warm brown eyes. "Even covered in dust you look good to me."

"Thanks, I think." She smiled and trudged on. "Will we ever get there?"

"Two more days and we'll be out of the desert. Then a couple days more and we'll get to Truckee."

"What an odd name."

"It's named after a friendly Piute Indian guide with a name that sounded like 'Tro-kay.' The white men dubbed him 'Truckee,' and the name stuck."

"Is it nice there?"

"You're going to love it. Think of tall pine trees ... fresh mountain air ... a river of clear water."

"What heaven! I can think of no greater pleasure on earth than to be able to wash all over."

"There will be plenty of fresh game, too, as well as fish from the lake, and ..." He hesitated. "Truckee will be a place where we can have some privacy and talk."

Her heart did a flip flop. Privacy! She and Clint could be alone. "What will we talk about?"

He cast a piercing gaze. "You know what we'll talk about."

"You mean Abner."

"You can't stay with that man. We'll talk when we get to Truckee."

Her heart swelled with hope. Could she dare dream she and Clint could be together? He didn't want to talk now. Well, she could wait. After all, what did a few more days matter? They walked another dozen steps before she felt enough in control to venture a change of subject. "Chad says he wants to go to a place called Hangtown."

"Not a good idea."

"Why not?"

"Because it's a rough, tough, lawless town where they'll hang a man for so much as spitting on the sidewalk."

"You've been there?"

"Yes. I won't be going back, though."

"Lucy, come here!"

Abner. She hadn't noticed, but the train had stopped and they'd come abreast of his wagon. "I must go."

Anger flashed in Clint's eyes. "I'd like to kick his teeth in when he yells at you like that."

"But you won't," she softly replied. "Good day. Nice chatting with you."

When she got to the wagon, Abner glowered down at her. "Come and drive these oxen. My leg hurts, and I'm tired."

"Of course." If there was one thing she'd learned in dealing with Abner these days, it was patience. She climbed to the wagon seat, picked up the reins, and cracked the whip. Had there ever been a time when she thought driving the oxen would be fun? Now she could holler "Gee! Haw!" and the other commands with the best of them, but she'd long since learned driving a team of oxen was a lot of sweaty hard work. "I see no reason why you can't help more, at least drive the oxen,"

Abner rubbed the remains of his leg, now a pitiful stump covered by his pinned-up pant leg. "Can't you see God has seen fit to make me a cripple? If God wanted me to—"

"Oh, be quiet." Patience be damned. "I don't want to hear about God from *you*." She took a good look at her brother-in-law. Since the accident, his body had grown slack, his shoulders slumped. His beard looked like a rat's nest, it was so unkempt.

He was more to be pitied than anything else, and she shouldn't argue with him. "Just go lie down."

Without a shred of remorse, she picked up the reins. She didn't care she'd let her disgust show when she spoke to Abner. She didn't want to think about him. All she wanted to think about was Clint. She cracked the whip again, her mind reeling with all that had been left unsaid between them.

She could hardly wait to get to Truckee.

For days, tortured by thirst and hunger, the train slogged through the barren desert until one day, around noon, Lucy sighted a shimmering dark green line of cottonwoods on the far horizon. Soon the thirsty oxen and cattle scented the proximity of water. They became so maddened that to prevent the teams from stampeding and wrecking the wagons, Clint and Charlie called, "Truckee River ahead! Everyone get those teams unhitched! Let 'em go!"

The crazed animals rushed pell-mell for the water. The thirsty humans, Lucy among them, followed close behind.

When Lucy reached the river, she pulled her boots off, waded in, and joyfully splashed around. Cupping her hands together, she scooped up the precious liquid and drank until she'd had her fill, letting it dribble down her chin. Ah, water! She'd never take it for granted again.

The low spirits of the exhausted, trail-worn party picked up when William Applegate and the council decided they'd stay two whole days in the beautiful mountain setting by the side of the Truckee River where there was plenty of water, lush grass, and an abundance of game. Lucy rejoiced along with the rest, then went to work. Starting with the baby, she washed practically everything in sight, including herself and her clothes. She also washed Abner's clothes, the dusty wagons, and everything inside that wasn't nailed down. What an exquisite feeling to be clean again!

That evening, for the first time since they started the trek across the desert, members of the wagon train gathered around a campfire. In a buoyant mood, they chatted, danced, and listened to Erasmus Butler play his fiddle.

Lucy heard the music from her wagon. Anxious to join in the fun, she laid Amy in her tiny bed—a box she'd soon outgrow, but fine for now. With a surge of affection, she looked down at the child. What a good baby she was. Amy might have been born early, but far as Lucy could see, she was perfect in every way. She didn't even cry much. At nearly two months old, she gurgled happily and showed the beginnings of a smile.

Lucy carried Amy, box and all, to the Applegates' wagon where the oldest girl, Jessie, had volunteered to watch the little ones. From there she walked a fair distance to Abner's wagon. In accordance with his new custom, he'd parked amidst the trees on the far perimeter of the campsite, isolating himself as far from the others as he could get. She found him sitting outside his wagon reading his Bible by lantern light.

"I'm going to join everyone at the campfire. Want to come along? There's singing and dancing, just what we need after what we've been through." She laughed to herself, wondering why she was being so kind to this horrible man. It all came down to pity, she supposed, inspired by a gentle upbringing that emphasized kindness and compassion. Not that anything she said would matter. She knew her brother-in-law would decline. He could manage well enough on crutches now, but since the accident, he had avoided human contact, much preferring to sit beside his wagon, read the Scriptures, and feel sorry for himself.

Abner looked up from his Bible and glared. "Dancing is a sin."

"Nowhere in the Bible does it say dancing is a sin."

" 'Thessalonians five, Verse twenty-two: 'Abstain from all appearance of evil.' "

"I hardly think ..." What was the use? Why waste her

breath? She could move a mountain more easily than she could change her brother-in-law's mind.

"What have you done with the baby?" Abner asked.

"Amy's quite safe with the Applegates."

"Then I suppose I can't stop you."

Why had she bothered? She might have known he'd throw up the same old obstacles when he had no right to stop her from doing anything she pleased. She'd grown thoroughly sick of Abner's constant negative attitude, especially since he'd put all the work on her since his accident. She wouldn't let him spoil her evening. She'd see Clint tonight, and nothing would stop her. She smoothed her blue muslin dress. Today she'd patched it, and it didn't look too bad. She touched her hair. Newly washed, it fell prettily over her shoulders. "Goodnight."

"Mind you're not gone long."

"I'm not your wife. It's not your place to tell me what to do."

He seemed not to have heard. "Stay away from Clint." His voice was harsh.

"I don't know what you mean."

"Oh, yes you do." Abner's eyes were lethally calm. "You think I don't see how you lust after him? You think you're fooling me?"

"I don't have to listen to you." She started away.

"You'd better listen to what I have to say."

Something in his voice made her stop and turn. "What do you mean?"

"I hear your dear friend Cordelia has decided not to farm."

What was he up to? "That's right. She and Chad plan to settle in one of the mining towns."

"So will we."

She stared at him tongue-tied.

Abner smiled, a mean kind of smile that conveyed his pleasure he'd shocked her. "Do you actually think I can farm now?"

She gathered her wits together. "I really don't know. You've got your crutches, although I must say, you don't use them much. You can always find plenty of hired hands—"

"We're going to the gold fields."

She stifled a gasp. "Why? You can hardly walk, let alone pan for gold."

"There's other money to be made in the mining towns. I plan to open a store."

"Have you decided where?"

"A placed called Downieville, on the fork of the North Yuba. I hear they've hit pay dirt there."

For a moment she stood silent, amazed and shaken. "When do you plan to leave?"

"When we reach the cutoff—in two or three days." He smiled benignly, as if dealing with a temperamental child. "I'll be taking my daughter, so if you want to come along, you'd better start saying goodbye to all your dear friends. If you don't wish to come, say goodbye to Amy."

"Who would take care of her?" Her voice was panicky.

"Not your concern." His smile disappeared, replaced by a look so menacing and downright cruel she wanted to cringe. "If you decide to come, don't forget your dearest of friends, Clint. Be sure to give him a fond farewell because you're never going to see him again."

In an agony of indecision, Lucy walked away from Abner's wagon, so shocked by his announcement she hardly noticed the slight breeze, scented with evergreen, that whispered through the tall pine trees. After the ordeal of the desert, she should have appreciated the coolness of the mountain air, but her agitated thoughts lay elsewhere. What was she to do? She couldn't go to Downieville with Abner. But how could she leave that dear little baby in his care? By now, she loved Amy as if she were her own.

If need be, she'd lay down her life for that child.

So here she was, right back where she started from, forced to let Abner run her life, only this time his hold on her was because of Amy, not poor little Noah.

Clint. She must find Clint. Maybe he could help somehow. She fervently hoped he could, because how could she say goodbye forever to the man she loved? How could she bear not seeing him again? Stepping carefully—there was only a sliver of a moon tonight—she walked to the campfire and stood in the shadows, just beyond the circle of light. For a time she listened to the lively strains of "Old Dan Tucker," played by Erasmus on his fiddle. Chatter and laughter filled the air. Some were clapping their hands to the lively tune; others were up dancing a reel. Where was Clint? She scanned the crowd but couldn't find him. She searched again and spied Charlie, but Clint wasn't with him. Perhaps his wagon? She slipped away, relieved no one had seen her, and walked to Clint's wagon. No trouble finding it. She always knew exactly where it was. Sure enough, as she drew closer, she could make out his form, sitting on the wagon seat, doing nothing, far as she could see, just staring into the darkness.

She came close. "Clint?" she said softly.

He looked down at her. She could barely see his face. "Lucy? Why aren't you dancing?"

"Why aren't you?"

He let a long moment go by before he spoke again. "I was waiting for you."

Now she was the one who remained silent. She couldn't get the words out, yet she knew she must. "I just talked to Abner."

"And?"

"He's decided not to farm. Instead he's going to Downieville to open a store, and he's taking Amy with him. Oh, Clint ..." She gulped, trying to curb the hysteria in her voice. "What am I to do? I can't let him take her."

In a flash, Clint sprang from the wagon and stood close, gripping her arms. "You're not going to spend the rest of your life with Abner."

"I could never leave Amy to his tender care."

"You won't have to."

"But how—?"

"You let me worry about that."

"That's what you always say."

"Have I ever let you down?"

No, he hadn't. She laid her hand lightly upon his cheek. "You know I trust you, but how can you possibly deal with Abner other than dispatching him with that huge knife of yours?"

"There are other ways."

"Like what?"

"Abner may love God, but there's one thing he loves more, and that's money."

"Are you saying—?"

"I'm saying Abner can be bought. Money-wise, he hasn't fared well on this journey. He had to dump all that whiskey. He sold his cattle for a song when he chose to take that lunatic shortcut. Now he's down to one wagon, four tired oxen, and whatever cash he has left." He cupped her chin tenderly in his hand. "Let me do the worrying and not let Abner ruin our night."

"But the money—"

"I said, don't worry. Charlie and I aren't in this business for fun, you know. We've earned a few dollars along the way. We've talked enough." He pulled her roughly, almost violently, into his arms. Heart pounding, she forgot about Abner and flung her arms around Clint's neck as his warm lips hungrily covered hers. Pressing against him, she rejoiced in the feel of every hard inch of him. It was as if a dam had broken, releasing their bottled-up passion in one enormous rush. For weeks she'd lived on the searing memories of their kiss in the woods and that rainy afternoon in the wagon. With every grinding step across the desert she'd wanted it to happen again, and now it had.

Their kiss continued. His ragged breathing told her that he, too, felt the excitement of this moment. A delicious shiver of wanting flowed through her, caused by his kiss, caused by that rugged buckskin, tantalizingly masculine smell about him that made her knees grow weak.

Finally he pulled his lips away. "How I've wanted this," he whispered, shaking his head in wonder. "Lucy, darling Lucy ..." Before she could answer, his lips found the pulsing hollow at the base of her throat. She tilted her head back, wanting more, and more ... oh, she didn't want him to stop!

At last he raised his head, stepped back, and gripped her arms. "Let this be our night." His strong, sure hands caressed her hair, ran down over her breasts, gripped her waist. "For one night let's not fight this ... this constant, damnable, overpowering desire that hangs between us. It is driving me mad. *You* drive me mad."

No way in the world could she say no to this irresistible man. From not far away, she heard Erasmus strike up a new tune. "We can't stay here."

He took her hand. "Come, I know a place where no one will find us."

Clint led her to a secluded spot by the river where he scooped her in his arms and laid her gently on a soft bed of pine needles. Overhead, faint light from the half moon filtered through a canopy of branches. Far in the distance she could hear the music of the fiddle, now nearly obscured by the soothing murmur of the river flowing by. At last they were alone, all those weeks of unfulfilled desire finally at an end. Clint lay half on top of her and laid a hand over her breast. Feeling the warmth of it through the fabric, she uttered an "Umm" and pulled him close.

Hungrily his mouth covered hers in an urgent, exploratory kiss that made her body tingle. Soon his tongue forced her lips apart. When it touched the tip of her tongue, an intense desire flared within her. He lifted his lips and whispered, "I want to see all of you."

She whispered back, "I want you to."

With maddening, delectable slowness, he unbuttoned the six buttons that formed a row down the front of her bodice. Quietly she lay beneath him, her aching need increasing as he bent to his task. When he finished, he laid open her bodice and caught his breath at the sight of her breasts exposed in the moonlight. "They're beautiful." He ran his hands over her nipples, touching them only briefly, but long enough that she yearned for their return. He kissed her lips again, this time using his tongue to penetrate deep inside her mouth. While he explored, she ran her tongue over his, another thrilling intimacy that made her want him closer still.

"Let's get these clothes off," he said. Swiftly they undressed each other. Soon, just as before, he was running his hands over her nakedness, stopping here and there to tease and explore. She grew increasingly aroused as he began a path down her body, kissing and licking as he went. She was acutely aware of every kiss, every flick of his tongue as it traveled until he reached her silky mound. "Spread your legs. I want to kiss you there."

With eager abandon, she moved her legs apart. What next? Jacob had never done more than just the one position. With him it was on and off quick and never a thought to her pleasure. Now Clint was going to kiss her *there*. With trembling anticipation, she awaited the touch of his tongue on the most private, intimate part of her, which now seemed the very center of all her currents of throbbing desire. When she felt its roughness, her whole body quivered from the exquisite sensation. "Oh, that's good, so very good."

"Then I won't stop." He continued on, his tongue bringing

her to ever higher levels of ecstasy. "You'd better stop. I'm about to explode."

He stopped at once. "Not that way." Again his hard body was atop her. "This way." She gripped his shoulders while he pushed his shaft into her, tantalizingly slow. When it was all the way in, with one quick, strong swoop, he turned them over so she now sat astride, gazing down at his face in the moonlight. She gave a joyous laugh. "You're full of surprises, aren't you?"

"Many. This is just the beginning."

Moaning with pleasure, she settled back on the long, hard length of him that pulsed inside her.

He raised his hands to caress the tips of her breasts. "Now you do the work."

"Like this?" She pushed on her knees, raised up, then slowly brought herself down, sliding over his hardness. It felt so good, she raised up and down again, then again, wrapped in a sensuous rhythm that sent her to new heights of arousal. At last, her body flooded with desire, she hurtled beyond the point of no return. "Oh, I'm going to ... it's ... oh, oh!"

The hot tide of passion that had built within her exploded, sending her into a paroxysm of shuddering ecstasy. The next instant, she heard him gasp, felt his grip tight on her thighs, and knew he had exploded, too.

They collapsed on the bed of pine needles, lying exhausted in each other's arms. Finally he propped himself up on one elbow. "How was it?"

"Mmm," she ran her fingers over his bare chest. "Until the day I die, I'll never forget this night. My sister was right."

"Right about what?" He ran a loving, leisurely finger along her cheek.

"She said that *that* part of a marriage is a beautiful thing. That's why I was so disappointed when Jacob ... well, he just didn't—"

"I know."

"Never in all the time I was married did I ..."

"But tonight?"

"Ah, yes." Clint would laugh if she quoted Sarah exactly, telling him she'd been carried away on the wings of love, but that's just the way she felt. Now, slowly returning to the real world, all the doubts and fears she'd forgotten for a precious while came flooding back. Would she never feel this way again in her whole life? She breathed a deep sigh. "You're sure about Abner?"

"Do you think I can let you go now?" Clint stroked her hair and trailed kisses across her cheek. "I love you. I never thought I'd say that to a woman. I used to think I'd spend the rest of my life in the wilderness, but that was before I fell in love with you."

His words made her blissfully happy, grateful just to be alive. "Do you think we could settle down somewhere?"

"Of course. After we're married, we'll decide where. You and I belong together, and Amy, too. God knows, he cares nothing for her."

Never to see Abner again ... how delightful to contemplate! "I dreaded the thought of going off to Downieville with him."

"You're coming with me."

"Tomorrow you'll talk to Abner?"

His voice was full of confidence. "Charlie and I are going hunting in the morning. As soon as I get back, I'll have that chat with Abner."

Chapter 20

When Lucy returned from the river, she could still hear the music from the campfire. Approaching the Applegates' wagon to pick up Amy, she couldn't contain herself and danced a happy step along the way. She was about to see the last of Abner! Amy would soon be all hers, and—best and most delightful of all—Clint loved her, she adored him, and they were going to be together for the rest of their lives. How incredibly wonderful. How incredibly happy could she be?

At the back of the Applegates' wagon, she knocked softly. Young Jessie stuck her head out. "The baby's not here. Mister Schneider came and got her a while back."

Since when did Abner have the faintest interest in caring for his own child? "Where did he take her?"

"To his tent, Mrs. Schneider. I know because I had to carry her, him being on crutches and all."

Lucy managed a polite thank you, not easy when a wave of apprehension was sweeping through her. She no longer felt like dancing as she headed toward the far end of the campsite where Abner had parked his wagon and pitched his tent alongside. When she reached it, she saw a figure looming in the darkness. "Abner?"

"Where have you been?" His voice was hard and low, barely above a whisper.

"At the campfire."

"No, you weren't." Leaning on his crutches, he took a step toward her. "You whore! You've been with Clint, haven't you?"

He knew! She gasped from the shock. Her mind raced. What should she say? She must think of an excuse ... something ... but before she could frame a reply, he tossed one of his crutches to the ground and grabbed her arm. In a flash, he twisted it behind her, causing her to spin around and gasp at the sudden pain. She was half bent over.

"What are you doing?"

"If ye shall still do wickedly, ye shall be consumed," he hissed. He bent her arm up, only a little, but the pain was incredible. "Admit you were with Clint!"

She gritted her teeth. Tears welled in her eyes. "Please, you're hurting me!"

He bent close to her ear. "I can smell him on you. Confess! Or I'll twist your arm clear off."

The music stopped. Lucy heard people still chatting around the campfire. If she screamed, they'd surely hear and come running, but she didn't want to scream. She'd die of mortification if anyone witnessed this ugly scene.

"Tell me!" Again, Abner jerked her arm up. She thought she'd faint from the pain. From inside the tent, she heard a sudden wake-up wail from the baby. "There's Amy. Let me go to her."

He tightened his grip. "Admit you were with Clint."

What with the pain and Amy crying, she knew she couldn't fight anymore, and besides, there was no sense lying. "All right, let me go, and I'll tell you."

He let go and shoved her hard up against the wagon, his hand pressing against her throat. "Talk!"

"I can't when you're choking me."

He removed his hand but remained so close she could feel his hot breath upon her face. What could she say? He could easily kill her, and probably would if she spoke the truth. Perhaps she could reason with him. "First, you need to calm down." She tried to assume a reasonable tone. "I must go see about Amy. She's crying."

He was still in her face. "You'll never see her again if you don't confess your sins."

She had no choice. It was time for the truth. "All right, step back and I'll tell you."

"I'm listening."

She took a deep breath. "Listen carefully. I love Clint, and he loves me. We want to be together, with Amy, too. You know you can't care for her properly. She'll be so much better off with—"

"You ... you strumpet!"

His hands dug hard into her shoulders. She twisted, trying to knock them away. "Now let me go. The baby—"

"I ought to kill you." His hands went around her throat again. She waited, her insides trembling, not knowing if these moments might be her last. He dropped his hands. "Get in the tent." His voice was so absolutely devoid of emotion it chilled her to the bone.

Without another word, she entered the tent and picked up Amy, who by now was crying lustily. Cuddling the child, she whispered softly, "Now, now, sweetheart, you mustn't cry."

Abner hobbled in behind her. Without warning, he swept Amy out of her arms.

"What are you doing?" She reached for the baby, but Abner moved back, jerking the tiny bundle out of her reach.

"Not so fast." His lips twisted into a cynical smile. "Wouldn't it be a shame if something happened to the child?"

Icy fear twisted around her heart. "You wouldn't—"

"Accidents happen." He smiled. "Sometimes babies get sick or run over by a wagon, or they smother ... like this."

Lucy watched in horror as Abner slowly, deliberately, covered the baby's face with the palm of his hand. "Abner, stop! You wouldn't!" She threw herself at him, tried with all her might to wrench the child from his arms, but even in his weakened condition, Abner was much stronger than she. Easily he pushed her away.

"You'll never get away with this!"

"I won't? Babies die all the time." A satanic smile spread over his thin lips. He nodded toward the campsite with a taut jerk of his head. "You think those people care? They wouldn't lift a finger to help. All they want is to get to California. Besides, who'd take a mere woman's word against mine?"

What he said was true. Even if everyone knew the truth, what justice could she expect on a wagon train? A sick realization crept over her. Abner was not making an empty threat. She had thought him a bit strange, as did everyone, but now she could see from the crazed look in his eyes he'd crossed a line from eccentricity to insanity. Or had he been insane all along? It didn't matter. He meant what he said. He'd kill little Amy if had to. "All right, you win. I'll do anything you want."

He lifted his hand. The false smile disappeared, replaced by an expression of viciousness mixed with hate. "Pick up my Bible."

She did.

"Get on your knees."

Desperate, her heart pounding, she hastened to obey.

"Now swear on the Holy Bible you'll never leave me, or by God ..." his hand covered the baby's face again.

Did Abner mean what he said? How could he possibly harm his own child? How could he force her to such degradation? She knew him now for the cold, ruthless man he really was, and insane besides. Deep in her soul she knew the truth—he would do anything, no matter how horrible, to get his way, and she could not let that happen.

She clutched the Bible in her shaking hands and whispered, "I swear I won't leave you."

"Louder!"

She raised her voice. "I won't leave you!"

"You'll have nothing more to do with Clint Palance."

At this point he had her so terrified she would swear to anything. "All right, I'll have nothing more to do with him."

"Swear it."

"I swear, I swear!"

"Get back on your feet."

When she stood, he asked, "How much flour is left in the barrel?"

At first she didn't understand. What could flour matter at a time like this? His meaning dawned on her. "Abner, it's mine. You can't."

"Go get it."

As if in a dazed nightmare, she hurried to her wagon and retrieved the bag of five dollar gold pieces Jacob had hidden at the beginning of their journey. Soon she faced Abner again, the bag in her hands. She felt sick to think Jacob must have told Abner, but she should have known he would. Here she'd counted on that money. It was all she had—her security, her hope for the future. "This money isn't yours. How dare you take it."

"What was Jacob's is now mine." Abner gave her body a raking gaze. "Including you." Taking the bag of coins, he thrust Amy back in her arms. "Take her." His flat, passionless eyes drilled into her. "Remember, if ever you disobey me, she'll die."

"Yes, I understand."

"Pack up. We leave for Downieville at dawn tomorrow."

"We're leaving the wagon train?"

"Don't you ever question my decisions." His voice hardened. "Woman, you will obey me from now on. Swear it!"

"I swear." Lucy answered in a very small voice. Never in her life had she felt so low, so defeated, so totally without hope. She hugged the baby tight, tears of humiliation running down her cheeks.

❧❧

"Mister Palance?"

Beside his wagon, Clint raised his head from the wash basin. He and Charlie had just come back from hunting. In another minute, he'd be off for that much anticipated talk with Abner. "Yes, Chad?"

"This is for you." Chad held out a sealed note. "Mister Schneider said I should deliver it to you after they left."

After they left? "Thank you." Clint took the note, sank down by the campfire and ripped it open.

Dear Mister Palance,

I am writing this to inform you Abner Schneider and I have left the wagon train for good. It is my wish that I never see you again. If I gave you the impression I felt otherwise, I apologize.

Please don't come after me. It will be a waste of time if you do.

Sincerely yours,
Lucy Schneider

Charlie, newly returned from dressing the deer they'd shot, took one look at Clint "What's the matter? You look like you lost your best friend and your horse besides."

"She's gone off with that bastard." Clint's voice nearly broke with huskiness. "I can't believe it."

"Jehosaphat!" Charlie let out a soft whistle. "What would she want to do a fool thing like that for?"

Clint retained a tight-lipped silence, the note still clutched in his hand.

"I see the Schneiders' wagons are gone." Charlie gazed around the camp site. He raised an inquisitive eyebrow. "You ain't planning on doing anything crazy, are you?"

Clint balled a fist. "That fucking lunatic must have forced her."

"Reckon he did. Why else would she go off with him?"

"I'd wager the baby had something to do with it. I'm going to find her."

"Well, I think you should, but first you'd better find where she's headed."

Which way did she go? She'd told him Downieville, but he'd better make sure. At this point in the journey, several families had already left the train bound for any one of the many gold mining camps that dotted the Sierra Nevada Mountains. After making inquiries, Clint found two people who'd been up early enough to see the Schneider wagons leave. "I saw the Johnson and Lehman wagons leave also," one woman said. "Don't know about the Lehmans, but the Johnsons said they were headed north for Downieville. The Schneider wagons were right behind them, all of them after the gold."

"I heard Abner say he was going to Downieville," said another. "Heard him plain as day."

"So, you're headed north," Charlie said when Clint returned. He watched his friend saddle up. "You're sure they're going to Downieville?"

"Almost positive. I'm going to find her. I won't come back without her."

Hours later, Clint caught up with the Johnson wagon. They were alone. "I ain't seen them." Samuel Johnson scratched his head. "Maybe they went with the Lehmans when they turned off."

Clint tried to hide his frustration. "Where were the Lehmans heading?"

"Well, Sierra City, of course. They heard there's gold in the streets there, too."

Dammit, he'd have to backtrack for miles until he reached the Sierra City turnoff and then catch up as fast as he could. This was going to take time. Longer than he'd thought.

❧❧

After leaving the camp at the crack of dawn, Abner followed the Johnson and Lehman wagons a short way north. When they came to a fork along the faint trail, to Lucy's astonishment, they turned south, not north. "Aren't we going to Downieville?"

"No."

"But you said—"

"I know what I said. That was just in case anyone should want to track us down."

In the back of her mind, she was hoping Clint would come after them. Now, even if he did, he'd be heading in the opposite direction. "Then where are we going?"

"Hangtown."

Her heart sank. From all she'd heard, Hangtown was a terrible place. How was Clint ever going to find her?

As the day wore on, she felt such an acute sense of loss she hardly cared. In a numb haze, she drove the wagon, cared for Amy, and fixed the meals over the campfires she'd built. All day she sought to absorb the events of the night before, which had shaken her world and changed her life. How had this happened? How could she have allowed herself to be so intimidated by Abner she'd lost the man she loved, along with her freedom, and was now heading to a wild, lawless gold mining town, the last place in the world she'd ever wanted to go? She was plagued by guilt and self-recrimination. She should've stood up to Abner, screamed for help, done something—anything!—instead of allowing him to ruin her life. But then ...

Each time she told herself what a cowardly fool she'd been, she remembered that crazed lunatic gleam in Abner's eye when he held his hand over little Amy's face. No question, he would've carried out his threat, had she not given in. *I've ruined my life, but I did the right thing.*

That night they made camp in a grove of tall, majestic redwood trees. In the background, the snow-covered peaks of the Sierra Nevadas towered over them. She was unmoved by the beauty of the site. All she could think about was how she'd fallen into the clutches of a man so ruthless, so heartless, he would commit murder to get his way. She realized now that he was more than a touch insane. In the past, despite his eccentricities, she'd considered him a rational human being. Now she knew he was not.

She had more on her mind than grief over losing Clint and fears for Amy's welfare. Up to now Abner had never so much as looked at her in a suggestive manner. She suspected she'd been safe because she was his brother's wife, and therefore on sacrosanct ground. But here, all alone in the wilderness, would Abner make advances? Demand she submit? Dear Lord, she hoped not. She could think of nothing more loathsome than making love to Abner. She gave a shudder, just thinking about those thick, moist lips pressed to hers, the coarse hairs of his scruffy black beard rubbing against her skin. What could be more revolting? She recalled the intimacies she'd shared with Clint. Was it only last night they'd made love? So much had happened since then it seemed like another lifetime, back when happiness had seemed within reach. The memory of his loving hands stroking her body sent a warm shiver of feeling through her. The thought of Abner's hands doing the same filled her with disgust.

Please find me, Clint, please!

That night after dinner, Abner sat silently watching as she washed the dishes, put them away, and stomped out the campfire. If all went as she fervently hoped, he'd soon say goodnight and retire to his wagon for the night. She would go to her wagon and all would be well. Something in the way his eyes boldly raked over her while she worked gave warning she'd better be prepared for the worst. How should she handle this man she despised? All day the question had hammered at her.

Later on, after she stomped out the campfire, Abner stood, adjusted his crutches, and hobbled toward her. "Come along."

"Come along where?"

His stern expression didn't waver. "To my wagon, of course. In case you've forgotten, you swore to obey me."

Her mind raced. Would she give in to his revolting demands? She regarded her brother-in-law, dwelling on those flat, cold eyes that held no hint of love or compassion. Impossible though he'd been before his accident, now he was ten times worse. There was no way she could reason with him. Why even try? At that moment, she made the only decision that would allow her to retain a modicum of self-respect.

"No."

His eyes went wide. "What do you mean, no?"

She stepped back and crossed her arms. "Last night I promised not to leave you, and I won't."

"You promised to obey me, too."

"Yes, I did." She forced herself to sound calm and reasonable. "I will obey you in all ways but one."

"You will obey me in all things!" He raised his hand as if to strike her, but she nimbly leaped away.

Out of range, she faced him, fists clenched. "I will cook and clean for you. I will care for your child. I will not share your bed, not now, not ever. I don't care what you say or do."

For a moment, Abner sputtered, shocked by her defiance. Soon his mouth spread into a thin-lipped smile. His curt voice lashed at her. "Have you forgotten our discussion concerning Amy?"

The mention of Abner's threat to kill the baby strengthened her resolve. "Wait right here." She went to her wagon, hopped on the long yoke, and climbed inside. Jacob's two Hawcan rifles still stood propped behind the flour barrel. She grabbed one and carried it to the front of the wagon. Kneeling down, she faced Abner, who stood waiting by the smoldering campfire. She aimed the rifle at his head. "You see this rifle? If you ever try to touch me, I shall get this rifle and blow your head off. Is that clear?"

Abner's jaw dropped. When her words sunk in, he sneered. "You wouldn't dare."

"Oh, wouldn't I?" The mere act of holding the rifle in her hands gave her a feeling of power she wouldn't have thought possible. No longer was she shaking or filled with fear. Instead, a calm confidence came over her. She bent her head and sighted along the barrel. "In case you've forgotten, I've already killed one man with this rifle—shot him square between the eyes. You think I couldn't do it again?"

"It was only an Indian."

"A man, nonetheless."

For a long time, Abner stared at her, no doubt searching for an appropriate answer. Coward that he was, she could see he was flabbergasted, unsure what to do. "I won't tolerate your disobedience. But for now, I shall let it go because you're tired and don't know what you're saying." He turned to leave. "We shall discuss this in the morning."

"Yes, we'll do just that." She felt a glow of triumph because she knew she'd won. The glow soon faded. What had she gained other than putting Abner off for the night? She was still obligated to the man. Her heart twisted with anguish. How could Clint find her when he had no idea where she was? What if she'd lost him forever?

❦

Late the next day, Clint returned to the camp at Truckee empty-handed. "I couldn't find her." He wiped a weary hand over his brow.

"That son-of-a-bitch must have lied. Most likely he said he was going one way, then went the other. Trouble is, she could be in any one of dozens of gold mining camps by now."

"I've got to find her. Even if I have to search every gold mining camp in the Sierras."

"I know." Charlie had been sitting by the campfire. He started to stand but sat down again, wincing in pain.

"What's wrong?" Clint asked.

"It's my back. Must've wrenched it hauling that deer carcass. Right now I can't even get on my horse." Charlie regarded Clint with pain-filled eyes. "I'll be fine. You go ahead. You've got to find her."

With all his heart and soul, Clint wanted to continue his search for Lucy, but he didn't hesitate. Loyalty to his partner came first, obligation, plus what it came down to was doing the right thing. He swung from his horse. "You're not fine. "I'm taking over. You go lie down."

"But, Clint—"

"You heard me. You old fool. I know you won't admit it, but you damn well are going to need my help." With an effort, he stripped all bitterness and frustration from his voice. "Don't concern yourself. When we get to Sacramento, I'll start looking again. That should be soon enough." Would it be? Already he knew he'd be half out of his mind with worry, but for the moment, there was nothing he could do except pray that Lucy's courage and resourcefulness would be enough to keep her safe.

Chapter 21

*H*angtown. Never had Lucy imagined such a place existed.
The contrast between staid, respectable Beacon Hill and
this roaring, wide-open mining town amazed her. Where else
did fortune seekers from the four corners of the earth jam the
stores, whorehouses, and gambling halls, each with high hopes
he'd strike it rich? They spoke in at least a dozen languages,
bargaining in the coin of whatever country they came from.
Mexican gold Orzas mingled with silver dollars, but at sixteen
dollars per ounce, the gold dust dug from the nearby hills
remained the main coin of the realm. Nearly everyone carried
small bags of gold dust in this busy, brawling, sinful town.

Justice came swiftly in Hangtown, a place aptly named. A
man accused of a serious crime got a fast trial, held in one of the
saloons or occasionally in the street. If found guilty, and he
usually was, he was immediately hauled in a wagon to a large
oak tree that grew just outside town and hanged.

When Lucy and Abner arrived, Hangtown consisted of just
two rows of buildings with a street in-between, but it was
constantly growing. Hundreds of emigrants arrived daily, not
only to stake claims in the surrounding hills but to take up lots
to build homes and businesses.

Abner was among them. The very day he arrived, he found
a store for sale and bought it with the remainder of his cash.
Taking Lucy along, he went to the town's only bank and
deposited most of Jacob's hoard of gold coins, keeping just
enough to buy new inventory.

Americus Washburn, owner of the bank, gave them a grand welcome. "I trust you and your lovely wife will enjoy living in Hangtown, Mister Schneider."

"My wife and I surely will."

Lucy silently bristled. *I am not your wife. How dare you!* Best not say anything. At least for the moment.

Within a week, the two-story, wooden frame structure situated next to the Gold Dust Saloon became Schneider's General Store, open for business. An instant success, it stocked a variety of miners' equipment as well as general merchandise. The store occupied the first floor. The Schneider family lived on the second floor. Soon Lucy found herself racing up and down the stairs, helping in the store and taking care of Amy at the same time.

On the third day after the store opened, Lucy was working behind the counter when she heard someone call, "Lucy! I can't believe it!"

That voice. "Cordelia!" Lucy fairly ran around the counter to hug and greet her friend. "I had no idea you were here."

"It was Chad's idea. Remember how he said he wanted to come to Hangtown? Well, here we are, and now I'm looking to open a boarding house."

Lucy took her friend upstairs and gave her a tour of the two bedrooms, living room, and kitchen that made up her new living quarters. Located out back, the privy seemed the height of luxury after the inconveniences endured on the trail. "I thank my lucky stars I'm not living in a wagon anymore. Don't you feel the same?"

"Of course," Lucy answered, almost by rote. Her joy at seeing Cordelia was short-lived. These days, try as she might to conceal it, a constant heaviness hung over her heart. When she lost Clint, she lost her spirit. Nothing, it seemed, could ever bring it back.

Cordelia seemed to perceive something was wrong. "I

wondered where you'd gone. Everyone did. But Hangtown? With Abner? Don't tell me you married that awful man."

"No, but everybody thinks I did." Lucy proceeded to tell her friend about Abner's threat to murder the baby. "He meant it. I know he did."

Cordelia listened with increasing horror. "You must leave him at once. The man's a maniac. You're not safe."

"I can't afford to leave." Lucy's smile was rueful. "I had some money—gold coins Jacob had left—but Abner took everything I had."

"What about Clint? Why hasn't he come after you?"

"When we left, Abner told everyone we were going to Downieville. If Clint went after me, he doubtless went in the wrong direction. He has no idea where I am."

"How monstrous." For a time, Cordelia sat silent. "Perhaps you could send him a letter?"

"And how should I address it? To Mister Clint Palance, The Sierra Nevada Mountains, somewhere between Truckee and Sacramento?"

Cordelia gave a sigh of defeat. "When I open my boarding house, you can come and stay with me."

Lucy raised her chin high. "Thank you. You're more than kind, but I won't be a charity case. Don't you worry. I'm fine for now." *But for how long?* Silently she vowed that from now on, she would only grieve on the inside, not just for Clint but for the loss of her independence, the end of her dignity and self-respect. Abner had taken all that away, leaving her with nothing but a numb emptiness in her heart. She put on a bright smile. "As you can see, I'm making the best of it."

"So how does Abner feel about living next to the Gold Dust?"

Lucy laughed aloud, a rare occurrence these days. "He's quoting his Bible verses again." She stood and assumed Abner's prophet pose. In a deep voice she pronounced,

" 'The drunkard and the glutton shall come to poverty.' I believe that's Proverbs something-or-other. Oh, and you know how he feels about all the fancy women in town? 'Do not prostitute thy daughter, to cause her to be a whore lest the land fall to whoredom, and the land become full of wickedness.' "

Cordelia broke into laughter. "Then I guess Hangtown fell into wickedness a long time ago, what with all those fancy women we've got around here."

During the days that followed, Cordelia visited often, each time reviving Lucy's lagging spirits. One day Cordelia came had a strange look on her face. "Is there something wrong?" They sat at Lucy's kitchen table.

Cordelia opened her mouth to speak, then shut it again.

"You were going to say something?"

"Uh, no, nothing."

Lucy was about to insist Cordelia speak when the baby started to fret. She took Amy from her cradle and cuddled her in her lap.

"She's so darling." Cordelia wasn't exaggerating. At nearly four months old, Amy was a rosy-cheeked baby with her father's dark hair and her mother's big blue eyes. She hardly ever cried, but instead spent her waking hours cooing contentedly, reaching her little fingers out to explore her new world.

"I hate to leave her for a minute, but Abner wants me to work in the store. I've hired Molly Sawyer, the doctor's daughter, to watch her while I'm downstairs. She's only thirteen but quite responsible."

"I know who you mean. A pretty little thing. The doctor dotes on her."

They chatted for a while, mostly about the tea party Cordelia planned to give in the parlor of her new boarding house. "I feel it will be an uplifting event for Hangtown. We could do with a bit of culture around here."

Tongue in cheek, Lucy asked, "Are you inviting the ladies from the Gold Dust?"

Cordelia pretended to bristle. "Most certainly I am not! Only genteel ladies, if you please."

"That won't leave many." Despite Cordelia's newfound tolerance, Lucy knew the town's "painted women," as Abner sneeringly called them, would never get invited to her parlor for tea.

Again, a peculiar look crossed Cordelia's face. Again she started to speak, then seemed to think better of it.

Lucy looked her square in the eye. "Out with it. What do you want to say?"

"Nothing ... well, I don't know if I should tell you or not. It's just a rumor."

"Now my curiosity's aroused. You've got to tell me."

"I'm not one to gossip."

"Of course not."

"It's about Abner, and you really should know."

"Just tell me."

"You know how men are."

"Indeed I do. Now for heaven's sake, tell me."

"Sometimes I overhear the men talking at my boarding house. They say ... well, Abner has been seen coming out of the ... you know, the places of ill repute."

"Whorehouses?"

"Yes, whorehouses, and just about every night."

Pious, sanctimonious Abner? She couldn't believe it. "That can't be true. Abner would never ... They must be wrong. Yes, of course they're wrong. They must have mistaken him for someone else."

"Perhaps, but on the other hand, how many tall men with a peg leg and a long black beard could there be in Hangtown?" At Lucy's stunned silence, Cordelia continued, "I do believe it to be the truth, much as I hate to say it. May I ask a very personal question?"

"Go ahead."

"You sleep in separate bedrooms?"

"I sleep in Amy's room." Lucy smiled. "I once threatened to blow his head off if he touched me. Apparently, he hasn't forgotten."

Cordelia screeched with laughter. "Then that might explain ..." She screwed up her face, as if a battle raged within. She finally heaved a resigned sigh. "Since I've come this far, I may as well tell you everything. I guess you know Abner is a lusty man, with strong appetites for ... you know."

"Abner? I had no idea."

"Well, here's what you don't know. While we were on the trail, Abner got himself a bad reputation for bothering the women. He was always touching where he shouldn't, getting up too close, making suggestive remarks. His actions made us angry, especially because he was so sneaky about it, always going around with that pious, holier-than-thou attitude." Cordelia paused, apparently gathering her thoughts. "I never told you this, but Abner had the nerve to come to my wagon the night after Nathaniel died and ... it was just awful. He actually thought I would welcome his advances. He said he wanted to 'comfort' me and help me find solace in God. I was horrified."

"Why didn't you speak up and complain? Why didn't *anyone* complain?"

"Far as I know, none of the wives ever said anything. You know what it's like on a wagon train, what with the men's tempers so short anything could set them off. Something like that ... well, you know they all have guns. It could have led to bloodshed."

"I had no idea."

"Nobody wanted to tell you, but at this point, I think you deserve to know. I suppose you can't stop him, but you should be aware of what he's up to every night. Quite frankly, I think we should all keep an eye on him. He doesn't quite seem normal to me, like he's some kind of pervert or something."

"Thanks for telling me. I needed to know."

Cordelia eased into a warm, friendly smile. "Let's get on to more pleasant topics, shall we?"

"Yes, let's." Lucy didn't want to think about that loathsome man any more than she had to.

"Don't forget my tea party." Cordelia rose to leave. "Next Thursday afternoon. Perhaps you might ask Molly to watch the baby while you take some well-deserved time for yourself."

That night, like every night, Lucy strained to keep the conversation pleasant between Abner and herself. It wasn't easy; that horrible moment when he had put his hand over the baby's face remained etched forever in her memory. Now this latest news ... Cordelia's revelations simply gave her yet another reason to detest Abner.

"You overcooked the roast," Abner announced when dinner was done.

"Really?" These days she wouldn't dream of apologizing. Abner rose from the table and hobbled to the coat rack. A Hangtown doctor had fitted him with a peg leg, which thumped annoyingly across the wooden floor. He donned his coat and hat and headed for the door. "I'm going out."

"All right." She'd wondered where he went every night. Now she knew and couldn't care less. The more time he spent out of the house, the better, as far as she was concerned. She could hardly stand him anymore. Most of the time he treated her like a lowly servant. Only when they worked together in the store did he make any show of affection, all of it false, just meant to create a false impression that they were a loving, congenial couple. Oh, what a hypocrite he was!

She went to the baby's room, where she could always find peace and comfort. With a troubled sigh, she sank into the rocking chair by Amy's crib. *Trapped*. She gazed at the sleeping baby. She could run away, she supposed, but without any money, where could she go? Back to Boston in disgrace? She'd rather be dead.

Besides, how could she escape when she had a baby to care for? Amy came first, always.

If only Clint would find her! Was he looking? Did he care? No day went by when her agonized thoughts didn't dwell on Clint. Was he well? Sick? Happy? Sad? Had he found someone else? Was he dead? What torture never to know.

The trunk she'd brought clear from Boston stood in the corner. On an impulse, she went and opened the lid. On top lay the pair of moccasins the Indians had traded for her pan of biscuits. That night on the trail seemed ages ago, almost another lifetime. She carried the moccasins back to the rocking chair. In the darkness, she started to rock, tenderly holding the soft, embroidered buckskin to her cheek. Clint had touched them once. *Clint*. Her heart swelled with longing. How could she live knowing he was gone forever?

She continued rocking, her tears dampening the moccasins still pressed to her cheek until, from out of nowhere, she remembered something Charlie Dawes had said.

"Did it ever occur to you that you should do what's best for you? There ain't no person on this earth should have to be beholden to someone else. That includes you, even if you are a woman."

Lucy sat straight up. By God, Charlie was right. Out of her own fear and guilt, she'd let Abner take the upper hand. Well, no more. "Follow your heart," Hannah had said. Damned if she'd spend the rest of her life with Abner. Now wasn't the time, what with the baby still so little, but the day would come when somehow, some way, she'd leave this place and go find Clint. It might take years. She might have to search the continent over, but once she escaped, she'd either find him or die in the attempt.

On the day of Cordelia's tea party, Lucy spent the morning downstairs waiting on customers alongside Abner. Chad was there, too. When he wasn't helping his mother, he enjoyed working in the store. As usual, gold seekers swarmed the aisles, buying everything from pick axes and shovels to tents, blankets, and food. For the most part, the miners were a rough, tough lot, but even the most uncouth showed her the utmost courtesy and respect. If she heard the occasional stray curse word, she simply smiled to herself. After the Butler Brothers, nothing could shock her.

Before she left for Cordelia's, she ran upstairs to check on the baby and found Molly cuddling her. "I'll be at Mrs. Benton's tea party. If you need me—"

"Now, you just run along." Molly looked up and gave her a bright smile. "Don't you worry. We'll be fine."

"I'm sure you will." Although Lucy never liked to leave the baby, she trusted Molly implicitly. At just thirteen, the doctor's pretty daughter showed a maturity beyond her years. Soon she'd be a real heartbreaker with her rose petal cheeks, wealth of dark hair, and full red mouth.

Descending the stairs, Lucy felt a spark of anticipation. After weeks of nothing but hard work, how nice to be going to a real indoor, sit-in-the-parlor tea again. She drew Abner aside. "I'm going to Cordelia's for her tea party."

Lines of annoyance instantly furrowed Abner's forehead. "You can't go. We're busy today."

She might've known Abner would attempt to spoil her first real social event since she'd left home. Damned if she'd let him. She leaned her head back and looked straight into his eyes. "I'm going to the tea. You can get along without me for an hour or two."

She'd always found it amusing when, at the least provocation, Abner's face turned red. A deep crimson she could see through his beard crept over his cheeks, deepening by the moment. Mindful of nearby customers, he gritted his teeth. "How dare you disobey me?"

"Oh, I dare all right." Amazing what last night's remembrance of Charlie's words had done for her. "I may have to live with you, but you're not going to order me around. Is that clear?"

She turned away and marched out the door. He must be livid, but he'd have to get over it. No longer were they on the trail. They were in a civilized place where getting away with murder wouldn't be so easy. She wasn't going to be his slave anymore.

"My, what delightful tea, Cordelia. Is it oolong? What delicious cookies. I *must* have the recipe."

Sitting in Cordelia's frilly parlor, Lucy savored the pure pleasure of mingling with a group of ladies who held their cups gingerly and didn't slurp. Cordelia's guests included the cream of Hangtown society: Edwina Sawyer, the doctor's wife and mother of Molly; Carolyn Washburn, wife of the town's one-and-only banker; several wives of the town's leading merchants; and the new school teacher who boarded with Cordelia.

Lucy thoroughly enjoyed the idle, feminine chatter. What a lovely change from having to listen all day to the rough talk of men.

"We ought to make this a regular event," Edwina Sawyer said. "Why don't I be the hostess for our next tea? We could discuss forming a lady's benevolence society, as well as ... what was that?"

From outside, Lucy heard men shouting. Cordelia went to the window, drew back the lace curtain, and looked to her left, toward Schneider's General Store. "I declare, there's a crowd gathering in the street. They seem angry. My gracious, they appear to be directly in front of your store."

Lucy hastened to the window. Dozens of shouting men had gathered in the street. Even as she watched, the crowd grew larger. She set down her teacup. "What on earth? I'd better find out what's going on." She started for the front door.

Frowning, Cordelia shook her head. "Perhaps you shouldn't go out there. Those men look mighty angry to me."

"I must see about Amy." Lucy hurried through the door, down the steps, and into the street crowded with men, their faces twisted with rage, shouting, thrusting fists in the air. In a state of growing anxiety, she made her way up the street to where the crowd seemed most heavily congregated, directly in front of Schneider's General Store. Spying portly Americus Washburn, the banker, she shoved her way to his side and grabbed his arm. "What's going on? Why are they gathered in front of our store?"

"Why, they—" The dignified banker stopped abruptly when he saw who it was. "Uh, I really don't know."

Just then, a rough voice called, "Come out, Abner Schneider!" The crowd immediately picked up the phrase and started chanting, "Come out, Abner Schneider!" over and over, in a chillingly growing roar.

Something was wrong, really wrong. Lucy pushed her way through the crowd and raced up the wooden steps of the store. The front door was closed. Strange. It was never closed in the middle of the day. She turned the doorknob, but the door wouldn't open. Why was it locked? She peered through the glass. The store seemed empty, but there had to be someone inside. "Let me in!" She started pounding. Behind her, the angry shouts grew louder. She called out again and kept on pounding. Finally she saw Chad through the glass. "Chad, let me in." By now she was beating on the door with both fists. The young man came to the door. She could see his face, white and frightened. "Let me in. You must let me in!"

Chad unlocked the door and cracked it open. "Quick!" His

voice was urgent. In an instant, she slipped inside. The boy slammed the door shut behind her and quickly locked it again. He was trembling.

"What is this? Why is there a crowd outside? Where's Mister Schneider?"

Chad shook his head. "All I know is, after you left, Mister Schneider asked me to watch the store while he went upstairs. Then, not long after, Molly came running and screaming down the stairs." He bit his lip, looking as if he wasn't sure he should go on. "She had blood on her face, and her clothes were torn." Dismally he added, "I'm real sorry. Molly ran screaming out the door, home I reckon. Not long after, this crowd started gathering. I guess they're after Mister Schneider for something he did."

She spoke as calmly as she could. "Where is Mister Schneider?"

"He's upstairs, ma'am. I think the baby's room."

She thanked Chad, lifted her skirts, and raced up the steps to the second floor. In the baby's room, she found Amy safe and asleep in her crib. Abner cowered in a corner, his left eye bruised and swollen.

The roar of the crowd grew louder. Over the shouts of, "Come out, Abner Schneider!" she asked, "What happened? Why are they after you? What happened to your eye?"

Ashen-faced, Abner cringed against the wall, hugging himself. His lips trembled. "They're mad, Lucy, mad! I've done nothing wrong. That girl is telling lies." A sudden, jarring crash came from downstairs. "Dear God, they've thrown something through the window!"

Lucy gripped Abner's shoulders. "For God's sake, what did you do?"

"Mister Schneider?"

Lucy turned to see Tom Stewart, the town's newly appointed marshal, standing in the doorway. A tall, imposing figure with a star on his vest and gun on his hip, he addressed Abner. "I've been delegated to come get you."

Abner's eyes grew wide with terror. "Never! You have no right to come in here."

"Chad let me in, sir." The marshal shrugged dismissively. "An angry mob like this isn't concerned over your rights. Didn't you hear? Already they've broken a window. If you don't come out, they'll come in. Do you want that? Do you want them busting up your store?"

Abner spoke in a quavering, almost childlike voice. "What will they do to me?"

"Give you a fair trial. That's all I can promise."

"Fair trial?" Abner laughed hysterically. "In Hangtown?"

"It's the best you're going to get. Now come along."

The blood-thirsty crowd was screaming as Tom Stewart led Abner through the front door of Schneider's General Store. Shouting men surged forward, but when the steely-eyed Marshall raised his hand, they held back.

"This man deserves a fair trial, and long as I'm marshal, he's going to get one." He laid his hand over his gun. "If there's any man not agreeing with me, he'd better step forward."

The crowd made way for the marshal as he pushed Abner forward, down the steps, onto the street. The noise picked up again as Tom escorted his prisoner next door to the Gold Dust Saloon.

Numb with shock, Amy in her arms, Lucy trailed behind the ever-growing mob. When she went up the steps of the Gold Dust, Cordelia came alongside. In a horrified voice she asked, "Oh, Lucy, what has he done?"

"It has something to do with Molly."

Someone shouted, "Americus Washburn's been appointed judge!"

Cordelia shouted out, "And just who appointed him?"

"The crowd, ma'am."

Inside the Gold Dust, two rows of six chairs each had been hastily set up for the jurors, a chair and a table up front for the judge, and a chair for the witnesses. After seating Abner in another chair up front, Tom Stewart stood behind the judge.

Lucy and Cordelia found two seats in the back. Holding Amy tight, Lucy watched the unruly crowd choose the jurors. The selection proved easy enough. Without asking a single question, they pointed to the first twelve men who stepped up and volunteered. The whole process took less than two minutes.

Someone in the crowd called, "Where's his lawyer?" but was quickly stilled by hisses and boos.

"I guess it's just the judge, Abner, and the jury," said Cordelia.

"This can't be happening." Abner was about to be hanged? She couldn't get it through her head.

Cordelia squeezed her hand. "You must be brave. There's nothing you can do now except pray." She flicked Lucy a glance. "That is, if you want to pray."

In a daze, Lucy sat and watched what passed for a fair trial in Hangtown. The jurors were immediately sworn in. The marshal called the first witness, Doc Sawyer, who swore to tell the truth with his hand on the Bible and seated himself in the chair beside the judge.

"Doc, tell us what happened," said Americus.

The town's only doctor, ordinarily a pleasant man with kindly eyes and an easy manner, today sat clutching his fists as he testified, his mouth set in an angry line, a muscle twitching along his jaw. "This afternoon my daughter, Molly, was watching the Schneider baby. I was working in my office, which, as you know, is in my home. All of a sudden, I heard screaming. It was Molly. She burst into my office. She ..." The doctor choked up. He needed several seconds to pull himself together. "She said Abner Schneider came upstairs and threw her to floor, demanding she submit. My daughter refused and started to fight him off. It was then he tore her dress and hit her in the face. I saw the blood!" Eyes blazing, the doctor stood, raised his arm, and pointed an accusing finger at Abner. "That man tried to rape my daughter!"

The room exploded into angry shouts. Not having a gavel, the judge pounded on the table with a heavy whiskey glass. When the noise died down, he asked, "How did Molly get away, Doc?"

"She hit him in the eye and ran."

"So he didn't—?"

"No, he did not."

"How's she doing now?"

"Fine, but she'll be doing a lot better when they put a noose around that bastard's neck."

"Hang him!" came incensed shouts from the crowd. Americus had to bang the whiskey glass again.

When the doctor stepped down, young Chad Benton was sworn in and took his place in the witness chair. More composed now, he looked expectantly at the judge, waiting for a question.

"Tell us what happened, lad."

"Well, uh, Mister Schneider and I were working in the store. Then he went upstairs. Then pretty soon Molly came running down and out the door."

"Was she screaming?"

"Yes, and her dress was torn."

"Did you see any blood?"

"On her face I did."

"Then what happened?"

"Mister Schneider came downstairs. He acted like nothing was wrong, but he looked terrible, like he was upset about something. His eye looked awful, real red like somebody punched it."

"Anything more?"

"Pretty soon I heard yelling outside. So did the customers. When they all went outside to see what the yelling was about, I got scared and locked the door. Then Mrs. Schneider knocked, and I let her in. Then I let the marshal in, and he took Mister Schneider away. That's about it."

Chad had nothing more to add. When he left the witness chair, the judge addressed Abner. "What have you to say for yourself?"

Abner stood and faced the crowd. "All lies! I never touched the girl. I didn't do it." His gaze swept the room until he spied Lucy. "Strumpet! Harlot, this is all your doing." He pointed an accusing finger, quoting a verse she recognized from the Book of Obadiah. " 'As thou hast done, it shall be done unto thee.' "

"String him up!" came shouts from the crowd, but Americus again pounded for order.

The marshal leaned over his shoulder. "They can't hang him yet, Judge. The jury's got to give its verdict."

Americus addressed the jury. "We'll find a room for you if you want to deliberate."

One of the jurors, a seasoned old miner with a straggly gray beard, stood and spoke. "T'won't be necessary, Judge. I think we all agree." He turned to his fellow jurors. "What do you say, boys?"

"Guilty!" came from the throats of eleven men.

"Then we all find him guilty, Judge, and we think he ought to hang."

The marshal bent and spoke to Americus again. Above the noise of the crowd, the judge declared, "Tom says we've got to do this right. We need a vote from the spectators, as well as the jury's decision. Now, who makes a motion this man be hanged?" The motion was instantly made and seconded. "Should Abner Schneider be hanged?"

A vengeful, rancorous, roaring "Yes!" issued from the

throats of hundreds of men, both in the Gold Dust Saloon and gathered outside in the street. Immediately, a group of men lifted Abner over their heads to carry him outside. They were jabbing, punching at him, and shouting terrible things.

"Lucy, they're taking him to the hanging tree," Cordelia shouted over the noise of the crowd. "Do you want to follow?"

"No, I don't." Lucy shook her head decisively. She knew this trial was a farce. She knew no one should be hanged in such a manner. Yet, when she thought of all the people Abner had hurt, including herself ... his sanctimonious, superior attitude ... his cruelty ... she couldn't pretend to care and wasn't going to try. "I've seen enough. Let's get out of here."

They returned to Cordelia's boarding house and sat in the parlor, both numb with disbelief. Holding the baby tight in her arms, she fought for whatever fragile control she had left, telling herself she couldn't afford to break down now. In the distance, she could plainly hear the noise of the crowd. Suddenly a jubilant roar went up.

"Oh my Lord," Cordelia exclaimed, "he must be swinging from that tree right now. Sorry, but I can't cry."

"Don't apologize. I can't cry either. All I can say is, may God have mercy on his wretched soul."

"At least you still have the store. You can run it every bit as well as Abner ever could."

The store! In all the tumult, Lucy had forgotten. "I'd better pull myself together." She handed Amy to Cordelia. "Will you watch her for me? It just occurred to me the store has been left untended."

The first thing Lucy saw when she stepped from the boarding house into the crowded street was a wisp of black smoke curling toward the sky. It came from the direction of the store. As it grew heavier, she choked back a cry. It couldn't be! Not ...

"They've set Schneider's on fire!" someone shouted.

Oh, God, no! Lucy picked up her skirts and ran. By the time she reached the store, she found it engulfed in flames, the volunteer fire department only now arriving. An unruly crowd milled around in the street in front, some holding merchandise they'd looted.

Lucy watched in stunned horror as the store burned to the ground. Was it only hours ago she was having a lovely day, taking tea in Cordelia's parlor with the cream of Hangtown society?

But now?

Abner gone ... the store gone ... in the wink of an eye she'd lost everything except Amy and the clothes on her back.

Chapter 22

Sacramento, California

Charlie Dawes smiled gratefully at his partner. "You were right. Guess I did need a little help."

Clint suppressed a smile. Charlie's back had been in such bad shape he had laid in the back of the wagon most of the way to Sacramento. "I'm glad you're better now."

"Yep, I can get on my horse again. I know how anxious you are to find Lucy, and I surely appreciate—"

"You'd have done the same for me." Anxious was hardly the word. Since the day they began the last leg of their journey—the trek out of the Sierras to the flatlands of Sacramento—he'd had to curb his desperate urge to find her. "Now that you're all right, I'm going back. Leaving today. Right now."

"Well, I sure hope you find the little lady." Charlie's bushy white brows drew together in a frown. "Where will you look? There are mining camps all over the Sierras, and she could be in any one of them. Angel's Camp. Dutch Flat. Rough and Ready—"

"I'll find her." A mixture of rage and frustration welled up within him every time he thought of Lucy in the hands of that sick bastard, Abner Schneider. "I'll find her if it takes the rest of my life."

Had it not been for Cordelia, Lucy didn't know how she would've survived. What would she have done if Cordelia hadn't insisted she and Amy stay at her boarding house? For the first few days, she'd remained in such a state of shock she could hardly function. Cordelia stood by her, treating her like an honored and cherished guest. "Stay as long as you like. You have a home here. I'll help in any way I can." Lucy was grateful but soon realized she couldn't continue to accept her friend's charity. She began to help around the boarding house, cooking, making beds, washing clothes and linens, scrubbing floors. The hard work earned hers and Amy's keep, but she soon realized she couldn't work in a boarding house forever and must make other plans.

"Where would you go?" Cordelia asked when Lucy expressed her desire to leave. "I love having you here. Nothing would make me happier than if you made this your permanent home."

"I can't keep imposing."

"Imposing!" Cordelia declared indignantly. "You more than earn your keep, even though I've told you many times you needn't lift a finger."

"Even so ..." Lucy stifled a sigh. These days she had to fight to remain cheerful, especially when she felt as if the bottom had dropped out of her world. She didn't mourn Abner in the slightest, but since that horrible day he died, she couldn't keep herself from constantly wondering why so many things in her life had gone wrong. She had worked so hard—gone through so much—only to end up penniless and alone, living off the kindness of a friend.

Cordelia sighed. "If only you had a bit of money. You could rebuild the store and run it yourself. I know you could make a go of it. You were as responsible for the store's success as Abner was."

"I think so, too, but you know I lost everything in the fire."

A rueful smile curved her mouth. "Perhaps I could get a job as a dancing girl at the Gold Dust."

"No, you won't." Cordelia didn't return the smile. "And if you think all those girls do is dance—"

"I know. Only joking."

"You could always go home to Boston."

"If I did, I'd have to ask my father for our passage." Her spirits plunged even further, just picturing herself returning to Boston, appearing on the Beacon Street doorstep clutching the baby, ragged, penniless, a charity case depending upon Pernelia's benevolence for the rest of her life. "I could never go back."

"Didn't Abner have an account at the bank?"

Lucy was reminded of the bag of coins Abner had taken away from her—*stolen* from her and felt indignant all over again. If only she had them now! "He has an account there all right. Opened with my money, I might add."

"If it's your money, then why don't you just go get it?"

"I can't. Don't forget, I wasn't married to Abner. By law, the money will probably go to Abner's relatives back East."

Cordelia regarded her with astonishment. "So, he can send them *your* money?"

Lucy shrugged. "What else can I do?"

"Do?" Cordelia fairly leaped from her chair. "I'm surprised at you! Have you lost your spunk? Aside from me, does anyone in this town know you weren't married to Abner?"

"Not that I know of."

"Then you're going to get that money."

"But—"

"Grab your hat. We're going to the bank right now, Mrs. Schneider. Mrs. *Abner* Schneider."

"So what can I do today for you two lovely ladies?" Americus Washburn sent his most gracious smile across his desk to Lucy and Cordelia.

Cordelia cast a troubled glance at Lucy and patted her hand. "As you know, Mister Washburn, my dear friend has suffered a terrible loss." Lucy had never heard Cordelia talk with such a thick, cloying southern accent.

Americus looked properly grim. "A terrible, terrible thing. Mrs. Schneider, you know you have my condolences."

"Thank you. As you know, my dear husband opened an account here, and I thought—"

"You're wondering if we could put the account in your name," Americus interrupted. "But of course, we can."

"I'm familiar with the banks back East, so I'm wondering about papers to fill out ... legal procedures ..."

"This is Hangtown. I'll have that money in your name in about one minute flat."

"Thank you, Cordelia! I'm so glad you thought of it," Lucy bubbled on the way back to the boarding house. "It's wonderful to have money again. It was awful feeling so poverty stricken ... so utterly without hope."

"Now you can go back to Boston with money of your own."

"You know how I'd love to see my family again, but I shall stay right here in Hangtown."

"Waiting for Clint?" Cordelia gave a wise nod.

"I know he'll find me. If it takes forever, I shall wait right here until he does." Lucy's heart swelled with feeling. Never more than at that moment did she realize how strong and enduring was her love for Clint. He was going to find her, she was positive.

Days later, Lucy was surveying the blackened ruins of Schneider's General Store when she heard someone call her name. The voice came from a wagon halted in the street. When she saw who it was, she exclaimed, "William Applegate! What are you doing in Hangtown?"

"Looking for gold, what else?" William Applegate went on to explain that Agnes and the rest of the family were still at Angel's Camp, where he'd first gone to look for gold. "All the good claims were taken. Since then, I've traveled around, looking over several of the mining camps. That's why I'm here."

After they chatted for a while, Lucy asked the question uppermost in her mind. "I don't suppose you've seen Mister Palance, have you?"

"Clint?" William Applegate looked thoughtful. "I ain't seen him since he and Mister Dawes left for Sacramento with the rest of the wagon train."

She swallowed hard, trying to mask her growing consternation. "That was after I left?"

"That's right, ma'am, shortly after."

"He didn't say anything about wanting to search through the mining towns for ... well, anybody or anything?"

"Not that I know of. He seemed just his usual self, not caring about much of anything except leading the wagon train the rest of the way to Sacramento. I don't believe he was coming back. If he was, he surely didn't say."

Chapter 23

San Francisco

Waiting to board the clipper ship *Flying Cloud*, Lucy stood on the dock, Amy in her arms, taking in the incredible sight of a city caught in the madness of the gold rush. In the bay, she could see a tangle of masts where hundreds of ships lay abandoned, their entire crews having deserted to head for the gold fields. Behind her at least a thousand tents and canvas houses dotted the hillsides of San Francisco. Across the bay, the land rose gradually, lifting up into mountains in the distance and stretching off to where the peaks of the Sierra Nevadas were just visible, their snowy caps dotting the horizon. Strange to think that only a short time ago she'd been there.

Lucy inhaled a breath of tangy salt air while she listened to the harsh squawk of a passing seagull. So like Boston! Soon she'd be home again, safe in the arms of her family, able to hold her head high, thanks to Jacob's money. She ought to feel ecstatic right about now, but indeed, she didn't. Instead, grief and despair tore at her heart.

How wrong she'd been to think Clint would come after her. She could've sworn he would, but now, thanks to William Applegate, she knew better. Clint hadn't cared enough to conduct even the shortest of searches. He'd just gone on with his life, as if she'd been nothing more to him than a casual dalliance.

A seaman from *Flying Cloud* came by. "How long will it take us to get to Boston?" she called after him.

"Don't know for sure, ma'am. Did you know we sailed New York to San Francisco in only eighty-nine days? Broke the record."

Only eighty-nine days? Three months on the open seas seemed an eternity. Three months where she'd have nothing to do but think about Clint and how she'd lost him forever. At least, when she got home, she'd keep busy. She would never marry again, but she could spend the rest of her life doing good work. She would help with the poor—join an abolitionist group so she could do her part to free the slaves. She would—

"Out for a stroll, Mrs. Schneider?"

That voice! It came from behind her. She knew it couldn't be him. With her luck, nothing so wonderful could ever happen to her. She turned, all the same, and gazed into Clint's warm brown eyes.

A soft gasp escaped her. "Clint! How did you find me?"

He smiled. "By combing practically every mining camp in the Sierras."

"William Applegate told me you went on to Sacramento. You didn't look for me at all."

"William Applegate doesn't know everything." Clint proceeded to tell her how he had to stay with Charlie until they reached Sacramento. How he had rushed back and searched for any trace of her until finally he came to Hangtown. "Cordelia told me everything. How they hung Abner. How you'd booked passage on *Flying Cloud* and planned to go back to Boston. I haven't slept for two days, trying to get here before your ship sailed."

It was then she noticed his unshaven face, dust-covered boots, and the tiredness in his eyes. "When William Applegate said you'd gone on to Sacramento, I was devastated. I'd been so sure you were going to come after me."

"Not try to find the woman I love?" Clint's gaze shifted to *Flying Cloud* where it sat gently rocking in the bay. "You're not going home to Boston."

"I'm not?"

"We're going back to Hangtown, where we're going to get married and settle down."

"I thought you weren't a marrying man."

"That was before I met you." He looked deep into her eyes. "So, what's it to be? Boston or me?"

"You know the answer to that." Amazing how, in the course of only a few seconds, her outlook on life had changed from bleak resignation to the rosiest optimism. Life was full of surprises, a fact she should ponder, but later. As for now ...

She smiled up at the man she loved, eyes filled with joy and contentment. "Come. Let's find a place where I can put the baby down. I want so much to kiss you!"

Shirley Kennedy has published Regency romances for both Ballantine and Signet. Born and raised in Fresno, California, she has lived in Colorado, Texas, California, Bogota (Colombia) and Calgary (Alberta, Canada), where she earned a BS in Computer Sciences. Before returning to her first love, writing, she worked as a computer programmer/systems analyst for several years. Shirley currently resides in Las Vegas, Nevada where she belongs to The Romance Writers of America, Sisters in Crime, and Las Vegas Writers Group. Currently she's working on another western historical novel. You can find Shirley online at www.shirleykennedy.com.